# EMPEROR
## OF THE
## EIGHT ISLANDS
### The Tale of Shikanoko

**Lian Hearn**'s beloved 'Tales of the Otori' series, set in an imagined feudal Japan, has sold more than four million copies worldwide and has been translated into nearly forty languages. It is comprised of five volumes: *Across the Nightingale Floor*, *Grass for His Pillow*, *Brilliance of the Moon*, *The Harsh Cry of the Heron* and *Heaven's Net is Wide*. The series was followed by two standalone novels, *Blossoms and Shadows* and *The Storyteller and His Three Daughters*, also set in Japan. Lian Hearn's new series, 'The Tale of Shikanoko', is made up of two books: *Emperor of the Eight Islands* and *Lord of the Darkwood*.

Lian Hearn has made many trips to Japan and has studied Japanese. She read Modern Languages at Oxford and worked as an editor and film critic in England before emigrating to Australia.

Also by Lian Hearn

TALES OF THE OTORI

*Across the Nightingale Floor*
*Grass for His Pillow*
*Brilliance of the Moon*
*The Harsh Cry of the Heron*
*Heaven's Net is Wide*

*Blossoms and Shadows*
*The Storyteller and His Three Daughters*

# EMPEROR
## OF THE
# EIGHT ISLANDS
## The Tale of Shikanoko

## LIAN HEARN

PICADOR

First published 2016 by Hachette Australia

First published in the UK in 2016 by Picador
an imprint of Pan Macmillan
20 New Wharf Road, London N1 9RR
Associated companies throughout the world
www.panmacmillan.com

ISBN 978-1-5098-1247-9

Map artwork by K1229 Design

3 5 7 9 8 6 4 2

A CIP catalogue record for this book is available from the British Library.

Printed and bound by CPI Group (UK) Ltd, Croydon, CR0 4YY

Visit **www.picador.com** to read more about all our books
and to buy them. You will also find features, author interviews and
news of any author events, and you can sign up for e-newsletters
so that you're always first to hear about our new releases.

*For my family,*

*For my friends,*

*For fans of the Otori around the world.*

Frail indeed must be
cross threads of frost and drawn threads
fashioned of dewdrops,
for brocades in the mountains
are woven only to scatter.

*Kokin Wakashū*
TRANSLATED BY HELEN CRAIG MCCULLOUGH,
STANFORD UNIVERSITY PRESS 1985

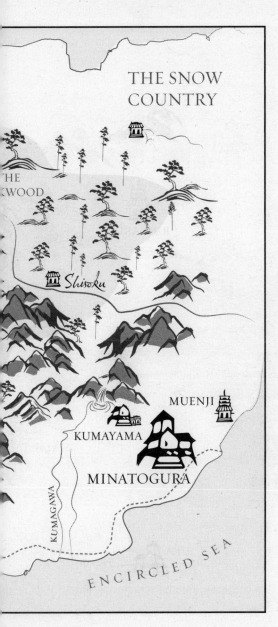

THE SNOW
COUNTRY

THE
KWOOD

*Shisoku*

MUENJI

KUMAYAMA

MINATOGURA

KUMAGAWA

ENCIRCLED SEA

------ ROADS

——— RIVERS
AND STREAMS

 CONVENT
OR TEMPLE

 HUT

 SHRINE

 ESTATE

 TOWN

# LIST OF CHARACTERS

## MAIN CHARACTERS

**Shikanoko (Shika)**, first known as Kazumaru, the son of Shigetomo and nephew of Sademasa, lords of Kumayama

**Akihime (Aki)**, daughter of a nobleman, Hidetake, foster sister to Yoshimori and Kai

**Kiyoyori**, the lord of Kuromori

**Tama**, his wife, originally married to Masachika, mother of Tsumaru and stepmother to Hina

**Masachika**, Kiyoyori's younger brother

**Hina**, sometimes known as Yayoi, daughter of Kiyoyori

**Tsumaru**, Kiyoyori's son

**Bara** or Ibara, Hina's maid

**Yoshimori (Yoshi)**, the true Emperor, heir to the Lotus Throne

**Takeyoshi (Take)**, also Takemaru, son of Shikanoko and Akihime

**Lady Tora**, mother of the five children born to five fathers

**Shisoku,** the mountain sorcerer
**Sesshin,** an old scholar and sage
**The Prince Abbot of Ryusonji**
**Akuzenji,** King of the Mountain, a bandit
**Hisoku,** Lady Tama's retainer

## THE MIBOSHI CLAN

**Lord Aritomo,** head of the clan, also known as the **Minatogura Lord**
**Takaakira,** lord of the Snow Country, friend and confidant to
  Lord Aritomo
**The Yukikuni Lady,** his wife
**Takauji,** their son
**Arinori,** lord of the Aomizu area, a sea captain
**Yamada Keisaku,** Masachika's adoptive father
**Gensaku,** one of Takaakira's retinue
**Yasuie,** one of Masachika's men
**Yasunobu,** his brother

## THE KAKIZUKI CLAN

**Lord Keita,** head of the clan
**Hosokawa no Masafusa,** a kinsman of Kiyoyori
**Tsuneto,** one of Kiyoyori's warriors
**Sadaike,** one of Kiyoyori's warriors
**Tachiyama no Enryo,** one of Kiyoyori's warriors
**Hatsu,** his wife
**Kongyo,** Kiyoyori's senior retainer
**Haru,** his wife
Chikamaru, later Motochika, **Chika,** his son
**Kaze,** his daughter
**Hironaga,** a retainer at Kuromori
**Tsunesada,** a retainer at Kuromori
**Taro,** a servant in Kiyoyori's household in Miyako

# THE IMPERIAL COURT

**The Emperor**
**Prince Momozono,** the Crown Prince
**Lady Shinmei'in,** his wife, Yoshimori's mother
**Daigen,** his younger brother, later Emperor
**Lady Natsue,** Daigen's mother, sister to the Prince Abbot
**Yoriie,** an attendant
**Nishimi no Hidetake,** Aki's father, foster father to Yoshimori
**Kai,** his adopted daughter

## AT THE TEMPLE OF RYUSONJI

**Gessho,** a warrior monk
**Eisei,** a young monk, later one of the **Burnt Twins**

## AT KUMAYAMA

**Shigetomo,** Shikanoko's father
**Sademasa,** his brother, Shikanoko's uncle, now lord of the estate
**Nobuto,** one of his warriors
**Tsunemasa,** one of his warriors
**Naganori,** one of his warriors
**Nagatomo,** his son, Shika's childhood friend, later one of the
    **Burnt Twins**

## AT NISHIMI

**Lady Sadako** and **Lady Masako,** Hina's teachers
**Saburo,** a groom

## THE RIVERBANK PEOPLE

**Lady Fuji,** the mistress of the pleasure boats
**Asagao,** a musician and entertainer
**Yuri, Sen, Sada** and **Teru,** young girls at the convent
**Saru,** an acrobat and monkey trainer
**Kinmaru** and **Monmaru,** acrobats and monkey trainers

## THE SPIDER TRIBE

**Kiku**, later Master Kikuta, Lady Tora's oldest son
**Mu**, her second son
**Kuro**, her third son
**Ima**, her fourth son
**Ku**, her fifth son
**Tsunetomo**, a warrior, Kiku's retainer
**Shida**, Mu's wife, a fox woman
**Kinpoge**, their daughter

**Unagi**, a merchant in Kitakami

## SUPERNATURAL BEINGS

**Tadashii**, a tengu
**Hidari** and **Migi**, guardian spirits of Matsutani
**The dragon child**
**Ban**, a flying horse
**Gen**, a fake wolf
**Kon** and **Zen**, werehawks

## HORSES

**Nyorin**, Akuzenji's white stallion, later Shikanoko's
**Risu**, a bad-tempered brown mare
**Tan**, their foal

## SWORDS

**Jato**, (Snake Sword)
**Jinan**, (Second Son)

## BOWS

**Ameyumi**, (Rain Bow)
**Kodama**, (Echo)

*Part One*

# EMPEROR OF THE
# EIGHT ISLANDS

# I

# KAZUMARU

'Did you see what happened?'
'Where is your father?' Two men were standing above him, their shapes dark against the evening sky. One was his uncle, Sademasa, the other Nobuto, whom he didn't like.

Kazumaru said, 'We heard a funny noise,' and he mimed placing stones on a board. 'Clack, clack, clack. Father told me to wait here.'

The men had come upon the seven year old hidden in the long grass, in the sort of form deer stamp out for their fawns. The horses had nearly stepped on him. When his uncle lifted him up the grass had printed deep lines on his cheek. He must have been there for hours.

'Who brings a child on a scouting mission?' Nobuto said quietly.

'He can't be separated from him.'

'I've never seen a father so besotted!'

'Or a child so spoiled,' Sademasa replied. 'If he were mine . . .'

Kazumaru did not like their tone. He sensed their mockery. He said nothing but resolved to tell his father when he saw him.

'Any sign of his horse?' Sademasa asked Nobuto.

The older man looked towards the trees. 'The tracks lead up there.'

A small group of stunted trees clung to the side of the volcanic mountain. Some were dying, some already stumps. The air smelled of sulphur, and steam hissed from vents in the ground. The men went warily forward, their bows in their hands. Kazumaru followed them.

'Cursed-looking place,' Nobuto said.

The larger tree stumps were crisscrossed with faint lines. A few black stones, a handful of white shells were scattered on the ground.

'Something bled here.' Nobuto pointed at a splash on a pale rock. He crouched and touched it with his finger. 'Still wet.'

The blood was dark, almost purple.

'Is it his?' Sademasa whispered.

'Doesn't look human to me,' Nobuto replied. He sniffed his finger. 'Doesn't smell human either.' He wiped his hand on the rock and stood, looked around, then suddenly shouted, 'Lord Shigetomo! Where are you?'

'You, you, you,' came back the echo from the mountain and behind the echo another sound, like a flock of birds beating their wings.

Kazumaru looked up as the flock passed overhead. He saw it was made up of strange-looking beings, with wings and beaks and talons like birds, but wearing clothes of a sort, red jackets, blue leggings. They looked down on him and pointed and laughed. One of them brandished a sword in one hand, a bow in the other.

'Those are his weapons,' Nobuto cried. 'That is Ameyumi.'

'Then Shigetomo is dead,' Sademasa said. 'He would never have surrendered the bow alive.'

Afterwards Kazumaru was not sure what he remembered and what he dreamed. His father and his clever, witty mother often played Go in the long snowbound winters at Kumayama. He had grown up with their sounds, the quiet clack of stones on the boards, the rattle in the wooden bowls. That day he and his father heard them together. They had ridden far ahead of the others. His father always liked to be in the lead, and the black horse was strong and eager. It had been a present from Lord Kiyoyori, to whom the family were vassals and on whose orders they had ridden so far north.

His father reined in the horse, dismounted and lifted him down. The horse began to graze. They walked through the long grass and almost stepped on the fawn, lying in its form. He saw its dark eyes, its delicate mouth, and then it was on its feet and leaping away. He knew the other men would have killed it, had they been there, but his father laughed and let it go.

'Not worth Ameyumi's time,' he said. Ameyumi was the name of his bow, a family treasure, huge, perfectly balanced, made of many layers of compressed wood with intricate bindings.

They went stealthily towards the trees where the sounds came from. He remembered feeling it was a game, tiptoeing through the grass that was as tall as he was.

His father stopped, holding his breath, so Kazumaru knew something had startled him. He bent and picked him up and in that moment Kazumaru glimpsed the tengu playing Go beneath the trees, their wings, their beaked faces, their taloned hands.

Then his father was striding back to the place where they had found the fawn. He could feel his father's heart beating loud through his chest.

'Wait here,' he said, placing his son in the trampled grass of the form. 'Be like the deer's child. Don't move.'

'Where are you going?'

'I am going to play Go,' he replied, laughing again. 'How often do you get the chance to play Go against tengu?'

Kazumaru didn't want him to. He had heard stories about tengu, mountain goblins, very clever, very cruel. But his father was afraid of nothing and always did exactly as he pleased.

The men found Shigetomo's body later that day. Kazumaru was not allowed to see it but he heard the shocked whispers, and remembered the beaks, the claws as the tengu flew overhead. *They saw me*, he thought. *They know me.*

When they returned home Sademasa reported his older brother had been killed by wild tribes in the north, but Kazumaru knew, no matter who actually killed him, he had died because he had played Go with the tengu and lost.

•

The news of his father's death plunged Kazumaru's mother into a grief so extreme everyone feared she could not survive it. Sademasa pleaded with her to marry him in his brother's place, saying he would bring Kazumaru up as his own son, even swearing an oath on a sacred ox-headed talisman.

'Both of you remind me of him all the time,' she said. 'No, I must cut my hair and become a nun, as far away from Kumayama as possible.' As soon as the winter was over, she left, with hardly a word of farewell, beyond telling Kazumaru to obey his uncle.

The family held a small parcel of land, confirmed by Lord Kiyoyori, on the side of the mountain known as Kumayama. It was made up of steep crags and deep sunless valleys, where a few rice paddies had been carved out on either side of the rivers that tumbled from the mountain between forests of cypress and cryptomeria, full of bears, wolves, serow and other deer, and boars, and groves of bamboo, home to quail and pheasants. It was seven days' journey east of the capital and four days in the other direction from the Miboshi stronghold of Minatogura.

As the years went by it became apparent that Sademasa was not going to keep his oath. He grew accustomed to being the Kumayama lord and he was reluctant to give it up. Power, along with unease at his own faithlessness, unleashed his brutal nature. He treated his nephew harshly, under the pretext of turning him into a warrior. Before he was twelve years old, Kazumaru realised that each day he lived brought his uncle fresh disappointment that he was not dead.

Some of Sademasa's warriors, in particular one Naganori, whose son was a year older than Kazumaru, were saddened by the harsh treatment of their former lord's son. Others like Nobuto admired Sademasa for his ruthlessness. The rest shrugged their shoulders, especially after Sademasa married and had children of his own, thinking that it made no difference as Kazumaru would probably never be allowed to grow up, let alone inherit the estate. Most of them were surprised that he survived his brutalising childhood and even flourished in some ways, for he practised obsessively with the bow and from his rages came a superhuman strength. At twelve years he suddenly grew tall and soon after could string and draw a bow like a grown man. But he was as shy and fierce as a young wolf. Only Naganori's son, who received the name Nagatomo in his coming of age ceremony, was in any way a friend.

He was the only person Kazumaru said goodbye to when, in the autumn of his sixteenth year, his uncle announced he was taking him hunting in the mountains.

'If I don't come back, you'll know he has killed me,' Kazumaru said. 'Next year I come of age, but he will never step aside for me. He has grown too fond of being the lord of Kumayama. He intends to get rid of me in the forest.'

'I wish I could come with you,' Nagatomo said. 'But your uncle has expressly forbidden it.'

'That proves I am right,' Kazumaru replied. 'But even if he doesn't kill me I will not be coming back. There's nothing for me here. I've only the vaguest memories of what it was like before. I remember not being afraid all the time, being loved and admired. Sometimes

I daydream about what might have happened if my father had not died, if my mother had not left, if more of the men were loyal to me ... but that's the way it turned out. Don't grieve for me. I can't go on living in this way. I pray every day to escape somehow – if the only way is through death, so be it.'

## 2

# KAZUMARU/SHIKANOKO

The summer storms had abated and every day the stain of red leaves descended further from the peaks. That year's fawns were almost full grown but still followed their mothers through the shade-dappled forest.

There was a famous old stag with a fine set of antlers that Sademasa had long desired but the creature was cunning and cautious and never allowed itself to be encircled. This would be the year, Sademasa declared, that the stag would surrender to him.

He took his nephew, his favourite retainer, Nobuto, and one other man. They went on foot, for the terrain was too rough even for the sure-footed horses that grazed on the lower slopes of Kumayama. They lived like wild men, gathering nuts and berries, shooting pheasants and setting traps for hares, every day going further into the pathless forest, now and then catching glimpses of their prey, then losing it again until they came upon its tracks in the soft earth or its brown compact scats. Kazumaru expected his uncle to grow impatient, but instead Sademasa became almost jovial, as though he were about to be relieved of a burden he had carried for a long

9

time. At night the men told ghost stories about tengu and mountain sorcerers, and all the ways young boys had disappeared. Kazumaru swore he would not let himself be killed along with the stag. He hardly dared sleep but sometimes fell into a kind of waking dream and heard the clack of Go stones and saw the eagle eyes of tengu turned towards him.

They came one afternoon to the summit of a steep crag and the stag stood before them, its antlers gleaming in the western rays of the sun. Its flanks were heaving with the effort of the climb. The men were panting. There was a moment of stillness. Sademasa and Kazumaru both had their bows drawn. The other two men stood with knives ready. Sademasa gestured to Kazumaru to move around to the left and drew his bow. Kazumaru was about to draw his, seeing where he would aim, right at the heart. The stag looked at him, its eyes wide with exertion and fear. Then its gaze flickered towards Sademasa and Kazumaru followed it. In that instant he saw his uncle's bow was aimed not at the stag but at him. Then the stag was leaping straight at him in its desperate lunge to escape. The arrow flew, the stag collided with Kazumaru and sent him crashing down with it into the valley below.

The animal broke his fall. As they both lay unmoving, winded, he could feel the frantic beat of its heart beneath him. He reached for the antlers and grasped them, then stood, fumbling for his knife. The deer was wounded, its legs broken. Its eyes watched him, unblinking. He prayed briefly and slit its throat, the hot blood pouring from it as its life slipped away.

Thick bushes hid him from the men above. He could hear their shouts but made no sound in response. He wondered if his uncle's desire for the antlers would be so great he would follow him down the cliff, but the only way was to jump or fall. When silence returned he dragged the stag as far as he could, finding a small hollow under a bank filled with dry leaves. He lay down with the dead beast in his arms, slaking his thirst in its blood, reliving the moment on the cliff. It would have been easy to tell himself it was an accident but it seemed important to face the truth. His uncle had aimed at him but the stag had taken the arrow. It had saved his life. And then he felt again his own fall, the astonishment of flight, his hand gripping the bow as if it would hold him up, too young to believe in his own mortality yet expecting incredulously to die.

All night he sensed wild animals circling, drawn by the smell of blood. He heard the pad of their feet, the rustling of leaves. The sky was ablaze with stars, the River of Heaven pouring light.

At dawn the stag had cooled. He moved it into the clearing and set about skinning it, carefully cutting out the brain pan and the antlers, regretful for the way life had vanished so quickly from the eyes and face, wishing it could be restored, all the time filled with gratitude.

He found flint-like stones and spent the morning scraping the skin clean. The sun came round the valley and for a few hours it was hot. In the early afternoon he carved several strips of meat from the haunches, thin so they could dry quickly, and threaded them on a shaft cut from an oak tree, placing leaves between them. He left the rest of the carcase for the foxes and wolves and began to walk towards the north.

Mostly he walked all night; the moon was waxing towards full, bringing the first frosts. He slept for brief periods in the middle of the day, after softening the deer hide with water or his own urine and spreading it out to dry. He saw no one but on the third day he became aware an animal was tracking him. He heard the pad and rustle of its tread and saw the green gleam of its eyes. Several times he set an arrow to the bowstring but then the eyes vanished and he did not shoot. He did not want to lose an arrow in the dark.

It seemed to be guiding him or, he reflected uneasily, herding him. From time to time he thought it had gone but at nightfall it always returned. Once he caught a glimpse of it and knew from its size and colour it was a wolf, drawn by the scent of the deerskin and the meat. He and his uncle had pursued the stag to the point of exhaustion and now the wolf was doing the same to him. It was driving him further and further into the forest and when he was exhausted and weakened by hunger it would spring at his throat. He tried to outwit it, pretending to sleep then rising soundlessly, changing direction, but it seemed aware of his intentions even before he was. He saw its green eyes shining in his path.

One morning at dawn he stopped beside a stream that flowed through an upland clearing from a spring further up the mountain. He had eaten the last of the dried meat a day ago. A path had been worn through the grass and there were tracks at the water's edge. He saw that animals came to drink there: deer, foxes, wolves. He slaked his own thirst warily, gulping quickly from cupped hands. Then he hid upwind with arrow drawn.

He must have dozed off, for a sudden movement woke him. He thought he was dreaming. Two animals appeared walking awkwardly side by side, their heads turned towards each other. They were carrying something between them in their mouths. They walked strangely as though they were not quite alive. Their heads were lacquered skulls, their teeth sharp and glistening, their eyes bright shards of lapis lazuli. Their skins did not cover flesh but seemed to be packed with straw and twigs. He caught their smell of smoke and putrefaction; his stomach heaved and his guts twisted.

As they came closer he saw the object they carried in their mouths was a two-handled water jar. They stood in the pool and lowered the jug into the stream. When it had filled they turned and walked back along the path, staggering a little and spilling water as they went.

Kazumaru followed them as though in a dream, without questioning but not without fear. He could hear the thump of his blood in his skull and chest. He knew he was approaching the lair of a mountain sorcerer, just as his uncle's men had described. He wanted to flee, yet he was driven forward not only by his own curiosity and hunger but also by the wolf, which now padded openly behind him.

He passed a rock that looked a little like a bear and then a tree stump with two jagged branches like a hare's ears. Closer to a small hut, which stood in the shelter of a paulownia tree, the forms became more lifelike and precise: statues carved from wood and stone, some with the same lacquered skulls, some draped in skins or decorated with antlers; owls, eagles and cranes with feathers; bats with leathery wings.

The hut's roof was thatched with bones, its walls covered with skins. A strong smell of urine came from a large bucket by the door. One detached part of his mind thought, *He must use it for tanning hides*, just as his own urine had softened the stag's skin. Two fox cubs, real, were snarling at each other over a dead rabbit. The wolf sat on its haunches, panting slightly. The two beasts Kazumaru had been following stopped in front of the hut and whined. After a few seconds the sorcerer emerged. He took the jug from their mouths and made a gesture for them to sit as if they were dogs. His skin was tanned like leather, his hair long, his beard wispy, both deepest black with no sign of grey. He seemed both old and young. His movements were as deft and free of thought as an animal's but his voice when he addressed Kazumaru was human.

'Welcome home. So, you have come back to Shisoku?'

'Have I been here before?' Kazumaru said. Behind him the wolf howled.

'In this life or another.'

And maybe he had. Who knew where the soul voyaged while the body slept? Perhaps it had the strange familiarity of dreams.

'Did you bring the shoulder blades?' the man called Shisoku asked abruptly.

'No, I . . .' Kazumaru began but the sorcerer cut him off. 'Never mind. No doubt they'll turn up one day. Give me the antlers. We still have time.'

'Time for what?'

'To make you the deer's child. That's why you came.'

'What does that mean?'

'Your life is not your own. You will die to one life and rise to another, to become what you are meant to be.'

He turned at that moment and tried to run but the sorcerer spoke words in a language he did not know and then said, 'You will stay!' and the words were like bars closing around him. He felt bony hands grasp his forearms, though the sorcerer stood some distance from him. Shisoku stepped slowly backwards and Kazumaru was drawn into the hut.

•

He was not sure if he was in a dwelling, a workshop or a shrine. There were scents of lacquer, camphor and incense, not quite masking the stench of dead things. In the hearth a fire blazed under an iron pot in which bubbled an unrecognisable brew. Carving tools and paintbrushes lay on a smoke-blackened bench. The floor was of packed earth but at one end, in front of a sort of altar, rugs and cushions had been spread surrounded by glittering lamps and candles. Carved figures of deities, all with lacquered and painted faces, stood on and around the altar, and on the wall hung many masks and animal heads, together with their skins. He could see at least two human skulls. He realised he had arrived at one of those places where the worlds mingle, like the place that had haunted his childhood dreams where his father met the tengu. He began to tremble but there was no escape. Outside, the hut was surrounded by animals, both real and counterfeit. Inside was the sorcerer.

Without knowing how it happened he was lying before the altar, naked, covered only by the deer skin. He looked up at Shisoku with the same eyes as the stag, widened and resigned in the face of death. Shisoku gave him a drink of mushrooms and pine needles, mixed with lacquer and cinnabar, which would ordinarily kill a man but put Kazumaru into a deep trance. Time stopped.

Kazumaru watched him take the antlers and the half-moon-shaped brain pan and begin to create a mask, chanting as he worked, some mysterious sutra that Kazumaru had never heard before. Slowly day turned to night. Outside, the animals stirred and cried out. It seemed to Kazumaru that a woman lay next to him. He was filled with fear, for he had never been with a woman, had avoided the knowing glances of the maids at Kumayama, suspicious of all they seemed to offer, wary of the ways humans hurt each other. But she led him on to embrace her, many times that night and the following ones, his cries mingling with the animals'. He knew his body, his strength, his maleness, were being used for purposes he did not understand, against his will. Nevertheless his own lust rose to meet hers.

In the day he lay unable to move and watched Shisoku as he painted the mask with layer upon layer of lacquer and the red and white fluids produced by the lovers. He dried each layer by passing it through smoke from the incense, chanting a different spell each time. He made lips and a tongue from cured leather painted with cinnabar, carved out hollows for the eyes and fringed them with black lashes cut from the woman's hair. He polished the antlers until they shone like obsidian. The moon waxed to full and waned into nothingness. When it was next half-grown the mask was finished.

Shisoku fitted it to Kazumaru's face. It clung to his features like a glove to a hand. He felt rush through him the strength of the stag and all the ancient wisdom of the forest. The woman came to him one last time. His cries echoed like the stag in autumn. She held him tenderly and whispered, 'Now your name is Shikanoko, the Deer's Child.' A distant memory came to him – a fawn, his father's voice – and he knew he would never take another name. Then he fell into a deep sleep. When he awoke he was clothed again, the woman had gone and the stag's mask lay in a seven-layered brocade bag on the altar. It did not seem possible that it should fit in a bag that size, but it was one more aspect of the spells that Shisoku had cast on it.

•

Shisoku practised a kind of haphazard, offhand magic. He made a vague gesture towards the fire, which sprang into life seven times out of ten and the other three sulked in disobedience. The live foxes and wolves occasionally appeared when he summoned them but more often went on with their wild lives as if the sorcerer were not living among them. Sometimes the artificial animals did what was expected of them, fetched water in the jug, gathered firewood, but shards of pottery at the water's edge indicated how many times they had failed. Shikanoko collected firewood himself and as winter wore on went out hunting to feed them both. He made new arrows and fletched them with eagle's feathers, but though he spotted and followed many deer he never killed one again.

Shisoku ate very little, but spent his days skinning and plucking, preserving skins and plumage with camphor and rue, boiling up skulls and bones to get rid of every last trace of flesh. Then painstakingly he recreated the dead animals as though he were some kind of creator spirit, stuffing the skins with clay and straw, building frames of bamboo and cord to hold the skeletons together. His creations stood in rows under the eaves, the snow drifting across them. For many weeks the frost preserved them but when spring came insects returned too. Eggs hatched into grubs and most of the crawling mass had to be burned. One or two survived, by luck, skill or magic, and came to life and joined Shisoku's collection.

The snows melted high in the mountains and the stream flooded almost up to the door of the hut. After it receded, grass and wild flowers covered the clearing. Every night Shisoku placed the mask on Shikanoko's face and taught him the movements of the deer dance.

'This dance unlocks the secrets of the forest and releases its blessings. It is a powerful link between the three worlds of animals, humans and spirits. When you have mastered the dance you will gain knowledge through the mask. You will know all the events of the world, you will see the future in dreams and all your wishes will be granted.'

The movements awakened something in him that he both craved and feared, but he thought it was probably unreliable like all Shisoku's magic and he only partly believed it.

•

Just after the full moon of the equinox a band of ten horsemen came into the clearing.

'It is the King of the Mountain, Akuzenji,' Shisoku said. He did not seem alarmed.

Shikanoko took up his bow anyway. He was sure the woman who rode with them was the one who had accompanied him through his initiation and the creation of the mask, but she gave no sign of recognising him. He was filled with intense curiosity about her and sudden shyness in her presence. He wanted to ask her a hundred questions, but could not find the words for one.

Akuzenji dismounted and added a stream of urine to Shisoku's bucket, saying, 'My contribution to your work. I'm sure it has magic properties.' He was a broad squat man with tangled hair and beard. He wore a shabby corselet of leather plates laced with faded green cords and carried a huge sword – both looked as if they had been stolen from some ambushed warrior. He said to Shisoku, 'I've just come to check you are keeping safe the treasure I entrusted to you.'

'I placed it under a binding spell,' Shisoku replied. 'Shall I release it to you?'

'Not yet. Business is good, I've no need of it. But I'd like to take a look at it.'

Shisoku bowed in his offhand way, and waved him towards the hut. He followed Akuzenji inside while the other men dismounted, urinated into the bucket in turn, and squatted down by the fire. After a while Akuzenji came out, a smile of satisfaction on his face, and sauntered towards Shikanoko.

'And who might you be?'

'I was Kumayama no Kazumaru, but now I am Shikanoko.'

'The boy who fell off the mountain last year? You were believed to be dead.'

'I came here and the sorcerer looked after me.'

'Did he?' Akuzenji's shrewd black eyes took in the bow and the fletched arrows. 'I don't suppose your uncle will pay a ransom for you, will he?'

'He would be more likely to pay for confirmation of my death,' Shikanoko said, wondering if he had just invited the King of the Mountain to kill him.

'What about Lord Kiyoyori? He'd be your liege lord, wouldn't he? Would he pay anything for you?'

'I don't suppose so,' Shikanoko replied. 'What use would I be to him?'

'A pawn has many uses, but only if it is alive,' the woman said.

It was her – he recognised her voice. It roused both anger and fear in him, at the way she and Shisoku had used him, but he also felt a pang of longing for that deep intimacy when their bodies had been joined as one and an object of beauty and magic had been created.

Akuzenji frowned and scratched his head, studying Shikanoko with a probing look. 'How old are you?' he said.

'I turned sixteen in the new year.'

'Can you use that bow?'

'I can, but I will not kill deer.'

'But will you kill men?'

'I have no objection to killing men,' he replied.

'Then I will tie up your hair, you can swear allegiance to me, and come with us.'

Shikanoko sought Shisoku's eyes. Was he to go or stay? The sorcerer did not return his gaze.

It was not the coming of age ceremony he had expected: he had thought he would kneel before the Kuromori lord, Kiyoyori, in the presence of his uncle and all their warriors. Instead there was the spring clearing, the wood smoke in his eyes, the rough lord who took him into his service, the animals half-living and dead. When it was done he placed some of the arrows in his quiver, tied the rest in a bundle, and took up his bow. Shisoku went into the hut, came out with the seven-layered bag containing the mask and gave it to Shikanoko.

The woman unloaded sacks of grain, rice, millet and bean paste from one of the horses and took them into the hut. The men were gathering up any usable skins and feathers. Akuzenji eyed the seven-layered bag.

'What's that?'

Shisoku gave him no answer.

'Show me,' Akuzenji demanded and, after a moment's pause, Shikanoko drew the mask from the bag and held it up.

Akuzenji took a step back, silenced, angry. When he could speak, he said, 'This is the sort of thing I've always wanted from you. When am I going to get it? For years I've been begging you. I want a skull of divination to be my oracle, to tell me all things. You know the secret techniques and rituals; why do you keep denying me?'

'It is not me who denies you,' the sorcerer muttered, but Akuzenji was in full flow.

'I have brought you many skulls. Surely no one has brought you as many. What did the boy bring you? Why did you favour him?'

'He came at the right time,' Shisoku said. 'I'm sorry.'

'So when is the right time?'

'It is when the time is right. The skulls you bring are worthless – dull peasants or desperate criminals or warriors steeped in blood. Bring me a wise man or a shrewd minister, an ascetic or a great king.'

'Is that what the boy brought you?' Akuzenji was incredulous. 'How?'

'He is Shikanoko, the Deer's Child. What he brought was for him alone.'

Akuzenji stuck out his lower lip and narrowed his eyes. 'What about Kiyoyori's skull? What if I brought that?'

'Kiyoyori is undoubtedly a great man,' Shisoku replied. 'But he is not going to let you take his head.'

The woman spoke again, 'Kiyoyori's skull is not for you, Akuzenji. If you try for it you will lose your own.'

She and Shisoku exchanged a slight glance, a fleeting smile, making Shikanoko shiver as he caught a glimpse of the secret worlds they moved in, worlds that he was now part of.

He knelt in thanks before the sorcerer, who smiled slightly, and brushed him away.

He looked back as they rode off. One of the wolves had approached the hut and the sorcerer stood with his hand on its head.

The rider next to him laughed. 'Old Four Legs! Did you learn any useful tricks from him?'

He waggled four fingers in Shikanoko's face. 'Did he turn you into a four legs too?'

There was a flash of lightning, a sudden crack of thunder. A pine tree in their path split in half, smoking. The horses reared and plunged to the side, nearly unseating them.

'Make sure you are far away before you speak ill of the sorcerer,' the woman said quietly.

The man looked chastened and Shikanoko was glad the magic had for once been effective. He rode behind the woman, knowing that he had indeed embraced her many times, that together they had made the mask, but at the same time not understanding how that was possible. How would she make such a journey night after night? Did she have magic powers or had he lain with a spirit woman, summoned by Shisoku? Had he lain with a demon?

# 3

# KIYOYORI

Lord Kiyoyori was twenty-eight years of age, the time when men approach the height of their physical and mental powers. He was descended from the Kakizuki family, who took their name from the persimmon-coloured moon of autumn. Their founder was the son of an emperor who renounced his imperial rank and took an ordinary surname and whose sons and grandsons prospered, becoming skilful statesmen, gifted poets and fine warriors, while his granddaughters became wives and mothers of emperors.

Though Kiyoyori's family were younger sons of younger sons and so not of the highest rank or importance, his father, Kiyomasa, had always had the deepest respect for his name and had done his utmost to preserve it. He had endeavoured to bring his sons up as perfect warriors, experts with horse, bow and sword and unquestioningly obedient to their father's will.

Kiyomasa frequently visited the capital, Miyako, and kept himself fully abreast of all the politics and intrigues of the court. The Kakizuki family held many important posts but so did their rivals, the Miboshi, also of imperial descent. Kiyoyori's grandmother had been a Miboshi, for in more peaceful times the two great families had often intermarried. But recently relations between them had been less cordial.

For years the Miboshi had been fighting the Emperor's battles in the east and north of the Eight Islands, bringing clans under their control and subduing various barbaric tribes. Their lord, Aritomo, had established himself in Minatogura in the east, but many of his warriors were turning up in Miyako, expecting rewards for their services, including court positions, new ranks and land.

There were not enough of any of these to go round.

Warrior families, aware of intrigues in the Emperor's court and in the government, were striving among each other for position and influence. Kiyomasa tried to arrange advantageous marriages for his sons, and at seventeen Kiyoyori had been married to a woman from the domain of Maruyama in the west, whose father was a counsellor in the Kakizuki government. The marriage had worked out well, a child was born, and then another, but this second one took the life of her mother, and then slipped away after her, across the River of Death, leaving Kiyoyori grief stricken. He had loved her deeply and felt he would never recover from her loss. His only consolation was their first child, a daughter, whose pet name was Hina.

The younger brother, Masachika, had also made a desirable marriage to the daughter of a neighbour who owned an extensive and productive estate known as Matsutani, Pine Valley. It was all destined for Lord Matsutani's son but, the day after his sister's marriage, on the journey home, the young man had attempted to swim his horse across the swollen river, had been swept away and drowned. There were no other heirs and it seemed everything would go to Masachika's new wife. Masachika himself assumed his father-in-law would adopt him, giving him a far greater and richer estate than his older brother's.

However, his father had other plans, which he announced a few months after the death of Kiyoyori's wife. Kiyoyori was twenty-one, Masachika nineteen. The brothers were summoned to a meeting in one of the secret rooms in the house at Kuromori, a fortified residence built mainly of wood in an inaccessible position on a mountainside surrounded by the Darkwood from which they took their name. It had several hidden rooms; this one faced south and was the warmest. Perhaps for this reason it had been taken over by a man of indeterminate age and unremarkable appearance who had the reputation of being a great scholar. He certainly spent a lot of time reading and the room was filled with his scrolls and manuscripts which he collected from the eight corners of Heaven and which were in many languages. He had a monkish sort of name, Sesshin, and could sometimes be heard chanting. Nobody took much notice of him. Kiyoyori found his presence vaguely reassuring, like that of an old dog.

It was a showery autumn day, rain sweeping across the valley. The shutters were closed, the room dim even though it was not yet mid-afternoon. The thought of winter approaching filled Kiyoyori with gloom. He could not shake off the sadness that had fallen on him since his wife had died.

He had been outside the stables when his father sent for him. He wanted to start teaching Hina to ride and had been trying out a suitable pony, with the help of most of the children of the estate. For some time he had feared that his father was going to announce he had found him another bride. Naturally he would have to marry and produce an heir, but at the moment he felt more inclined to cut his hair and become a monk. Only Hina kept him from such a decision. He came to the meeting with some apprehension, which increased as they sat waiting for his brother. The shutters rattled as gusts of wind shook them and rain beat heavily on the roof. His father kept giving impatient glances up from under his heavy eyebrows and sighing heavily.

Eventually Masachika appeared, full of excuses for his tardiness. He had an air of expectation, as though all his desires were at last to be confirmed.

Their father began to speak. 'I know you believe as I do that our most important aim must be the survival and increase in influence and power of our family. I believe we are approaching very dangerous times. There have been many evil omens in the capital and diviners predict warfare and chaos. Our estate is too small to support sufficient warriors to give us much influence. Now fate has given us the opportunity to merge with Matsutani.'

Masachika nodded and a faint smile appeared on his well-shaped mouth.

'But I cannot dispossess my eldest son,' their father continued, 'for whom I have such a high regard, and to give the greater estate to the younger son is asking for conflict. Therefore, I have decided that you, Masachika, will put aside your wife and will go to our Miboshi relatives in Minatogura. My cousin has one daughter only and has agreed to adopt you as his son. Kiyoyori will marry your former wife and will inherit both estates. Her father is in complete agreement. This way, if war does erupt between Kakizuki and Miboshi, whichever side prevails, one of my sons will be among the victors.'

For a few moments neither of them spoke. Then Masachika said, trying to control himself, 'I am to give my wife to my brother? I am to lose her and Matsutani?'

'There is no need to be so drastic, Father,' Kiyoyori said. 'Let my brother keep his wife. I will renounce my claim to both estates. I wish to retire from the world . . .'

'Don't be a fool,' his father snapped. 'You are my eldest son and heir. Do you think I would allow you to humiliate yourself and become a monk? A man does not flee from the world. He bears up under its sorrows and does his duty. Yours is to me and your family. After all, you have your daughter to consider.'

Kiyoyori tried then and later to dissuade his father from making the two brothers enemies in such an irretrievable manner. He dared to admonish him, citing many instances from classical literature where brothers had destroyed each other and whole kingdoms, but Kiyomasa would not brook any contradiction. Masachika had to hide his rage and resentment and Kiyoyori his reluctance, and both had to submit.

Later, after Masachika had left for Minatogura, his father said to Kiyoyori, 'I believe you will improve the land and defend it. Masachika wanted only to enjoy it. It would have been swiftly taken from him. Old Matsutani knows that, which is why he agreed with me. Besides, the men prefer you and you know how to treat them.'

•

It was a time of troubles and opportunities. In the capital the Emperor was weak, his sons rivals. His brother-in-law, the Prince Abbot at Ryusonji, was regent in all but name. He favoured the Emperor's younger son and carried on endless intrigues against the Crown Prince.

In the provinces the Kakizuki extended their power in the west and the Miboshi in the east while both strove for influence in the capital. Warlords fought constant skirmishes seeking always to increase their land. More land meant more warriors who in turn could be used to gain more land. Retainers were persuaded to swear undying loyalty, but they expected much in return. If they felt badly treated or overlooked, their loyalty was eroded; they could be seduced away to another warlord's service, someone who appreciated them and offered greater rewards.

•

Kiyoyori was all too aware that no one had asked Tama, the woman who had been Masachika's wife and was now his, for her consent or even her opinion. She was as obedient to her father as her husbands were to theirs. Kiyoyori waited several weeks to make sure she was not pregnant, and when he did approach her he felt as shy and awkward as an adolescent. She responded dutifully but without any real passion, and while he knew he could not blame her for this, it still wounded his pride. He felt his younger brother would always lie between them. Even his delight and gratitude when she gave birth to a son could not break down the barriers between them. She nursed the baby herself, used this as an excuse to keep him away and from then on they slept apart. Kiyoyori continued to feel obscurely guilty about her and treated her with excessive courtesy, masking the absence of real warmth and intimacy. It was for her sake that he moved to Matsutani, for she loved her childhood home and put all her energies into making the residence more beautiful and the estate more productive than ever. Kiyoyori took his horses and his dogs and somehow the old scholar went with them, along with all his books. Matsutani was certainly more comfortable and more convenient, but no one ever referred to its owner as anything other than the Kuromori lord. The Darkwood was his true home.

In the following years both fathers left this world to cross the Three Streamed River for that place of underground springs and caves where they would face the judges of Hell. Kiyoyori was, as his father had predicted, a good leader of men, as well as being both courageous and astute. He was quick to anger and impulsive, acting swiftly on instinct, but his instincts were usually correct and his anger, together with a degree of ruthlessness, meant he was feared as well as admired. His fame spread. He fought several small but well-planned skirmishes that subdued his neighbours and rivals, not only holding on to his own lands but also extending them. The twin estates of Kuromori and Matsutani seemed blessed. Some said it was karma due to good deeds in a former life; others that the estates must be protected by powerful magic and charms.

One dawn in the ninth month when he was walking towards the horse lines, for it was his custom to ride every morning with two or three retainers or young pages, Kiyoyori realised he did not have his whip. He must have left it somewhere in the residence. He thought of sending a groom back for it but, not being sure exactly where it was, decided it would be quicker to fetch it himself.

He stepped onto the wide verandah and pushed up the bamboo blind. The wooden shutters had already been opened as the day promised to be fine and warm. There was someone in the room, one of the servants, he thought at first, but the person did not bow or glide respectfully away. Instead whoever it was sat down cross-legged as if he planned to stay for a while and said, 'There you are! I have been waiting for you.'

'It would have been a long wait,' Kiyoyori replied, ignoring the familiar tone. Eccentric old men could be allowed a few liberties. 'On a beautiful day like this I might have ridden until midday.'

'I knew you would return for this.' The whip lay in the old scholar's wrinkled palm.

'Well, thank you, Master Sesshin.' Kiyoyori stepped forward to take it, but without him quite seeing how, the whip switched sides and now lay on the other palm. All his senses came alert. He knelt in front of Sesshin, keeping his eyes fixed on his face. He realised he had hardly spared the old fellow a glance in all the years they had lived under the same roof. Indeed he had averted his eyes and made efforts not to notice him, finding his slovenly appearance vaguely affronting and his body odour disconcerting. The thought came to him that maybe the old man had kept himself concealed in some way and now for the first time he was allowing Kiyoyori to see him.

The skin was like ancient silk, drawn taut over the bones. The eyes returned the lord's gaze guilelessly but they held an unfathomable depth. They had looked on worlds he had not even dreamed of and into mysteries he would never understand.

He spoke brusquely to hide his unease. 'Do you have something to say to me? If you wanted to speak to me why did you not send a message?'

Sesshin laughed, a dry crackling noise like old wood burning. 'You would have put me off and gone out today, and then it would have been too late.'

'What do you mean?'

'There is a bandit, Akuzenji. He calls himself the King of the Mountain.'

'I know who Akuzenji is. I have no quarrel with him. As long as he stays on the mountain, does not extract excessive amounts from merchants and deals with his rivals swiftly he is causing me no harm. I don't have enough men to place guards on the whole length of the North Mountain Road. Let Akuzenji do my work for me; I don't have to pay him.'

'He is going to demand a high price from you. He has taken a fancy to your skull.'

Kiyoyori laughed. The idea that a bandit would dare to attack him, the Kuromori lord, amused him. 'Give me my whip and I'll be on my way.'

'Well, if you must ignore my warning, take extra men and be on your guard. Or tonight your head will be in a pot, the flesh boiling from it, and before the next moon your brother will be back in Matsutani and your children will be dead.'

'Is my brother plotting with Akuzenji? Is that what you are trying to tell me?'

'Plotting is not perhaps quite the right word. Akuzenji has no personal enmity towards you. He simply wants the skull of a great man. He is an undiscerning fellow. He boasts of every exploit before and after its achievement. He may never have seen you but he knows you to be great because your fame spreads more widely every year. Your brother is an opportunist. He prays for your death before your son is grown so he may take back what he believes you stole from him.'

'Akuzenji seeks the skull of a great man? For some kind of dark magic?'

'I believe so,' the old man said.

'I should offer him yours!'

'Certainly my skull would be extremely powerful, as would all parts of me. Luckily for me, Akuzenji does not know of my existence, nor does anyone else. That is why, Lord Kiyoyori, it is in my interests to keep you alive.'

'How do you know these things? Who are you?'

'Don't you wonder why you never thought to ask me before?'

'You have always been around ever since I was born,' Kiyoyori said slowly. 'You were part of the household like an old chest or a tree in the garden.' He could have said, *like a dog*, but he realised the dogs died one after the other, at their allotted time, but the old man had lived on and on.

'Kuromori became my home when your grandfather was lord. We were friends. He arranged I should stay on after his death throughout your father's time. The place suited me, and Matsutani is even better; it's perfect for my studies and research. In return I have been able to perform certain rituals that have ensured the safety and prosperity of your domain.'

'And I thought it was all due to my hard work and good management!'

'You have played your part. I would not have wasted my efforts on an inferior person. Spells can only go so far.'

Kiyoyori said nothing for a few moments. Outside a kite was mewing, the wind soughed in the pine trees, a horse neighed impatiently from the stables.

Sesshin said, 'You say you cannot afford to guard the North Mountain Road, but if you removed Akuzenji and his bandits the merchants would pay you for their safe passage.'

'Akuzenji is as cunning and elusive as a wolf,' Kiyoyori replied, 'but if he can be enticed by my skull I may take him by surprise.'

'Wear armour under your hunting robe,' Sesshin said. 'And send someone as a decoy on your horse: Tachiyama no Enryo for example.'

'Enryo? Why do you name him?'

'He sends messages occasionally to your brother in Minatogura.'

'Does he now?' There was another short silence. 'His wife is a great favourite of my wife. They have been friends since childhood.' Was Tama also in touch with his brother, her first husband? Kiyoyori could feel fury building within him.

# 4

# SHIKANOKO

Shika, as the bandits called him, was neither happy nor unhappy in the service of the King of the Mountain, in the high fastness that was Akuzenji's base. From time to time he wondered if this was to be the rest of his life or if he should return to Kumayama and confront his uncle. On the whole it seemed better to let everyone in his old life believe him to be dead.

He felt he was waiting every day to see what would happen to him. Akuzenji called himself King of the Mountain, just as pirates styled themselves Kings of the Sea, but in the eyes of most they were still pirates and Akuzenji no more than a bandit. Shika learned how he protected merchants and their goods on their way to the north and west, trading out of Kitakami and other sea ports, where ships loaded with copper coins, iron, textiles and medicines came from Silla and Shin on the mainland. Akuzenji fought off other marauding bandits and made life safe for the woodsmen who cut trees on his mountain and sent the logs downstream to Lake Kasumi and then on to the capital. He had always been a superstitious man who liked to keep a number of shamans and sorcerers on the mountain and in the forest to consult about dreams and omens. Now he had become obsessed with obtaining a suitable skull for Shisoku's magic and had settled on the Kuromori lord.

He soon realised Shika could move as silently as a deer, with the same keen eyesight and hearing and began to send him on scouting missions to the land around Matsutani. Shika came to know Lord Kiyoyori well: his favourite horse, a tall black stallion; his manner of riding; and the retainers and pages who accompanied him, to whom Shika assigned nicknames in his mind: Gripknees, Wobbly, Neversmile.

When he was not scouting he practised archery, shooting endlessly at the straw targets, or made arrows from close-jointed bamboo, some with humming bulbs carved from magnolia wood. He fletched them with feathers he found in the forest or took from birds he hunted, eagles and cranes. He also carried out the countless chores that were laid on him as the youngest of Akuzenji's men, feeding and grooming the horses, including Akuzenji's white stallion, Nyorin, fetching water from the well and firewood from the forest, skinning and butchering dead beasts.

Only when he was alone and certain no one was watching did he take out the mask made from the deer's skull. He placed it over his face and tried to meditate. But what stirred within him was the ancient power of the forest, the stag's drive to mate and make children. There were many women in Akuzenji's fortress, but they already had husbands, lovers or other protectors and favourites and were out of his reach. And then there was the one who had ridden with the bandit to the mountain sorcerer's hut, whose name he discovered was Lady Tora. Men lowered their voices when they spoke it and whispered about her among themselves. She had some power that terrified them, though they would never admit it. He knew the mask was powerful in the same way but he had not yet learned to turn that power to his own advantage and it left him disturbed and confused.

One warm sultry evening he went deep into the forest and came upon a waterfall that fell white in the twilight into an opaque black pool in which was reflected the thin sickle of the new moon. Hot and restless, he took off his clothes, laid them on a rock with the brocade bag that held the mask and plunged into the water. When he surfaced, shaking drops from his eyes, he saw some creature moving on the bank. He thought it was a deer coming to drink but then he saw the long black hair and the pale face and realised it was a woman.

Lady Tora stood where he had left his clothes. She bent down and took the mask from the bag. She beckoned to him. He came naked out of the water, his skin wet and cool. She placed the mask on his face and kissed the cinnabar-coloured lips. Beyond the rocks was a mossy bank and here they lay down together.

She was without doubt the same woman who had come to him in the sorcerer's hut. She was using him for some purpose of her own, just as the sorcerer had used him to create the mask, but as then he had no will to resist. Skilfully she led him into the Great Bliss and together they heard the Lion's Roar. A sudden gust of wind drove spray over them, soaking them.

Then Tora took the mask off and kissed the real lips, the real eyes. 'Now you must lie with no one, woman or man, until you wed the one who is meant for you.'

'Will I never lie with you again?'

'No, our work together is finished.'

She stroked his face tenderly as though he were her child.

He was so unused to affection he felt near tears.

'That was part of my mission, which one day you will understand,' she said. 'And it was the final ritual of the mask. Love is bound into its creation but so is lust, the force that drives the world to recreate itself, unconstrained by human rules.'

'I understand nothing,' he said.

'Use the mask carefully – it will bring you wisdom but it will also lead you into danger. Practise abstinence and all the other disciplines our friend taught you in the forest. Subdue your body and mind so when you meet her you will recognise her.'

'Who is she?'

She did not answer him, but told him to bathe himself again. The water was like ice on his body. When he came out she was gone.

•

The next morning just after daybreak Lady Tora rode out with Akuzenji and his men. She gave Shikanoko no sign of recognition, no glance, no smile. It was as if there were some other realm in which their meetings took place far removed from the conventions and relations of the everyday world. He wondered what Akuzenji's reaction would be if he knew; he was a violent man and Shikanoko had already seen the punishments he handed out for minor disobedi-ence: an eye torn out, a hand amputated, brandings . . .

He shivered and kicked the brown mare he was riding. She still lagged behind the others. She was the oldest and slowest horse in the group, given to him because he was the newest arrival and the youngest. There was something about him that unsettled her, as horses were often alarmed by deer, and she tried many ways to rid herself of him, rubbing his legs against posts or walls, carrying him under low-hanging branches, taking him by surprise by shying or bucking. Her name was Risu. He had lost count of the number of times he had fallen off, a source of endless entertainment to the other men.

In her contrary way Risu had formed a bond of affection for her previous rider, a lanky man called Gozaemon, and whickered after him as he cantered ahead on the sturdy dark bay horse he had been promoted to. Now she swung her head back and tried to bite Shika's foot.

Akuzenji was leading his men down the forest-covered slope towards the trail through the valley where Lord Kiyoyori rode every morning. The rest of the group were some way ahead, out of sight. Risu lifted her head and neighed as Gozaemon came trotting back.

'Hurry up,' he said. 'Lord Akuzenji wants you to kill someone.' He grabbed Risu's rein and led her alongside his horse. She moved faster than she had all morning.

Akuzenji and his men had concealed themselves in a grove of bamboo on a rocky outcrop above the trail that ran between the forest and the cultivated fields. The rice had been cut and was hanging in sheaves to dry. Farmers were already at work, spreading manure and mulch. Akuzenji beckoned to Shika and said, 'Get off your horse and take up position. I want you to shoot him in the neck or the chest. Don't hit his head whatever you do.'

They could hear the sound of horses approaching. At the same time Shika became aware of a woman calling in the distance. She was running across the rice field, shouting and waving both arms. She looked awkward, almost comical, a noblewoman not used to running, her layered robes tangling round her legs. She slipped and fell sprawling into the manure.

Why was she running? He frowned, trying to work out what was going on.

The riders, a small group, not wearing armour, swept into view, the black stallion in the lead.

'Now,' Akuzenji breathed. 'Shoot him!'

'Shoot who?'

'The Kuromori lord! On the black!'

'That is not the Kuromori lord,' Shika said, lowering his bow slightly. 'It's his horse but it's not him.' It was the man he called Neversmile.

'Shoot!' Akuzenji screamed in his ear.

Shika shrugged and obeyed. The arrow slammed into the unprotected neck. The blood sprayed in an arc of scarlet glistening in the first rays of sunlight. Dust rose in golden motes as the horse reared and the man fell.

The other riders halted and fell back as the bandits surged forward, Akuzenji in the lead. He had slid from his horse, seized the topknot of the fallen man with a yell of triumph, and was in the act of severing the head when there came a pounding of hooves, the shouting of men, and a host of armed warriors appeared. At their head was Lord Kiyoyori.

# 5

# KIYOYORI

Kiyoyori was possessed by both rage and exhilaration as he surveyed the kneeling prisoners. All that day they had been held in the riding ground between the stables and the residence, under a chill wind, for the weather had changed suddenly bringing the first intimation of winter.

The rage was against the disloyalty of his retainer, Tachiyama, who had taken his horse and died in his place. The exhilaration was for his survival, the stallion's survival, for the painful deaths already suffered by some of those who had wanted his and for the imminent execution of the rest.

Tachiyama's wife had revealed everything before she died: Akuzenji's scheme to take Kiyoyori's head, letters between Tachiyama and his brother, Masachika, their desire to see Akuzenji's plan succeed and to seize the opportunity to regain the estate. His rage extended to his own wife whom he had not yet questioned though she had been waiting for him, pale but dry-eyed, when he returned from the skirmish. She had expressed appropriate amazement at the audacity of the attack and equally suitable relief at her husband's survival, yet he felt she was lying. Of course it was not her fault that two old men had agreed to trade her between two brothers, but since she obviously had no deep feelings for him it was not unreasonable to suspect she might still harbour some for Masachika. She stood to benefit as much as anyone from Kiyoyori's death.

He thought for the thousandth time of his dead wife. If only Tsuki had lived!

*If I had, you would not own Matsutani – would you really be willing to pay such a price?*

He heard her teasing laugh and, looking across the riding ground, saw her standing in the front row among the prisoners. Surely it was her? The long black hair reaching to the ground, the slender form . . . he would recognise them anywhere even after eight years.

'I am sorry, lord,' one of his men, Hachii Sadaike, said at his side. 'She refuses to kneel; she has stood like that all day.'

*Oh my beloved! You must be cold. One day in the frost and eight years in the grave.*

'Lord Kiyoyori?' Sadaike said.

He came back to his senses. 'Who is she?'

'A woman who rode with the bandits.'

He looked at her and saw she was not Tsuki, though there was a resemblance. While he wondered at it, their eyes met. Once he had been close to a lightning strike and had felt all his hair stand on end. He experienced the same jolt now.

The woman bowed her head and fell to her knees before him. She would kneel for no one else but she would for him. An almost uncontrollable passion seized him, a desire stronger than he had ever known. He would have the whole band executed at once and then he would have her brought to him.

He had thought to devise some special punishment for Akuzenji, boiling him alive or sawing his head off slowly, to dissuade anyone else from daring to attack the Kuromori lord, but now his impatience would brook no delay. He was about to order Sadaike to take the woman aside and remove the heads of the rest, when the sky darkened and a shadow loomed over the riding ground. It swooped low over Kiyoyori's head and then rose to sit on the gable of the roof behind him. As he spun round to look at it, it began to call in a voice so ugly everyone whose hands were not tied behind their backs immediately covered their ears.

Kiyoyori called for archers to shoot it down and his best bowmen came forward, eager to compete and win the lord's favour, but it was obviously an evil creature with supernatural powers for their eyes were dazzled by the sun and their arrows clattered uselessly on the tiles. It was hard to perceive clearly: one moment it seemed dense and black, the next Kiyoyori thought he saw golden eyes like a monkey's above the needle-sharp beak. Its tail was long and sinuous like a snake and its legs were striped with gold, reflecting its eyes. It mocked them in a voice that was close to human, but inhuman, filling their souls with dread.

'Go to Master Sesshin,' Kiyoyori instructed one of his pages. 'Ask him what this creature means. Is it a sign that I must spare Akuzenji's life?'

He had spoken quietly but the woman heard him.

'Do not send for the master,' she said. 'The bird has nothing to do with Akuzenji. Let Shikanoko kill it now at once.'

Her voice thrilled him. He made a sign that she should approach him. 'Who is Shikanoko?'

The woman walked towards him, then turned and called, 'Shikanoko!'

*Oh that she would call me like that! She will! She will!*

'It was he who shot your decoy,' she said to Kiyoyori.

'He would have killed me! I should put a bow in his hands now?'

'He spared your horse,' she said gravely. 'He is a good marksman.'

'I suppose I cannot argue with that,' Kiyoyori said, elation sweeping through him at her proximity.

The boy came forward, a young man on the cusp of adulthood. Fairly tall, thin, brown skinned, he moved, despite his cramped limbs, with spare grace like an animal. Kiyoyori studied him with narrowed eyes. He did not look like a bandit. He was surely a warrior's son; perhaps he had been kidnapped. If he could kill the bird he would be spared and Kiyoyori would find out who he was and restore him to his family or take him into his service. If he failed he would die along with the rest of them, which would serve him right for keeping such bad company.

'Give him his bow and arrows,' he ordered.

He could tell his men did not like this command, nor did they relish the likelihood of being shown up by a stripling. There was a short delay while the bow and quiver were located among the piles of weapons that had been taken from the bandits and then they waited for Shikanoko to restring the bow. The bird called gratingly all the while, swinging its head from side to side and peering down with golden eyes, seeming to laugh in greater derision as Shikanoko drew the bow back, squinting against the sun. He lowered it as if the mocking intimidated him.

*He will die tonight,* Kiyoyori vowed.

Shikanoko whispered in the woman's ear.

'Something else was taken from him,' she said to Kiyoyori. 'It must be returned to him before he can shoot. A seven-layered brocade bag containing a mask.'

'Find it,' Kiyoyori commanded, barely able to control his impatience.

One of his men produced the bag a little shamefacedly.

The boy received it without speaking, his demeanour relaxing noticeably as he felt the contents of the bag.

'Tell him to show me what's inside,' Kiyoyori said to the woman. He liked the idea of speaking through her as though the boy were a barbarian who needed an interpreter, as though he bound both of them closer to him by this means.

She said, 'Show the lord.'

Shikanoko drew out the mask and held it in both hands towards Kiyoyori, who gasped without meaning to at the almost living power of the face, the dark lashes over the eye sockets, the reddish lips and tongue. He saw the brain pan from which it had been formed and was conscious suddenly of his own skull, so hard yet so fragile. The mask seemed to float between woman and boy like an infant. He realised they had both taken part in its creation and jealousy flooded through him. The woman's eyes met his and he knew it was for this that Akuzenji had wanted his head, to turn it into a magic object of power.

He gestured upwards with his head and Shika put the mask away, giving the bag to the woman to hold. The bird had fallen silent, peering down at them. Now it launched itself into flight but it was too late. The arrow sped true from the bow, humming as it went. Its sound merged into the bird's cry of despair as it pierced the heart. Blood burst from the wound falling in sizzling drops. Then the creature plunged headfirst to the ground.

'Bring it to Master Sesshin,' Kiyoyori said. 'He will know what it is.'

•

Even the most hardened warriors were reluctant to touch it, so Shikanoko, after drawing out the arrow and returning it to his quiver, wrapped it in the woman's shawl and carried it in both hands into the residence. Kiyoyori led the way to Sesshin's room. It was the first time he had been in it since the move to Matsutani, and the differing scents of old books, ink, lamp oil and some sort of incense made his senses reel even more.

'It is a werehawk,' Sesshin said, after inspecting it carefully. 'How strange that it should come here now.'

'What does it mean?' Kiyoyori demanded.

'I shall have to practise some divination to find out.' The old scholar looked slightly perturbed. 'What a mysterious coincidence of events. I knew something was awry but I thought it only affected you. Now I fear there are wider forces converging, with far-reaching consequences.'

He fell silent, gazing on the dead bird.

Kiyoyori felt suddenly weary. It seemed days ago that he had returned for his whip. He wanted above all to lie down with this woman and wipe out the reproaches of the dead.

From outside came the sound of heads falling one by one as the bandits were executed. Most of them were resigned to their fate, not unexpected given their calling, and died quietly, some speaking the name of the Enlightened One, but a few struggled and cursed, wept and pleaded. It was a pitiful sound.

Shikanoko quivered at each sword blow, tears in his eyes. The woman remained calm, watching Sesshin carefully.

A great yell of defiance that could only be Akuzenji echoed like a thunderbolt. Shikanoko gasped as if he were about to sob.

'Lord Kiyoyori may leave now,' the old man said. 'And the woman had better take this boy away before he faints.' His tone was dismissive and he hardly looked at Shika, continuing to stare at the dead werehawk, a frown creasing his brow.

'We will stay with you,' said the woman.

Kiyoyori and Sesshin spoke together. 'That will not be necessary.'

'I think you will find it is,' she replied. 'Please leave, lord.' She looked from one to the other though only Kiyoyori returned her gaze. She said no more, just waited calmly for him to obey her.

He said, 'But you will come to me later? We will be together?'

'I promise we will,' she said.

# 6

# SHIKANOKO

After the lord left, Sesshin looked from the dead bird to Lady Tora and then to Shikanoko.

'I don't understand why you are here. I usually conduct my divinations in private. They involve secrets that only the initiated are permitted to see.'

'We have something that will save you some time,' Lady Tora said. 'Shikanoko is an initiate. And I have taken part in rituals far more esoteric and dangerous than anything you can imagine, even though you are a great scholar and magician. Shikanoko, give the master the mask.'

He handed it over, suddenly reluctant to expose Shisoku's creation to the scrutiny of another sorcerer, but Sesshin took it from the bag with reverent hands and studied it intently. 'What a wonderful thing! Who made it?'

Lady Tora said, 'The mountain sorcerer, Shisoku. It was made for Shikanoko because he is the son of the stag.'

Sesshin looked swiftly at Shikanoko as if seeing him for the first time. There was a flash of something – surprise, recognition. The old man shook his head.

'Well, well,' he said quietly. 'Let him put it on.'

Shika recalled Shisoku's instructions and allowed the movements of the deer dance to flow through him. The others watched intently. He could still see them in the room. He was aware of his own figure, wearing the mask, looking through its eyes. The room took on the dappled light and the rich leafy smell of the forest. And then he was the stag stepping lightly between the trees, ears pricked, nostrils flared. Hawks flew overhead, shrieking loudly. The stag bounded after them. Each bound covered miles.

Shika saw the hawks fly over a great city and under the eaves of a temple set in a deep grove, beside a lake, not far from the river bank. He read its name board: Ryusonji. He stood on the verandah and saw, through the open doors, the hawks alight on the shoulders of a man dressed in brocade and silk robes, embroidered with dragons. They opened their beaks and sang to him in human voices.

The man peered into the brightness and said, 'I am the Prince Abbot of Ryusonji, the Dragon Temple. But who are you?'

Then Sesshin was shaking him and he was once again in the old man's dusty room.

'Don't speak! Don't say who you are!'

'I wasn't going to.' Shika removed the mask, held it to his brow and thanked it before returning it to the seven-layered bag.

'I saw your lips move. You were about to speak. Never mind; who was there?'

'The Prince Abbot at Ryusonji,' Shika said. 'The hawk was a messenger from him. The hawks speak to him in human voices.'

Sesshin breathed out slowly. 'Why would the Prince Abbot be turning his attention to Kuromori?'

'Perhaps he is looking for you,' Lady Tora suggested.

'I sincerely hope he doesn't know who or where I am.'

'Don't be so modest, Master. Surely at one time you knew each other quite well?'

'Years ago we studied together. He will have forgotten me by now.'

'Something must have reminded him. Unless it is the Kuromori lord who has attracted his attention.'

Sesshin scratched his head with both hands. 'I just want a quiet life,' he complained. 'I don't want to come to the attention of the Prince Abbot. He's going to be very angry at the loss of his werehawk. It is dead, isn't it?' He poked at the bird but it gave no sign of life. 'You shouldn't have killed it.'

'Only Shikanoko could have killed it, and he was there,' Lady Tora said. 'Doesn't that suggest some deeper working of fate than your desire for a quiet life?'

Sesshin buried his head in his hands. 'I would like you to go away now while I consider what this means and how I should advise Lord Kiyoyori. I have a horrible feeling it is not going to turn out well, least of all for me.'

'Shikanoko can leave now but I will stay. There is something else that needs to be done before I go to Lord Kiyoyori.'

Shika wanted to stay with them, wanted to talk about what had happened to him, what it all meant, who was the priest who had seemed so alarming and so attractive at the same time. He sensed they knew so much they could teach him and he was seized by a ferocious hunger to swallow up all this knowledge before it was too late.

'Go,' Lady Tora said, but he lingered outside, aware of the fragrance emanating from her, mingling with the lamp oil and incense. He heard the old man say, as if with foreboding, 'What do you want from me?'

'That which you have not given to earth, water, air or fire, to neither man nor woman, for forty years,' she replied. 'I am going to make you a father.'

'You'll have no luck with me,' he said, trying to joke. 'It's all withered away.'

'You will be able to give me what I need. Don't look so apprehensive, my dear Master. I promise you will find it enjoyable.'

Shika walked away. He did not know if he was feeling jealousy or some other deep emotion. He felt a sob rise in his chest – was it grief? But why would he weep for Akuzenji or for any of the others who had teased and bullied him? Yet, he was close to tears for them, and felt he should make some effort to honour their deaths and placate their restless spirits. He could hear chanting in the distance. Following the sound he made his way to the small shrine at the end of the lake, and knelt there beneath the cedars.

# 7

# KIYOYORI

The last of the bodies were stacked in a pile, covered with brushwood and set on fire. It was a long time since the smell of burning flesh had floated over the peaceful dwellings and fields of Matsutani. Kiyoyori was impatient, racked by desire, but he would not let this distract him from what had to be done. He dispatched groups of retainers with the heads to display them on sharpened posts at the Shimaura barrier and at crossroads and bridges along the North Mountain Road. Then he turned his attention to the problems that the deaths of Akuzenji and his band presented. The most urgent matter was to launch an attack on their mountain fortress and secure for himself their means of controlling the road and the merchants who travelled along it. This seemed like a straightforward exercise that could be carried out by his retainers. Then arrangements had to be made to purify the riding ground from the pollution of death and to make offerings to placate the spirits of the departed. When he had issued his instructions and spoken to the priests he sent for his wife. By then it was approaching dusk.

'Your eyes are red,' he addressed her. 'Were you weeping because I was not killed?'

'Forgive me, lord. I was overcome by shock and grief that such an attempt should be made on my husband's life.'

'And you are no doubt affected by the death of one of your waiting women?'

'If she was in any way part of the intrigue I rejoice at her death. My tears are for no one but you.'

'I would like to believe that.'

'It is true.' An expression of fear flickered into her eyes as though she had suddenly realised the danger of her position.

'You did not for a moment allow yourself to hope that you might be returned to your first husband?'

'How can you say such a thing? He is as dead to me. Have I not been a faithful wife to you? Everything that was mine is now yours. I have given you a son; I have been a mother to your daughter, as far as she would let me. I would have gladly given you more children, but you seem to have grown cold towards me.'

He made no reply, studying her carefully. She met his gaze with frank eyes.

'My lord must be tired and hungry. Let me prepare a bath and some food. What is your pleasure?'

'Did you know that my brother had been sending letters to Tachiyama?'

'I swear I did not. I would have told you at once. Please, take a bath and relax. Shall I bring the children to see you?'

The cedar-scented smoke from the bathhouse masked the smell from the pyre and in the hot water Kiyoyori felt himself cleansed in body and spirit. He ate with his children, who were thrilled and grateful to be included in the special feast his wife prepared: rice with chestnuts and quail, hen's eggs simmered in broth, fresh water fish grilled with taro. They were well behaved and confident. Both seemed intelligent, especially Hina, who he could see was growing more like her mother every day. She showed a great interest in the events of the day and questioned him closely about what they all meant, what would happen to the boy who shot the bird, and what her father would do with all the extra horses.

He could find no fault in their upbringing. But how would he feel if their mother was betraying him. He recalled Sesshin's words. *Your brother will be back in Matsutani and your children will be dead.*

This had become the usual behaviour of warlords and warriors. Was it not how he had dealt with Akuzenji? Even now his men were clearing out the mountain fortress as though ridding it of vermin. If Akuzenji had children there none would remain alive. He felt a moment of futile regret, which he tried to put from him. He could not show any weakness or he would be exploited by those he spared or by the others among whom he strove to be first, most important, most powerful. He would reap the benefit of his victory today and bestow the land and resources he gained as a reward to one or other of his men to bind them closer to him. He wondered, as he did from time to time, what his life would have been like if his father had agreed to his request to become a monk. He might have known greater peace and fewer regrets, he would have no suspicions of his wife or rage against those who sought to betray him, but he would not taste the incomparable elation of success or the restless anticipation of his next encounter with the new woman.

After they had finished eating, his wife told the maids to prepare the bedding and take the children away. When they were alone she encouraged Kiyoyori to lie down and he saw that she wanted to lie alongside him and make love to him. But she was not the one he desired, and he felt ashamed of sleeping while his men were still out risking their lives.

'I think I will go to the shrine for a while,' he said. 'I cannot come close to you when death and blood lie so heavy on me.'

'Whatever Lord Kiyoyori wishes,' she said, trying to hide her disappointment, but failing.

•

The priests were chanting, incense burned and bells rang. Kiyoyori noticed a solitary figure kneeling at some distance from the shrine steps beneath the tall shadowy cedar trees. He washed his hands and rinsed his mouth at the cistern. An attendant rushed forward with a mat for him to kneel on. After he had prayed for his victims' souls he asked to have Shikanoko sent to him.

He spoke some words to comfort him. 'I made arrangements for prayers to be offered. May their souls have a safe onward journey.'

'I cannot believe they are all dead,' the boy said in a low voice. 'They are all dead and I am alive. Though perhaps it is your intention to send me to join them.'

'Tell me who you are and how you came to be with them, and then I will decide what to do with you.'

Shikanoko told him his story briefly and when he had finished Kiyoyori said, 'That is rather inconvenient as your uncle is one of my chief allies. He swore allegiance to me and I confirmed him in the estate after you were presumed dead.'

'But Kumayama is mine,' Shikanoko replied.

'Nevertheless your uncle, Jiro no Sademasa, has been loyal to me. I cannot simply evict him in your favour.'

'Even though he tried to kill me?' Shikanoko said stubbornly.

'We only have your word for that. Your uncle's version is you slipped and fell. In his opinion it was a result of your wilful and impetuous character, and was an accident that would have happened sooner or later. Furthermore, why should I or anyone else believe you? You could be an impostor, put up to this claim by your bandit master. What proof do you have that you are Kazumaru?'

'People will recognise me. My men will know me.'

'Your men are quite happy with your uncle. Boys change in the year between sixteen and seventeen. The boy who disappeared was a child. I see before me a man with all the appearance of an outlaw.'

'So, you do intend to kill me?'

'I have not yet decided.'

The boy said nothing. He did not plead or argue and Kiyoyori liked him for that. He was disposed to spare him – good bowmen were always useful, and Shikanoko had possibly done him a favour by shooting down the werehawk.

'Was anything revealed in the divination?' he asked.

'They sent me away after the mask showed us the bird's identity. There was another ritual to perform between Lady Tora and the master.'

*Lady Tora.* So, that was her name.

'What kind of ritual?' Kiyoyori said.

Shikanoko did not answer for a moment but shot a strange look at the lord as though their roles were reversed and Kiyoyori was the youth whose life hung in the balance.

'And just who is the so-called lady?' Kiyoyori said. *A bandit's woman*, he was thinking. *Mine by right of conquest.*

'Lord Kiyoyori should be wary. Lady Tora is not what she seems.'

Night was falling and it had grown much colder. The wind had swung round to the north and dark rain clouds were slowly covering the sky. A sudden gust sent dead leaves swirling beneath the trees.

Kiyoyori stood. 'Let us go and learn the results of the divination.'

He was seized by impatience and alarm that the 'ritual' might be a euphemism for something unbearable – and so it was. When he strode into the room and saw the woman and Sesshin lying in disarray and realised what they had been doing, his rage was so great he felt like killing them both. But Lady Tora smiled and said, 'And now, lord, I am yours,' and prostrated herself before him as she had done before. The same lust erupted within him. He grabbed her hand and led her through the garden where she seemed to fly behind him, so light was her hold on his. He took her to a building on the lake shore, the summer pavilion.

Rain drove against the shutters. Drops fell through the flimsy roof making the charcoal in the brazier smoke and hiss. Beneath the bearskin rugs Kiyoyori and Tora were remote in their own world. He had not lain with a woman for months; his wife no longer attracted him and he had been too preoccupied to seek pleasure elsewhere. Now he was possessed by the mindless lust of adolescence, the inexhaustible desire, yet it was more than lust; it was a passionate yearning to be completely absorbed by this woman, to surrender to her and let her take him to unimaginable destinations.

He had thought her the bandit's woman, a prostitute, and when he had walked into the scholar's room and saw that Sesshin, the old fox, had been making love to her, he had been angry but also strangely relieved. So, she was a whore; he desired her, he would take her, and when he was tired of her, he would have her executed along with the boy. But when the night was beginning to fade into dawn and his desire was finally sated, she stroked his hair and sang quietly, a song that was popular in the capital, and he felt he had found the other half of himself, that he would tire of his own body before he tired of her. He lay making plans for the future; he would build her a house and install her there as his second wife.

He foolishly did not consider that she might have her own plans.

# 8

# AKIHIME

The eldest daughter of the Nishimi family was traditionally
dedicated to the shrine of the All Merciful Kannon at Rinrakuji
to become a shrine maiden. The family was among the highest
rank of the nobility, related to the Emperor. The current head of
the household, Hidetake, was a close friend of the Crown Prince,
Momozono, and his wife was wet nurse to the Crown Prince's son,
Yoshimori.

Hidetake had had two daughters born some ten years apart. The
older one was called Akihime, the Autumn Princess, because she had
been born in the autumn, the same month as now when the maples
were turning scarlet and the gingko tree by the gate dropped swathes
of golden leaves. The younger one, born in winter, had died at birth.
It was because of this that her mother had been able to nurse the
young prince, the Emperor's grandson.

Aki was fifteen years old, not particularly beautiful but lively
and full of high spirits. In that autumn of her sixteenth year suitors
had begun to hover outside the house, wooing her with poetry and
music. Her mother both feared and hoped that one might find his

way in. It was the custom of that time: if a man came three nights in a row and made love to the girl it was considered a marriage. Aki had already made her vows of purity and she recoiled from the idea, yet was drawn to it at the same time. Were the men invited inside or did they force their way in? Did the girl have any choice in the matter or did she simply submit?

'I won't let anyone touch me,' she declared one morning when her mother was voicing her concerns. 'You know my father has taught me how to defend myself.'

'You can hardly fight off a young nobleman with a sword,' her mother exclaimed. 'That would be a terrible scandal.' Then she added with a sigh, 'Sometimes we don't want to defend ourselves. Men can be very persistent. But at least if that happened we could keep you at home.'

Aki could see her mother was close to tears. 'You will still have Yoshimori, and Kai who is like a daughter to you.'

They both looked over to the verandah where Kai was playing with Yoshimori. They had been born on the same day and were inseparable friends. Yoshimori was in his seventh year. He was an intelligent child, popular with everyone, adored by his father. When he was two years old a physiognomist had pronounced he would reign as Emperor. It had made a deep impression on him.

'Yoshimori will soon be lost to me,' her mother said. 'But I suppose I will never lose Kai, as no one will ever marry her.'

'You can't see her ears when her hair covers them. I think they are charming, like a little bird or a gecko.'

'A gecko! Don't say such things!'

Kai's mother, one of the women of the household of whom Aki's mother had been particularly fond, had died in childbirth. Her baby girl had tiny ears like the whorl of a shell. When the midwives saw her they had exclaimed in fear and the baby had been wrapped in a cloth and left in a corner. It had been a terrible day with the deaths of a mother and a child and the birth, earlier than expected, of the young prince. Kai's mother was buried the same day as Aki's little sister, while the baby prince was given to Aki's mother to nurse. Everyone forgot the other baby, but she clung to life until Aki's mother heard her whimpers and demanded to see her. She was moved to pity and insisted that she would bring up both children together.

They were afraid she might be deaf but she could hear perfectly well though she had a way of frowning and looking intently at people's mouths when they spoke to her. She was prettier than Aki, with a sweet plump face and delicate limbs, and the women of the household often bewailed the fact that she might have made a wonderful marriage or other alliance, maybe even with Yoshimori himself, but for her ears.

No one knew what the future would bring for her, but Yoshimori adored her, insisted that she be with him at all times, and often would only be calmed and consoled by her. She had a lively imagination and made up stories and games, keeping him entertained in what was otherwise a tedious existence for a young child. He was not allowed outside – the verandah was as far as he went – and he was carried everywhere within the palace. He saw his own parents rarely and then had to be carefully trained in the correct etiquette and elaborate language of the court. Already he was expected to take part in the long complicated rituals that were part of life in the imperial household and though he was not yet seven years old sometimes Aki saw on his face an expression of resignation and world weariness that moved her to pity. Only with Kai did he behave like an ordinary child. He ordered her around, squabbled with her, threatened to scream if he was separated from her, but they ate from the same bowl and slept side by side.

Aki knew his father, the Crown Prince Momozono, a little, though she was not allowed to speak of how. Her father had taken her to Rinrakuji several times. She had made her preliminary vows there and begun to learn her duties and the many rituals in the service of Kannon. She was taught self defence, how to ride a horse and use a bow. Her father practised sword fighting and studied the art of war with an old monk who had once been a famous warrior. Sometimes Prince Momozono was there too, in disguise. Rinrakuji's monks had the reputation of being bold and belligerent and Aki knew without being told that her father and the Prince were preparing for war.

The Emperor, Momozono's father, was ailing. He had designated his oldest son as his heir, but the Prince Abbot, the powerful priest at the temple of Ryusonji, favoured the second son, Daigen, whose mother was the Prince Abbot's sister. He had taken an implacable dislike to the Crown Prince, taking every opportunity to undermine him, trying to persuade the Emperor to disinherit him. Aki knew that Prince Momozono was preparing to fight for the throne if necessary, but that no one must reveal this, for if it came to the Prince Abbot's ears it would be called rebellion.

'Look!' Yoshi called, pointing into the garden. 'Look at that strange bird.'

Aki stared out and saw a large black bird had landed clumsily in one of the maple trees, scattering leaves and twigs. It gave a curious call, both compelling and repulsive, and swung its head towards Yoshimori as if studying his features with its hard golden eyes. It seemed to recognise him, for it bowed its head three times in a way that was both respectful and mocking.

Aki's mother and her attendants were seized by horror, for it seemed a terrible omen, but Kai, unafraid, cried, 'Let's give it something to eat.'

'Yes, bring food!' Yoshimori commanded.

One of the ladies in waiting went inside, pale-faced and trembling, and came back with a bowl of rice cakes. Kai took one and went slowly into the garden. Yoshimori tried to follow her but at least three pairs of hands restrained him.

Kai held the rice cake on her open palm. The bird peered down. When it did not descend she placed the cake on the ground and took a few steps back. The bird hopped from the tree, picked up the rice cake in its claws, inspected it carefully then swallowed it in a gulp. It fluttered to the pond and drank. Then it flew back to the maple, preened its breast feathers, and continued to watch balefully, occasionally uttering a loud shriek.

'I don't like it,' Yoshi said. 'Make it go away.'

The women clapped their hands and raised their voices, but the bird would not be dislodged.

'Go call your father,' Aki's mother said. 'It's giving me a headache. And what terrible disasters does it portend?'

Aki found her father and told him the news, then asked, 'Should I bring my bow?' It was the ceremonial catalpa bow she had been given at the temple, along with a ritual box that held a doll, a weasel's skull and her prayer beads.

'Yes, and I'll bring mine,' her father replied, but when he saw the bird he laid the bow aside quickly, even furtively. He stepped out into the garden and said angrily, 'How dare you come here? Go tell your master to cease trying to spy on me!'

Aki raised her bow and twanged the string as she had been taught, to alert the spirits. The bird swung its head towards her, gave a scornful cry and flew away to the north.

'What was it, Father?' Aki said, going to stand at his side, following his gaze as the bird disappeared.

'A werehawk, a sort of magic hawk. The Prince Abbot has

several at his command. They have speech of a sort that only he can understand. Vile birds! I hate them!'

'You should have shot it, Father.'

'I did not want to show I am armed and prepared to use my bow. They are almost impossible to kill anyway.' He said in a quieter voice, 'He is suspicious of me. What will he do next? I am glad you will soon be at Rinrakuji. You will be out of his reach, and what you learn there may help us in our struggle against him.'

Aki shivered as if she sensed a dark shadow stretching out over the city from Ryusonji.

# 9

# TAMA

Like most girls of that time who lived in the provinces, Tama had been taught to ride and fight with a lance. When she came of age her mother had presented her with a dagger so she could defend herself or take her own life if necessary. The only time she had been tempted to use it was when she and the estate she had inherited had been taken from her husband and given to his older brother. She had lain awake at night, furious in her helplessness, imagining plunging the dagger into the throat that lay exposed next to her. She had never contemplated killing herself, for to do so would be to lose Matsutani, the family home where she had grown up and which she loved passionately.

She waited for love to develop for Kiyoyori. She could see rationally that he was an admirable man. He was courageous and intelligent, kind to his daughter, good looking in a way, though not as handsome as his younger brother. But love never came; it had come once for Masachika and her heart refused to be unfaithful though her body had to be. Even after their son, Tsumaru, was born, she felt only indifference for her husband.

Now she was also afraid of him. Since the attack by Akuzenji and the apparent disloyalty of Tachiyama and his wife, his suspicions of her increased. She had to conceal her grief for her friend and her anger at her husband. She was determined that she would give him no excuse to kill her.

She knew she did not love Tsumaru passionately as some mothers seemed to, and Hina was always cool towards her, but she made sure the children were brought up properly. She prided herself on carrying out her duties. She oversaw the running of the household, the making of clothes, the supplies of food and charcoal, the pleasure gardens, rice paddies and vegetable fields. She made the most of the life that had been given to her, tried to shut away all memories of Masachika, and was not unhappy, until the arrival of the sorceress who had enthralled Kiyoyori with a single look and who now lived in the summer pavilion.

Tama hated this woman for her supernatural beauty and strangeness, for her self confidence, her indifference to everyone but Kiyoyori, for the way she had taken up residence as spiders and foxes move into deserted houses. Sometimes Tama took out the dagger and felt its sharp edge, and imagined slashing that beautiful face to ribbons. She imagined setting fire to the pavilion, and ordered the winter's firewood to be stored along its southwestern side. Her loathing embraced the old scholar. Until now she had paid little attention to him though his presence in her well-ordered home irritated her. He had come without permission or invitation; he upset the maids by never allowing them to clean his room, and she disliked his sharp eyes and his air of superiority. Now she suspected him of some close connection with Kiyoyori's woman. She sensed that they were two of a kind, both involved in sorcery. Her dislike included Shikanoko, even though Hina and Tsumaru admired him and followed him around while he cared for the horses and carried out Lady Tora's orders. He seemed to tolerate their company and was patient with them, but Tama still disapproved and tried to forbid it. The children, however, were adept at disappearing outside and Hina, she was sure, took pleasure in disobeying her.

She began to watch Shikanoko obsessively, following him as much as the children did, resenting how assiduously he served Lady Tora. She saw how, after Kiyoyori had decided he should live, Shikanoko had been given the choice of Akuzenji's horses and had taken the white stallion for himself, as well as the brown mare. She thought the horses gave him undeserved status, the right to be fed along with the rest of Kiyoyori's men; she knew he slept on the verandah outside the summer pavilion while her husband was within, and that he was aware of her as she prowled jealously through the gardens.

•

In the tenth month Kiyoyori decided to go to Miyako. It would probably be the last chance he would have before the snow came, and he had said he was disturbed by rumours of intrigue and unrest, which he wanted to investigate for himself. Hina moped and had bad dreams. A few days after his departure the weather was suddenly fine and warm and, feeling it was the last of the pleasant autumn days, Tama allowed the children to play outside. They did not return for the midday meal but she assumed they were eating with their former nurse, Haru. Haru had two children of the same age, Chika and Kaze, and the four often played together. She was busy overseeing the fulling of cloth, and reflecting, as the heavy sound rang out in the still air, how peaceful Matsutani was, when one of the maids approached her.

'Lady, the children are not back yet.'

'Where is Shikanoko? They are probably trailing after him somewhere.'

'The men say he went out earlier with his horses,' the girl replied. 'He didn't take the children.'

'They must be at Haru's. Go and get them; it will be dark soon and it is time they came home.'

'Lady,' the girl said nervously. 'I have been to Haru. They are not there. They called at her door in the morning but her two children are sick, so she told them not to come in. She thinks they might have gone up towards the Darkwood. Her husband is out looking for them.'

The first sense of unease pricked her and immediately she began assigning blame. Kiyoyori should not have left them so unprotected; he should never have let that woman into their home, or, come to that, the old man Sesshin. Some sorcery was at work. Shikanoko had stolen them. They had been abducted by foxes or wild mountain men for secret rituals, to be carved up or eaten. She began to run towards Haru's house. From the forest she could hear men's voices calling hauntingly. *Tsumaru! Oh-e! Hina!* But the only response was the whir of a startled pheasant and the hooting of owls as dusk fell.

Then from the other direction, from the road that led west, she heard shouts that were more relieved, joyful in tone.

*They have been found!*

She ran back to the west gate and saw a cluster of people hurrying towards her, carrying ... *Oh Merciful Heaven, not a corpse! And only one? Where is the other?*

It was Hina; she looked limp, lifeless and Tama feared the worst. Her heart was threatening to choke her, but the child stirred when she took her in her arms. She was alive. She had been struck on the temple, the bruise already darkening the pale delicate skin. She opened her eyes and stared vacantly at her stepmother. Her pupils were dilated and she did not seem to know where she was.

'Hina,' Tama cried. 'What happened? Where is Tsumaru?'

Light came back into the child's stare. 'Mother,' she said haltingly. 'Men took him. I tried to stop them. One of them smacked me.'

'What sort of men? What did they look like? Was Shikanoko with them?'

'No! He would have protected us. It wasn't him. Oh, my head hurts so much!'

Kongyo, Haru's husband, arrived at Tama's side. 'Lady, I would it had been my son.'

'Why was no one watching them,' she said in anger. 'How can one child be snatched away and the other left for dead, and no one saw?'

'They often hide,' Kongyo said. 'It's no excuse, I know, but it's a game they play. They can cross the whole estate without anyone seeing them.'

'Your children taught them this! They must be punished!'

'Whatever my lady commands.'

'Ride to the capital,' she cried, with a mixture of dread and anger. 'Lord Kiyoyori must be told.'

'It is almost dark, Lady Tama.'

'Take torches! Ride all night! And remember, your children are now hostages to me.'

She herself carried Hina inside and then gave her to her waiting women, who laid her carefully down and began to apply compresses soaked in vinegar to the bruise. The girl vomited once or twice, pale pearl-hued strands unlike any food she might have eaten, and then fell into a deep sleep.

Tama stared obsessively at the black eyelashes quivering against the fragile skin, through which she could see the faint blue veins where the blood pulsed slowly, and listened to the unnaturally heavy breathing. She shook Hina gently, but the girl did not waken. Slowly the conviction grew within Tama that her stepdaughter had been placed under a spell.

'Where is Shikanoko?' she cried. When she was told he had not returned, she commanded, 'Bring the old man to me.'

# 10

# SHIKANOKO

Shikanoko had taken the horses out in the late afternoon, as he often did, training Nyorin to know his voice and respond to his commands. He had just got back and was feeding them, planning to go next to Lady Tora to see if she had any requests for him before night fell, when he saw Sesshin, already in his night attire, being escorted to Lady Tama's rooms. A tense atmosphere had descended over Matsutani. Grooms were preparing horses and blazing torches. He saw Kongyo ride off at a gallop with three other men. Nyorin whinnied loudly, watching their departure with raised head and nervous eyes.

Tora stepped out of the summer pavilion onto the narrow verandah. Shikanoko saw the curve of her belly against the western light.

'What's happened?' he said.

'Lady Tama's son has disappeared. I suppose someone has taken him to persuade his father to submit to his will.'

He glanced up at her face, disconcerted by the indifference in her voice.

She smoothed the robe over her belly. 'I will give him more sons,' she said. 'You had better follow Master Sesshin and make sure he comes to no harm.'

Shikanoko went to the residence. In the confusion no one had thought to close the shutters and from where he stood outside he could clearly see and hear everything that was happening within.

He heard Tama's voice. 'You are so wise, Master Sesshin, and my husband admires you so much. Why have you repaid him in this vile way?'

'Lady,' the old man replied. 'This has nothing to do with me. If I can be blamed for anything it is my failure to put adequate protection around Lord Kiyoyori's children, which I regret deeply.'

'That is crime enough – you admit you could have protected them and did not?'

'Even I cannot foresee all the evil deeds of men,' Sesshin said. 'Don't be too anxious. The boy must have been taken for a purpose. Therefore he is in no immediate danger.'

'How do you know this? You are involved! Shikanoko took them, didn't he?'

'I am simply making deductions. Neither Shikanoko nor I had anything to do with it.'

Tama stared at him for a moment and then said abruptly, 'Release Hina from the spell she is under.'

'Let me look at her,' the old man said, and then, 'She is concussed. It is not a spell. She will wake in the morning, fully recovered. Your women have done the right thing – vinegar compresses, nothing better. I believe you have sent for Lord Kiyoyori. There is nothing else that can be done now. We should all get some sleep. Forgive me, as I grow older my eyes grow weary.'

Shika heard something snap in the lady's voice as she replied. 'Weary? Oh, let me cure you of that. Let me show you how it feels to lose the light of your eyes, that which is dearest to you.'

She turned to the men who had brought Sesshin to her. 'Put them out.'

They did not understand. 'Lady?' one queried.

'Put out his eyes.' She drew out her dagger and held it to her throat. 'Do as I say or I will take my own life. Explain that to Lord Kiyoyori when he returns.'

Shika wanted to call out: *Don't obey her! Let her kill herself. You will be doing the lord a favour.* But they were retainers from her household, accustomed to following her commands without question, and besides, he thought, seeing their faces, there was not one among them that shrank from the idea of blinding a man accused of sorcery.

He heard one sharp cry of agony, then another. He could not prevent himself running forward. The men pushed Sesshin, his face streaming blood, off the verandah and threw the useless globes after him. Lady Tama came forward to watch the old man scrabble in the dirt. When she saw Shikanoko approach him she called out, 'You, take him away! Let me never see either of you again!'

'My books, my books! I will never read again!' Sesshin's chest was heaving as he moaned.

Shika knelt beside him, his heart expanding and contracting with such force he felt it would burst from his chest. He was engulfed by pity and horror. 'I will get some for you. I will read to you. Tell me what I should bring.' His reassurances sounded futile and hollow in his own ears. He said dully, 'It is I, Shikanoko.'

'You will take nothing,' Tama commanded. 'I will burn it all. Now go before I add you to the fire!'

Sesshin reached out, feeling for him, and grabbed his arm. 'Shikanoko,' he whispered. 'Pick up my eyes and bring them. And fetch a blanket or a jacket, the night will be cold.'

Shika gathered up the eyes, his heart twisting in pity. No one came near him or offered any help. Indeed, they stood back and turned their faces away. Only a servant girl, who had often attended to the old man, brought a bowl of warm water and some clean cloths. Shika bathed Sesshin's face and tore a strip to make a bandage. He could feel him trembling from shock and pain. Then he washed the eyes, while tears streamed from his own and the girl wept.

'Fasten them to the west gate,' Sesshin said, 'so they may continue to watch over this place when we are gone.'

Shika had been ordered to take Sesshin away but now he was worried about Lady Tora. Lord Kiyoyori had commanded him to look after her. Leaving Sesshin for a few minutes with the girl, despite her protests, he ran to the summer pavilion.

He was able to release the horses but could not get any closer; it was surrounded by guards and some were already putting torches to the pile of firewood.

'Where is Lady Tora?' he said to one of them.

'Inside, we hope.'

'Lord Kiyoyori will have your heads for this,' he said in fury.

'And I'll have yours, you bandit's scum, if you don't get out of here.'

Windows and doors were all firmly fastened. There was no sign of movement within.

*She will have escaped*, he thought. *She would not let them trap her, especially not if she bears the lord's child. But where is she?*

He could stay and fight for her – if she was there – or he could escape with Sesshin. He made the decision, instantly regretting it, but not wavering. He hastened to collect his few possessions, sword and bow, the bag containing the mask, and saddled the horses. The servant girl met him halfway back.

'Hurry,' she said. 'They are talking of killing you.'

He lifted Sesshin onto Risu's back, tied him so he would not fall, and led both horses to the west gate. Risu was fretful; she did not want to go out in the dark, but the big stallion remained calm and where he went she followed.

There were many people milling around, carrying armfuls of books, boxes and flasks, maps and charts that he recognised from Sesshin's rooms. They were taking them to the summer pavilion and adding them to the firewood, already ablaze. No one looked at them as they passed under the gate.

Its transept was carved below the roof with curling dragons and flowers. Shika stood on Nyorin's back and found a niche into which he could slip the two eyes.

Sesshin had not uttered a word, but now he said, 'Make sure you behave yourselves. I am leaving my eyes to watch you, so don't think you can get away with anything.'

'Who are you talking to?'

'I put some guardian spirits in the gates when I came to Matsutani. Migi and Hidari are their names. They're quite effective but they need a lot of supervision.'

Shika was shivering when he sat down again and took up the lead rope. It was almost completely dark.

'Where shall we go?' he wondered aloud. As soon as it was light he could find food, but they would need water. It was too dark to ride all night – it was the time of the new moon. He thought of the woodland pools he knew where deer and other animals would come and drink at dawn and decided he would follow the stream that flowed into the lake from the northeast, and find one of its pools in the Darkwood.

They circled round the back of the residence following the wall, their way lit by the flames as the summer pavilion burned.

When they entered the Darkwood, Sesshin said, 'We have been delivered from the Prince Abbot in a truly miraculous way.'

'Miraculous? You have lost your sight and all your possessions. Lady Tora has vanished and we are fugitives!'

'But now we know the true nature of existence,' Sesshin said. 'And that is an inestimable gift.'

# II

# KIYOYORI

When he arrived in the capital Kiyoyori went first to the palace of the Kakizuki, to pay his respects to the head of his family, Lord Keita. He bowed to the great lord from some distance and received a gracious acknowledgment, and was then summoned to the apartment of one of his senior counsellors, Hosokawa no Masafusa, who was some kind of cousin to Kiyoyori's father.

Like all the Kakizuki, Masafusa lived in great luxury, wore robes of brocade and damask of the kind that were once reserved for members of the imperial family, served elegant food on gold and celadon dishes, and provided an endless supply of wine, music and entertainers.

Masafusa told him all the usual gossip in his barbed, amusing way, but Kiyoyori felt he had something more pressing, and at the end of the meal his suspicions were proved true.

Masafusa lowered his voice and said, 'Your brother has submitted a claim to the estate of Matsutani to the tribunal in Minatogura.'

'What tribunal?' Kiyoyori replied.

'It was set up by the Miboshi to deal with land disputes in an organised and legal way. You must know Miboshi Aritomo has a passion for legality and administration.'

'He can have all the passion he likes, that doesn't give him and his tribunal jurisdiction over Matsutani.'

'I don't think there's any cause for alarm, but you needed to be informed.'

'Even if the tribunal finds in favour of my brother, which I find hard to believe, he would have to resort to arms to get possession. I am perfectly capable of defending both my estates, Matsutani and Kuromori. And I imagine I could expect help from the capital. After all, Matsutani stands between Miyako and Minatogura. If it fell to Miboshi allies, it would leave Miyako wide open to attack.'

Masafusa nodded. 'Of course we are aware of all this.'

Kiyoyori mused for a few moments, then said, 'Why is the claim being heard now? Are the Miboshi so confident of being able to distribute land currently under Kakizuki control? Are they planning something?'

'The Emperor is not well,' Masafusa whispered. 'There is going to be a challenge over the succession.'

'But the Crown Prince is the most suitable, as well as the rightful heir.'

'Indeed. We have not seen a future Emperor of such talent and intelligence for many years. And his wife is Kakizuki, Lord Keita's eldest daughter. But certain persons – I do not want to name any names – favour his younger brother.'

*Certain persons who dwell in Ryusonji*, Kiyoyori thought.

'We are facing war,' he said, a statement rather than a question.

'You should be prepared for anything,' Masafusa replied. 'Our lord is aware of your loyalty and devotion.' He did not, however, make any commitments or offers of support in the way of armed warriors and horses.

Kiyoyori returned to the house he kept in the city, below Rokujo, angered and disturbed by this conversation. The Miboshi were preparing to challenge the Kakizuki in the capital itself. They were so confident of success they were already redistributing land in their law courts. And their most powerful ally, the Prince Abbot, had already turned his attention to Matsutani.

He felt he should return without delay to Matsutani but he was also needed in the capital. He was angered by Keita and Masafusa's apparent lack of concern. Would the Miboshi and the Prince Abbot really dare attack Prince Momozono? And would the Kakizuki have the ability and the will to defend him?

Even though he had sent some of his men on ahead, the house felt unusually cold and unlived in. Servants were often unreliable but it was unlike his steward to let him down. He remembered when the man, Taro from the insignificant village of Iida, had joined his household. He had seen something in his bold eyes and cunning expression that appealed to him and his trust had been justified. Taro could read and write well, had many connections in the city and was often a source of information that Kiyoyori would not have learned from anyone else. He was about to call for him when the man appeared, sliding open the inner door and saying, 'Lord Kiyoyori, a messenger is here for you from Ryusonji. The Prince Abbot has summoned you.'

'Now? At this time of night? What does he want?'

'I have not been able to find out,' Taro replied in a whisper, indicating the monk half-hidden in the shadows. 'But someone must have seen you arrive in the city and thought it important enough to inform the Prince Abbot.'

'I suppose I must go,' Kiyoyori said. 'But if I don't return you had better inform my wife what happened to me.'

*She will have Masachika restored to her*, he thought with pain. *And what will become of my children? And Lady Tora?*

The idea of never seeing Tora again was unbearable but he could hardly send messages to her through Taro. Surely she was thinking of him, as he thought constantly of her, and neither of them would die without the other knowing.

The horses walked nervously with pricked ears and exaggerated steps, shying at shadows. It was a cold night, the new moon a thin sliver in the east. He could smell the frost in the air, turning the breath of men and horses to cloud. The stars glittered, pin pricks in the curtain of the sky.

Ryusonji was close to the river and had been founded at the place where a dragon child fell to earth. The dragon's spirit lived in a lake in the gardens. People believed only the greatest magicians could summon it up and use its power. The Prince Abbot was one of them. He was the Emperor's brother-in-law and combined in his person all the prestige of the imperial family with the wealth and influence of the sect to which Ryusonji belonged.

They left the horses at the outer gate and walked through gardens and courtyards lit by oil lamps on stands. Guards and servants waited silently on the verandahs. One stepped forward and made a sign to Kiyoyori's men to stop, and he was led forward alone. He was half-expecting to be seized, interrogated and executed, which was what normally happened to people summoned to Ryusonji in the middle of the night. He had no idea what he had done but obviously he had somehow come to the attention of the Prince Abbot. First the werehawk had been sent, and now he himself had been brought here.

He was, however, treated courteously and shown into the reception room where the Prince Abbot sat on a small raised platform matted with fresh, sweet-smelling straw and decorated with purple and white silk cushions. On the walls hung scrolls of sacred texts and pictures of protective deities, predominantly dragons. A golden statue of the Enlightened One stood in an alcove, flanked by vases of chrysanthemums. Gilt and jewels glittered in the lamplight.

Kiyoyori bowed to the ground and waited for the priest to speak.

His voice was high pitched but measured as he gave Kiyoyori permission to sit up, every syllable enunciated clearly, his language that of the court. His face was rather long, his complexion pale. His shaven head was covered by a priest's cap, richly embroidered like his clothes. He thanked Kiyoyori for coming, commented on the night temperature (which was plummeting – there was no heating of any sort in the room), and then fell silent, contemplating the younger man's face.

Finally he said, 'Well, Lord Kiyoyori of Kuromori, tell me what you are up to in your Darkwood.'

'My lord?'

'You are dabbling in matters you do not understand. I want to know who is leading you astray.' His voice had not lost its calm politeness but there was menace behind the words.

'I am not sure what your Eminence is talking about. My estate is small and insignificant, but within it I am the master. If I go astray it is my own doing. No one leads me.'

'I know differently,' the Prince Abbot replied. 'Let me be frank with you. I am an adept in these matters. I see what is happening in all the worlds. I have messengers that fly throughout this realm and bring information back to me. Not long ago I sent one of these to Matsutani – I had become aware of powerful forces that threatened to come together in a way that bodes disaster for our Emperor's realm. It did not return, but, around the time it should have reached your estate, a stag came into my room at night and stared me in the eye. It disappeared before it could tell me who had sent it, but I believe it was someone from your house. I prayed and meditated on these events and came to the conclusion that you have within your walls – you probably have not even noticed: for all your boasts of independence you seem remarkably unperceptive – some being, or beings, possibly not fully human, who are practising evil magic.'

Kiyoyori could not prevent a shudder, remembering the hideous werehawk and the events that had followed its death. He realised that all he felt and thought was transparent to the priest.

*I must not think of Tora.*

But immediately passion swept through him and he longed for her. He knew he had failed to mask it when he saw the Prince Abbot's contemptuous smile.

'They have bought you with sexual pleasure? I would have thought the Kuromori lord's price would be higher.' He leaned forward. 'You are in grave danger, but you can save yourself. First those beings must be captured and handed over to me. My men will accompany you when you go home. Then you must be reconciled to your brother. His claim to Matsutani is very strong and the Miboshi will recognise it. Your father's decision was both foolish and high handed. No one blames you for it but you must return the estate and the wife. I suggest you retire from the world, shave your head and make atonement for all your father's mistakes and your own.'

Kiyoyori thought, *That was my original desire but it certainly is not now!* He said nothing, trying to judge how best to respond to this outrageous request, which he had no intention of obeying.

The Prince Abbot mistook his silence for acquiescence and after a few moments went on. 'The Kakizuki have been all-powerful in the capital for many years but their influence is waning. Their arrogance and lack of justice have turned many against them. Warriors flood the capital seeking compensation for their services but the Kakizuki spend all their money on their own ostentatious pleasures. The Miboshi rule by law and reward those who serve them fairly. I intend my nephew to be the next Emperor, and that may be sooner than was thought, very sadly of course. I am giving you a chance to be on the winning side. Take it for the sake of your children, if not your own.'

'I am amazed that your Eminence should concern yourself with my welfare,' Kiyoyori murmured.

Somewhere not far away a child was crying. It had been crying for some time but he had not registered the sound, partly because it had been so unexpected. Now his blood turned to ice; he thought he recognised it as his son. Disbelief and bewilderment shook him physically. He half-rose, gazing towards the interior of the temple.

'Don't be alarmed. We will not harm him, if you obey me.' The Prince Abbot struck a bronze bowl at his side and when a monk appeared commanded, 'Bring the child here. Sit down, Kiyoyori!'

Tsumaru was wearing his outdoor clothes, a jacket over a robe. They must have seized him while he was playing . . . but how was it possible? How had the children been left alone? Had someone in his household been involved?

'Father,' Tsumaru cried, struggling to get away from the burly monk who held him, but the man gripped him more tightly. Tears ran down the child's cheeks, but he struggled to control his sobs.

'He is a fine boy,' the Prince Abbot said, gesturing for him to be brought closer. 'What a slender neck! Can you imagine the ease with which a sword would sever it? In the event he lives, I will make him my acolyte and educate him.'

*If I concede to my brother, that will be his only future,* Kiyoyori thought wildly. *If I resist and am defeated he will die before me. I must buy time. I must agree for now. When I get home I will consult with Sesshin; he will tell me what to do.*

'It is gracious of your Eminence to interest yourself in such a worthless child,' he said, the false words scalding his tongue. 'If I have your word that no harm will come to him in your care I will do everything you request. I will return at once to Matsutani.'

'I suggest you go tonight, before dawn,' the Prince Abbot said. 'I do not want your departure to give rise to unsettling rumours.'

*In other words, the Kakizuki are not to be alerted. They are not to suspect that the Miboshi are to be handed a road straight into the capital.*

'Father, don't go!' Tsumaru wept, and then, 'Hina! Where is Hina?'

The monk put him down and he ran to Kiyoyori, burying his face against his father's side.

'May I ask, where is my daughter?' Kiyoyori said.

'I believe she is at home,' the Prince Abbot replied. 'She will be recovering now.'

He could feel the fury building within him. He held Tsumaru by the shoulders, looking into his eyes. 'Don't be afraid. Continue to be brave. Soon you will be home again too.'

Tsumaru took a deep breath and nodded.

Kiyoyori touched his son's hair briefly, bowed to the Prince Abbot and followed the monk to the outer gate where Tsuneto and Sadaike were waiting anxiously. They were joined by several more monks, one of whom carried a bird cage holding two of the same werehawks.

'We are returning to Matsutani,' Kiyoyori said to his men when they looked questioningly at him.

At his own residence he told Tsuneto to assemble the rest of the warriors and horses while he went inside. The burly monk who had held Tsumaru followed him, standing and watching him insolently.

Taro, the steward, was waiting inside the room. In the dim light Kiyoyori thought he saw something in his expression beyond his obvious relief.

'I am leaving at once,' Kiyoyori told him. 'Pack my things. I am not sure when I will return to the capital.'

'Shall I prepare some food?'

'Put something together for the journey but we have no time to eat now.'

Taro bowed, glanced at the monk and said, 'Lord Kiyoyori might wish to wash or use the privy before he leaves.'

'Good idea,' Kiyoyori replied.

'I will bring water and a lamp.'

The monk looked after him suspiciously as if he might scale the garden wall and escape but Kiyoyori was not followed and for a few moments he was alone in the darkness. Then Taro appeared with a lamp and a jug, set them on a shelf and helped Kiyoyori with his robe.

He said in a voice tinier than a gnat's, 'I can get your son away.'

'How did you know?' Kiyoyori whispered back.

'Someone came shortly after you left, and told me. He works in the gardens, saw the child arrive, and knew it must be your son when you were called to Ryusonji. He can show me how to get into the temple. I think I can rescue him.'

'They will be watching him day and night, and they will kill him if your attempt fails.'

'They will kill him anyway and you too once you have given them what they want. Trust me.'

'Your life will be forfeit to me if he dies.'

'You can take it. I give it to you freely. I did years ago when you gave me the chance to serve you.'

The monk's voice echoed, closer than he had thought. 'Lord Kiyoyori, we must leave.'

There was no time for further discussion, either to give permission or to withhold it. Taro poured the water over Kiyoyori's hands and held out a small cloth to dry them. His touch was impersonal and he did not speak again. Kiyoyori began to feel he had imagined the whole conversation. His last glimpse of Taro was the man standing on the verandah, the lamp in one hand, the other raised in a gesture of farewell. The first cocks were crowing as they rode away in the darkness.

They were halfway home when they met Kongyo. Kiyoyori brushed aside the man's shamefaced apologies.

'I have seen my son. He is alive. We have a little time.' He could not say more, for the Prince Abbot's monks rode on either side of him.

As they descended the last pass into Matsutani they saw the smoke rising in the valley. Kiyoyori urged his horse on and came at a gallop to the west gate. He did not notice the eyes in their niche, though they saw him, saw the monks that rode with him, and noticed how he checked his horse at the sight of the charred beams and the soot-blackened edge of the lake.

His wife came out onto the main verandah, Hina beside her. The child was pale and there were still signs of the bruise on the side of her face. Kiyoyori leaped from his horse and knelt before his daughter, tenderly touched her cheek and gazed into her eyes.

'I am sorry, Father,' she said. 'They took Tsumaru and I couldn't stop them.'

'Tsumaru is safe,' he said, 'He is in the capital at Ryusonji.' For the moment he must act as though it were true, at least until he could get rid of the monks, at least until he heard from Iida no Taro. 'You were brave and I am proud of you.'

He rose and looked at his wife, aware that if he spoke he would unleash a torrent of rage and grief. She met his eyes, and he saw a glint of some emotion in them, triumph, regret, remorse, a mixture of all three.

He mastered his own feelings and said, 'What have you done?'

'You will thank me. I have cleaned out the nest of sorcery that had infested my – our – home.'

'I may thank you but the Prince Abbot of Ryusonji certainly will not. He sent these monks to take the scholar and the lady back to the capital in exchange for our son's life.'

She took a small step back, glancing at the monk and then back at him. He saw her sudden dismay as she realised the meaning of his words.

He turned to the monk whose name he had learned was Gessho. 'Those you seek are not here.'

'Where are they?' Gessho demanded.

'The boy took the old man towards Kuromori,' Tama said. 'The woman, we believe, died in the fire.'

'Once they are in the Darkwood they are beyond anyone's reach. As for the woman, show us her bones,' Kiyoyori said, his voice steady. Surely Tora was not dead. He would know if she were.

'There was no trace; the fire was too fierce.' Tama's chin was raised, her eyes bright with defiance.

*She is not dead*, he thought.

The short winter daylight was already beginning to fade. When Kiyoyori did not reply Tama said, 'You must all be weary and it is getting cold. Come inside and I will prepare food.'

'We must search the house and grounds before it gets dark,' Gessho said obstinately.

Kiyoyori fought down the urge to execute the monks on the spot, send their heads back to Ryusonji and accept the consequences – Tsumaru's death, unless Taro had been successful, and an assault on his estates from both east and west. Grief threatened to overwhelm him – but surely she had escaped; surely he would see her again. He longed for her, he needed her.

There was no trace of either her or Sesshin. His wife had done her work well. The old man's room had been cleared out, the books, potions, flasks, bones, powders and everything else had been burned. Gessho made no effort to hide his annoyance. However, in his search he finally came upon the eyes.

He called Kiyoyori and they both stared at the globes that still shone, and moved and saw. While the monks, not daring to touch them, said prayers and chanted sutras, Kiyoyori went straight to Tama's rooms.

'What else did you do?' he said, 'Whose are those eyes?'

'The sorcerer had put a spell on Hina,' Tama replied without emotion. 'He had to be punished.'

'It was not a spell,' Hina said, as though she had repeated it several times. 'Someone hit me.'

'Is he dead?' Kiyoyori said to Tama. 'Master Sesshin?'

'No,' she replied. 'I told the truth. I spared his life and put him in the care of the last of the bandits, the young one.'

'Shikanoko is his name,' Hina said.

'I sent them both away.' She looked calmly at him. 'You would never have given them to the Prince Abbot, would you? Not even for our son's life.'

'I was trying to buy time,' he said. 'I cannot be coerced, but while the Prince Abbot thinks I can, he will keep Tsumaru alive. However, you have left me with nothing to offer him.'

'And you blame me?' she cried. 'None of this is my fault! Look to your own actions!'

She had never raised her voice to him before and her accusation fuelled his anger. He set guards at the doors to her rooms and took Hina to his own quarters. He wrestled, sleepless, with his thoughts, while Hina cried out in her dreams. He would kill his wife with his own hands; he would have her executed; he would force her to shave her head and become a nun.

He could hear the monks chanting all night as they kept vigil by the west gate. The next morning, a dull cold day, threatening snow, Gessho let the werehawks out. They circled the roofs shrieking and then flew off towards the Darkwood.

'I will follow them,' Gessho said. 'There is nothing to be gained by waiting here. These others will return to Ryusonji and tell our master what has happened. You will hear from him in due course. In the meantime I would advise you to do nothing more to arouse his displeasure.'

'If you find Sesshin and Shikanoko will my son be returned to me?' Kiyoyori asked.

'I cannot speak for my master,' Gessho replied.

'I will come with you and help you find them.'

Gessho brushed this offer away. 'As I said, do nothing.'

But this was the hardest thing to do, to wait day after day for news that never came. One moment he thought he must ride at once to the capital, the next that he must go in the other direction to Minatogura to press his own claim at Lord Miboshi Aritomo's famous tribunal. The thought of how his brother was undermining him in this way made his feelings towards Tama even colder, and he sought neither to comfort her nor to ask her advice. Sleeplessness made him irrational and his men began to fear the edge of his temper and question his judgement.

He had his wife confined to another pavilion, far out in the lake, accessible only by boat.

'You may have some items of worship,' he said. 'Spend your time in atonement.'

Her serving women packed up two golden statues, and silks and needles for embroidery. Every day one or other of them was rowed out to take food and keep her company, but at night she was alone.

# 12

# SHIKANOKO

Shikanoko and Sesshin stopped for a few hours on the stream's bank, huddled together for warmth. At dawn frost covered the blanket they shared and the horses' manes. They had nothing to eat and the water from the stream was so cold it made their teeth ache.

'Are you in pain?' Shika asked as he bathed the old man's face, carrying water in the flask the servant girl had thrust into his hands.

'Pain is a transient sensation. It will pass.'

'I suppose hunger is too, but I don't know if it is going to pass,' Shika muttered.

'I will teach you to conquer both hunger and pain,' Sesshin said, but his voice was faint.

The horses had cleared the ground of grass and were tearing at the tree bark. Shika saddled them and helped Sesshin onto Risu's back. He rode with his bow ready but nothing stirred in the forest, no birds, no rabbits, not even a squirrel. The cedars gave way to ancient beeches and live oaks. Beneath the beeches lay the autumn mast in hard reddish pods. Shika dismounted and gathered handfuls, cracking them open in his teeth, but the kernels were thin and barely nourishing.

'Don't you have some magic that will tell us where to go or where to find something to eat?'

'My boy, I have suffered a setback. I need to learn the lesson it has for me before my powers revive.'

'Should we return to Matsutani?' Shika wondered aloud. 'Maybe Lord Kiyoyori will be back by now.'

'We have been delivered from the Prince Abbot once. We should not put ourselves within his grasp again.'

'Well, he certainly won't find us here! No one will even find our bones!'

Later that day after they had left the stream and turned eastwards, Shika, riding ahead, came on a small clearing and was able to shoot a rabbit before it reached the cover of the undergrowth. He made a fire and cooked the animal, feeding pieces to Sesshin. A little water had gathered among the roots of two trees twisted together. He helped Sesshin drink and lapped at it himself, until the horses pushed him away. The food made him thirstier. It was going to be another cold night.

'Can you hear water?' he said to Sesshin.

'I can hear a waterfall very far away.'

'We must go at first light.'

'I will teach you a water meditation,' Sesshin said. 'Once you master it you can go without water indefinitely.'

'But can you teach it to the horses?'

Sesshin did not reply, but arranged himself, cross-legged on the ground, pulling the blanket around him.

After tethering the horses securely Shika sat down next to him.

Sesshin said, 'I sat under a waterfall for seven days and seven nights. The water entered my body and entered my bones and then my soul. I can call on it at any time.' His voice droned on while within Shika thirst began to build unbearably. His throat burned, his mouth dried out, his lips were stretched taut and parched.

'Come close to me and place your mouth on mine,' Sesshin said quietly.

Shika did so and a gush of cool water rushed into him, spilling over his lips.

*I am dreaming*, he thought, *I will awaken soon and be thirstier than ever.*

The flow of water stopped, his thirst was slaked and suddenly sleep overwhelmed him.

The next morning Sesshin was lethargic and feverish.

'I should not have done that,' he said, rambling a little.

'The water thing? Can you do it again?'

'Not for a while. You can see how it's weakened me.'

'Then we must ride on.'

'Let's rest for a day or two until I get some strength back.'

Shika studied the old man. 'I'll take the horses up to the falls while you rest here. I'll come back.'

'Very well. I won't be going anywhere.'

Before he left he made a pile of firewood so Sesshin could keep the fire alight. It was a steep climb up the ridge and took most of the day. Once he and the horses had reached the top and could see across the valleys, Shika realised where he was. The waterfall fell down the opposite cliff face, and the stream it formed flowed south towards Kumayama, his childhood home. To the north, beyond the mountains that lay in folds, violet in the evening light, was Shisoku's place. That would certainly be a refuge, but to get there he would have to fall down the cliff again. Still, knowing where he was made him feel better.

The horses caught the scent of water and began to scramble down the slope, crashing through the bushes and slipping on boulders. Shika clung to Nyorin's back, trusting him not to stumble.

Spray filled the air and the roar of the falls drowned out all other noise. The horses drank steadily. It was bitterly cold despite the winter sun, which had broken through the cloud cover and shone for a short while before dropping behind the mountains in the west. He would not get back before dark. The only vessel he had to carry water was the small bamboo flask. He found some roots of water plants, and a crab under a stone, and ate them both raw. Risu lay down and he settled beside her, his head on her belly. All night he was tormented by the idea of cutting her throat and drinking the warm blood. In the morning she looked at him reproachfully as though she knew what he had been thinking.

He mounted Nyorin and set off back over the ridge. He shot and wounded a hare on the slope and spent some time tracking it down. It took longer to get back and darkness overtook him again before he came to the clearing. He could smell the smoke and see the flames. His heart swelled with relief. If the fire was still alight, Sesshin was probably still alive.

The old man stirred at Shika's approach but did not seem able to speak. Shika dripped some water into his mouth and set about skinning the hare. After feeding Sesshin he held him in his arms all night, trying to keep him warm. In the morning he seemed a little better, but still could not move.

The next day Shika let the horses go, still saddled, for there was no way he could carry their harness. He and Sesshin could share the water he had brought if they rationed themselves, but the horses had to drink. They grazed in the clearing for a while, keeping an eye on him, and then they wandered away. For a while he heard the noise of their progress through the woods, then silence returned.

He hoped they would wait for him at the waterfall, but he couldn't help fearing he would not see them again.

Sesshin slowly recovered. Shika lost count of the days but one afternoon Sesshin said, 'I am sorry to have to tell you this, but someone is following us, guided by werehawks.'

Shika listened, but could hear nothing beyond the usual sounds of the forest. A wood pigeon was calling monotonously and the wind rustled the beeches.

'How can you tell?'

'I heard twigs break, and the cry of the birds.'

'How could you? I can't hear anything, with younger and sharper ears.'

'Once I underwent a ritual that was meant to give me farsight, so I could see into distant places. It failed, for reasons connected with the nature of light, but when I recovered I found my hearing had increased a hundred-fold. It was something of a burden – you may have noticed I used to plug my ears with wax – but now I am blind it will prove very useful. This is why you should never concern yourself over your fate; everything follows the laws of destiny and therefore happens for a purpose.'

'So, are we going to let this person, whoever it is, capture us, or is it our fate to escape?'

'I think we should make every effort not to be taken by one of the Prince Abbot's monks,' Sesshin said, struggling to his feet. 'I don't relish that prospect at all.'

'But can you walk?'

'I will lean on your shoulder.'

They made a slow painful progress up the slope towards the top of the ridge. Shika could see where the horses had been before them, the broken branches where they had torn at leaves, their hoof prints in the soft earth. When they came to the summit he spotted Nyorin's white coat through the leaves below. They had found their way down to the waterfall and were still there. His heart filled with joy, and he let out a loud whistle. Nyorin whinnied in reply, echoed by the mare.

A bird shrieked above him.

'Hurry,' Sesshin said. 'They are here.'

Pulling the old man after him Shika half-slid, half-scrambled down the slope. The birds swooped over his head twice, then circled away, calling loudly. When they reached the bottom Sesshin was trembling with fatigue. The horses trotted up to them, happy to see Shika. Risu's saddle had slipped round her belly and Nyorin had broken his reins. Shika quickly righted the saddle and lifted Sesshin onto the mare's back. He knotted the stallion's reins as best he could and swung himself up. There was no other way to go but downstream towards his old home, and in truth an irresistible longing had come over him to set eyes on it once more, before fleeing further into the mountains.

The valley widened and slowly signs of human life began to appear. Irrigation ditches ran into small fields that lay fallow under vegetable waste and manure. In every corner stood trees, leafless now, but he knew each one, peach, loquat, mulberry. Smoke hung in the still air and its woody scent brought tears to his eyes. Not until this moment had he realised how much he had missed it all. His heart was thick with emotion and it made him careless.

'Look out!' Sesshin cried, at the same time as Shika heard the arrow whistling towards him and the shriek of the werehawks as they dived at his head. He pulled Risu close, dropped the lead rein and sent her forward with a slap on her rump, then plucked an arrow from the quiver, brought Nyorin to a halt and spun round. One of the werehawks raked his cheek with its beak, drawing blood.

A man was riding towards him, bow drawn, shouting in a voice so loud it echoed round the valley.

'I am the warrior monk, Gessho, from Ryusonji! In the name of the Prince Abbot, surrender yourselves to me. I am commanded to bring you to him.'

Shika tried to shoot towards him but the werehawks flapped around his head, obscuring his sight; one seized the arrow in its claws and flew away with it. Nyorin, alarmed by the birds, gave a huge buck, and bolted after Risu.

Another arrow whistled past Shika's head. They came to a fork in the track, the horses turned to the left, and galloped into a group of armed men, led by Shika's uncle, Sademasa.

•

Sademasa recognised him at once, Shika was sure. His uncle's face, beneath the elaborate horned helmet, paled as if he had seen a ghost. He thought the men also knew who he was, but they surrounded him with drawn swords and he was afraid they would kill him and Sesshin without asking any questions.

'Uncle,' he called out, as he calmed Nyorin. 'It is I, Kazumaru.' He reached out for Risu's rein and spoke softly to her. Both horses were breathing heavily. Sesshin turned his bandaged eyes towards the voices, listening carefully.

'My nephew is dead,' Sademasa replied. 'Who are you, impostor, and how dare you ride up to me with such an outrageous claim?'

'You know who I am. You were there when I fell off the mountain a year ago. Lord Kiyoyori took me into his service.'

'If you serve the Kuromori lord what are you doing here with this sightless beggar?'

Above their heads the werehawks were shrieking in triumph. The monk, who had named himself as Gessho, rode up, shouting. 'Lower your swords. Do not harm these men. My lord, I am under orders from the Prince Abbot of Ryusonji to bring them directly to him, alive.'

One of Sademasa's men said, 'He does look like Kazumaru. What if it is him?' Shika knew him; his name was Naganori.

'Maybe he is a shapeshifter,' Gessho declared, 'who can take on the likeness of anyone, even the dead.'

'I don't need to be a shapeshifter,' Shika said. 'I am Kazumaru. Naganori, I remember you. Your son, Nagatomo, was my friend.'

The man's face lit up. 'Lord Kazumaru . . .' he began, but Sademasa rode his horse forward, barging between Shika and Naganori, and addressed Gessho. 'You can take them away. I'll send men with you to make sure they don't escape. As long as you remind your master of this service I am rendering him.'

'You will indeed be rewarded,' Gessho replied. 'And even more if you provide us with shelter. It is too late to ride on today. Let us rest at your house and we will leave in the morning.'

Shika glanced at Sesshin. If he had given one sign, made one gesture, Shika would have fought, no matter that he was outnumbered twenty to one. But Sesshin sat on the mare's back, calm and patient, as the warriors took the reins and led them away.

It was painful to return a prisoner to his own home and to be shut in the guard room, just inside the gate, where he had seen so many await punishment. Everything was taken from them, his bow and arrows, and the brocade bag that held the mask, which Gessho, who seemed reluctant to let his captives out of his sight, received with delight and awe and said many prayers over.

'This will please my master,' he exclaimed, opening it enough to peer inside.

'What is it?' Sademasa said, curious, but Gessho would not show him.

Until then Shika had kept his feelings under control but when the mask was taken from him he flew into a rage just as he used to when he was a boy. It took three men to restrain him. He was still raging when the guard returned with a bowl of gruel, and would have thrown it in the man's face, but Sesshin's voice calmed him. 'It is food. Eat. Isn't that what you wanted?'

'None of this is what I wanted,' he said, but he ate the gruel. He lay awake all night, vowing he would take revenge on his uncle and reclaim what was his.

•

There was no sign of the horses when they were brought out next morning and Shika was again afraid he would never see them again. The rage that he had kept simmering all night threatened to erupt once more. His uncle had stolen everything from him, even his horses.

Gessho said, 'Bring the horses. The prisoners can ride the mare, and the stallion will make a fine gift for my lord, the Prince Abbot.'

Sademasa, who had come out to bid farewell to the monk, said, 'We cannot get near them. One of my men has been bitten on the arm and another kicked in the head. I will have them killed. They will feed my men through the winter.'

'Untie the young prisoner,' Gessho said, after a moment's thought. 'Walk with me to the stables,' he said quietly to Shika.

A group of men followed them, bows ready, swords drawn.

'Don't try to escape,' Gessho said under his breath. 'Sademasa will seize any pretext to kill you.'

Shika realised it was less a threat than a warning. He looked at the warrior monk, seeing him properly for the first time. He was tall and broad-shouldered, with well-shaped features and almost copper-coloured skin. He carried a rattan-bound bow and a quiver of arrows fletched with black-banded eagle feathers. He had a long sword at his hip. Even if Shika had his own bow, and the mask, he did not think he could take on a man the size of Gessho.

The horses had been left in a small fenced area. The ground was churned up by their hooves and they were wild-eyed and sweating despite the cold. They whinnied in relief at the sight of Shika. They were both still saddled and bridled from the previous night and though they had been given food and water they had been too agitated to eat. Shika ran his hand over the stallion's flanks. He had lost weight during their flight over the mountains and his mane was tangled, his coat dirty.

He led Nyorin forward and Risu followed docilely, her head at Shika's shoulder.

Sademasa's men encircled them, but Gessho had his hand on his sword and they fell back to let them through. Shika hoisted the old man up on to Risu's back and then looked at Gessho.

'You may as well ride the stallion,' the monk said. 'Since it seems no one else can. But I will tie him to my horse.'

'Where are the werehawks?' Shika said, looking up. The clouds had cleared and the sun was shining from a pale sky.

'I sent them back to the capital,' Gessho replied. 'My lord Abbot will know I have accomplished my task and will dispatch men to meet us.'

Shika's heart twisted as they rode away from his home. No one looked at him, no one recognised him as the young lord of Kumayama. Yet he knew every tree, the pattern of their winter shadows, the outline of the mountains rising one behind the other, ever higher, to the snow-capped peaks, sharp and gleaming in the frosty air – they were all as familiar as his own hands.

At the boundary of his land Gessho told Sademasa's men to return home. They obeyed him – he was the sort of man, Shika realised, that would always be obeyed; as well as his gigantic build and strength he had powerful spiritual authority. After they had gone Gessho said, 'Lord Sademasa seems eager to get rid of you. Why should he be, unless your claim is true? That's what I've been asking myself.'

'It is true,' Shika said. 'Last year I fell while we were out hunting. I believe he tried to kill me then – but whatever his intentions he certainly left me for dead.'

'Did his men not recognise you?'

'At least one of them did.'

'Yet none of them came to your aid and most of them were prepared to take your life. He must rule his little domain with an iron hand and a cruel will. They are all afraid of him. He is Lord Kiyoyori's vassal, I believe. Are you?'

'I don't know,' Shika replied. 'We always served the Kuromori lords, and Lord Kiyoyori spared my life and took me into his household. But he was in two minds about it since my uncle, he said, is one of his staunchest allies.'

'Indeed. Just as Kuromori protects the capital, so it is itself protected by Kumayama.'

When Shika made no response Gessho said, 'I don't know what my master, the Prince Abbot, intends to do with you, but he rewards those who serve him well. Maybe one day your estate will be restored to you.'

*It will*, Shika promised himself.

•

Sesshin said very little on the journey. He seemed to have withdrawn inside himself. He made no complaints, though his body alternately burned with fever and shivered as though it would never be warmed again. Shika tended to all his needs, washed him and tried to feed him, though the old man would take hardly more than a mouthful of broth or hot water. From time to time he pressed Shika's hand in thanks. He did not speak to Gessho. Often his lips moved as if in prayer.

They followed the course of the Kumagawa as it flowed towards the sea. The river was fast and shallow, splashing over rocks and boulders, its noise constantly in their ears. The first night they came to the high road that ran along the coast between Miyako and Minatogura, and stopped at a small place on the corner. From here on there were a few scattered villages along the road, with stalls that supplied food and drink, wooden clogs, fur boots, cloths and other travelling needs, and one or two lodging places. After the first night they did not stay at these but at temples that belonged to Ryusonji and where the dragon child was worshipped. The rooms were austere and cold, the food meagre. The monks rose at midnight, and the dark hours till morning echoed with their chanting and the dull reverberation of gongs and bells.

On the third morning they came to a crossroads. To the south lay a small sea port where vessels plied between Akashi and Minatogura, and fishermen went out to the islands of the Encircled Sea. On the northern road two partially decomposed heads had been placed on stakes. Crows flapped around them, pecking at the rotting flesh. The eyes had been taken and the teeth were beginning their eternal grin. They were beyond recognition yet Shika knew them, remembered hearing them fall, when he thought his own would follow them.

'That is the road to Matsutani,' Gessho said. 'But we will not be going there.'

'Is Lord Kiyoyori there?' Shika asked.

'That is no longer a concern of yours,' Gessho replied.

Every morning Sesshin seemed smaller as though he were withering away. Not only physically: some inner light was fading from him. He was becoming an empty husk, an old bean pod ready for fire or earth.

Gessho never left them alone and at night tied their hands and feet, but even monks have to obey the calls of nature and the day they were to arrive at the capital, before he untied them, he went off to the privy at the back of the temple where they had stayed for the night. Sesshin spoke for the first time in days.

'Shikanoko! Come here, my boy. I must pass something over to you. Quickly, there is very little time.'

'What is it?'

'Remember the night you drank from my mouth? I have another gift for you. If I don't give it to you the Prince Abbot will take it from me. Come, place your mouth over mine.'

'What is it?' Shika said again.

'It is my power. I have concentrated it down into – well, into a sort of pellet. Take it inside you. It will grow like a seed. But be quick.'

Shika rolled over to the old man's side and placed his mouth over the other's, tasting the fever and the decaying flesh. Then he felt a smooth hard object on his tongue. Its flavour was sweet and fiery, bitter beyond words and smooth as honey at the same time. For a moment he thought he would gag on it but it slipped down his throat and, like wine, spread instantly. He felt hot and cold all at once. The fires of earth rushed from his feet upwards through his body where they crashed hissing into the freezing snows of Heaven that fell through his skull. His limbs bucked against the ties, throbbing. Snakes swam through his veins. A catlike animal purred in his brain. His skin sweated drops of ice.

He lay panting. Sesshin rested his brow against Shika's cheek. 'Good,' he whispered. 'I was afraid it might be too strong and would tear you apart. Don't do anything for a while. Just let it grow.' He began to speak more hurriedly. 'There is one more thing I must tell you. About Lady Tora.'

'She did not die in the fire?' Shika questioned, astonished as well as relieved.

'She escaped and has gone to the sorcerer in the mountains. She took something from me, and from you and Lord Kiyoyori, and from two others, I am not sure who they were. Maybe that bandit chief, and the old sorcerer himself. She needed it to make her children. From five fathers, five children will be born. Find them and destroy them. They will be demons. She is one of the Old People. I should never have succumbed to her. No wonder all these disasters followed. Well, I can do nothing about it now – but you can. You have shown me you have a kind heart despite your rough appearance and your bad temper. Don't be kind to the demons.'

Gessho returned with food and untied their bonds. As they approached the capital the meals had become more refined and flavoursome. This morning they had rice with grilled fish and pickled radish. For the first time Sesshin ate healthily. Gessho peered at him with suspicion.

'What's happened? He looks different.'

'Perhaps he is feeling better,' Shika said.

'I am the same as when you met me,' Sesshin said. 'A harmless old man, preparing to pass over to the next world, blinded for no reason by a poor woman driven mad by grief.'

A new merriment had come over him and indeed he seemed exactly what he said he was: an old man, joyful and serene at the end of his life.

Gessho ground his teeth in exasperation and, without giving them time to finish the meal, called for the horses. They set out immediately, riding at a gallop towards the capital.

•

They arrived at Ryusonji late in the evening. Guided by the Prince Abbot's men who had come to meet them, they did not ride along the wide avenues of Miyako but skirted through the hills of the northeast, passing many temples lit up by a thousand candles and oil lamps and echoing with the endless sutras that bound Earth to Heaven and kept the city safe.

The temple of Ryusonji lay a little way to the north of the capital near the river bank. In the low-lying ground between the temple and the river was the lake where the dragon child dwelt. As they passed through the great main gate and into the first courtyard, snow began to fall, making swirling patterns in the torch lights.

The horses, too exhausted to protest, were handed over to grooms, and Shika and Sesshin were taken to an outdoor hot spring where the dirt of the journey was scrubbed from them. They were purified with incense and dressed in old robes of bleached hemp, patched and darned but spotlessly clean. Shika's hair was untied, washed, combed and tied up again. All this was carried out by low-rank monks who worked silently and carefully with no sign of emotion, neither hate nor fear. Then Shika and Sesshin were led through a series of corridors and courtyards under great gates and through dark halls where carved images of the gods of Hell, saints, avatars and the Enlightened One himself glimmered faintly, until they came at last to the rooms of the Prince Abbot.

As the door slid open Shika saw Gessho was waiting inside. He had changed from his armour and travelling attire into temple robes. Silently and with an impassive face he put his hand on Shika's neck and forced him to his knees. Shika lowered his head to the ground and remained there for several minutes. He heard Sesshin say cheerfully, 'Ah, it's good to be clean. All thanks to you, mighty priest, whoever you are. Truly you follow the teachings of the Enlightened One. Your worship could be in the paradise of the pure land, but you have chosen to remain in this world and relieve the sufferings of the afflicted, as did the holy Jizo,' and he went prattling on, praising the Prince Abbot and recounting the lives and miracles of holy men. Finally his voice dwindled away and he sat nodding and smiling.

The Prince Abbot spoke to Gessho. 'What happened?'

'My lord, his eyes had been put out before we arrived. The Matsutani lady's anger was inflamed against him – she suspected him of involvement in the disappearance of her son. He and this young man had been turned out into the Darkwood. There was a woman whom Lady Matsutani accused of being a sorceress, though her judgement may have been clouded by jealousy, as the said woman was Lord Kiyoyori's concubine. She apparently burned to death in the fire that consumed the old man's books and instruments. I left Kiyoyori to deal with his wife and followed these two, catching up with them at Kumayama where the local lord, Jiro no Sademasa, was of some assistance. I said you would reward him, by the way. He was eager to get rid of the young man who it seems could be the nephew who was believed to be dead – you may remember?'

'Interesting. I do remember and we will come to that by and by. First I must consider my old friend here, Master Sesshin. We were novices together many years ago. Sesshin excelled in esoteric practices and eventually chose the way of a mountain hermit. I had not set eyes on him for years but from time to time I heard of some miracle, some challenge to the unseen powers, and knew it must be him. He would surface and then disappear. I tried to keep an eye on him but he vanished for many years until something drew my attention to Matsutani and there he was! So, it was your power at work, behind Kiyoyori, all this time?'

'Your Holiness must be confusing me with someone else,' Sesshin said. 'I knew all this attention was too good to be true. Well, that is the wheel of life. We all must pay for our misdeeds from past lives.'

'I am sorry, my lord Abbot,' Gessho said. 'I could not get him to you quickly enough. It was as if some change took place in him on the road. One moment you could see that despite his suffering he was a powerful sage; the next he had become this old fool.'

'What a pathetic end to our years of rivalry,' the Abbot said. 'Why did you not fight like a warrior of the spirit? I have dreamed of confronting you most of my life. Is this what you have become?'

Sesshin smiled and nodded. 'I am what I am and what I have always been, a poor soul on a journey.'

'Is he genuine, my lord, or a very good actor?' Gessho said.

'I sense nothing in him, no depth, no secrets. If he had any power he has divested himself of it utterly. We will keep him for a while and watch him. Treat him well, keep him occupied.'

'Perhaps he could join the blind lute player and the singers,' Gessho suggested.

'Ah, music.' Sesshin gave a deep sigh. 'To devote my final years to music, under the protection of the mighty Prince Abbot, in the holy precinct of Ryusonji! It is more than I could have dreamed of.'

Shika, by turning his head slightly, could see the Prince Abbot's disconcerted expression. One of the monks took Sesshin away. After a few moments he heard the priest's voice telling him to sit up and come closer. He shuffled forward on his knees.

'So, this is my young stag?' The Abbot placed his hands on Shika's head, gazed into his eyes and touched the side of his face, almost like a caress. Shika could not help trembling. He remembered the gaze and heard again Sesshin's voice, *Don't speak*. He lowered his eyes and remained silent.

'Well, you are pleasing enough to look at. I don't mind keeping you by my side for a while. Especially if you will show me the use of this lovely thing.'

He made a sign to one of the young monks who knelt behind him and the man stepped forward holding out the seven-layered brocade bag. The Prince Abbot drew out the mask. As always Shika felt a rush of pleasure at the sight of it, the long black lashes, the cinnabar-coloured lips, the polished antlers, the memory of its making, the knowledge of its power.

'Where did you come by this? Who made it for you?'

He did not reply immediately and then a false memory began to create itself in his mind. He saw himself coming upon the mask, it was half-buried in sandy ground, on the river bank.

'I found it. It must have been washed downstream after a flood.'

'You found it and then dared to use it? Just like that? Even I have not dared do that.'

'I thought it was mine since I found it.'

'That is a dangerous idea. Let's see what happens if just anyone puts it on.' The Abbot beckoned to the young monk without turning and held the mask out to him. 'Put it on.'

'Don't!' Shika said, suddenly knowing what was going to happen. 'He should not!'

The monk was very handsome with fine regular features and a smooth almost golden skin. He hesitated for a moment and then put the mask to his face.

Immediately he began screaming. He tried to take the mask off, his hands tearing vainly at it, but it clung to him. Gessho ran forward to help him, holding him still, pulling with all his great strength, but with no success. The young man broke away from him, shouting and crying. He rammed his head against the wall, and then, falling, on the floor. The Abbot stood, a movement shocking in itself, and stretched out his hand, speaking solemn words of power that unlocked rocks and summoned the dead back to life, but nothing shifted the mask until Shika went to the writhing figure and touched the polished surface. It slid into his hand. It was burning hot; it had only ever felt cool before. He felt its distress, its panic and pain, the fall from the cliff, the broken leg, the cut throat, the ebbing blood. *Nothing is ever lost*, it whispered to him. *It changes and takes a new form. All suffering mutates and persists.*

The young monk stared up at them. The skin of his face was stripped as if he had fallen into a fire, eyebrows and eyelashes singed away, cheeks seared purple, lips blistered. He wept helpless tears.

'Eisei, my poor boy, forgive me,' the Prince Abbot cried. 'I did not know it would be so extreme.'

Even Gessho looked shaken. 'Your Holiness might have tried it. What would have happened then?'

'Take Eisei away and tend to him,' the Prince Abbot said, his voice unsteady with shock. When the monks had done so he asked Gessho, 'Who still wields this ancient forest magic?'

'I don't know. I have never seen such a thing.'

The Prince Abbot handed the brocade bag to Shika and watched him put the mask away.

'This is what I think happened, Kazumaru – do you still call yourself that?'

'Now my name is Shikanoko,' Shika replied.

'Of course. The deer's child. As I was saying, you disappeared a year ago and during that time you met a mountain sorcerer who corrupted you with dark magic. He made you the mask from the skull of a stag, perhaps one you had killed, a wise old creature that bequeathed its power to you. But who else was involved? This mask has female power as well as male. Who was the woman? Was it the same one who bewitched Kiyoyori? That would be fascinating beyond words. Where is she now?'

'As Gessho said, she burned to death,' Shikanoko said, disturbed by the accuracy of the Prince Abbot's insights.

'If that is true, we have nothing to worry about. But if she escaped, it might be a cause for concern. This is a very powerful object.'

Shikanoko felt the power latent within him but he had no idea what to do with it. There was something very attractive, almost calming, about the priest's acknowledgement of the mask.

The Prince Abbot studied him with shrewd eyes as if he could read his mind.

'You do understand that I must take control of this sort of sorcery? We will find its author in the spring. In the meantime you will stay with me. Together we will discover exactly how much you know and what can be done with the mask. In return I will restore Kumayama to you. We will send a claim to the Miboshi and it will be confirmed in the courts of justice in Minatogura. In the coming war your uncle will be overthrown along with the Kuromori lord and all the Kakizuki.'

Somewhere in the distance a cock crowed, followed by another. A bell began to toll from the innermost hall of the temple.

'My lord, it is nearly dawn,' Gessho said.

'You may tell me your decision when we meet again. Give me the mask. I will take great care of it. I know you will not leave without it.'

'And if I refuse to cooperate with you?' Shika said as he reluctantly handed it over.

'You will be put to death and the mask will be destroyed. That will be your uncle's reward. But I don't believe you are willing to die yet.'

Gessho took him to a small room, where a thin mat lay on the wooden boards, and told him to lie down. Despite his exhaustion Shika could not sleep. Somewhere the bell tolled again and he heard the pad of feet as the monks assembled for prayer. He saw again the young monk's ruined face and felt the terror and power of the mask. He realised with some fear how little he knew of it or how to control it. Deep within him something – whatever it was that Sesshin had transmitted to him – continued to quiver. It had to be kept hidden but he had to learn how to use it. He knew the Prince Abbot was right. He was not yet willing to die, and he could not bear the thought that the mask would be destroyed. And part of him was already under the sway of the Prince Abbot's seductive personality. The priest's attention and interest reassured and flattered him.

Shika had just come to the conclusion that he had nowhere else to go when he fell into a deep slumber only to be woken abruptly after what felt like mere minutes. It was morning; a grey snowy light filled the room.

A monk was shaking him. 'Get up! Our lord Abbot wishes to speak to you.'

It was the same room, the same gathering of monks, though not the young man whom the mask had burned, but whereas previously the Prince Abbot had been uneasy but calm, now Shika sensed his rage.

'You are already working against me? You dared to strike, taking advantage of my lenience and generosity?'

'My lord?' he said.

'How did you do it? How did you spirit the boy away?'

'I don't understand. I thought about what I should do and then I fell asleep. How could I do anything else? Your Holiness has the mask. I was alone with your men watching me all night. Anyway, what boy are you talking about?'

'Kiyoyori's son.'

Shika could not hide his surprise. 'You had Tsumaru? It was you who took him?'

'I had him brought here. I thought to persuade his father to send you and the old man to me. Now I have you in my hands I intended to return him, but while I was occupied with questioning you last night, someone stole him away.'

'It was not I,' Shika said.

'You did not perform some magic that made the guards' eyes sightless or the boy invisible?'

'I have no idea how to do such things! Did you think I could?'

The Prince Abbot leaned forward and studied him. 'Well, I believe you. And I think you are capable of more than you have ever dreamed. That will be our work together. I take it you have agreed to serve me?'

It was this, not the threats or the promise of Kumayama or the granting of his life, but his desire to harness this power that persuaded Shikanoko to become the Prince Abbot's disciple in Ryusonji that winter, while ice froze the lake and the river, and snow blanketed the capital and the mountains.

# 13

# TAMA

The island pavilion had been designed by Tama's mother, a retreat on hot summer days, filled with poetry, music and laughter. It had been Tama's favourite place when she was a girl. Now it had been her cold, damp prison all winter. Every day she listened for her son's voice, for some sign that he had been returned alive, but as the weeks went by she began to feel she would never see him again. Often she wept in grief and rage, but only the guards who kept watch outside on the tiny verandah all night heard her and they were unmoved.

One morning, early in the new year, after the snow melted, she was woken at dawn by an earthquake. It growled like an angry beast approaching from afar, its roar growing louder and louder. The doors and screens rattled. A shutter broke loose and began banging like a drum. There were cries and shouts as the household awoke, the neighing of startled horses and frantic barking of dogs.

The guards took the boat and poled back to the shore. She watched them leave, saw the boat ground halfway to the shore, noticed the sudden flow of water towards the lake's outlet in the southeast. She dressed quickly, hiding her prayer beads in her sleeve and slipping the golden statues into a small bag. Her dagger she kept on her day and night, hidden under her clothes. By this time the water had receded even more. Stranded fish were flapping and struggling in the mud and stones of the lake floor. The rock wall that contained it had cracked and the water was pouring through it.

Tama walked away from her island prison leaving delicate footsteps in the mud like a fox woman's. Fire had broken out in the stables and the main residence and in the confusion no one saw her go.

Houses were destroyed all the way to the coast. Tama became one of the many homeless people seeking refuge and at the port of Shimaura she traded one of the statues for a berth on a temple ship, bound for Minatogura.

The winds were fresh from the southwest and the sea rough. Many passengers were afflicted with seasickness but Tama, even though she had never been on a ship before, felt as well as she ever had in her life, filled with a sense of freedom and excitement. She stood on deck hardly noticing the cold, watching the pine-covered islands, dotted here and there with the vermilion posts of a shrine. Sometimes they passed by close enough to see fragile white blossoms on the plum trees.

A group of women who were going on a pilgrimage befriended her. One of them had already shaved her head and was about to enter the convent at Muenji.

'It was founded by Miboshi Aritomo's wife, Lady Masa, before she died, as a refuge for widows and other women: some are fleeing from violent husbands, some have been turned out of their own land and are seeking justice from the Miboshi, some, like me, simply want to retire from the world and find peace and grace before death.'

'I am seeking justice,' Tama said. 'My first husband lives in Minatogura and serves the Miboshi. I was forced to leave him and marry his older brother, one of the Kakizuki. He treated me very badly, took over the estate I inherited from my family and kept me a prisoner. I want to recover what is mine.'

'Including your rightful husband, I suppose,' said Jun, the woman who was going to become a nun.

'I long for him day and night,' Tama said. 'I have never stopped longing for him. Also, my son was kidnapped and I have not seen him all winter. I don't know if he is alive or dead. I need someone to intercede for me.'

The women sighed in sympathy and wet their sleeves with their tears. Plovers cried mournfully from the shore.

'How pitiful,' Jun said. 'Come with us to Muenji and we will take care of you and support your cause.'

Tama watched the moon rise and set, seeing how it grew fuller every night, and on the fifth morning they came to the great port city where the Miboshi family held sway.

The women's temple was a little way out of town on the top of a hill overlooking the port. To the south lay the Encircled Sea, to the east the vast ocean where huge whales spouted and beyond which, in distant lands, men the size of giants hunted seals and wolves. Tama had been to the capital, Miyako, a few times, but Minatogura seemed even larger, and, from her vantage point on the hill, she could see clearly that it was a town preparing for war. Warriors thronged the streets, long horse lines stretched in every open space, armourers, fletchers and swordsmiths worked day and night, their fires blazing, their hammers ringing. Straw targets were set up in gardens and on the river bank and the angry whining of bulb-ended humming arrows filled the air. Flags and banners fluttered everywhere in the dazzling white of the Miboshi clan.

At Muenji, Tama was given shelter. Jun related her story to the Abbess and Tama was duly summoned and interrogated by a slender, graceful woman, much younger than Tama had expected. She thought the Abbess must be a former noblewoman; she had obviously been well educated, could read and write and had a careful and astute intelligence. She promised to make enquiries and a few days later Tama was called once again to her room.

'I have verified all you told me and have discovered your husband is living at the house of Yamada Saburo Keisaku, his father's cousin. Masachika has become his adopted son and is to marry Keisaku's daughter, as soon as she is old enough.'

'He is to marry her?' Tama felt weak with shock.

'Well, take courage. He is not married yet. He is, however, claiming the estate, currently held by his older brother, which you say is yours.'

'Matsutani. It is my family home. After my brother's death, it was given to me, and my husband – without me what right does either of them have?'

'They have the right of being male,' the Abbess said dryly. 'Whose idea was it to wrench you from one brother and give you to another?'

'Their father's, but mine agreed to it.'

'I hope they are both atoning in Hell for their blind, arrogant wickedness. But what do you want to do next?'

'I want Masachika back, I want my land, and I want to know if my son is alive or dead,' Tama said.

'Where is your son now?'

'He was taken as a hostage to Ryusonji. I don't really understand why. My husband, Kiyoyori, became involved in sorcery, with a woman. The Prince Abbot learned about it and wanted to bend Kiyoyori to his will. But Kiyoyori would never be swayed like that. He would sooner let his son die. I thought, if someone from the Miboshi were to approach the Prince Abbot, he might return Tsumaru to me, if he is still alive.'

'Is he your only child?'

'There is a stepdaughter, Hina. She has always been cold towards me. Her father spoils her, because she reminds him of his wife who died.'

The Abbess looked at Tama with her shrewd eyes. 'Are you sure you are not misjudging Lord Kiyoyori? Is no reconciliation possible? It is my duty to ask you this. The bonds between husband and wife spring from deep laws of destiny and should not be broken lightly.'

'I seek to restore a bond that was broken,' Tama said. 'The one with my original husband.'

'I will send a message to him,' the Abbess said.

Tama joined in the activities of the convent while she waited nervously, but even in prayer and meditation among the calm-eyed women her mind would not be still. She had not seen Masachika for seven years. She had aged, she had borne a child. Would he remember the young girl she had been, their nights of sweetness?

Two days later, around midday, Jun came and told her to walk in the garden, the outer one where visitors were permitted. She saw three horses outside the gate and two men waiting for him. So, he was already within somewhere.

Her heart was beating uncontrollably as she walked along the stone path towards a small thatched hut that overlooked the lake. It was a bright spring day though the wind came from the east, giving a chill to the air. Cherry trees surrounded the lake, pink budded but still a week from full flowering.

Masachika stood at the entrance to the hut. She studied him greedily. His clothes were new and made of fine silk; he wore a small black hat on his head. He had filled out; he was fully a man now, both like and unlike his older brother, taller and more handsome.

At the end of the path, boulders formed a step and yellow flowers blossomed between them. She caught their fragrance as she fell to her knees.

'Lord Masachika! My husband!'

He bent and lifted her by both hands and guided her into the interior. Then she was in his arms, remembering his smell, his hair, his skin. Neither of them spoke.

Finally he released her. They sat side by side on silk cushions. He said, 'Why are you here? Is my brother dead?'

'No, although, forgive me for saying it, I have wished many times he were. Terrible events occurred at Matsutani. He imprisoned me all winter. There was an earthquake and I ran away.' When he said nothing Tama went on. 'I know you were in contact with some of our old retainers – Tachiyama and his wife.'

'Kiyoyori had them killed, I believe,' Masachika said.

'Somehow he was forewarned that he would be ambushed in the hunt. He made Tachiyama ride his horse and take the arrow that was intended for him.' She remembered the desperate woman running. 'His wife tried to stop the attack. She was tortured to death.'

'He has become cruel,' Masachika observed.

'Cruel and selfish. There is – was – a woman too. She was a sorceress, and so was the old man.' Tama could hear her voice rising and stopped abruptly.

'What old man? Calm down, tell me slowly.'

'Master Sesshin.'

'My grandfather's friend? Is he still alive?'

She told him everything; he asked many questions and when her account was completed he sat gazing at the lake, deep in thought.

Tama said, hearing the pleading in her voice and despising it, 'In my mind and spirit I never stopped being your wife.'

'Seven years is a long time and a lot has happened.' Masachika did not look at her. 'I was sent away against my will but I have found a good life here. I am grateful now to my father for allying me with the Miboshi, with the side who are going to be the victors. My adoptive father is a fine man, very wealthy. He has treated me generously and I am betrothed to his daughter.'

'But she is only a child! She cannot give you what I once gave you, and will give you again, now, here, if you want.'

He tried to joke. 'You would cause the poor nuns some distress.'

Tama plunged on. 'You will take me to your home? We can live together? If only you knew how I have longed for you. Haven't you longed for me?'

'When we were separated,' Masachika said quietly, 'it was as though a limb had been wrenched from me. It would have been easier to bear if you had died. I would not have had to endure imagining you in my brother's arms, with all the pain and humiliation that brought me. I hated him more than I would have thought possible, and when I heard you had given him a son I hated you too.' He gave her a quick glance and then resumed his study of the lake.

'What could I do? I was helpless.'

'I thought you should have killed yourself with your mother's dagger rather than submit to him.'

'I thought of it,' Tama said, 'and I thought about killing him too. But I had the estate to look after. I had Matsutani.'

He shifted uncomfortably. 'You know I have made a claim to the estate in the judicial court here? The Miboshi set a great store by legality. Moreover, everyone knows Matsutani is the gateway to Miyako. It's no secret that the Miboshi intend to move against the capital. If Kiyoyori will not submit to the verdict of law, the Miboshi will support me in taking up arms against him and winning the estate in battle. They will have a staunch ally in a key position and I will have what was mine.'

'Your claim will be all the stronger if I am your wife,' Tama said. 'After all, it is my family who have owned Matsutani for generations.' He was making her uneasy. She wished he had not said he hated her. She was afraid he would no longer want her, now Kiyoyori's flesh had been imprinted on hers and contained within her.

'I am committed elsewhere,' he said. 'I can't easily escape from that commitment.'

'But she is only a child, as I said.'

'When we were first betrothed she was seven years old. I have watched her grow up and waited for her. Next year she will turn fifteen.'

*Fifteen*, Tama thought, *the age I was when I was betrothed to him.* Jealousy and misery welled up in her heart. No wonder he was reluctant to take her back. He would have both Matsutani and his young bride, and increased standing and respect among the Miboshi.

'Let's be patient,' Masachika said. 'Nothing will be achieved by acting in haste. Let's see how the court case is resolved. In the meantime you can stay here, I suppose?'

'Can you help me? I should have a waiting woman, I will need new clothes and of course I should make a donation to the convent.'

'It would be a little difficult,' Masachika said. 'I would have to ask my parents and I think it is better if they don't know you are in Minatogura.'

'But how long will I have to wait?'

'The court case will be heard before the end of the month.'

•

'He will not take me back,' Tama said later to the Abbess. 'I was a fool to expect it. Maybe I was a fool to come here, but what else could I do? I could not stay where I was, a prisoner in my own home, waiting for my husband to get rid of me. And I cannot go back to Matsutani unless . . .' she fell silent.

'Unless what?' the older woman prompted.

'Unless the Miboshi's famous justice system confirms me as the rightful owner. Why should I not also submit a claim?'

'It is possible,' the Abbess said after a moment's reflection. 'There are precedents.'

'Matsutani is a prosperous estate. I will be able to endow this convent for years to come. You must have important connections; you can advise me on how to set about it.'

The Abbess smiled slightly. 'Presumably you have documents recording your family's history?'

'Of course,' Tama said, 'unless they were destroyed in the earthquake, they are all there. Kiyoyori has copies but the originals are hidden in a place known only to me. I could send someone to get them . . . I would need a skilful thief.'

She looked at the Abbess. The other woman said, 'I'm afraid I have none in my acquaintance. Let us pray and meditate on how to proceed in these matters. I will give you my decision tomorrow.'

•

The following day the Abbess decided that the convent would support Tama's claim and a request was sent to the tribunal for permission to proceed. Then a long time passed in which she heard nothing. She was used to the constant activity of running a large estate; with nothing to occupy her, her mind buzzed with regrets for the past and plans for the future. Despite her words about Masachika to the Abbess and against her own better judgement, she could not help hoping and dreaming. She believed from the way he had held her that Masachika still loved her as she knew she still loved him. But the pretty features of a fifteen year old she had never met haunted her. If only she could regain Matsutani surely Masachika would return to her. If she had the support of the Miboshi maybe Tsumaru would be rescued. She was on the point of deciding she would go back to Matsutani to collect the documents herself when she was told the Abbess wanted to see her. She went at once to the tranquil room near the front entrance of the convent.

The Abbess led her quietly to the side verandah where they could see the gate and indicated a waiting man.

'Is that someone you know? He says he comes from Matsutani with a message from Lord Kiyoyori.'

Her heart plummeted. It could only be news of Tsumaru. But she did not recognise the man. Kiyoyori would surely have sent one of his senior retainers, Sadaike or Tsuneto. But Kiyoyori did not know where she was – no one knew except Masachika. Could he have sent this man to her, with some message, some promise? But why pretend to be from Matsutani?

'I've never seen him,' she whispered, as though he could hear her. 'I don't believe Kiyoyori sent him.'

'Then I will have him turned away,' the Abbess declared.

'No, he can only have been sent by Masachika. I must hear what he has to say.'

'My dear.' The Abbess gave her a pitying look. 'What if his purpose is more brutal than a mere message?'

'What do you mean? That Masachika would have me murdered?' Tama did not know whether to laugh or cry.

'Well, you are threatening to come between him and his estate.'

After a few moments in which she regained her composure, Tama said, 'If you turn him away we won't know for sure who sent him or if he might not strike again. Let him in and I'll give him a welcome he won't expect.'

'Be careful. We must avoid shedding blood. I will bring him to you myself.'

She waited for him in the same hut where she had met Masachika. She had her knife in her hand and had placed a halberd just inside the entrance. The man must have been lulled by the calm of the courtyards and gardens through which he had been escorted, as much as by the presence of the Abbess, for he stepped from the bright daylight into the darkness without hesitation. She had her knife at his throat before he had even seen her and when he lunged backwards, twisting away from her, he found himself up against the sharp blade of the halberd in the hands of the Abbess.

'Don't move!' said the Abbess. 'We don't want to have to kill you.'

The man fell to his knees. 'Forgive me,' he cried. 'I should never have come here.'

'Reveal the weapons you are carrying,' Tama said. 'Then I'll decide what to do with you.'

When he did not answer immediately, she put the knife to his throat again, the sharp blade piercing the skin.

He cried out.

'It's nothing,' she said, holding the knife steady. 'Not even a flesh wound. But don't misunderstand me. I will let your life blood out in an instant.'

He said, 'I left my sword at the gate. I am unarmed.'

'You are lying. I think you came to kill me. Were you going to strangle me with your bare hands?'

'I carry one hidden blade. In the breast of my jacket I have a leather garrotte, in the sleeve wax pellets that contain poison.'

'Is that all?' Tama said, swiftly locating each one. 'What about these?' She had located a tiny blowpipe and a set of darts in a miniature quiver. There was something almost intimate about searching him. Suddenly she was aware of him as a man.

'Take care,' he said, 'they are fatally poisonous.'

She heard real concern in his voice and realised with a flash of amusement that he found her attractive, that the situation pleased him.

'You thought to murder me,' she said. 'You say you come from Matsutani with a message from Lord Kiyoyori?'

'It was not he who sent me,' the man admitted.

'I know that. For a start he does not know I am here, and he would never send an assassin to murder his wife in secret; he would come here and kill me himself. He would do me that honour. He and I may have parted, we may hate each other but I hope we do not despise each other. It can only have been the one other person who knows where I am, Masachika.'

Her voice deepened with emotion.

'I am sorry,' he said. 'It was indeed Lord Masachika. I am employed by his family.'

'Really?' Tama's tone was scathing. 'Do they often send you on such missions? Killing defenceless women in convents? Is that the honourable way among the warriors of the east? Let me look at you.'

The Abbess raised the blinds on the western side and the evening light filled the room. Then she took up the halberd again.

Tama said, 'I am going to lower the knife now.'

He instinctively put up his hand to wipe away the blood.

'Don't move!' she said. She moved round to face him, and studied him for a moment.

'You seem to be a man of many talents,' she observed.

He fell to his knees and bowed to the ground. 'Lady, my name is Hisoku. All my talents are yours to command. I beg you to allow me to serve you.'

'Any man will make such vows at the wrong end of a halberd,' she replied. 'You were sent to kill me. Why should I believe your sudden change of heart?'

'I can hardly believe it myself,' he said, raising his head. 'I cannot explain it. I feel you have saved me from a terrible sin. If I had killed you I would never be able to atone for it. But now in your service perhaps I will find forgiveness.'

Tama turned to the older woman. 'My lady Abbess, do you think he is sincere?'

The Abbess gave the halberd to Tama to hold and knelt before Hisoku. She gazed into Hisoku's eyes and then her own eyes closed and an intense silence fell on the room. From the garden a bush warbler called, the first Tama had heard that spring.

'He is sincere,' the Abbess said with a note of wonder in her voice. 'It is almost like a miracle.'

'Of course I am sincere,' Hisoku cried. 'Do you not think I am capable of overcoming you both if I wanted to? But I am held back by my reluctance to commit murder in this holy place, as well as by my admiration for you.'

'It is a miracle,' Tama said. 'I need someone I can send to Matsutani to collect some essential documents. If you can do this for me, and if I regain my estate as a result, I will let you serve me.'

'Then tell me what you need,' Hisoku said, 'and I will leave tomorrow as soon as it is light.'

# 14

# KIYOYORI

Kiyoyori had been confined to Matsutani all winter by heavy snowfalls, cut off from any news of the Emperor's health or the fate of his son, Tsumaru. He heard neither from the steward Taro nor from Ryusonji. He tried to curb his impatience and anxiety by making meticulous preparations for the spring, which he was sure would bring some revolt or uprising, if not outright war. He did not speak to Tama, though he knew he could not put off a decision about her future for much longer. He could not forgive her for her actions at the beginning of the winter. As soon as the snows melted he sent men deep into the Darkwood, searching for any trace of Sesshin and Shikanoko, and, he hoped secretly, of Lady Tora.

One day Tsuneto returned with the news that the fugitives had been captured at Kumayama and handed over to the monk Gessho.

'They have been in Ryusonji all winter then,' Kiyoyori said. 'Why have I heard nothing?'

'If they are not dead, they will be prisoners,' Tsuneto replied.

'Did you speak to Sademasa at Kumayama?'

'I did.'

'You know Shikanoko claimed to be his nephew, the son of Shigetomo, the former lord of Kumayama? Did he have anything to say about that?'

'Sademasa referred to him as an impostor,' Tsuneto said. 'I gather he was more than happy to have him removed so conveniently. He is not expecting him to return to make any further claims.'

'So, the Prince Abbot has obtained what he sought from me – Master Sesshin. Why has he not returned my son?'

'Presumably he hopes to influence you in other matters,' Tsuneto said.

*Or he no longer has him*, Kiyoyori thought. *Taro succeeded in rescuing him. But where are they?* He heard over and over in his mind the child's farewell cries: *Father, don't go!* He remembered with startling clarity the evening after Akuzenji's attack when the bandits were executed and his wife had brought the children to eat with him. He had played with them and admired them, and then he had left and gone to Lady Tora and become enmeshed with her. Was that what had brought the punishment of Heaven down on him? Yet he would face ten times that punishment to be with her again. His grief welled up and threatened to overcome him. He forced himself to listen to Tsuneto's words.

'Sademasa was very close-mouthed about his own activities, but I noticed he has also spent the winter preparing for war. And he had several warriors with him whom I did not recognise. I wondered if they might have joined him from the east.'

'He is planning to betray us?'

'He is an opportunist. He hinted he expects great rewards from the Prince Abbot for handing over Sesshin and Shikanoko. If you and the Crown Prince prevail he will cleave to you, but if the Prince's defeat seems imminent he will join the Miboshi.'

'I need him to be staunch now more than ever. I must go to the capital myself as soon as possible and I don't like to leave Matsutani unguarded in these dangerous times.'

These and other worries meant that Kiyoyori hardly slept that night, and so he was awake when the earthquake struck, and was able to escape with Hina. Much of the main building collapsed and the stables were destroyed in the fire that followed. The stonework of the lake was broken in several places and the lake drained away, leaving a muddy floor in which, when he got around to looking at it, Tama's footprints were clearly visible. He lost twenty horses, including his favourite black stallion, and ten people died. He entrusted Hina to Haru, hoping she would be comforted by playing with the children, but later that day when he went to assess the damage to the west gate he found her there, poking through the rubble. The gateposts still stood erect but the roof and the transom had fallen to the ground.

'What are you doing there?'

Lost in some world of her own she was startled by his voice. He was shocked by her pale face and noticed for the first time how thin she had become. The earthquake was the most recent in a series of shocks for her – Tsumaru's disappearance, the blinding of Sesshin, her stepmother's imprisonment. He felt guilty that he had not been more considerate towards her all winter. He had left her to Haru's care. Now he spoke more gently.

'Stay away from the gate; the beams might fall on you.'

'I am looking for the eyes, Father. I had a dream I found them and put them in a treasure box. The gateposts were shaking with laughter. It was horrible. When I woke up the earth was shaking.'

He noticed she had been crying. He saw a slight gleam in the dust and bent to lift the carved transom that had been half-buried in rubble. The eyes stared back at him. They had lost none of their lustre.

'Ah,' Hina said. Two tears fell on the eyes, moistening them. She held out a carved wooden box in which she had placed a small piece of white cloth. 'Put them in here and I will keep them safe.'

He took the cloth and picked up the eyes with it, wrapped them and placed them in the box. She held the box awkwardly because she also had a sheaf of manuscripts, loosely bound with thread, clamped under one arm.

Kiyoyori gestured at the text. 'Give me that, you are going to drop it.'

She turned sideways so he could take it. It was a manuscript made up of folded pages, some yellow with black writing, some indigo with gold. He fanned through the pages, noting how some seemed to be glued together so he could not open them while others were so blurred they were impossible to read. Occasionally a drawing of an animal or a mythical creature appeared and he had the uneasy feeling their eyes were looking back at him. It resembled an esoteric text, the sort written by monks or healers.

'It's about medicine. Is it one of Master Sesshin's?'

'He gave it to me last year, after he saw me making potions for that dog that was so sick.'

This surprised Kiyoyori. He had not known Sesshin had ever spoken to Hina, let alone given her a text like this. 'Can you read it?'

'It's too difficult for me. But I like looking at the pictures. It's called the Kudzu Vine Treasure Store. That's because it's difficult and complicated like kudzu. Master Sesshin told me that. Sometimes I feel it doesn't want me to read it.'

'I will help you if you are really interested.' He made the promise knowing it was possible he would never keep it, that they would never have that sort of time together in the future, and again he deeply regretted squandering the time they might have had during the winter.

She nodded with a smile but then her face turned grave. 'Where is my stepmother?'

'I don't know. She walked away, probably early this morning.'

He went with Hina to the lake and showed her the footprints. Hina stared at them. 'Will she come back?'

'I don't think so.'

'Will Tsumaru?'

'I am going to tell you a secret about Tsumaru,' Kiyoyori said slowly. 'You know he was kidnapped to make me hand over Master Sesshin . . .'

His daughter fixed him with a gaze like steel. 'And Lady Tora?'

'I don't want to talk about Lady Tora with you; it is not fitting. When you are older you will understand.'

Hina flushed at the rebuke. Kiyoyori went on sternly, trying to mask his guilt and regret. 'Someone, one of our people, promised to rescue him. I don't know if he succeeded or not.'

'Who?' she said flatly.

'A servant in the house below Rokujo. Iida no Taro is his name.'

'If he did succeed, why has Tsumaru not come home?'

'I don't know,' Kiyoyori replied. 'But that is why I have to go to the capital, to find out.'

'You won't leave me here?'

'No, you can come with me.'

Hina said, 'Was the earthquake a punishment?'

He did not want to answer her. It was not right for children to judge their parents. But he feared that the earthquake was a punishment for the many terrible things that had happened at Matsutani, and it was certainly an ominous start to the year.

They camped in the undamaged part of the house while the funerals were held and the bodies burned and while Kiyoyori issued instructions for the rebuilding. He left two-thirds of his men to help with the work and guard Matsutani, and took the remainder with him to Miyako.

Hina took the text called the Kudzu Vine Treasure Store and the box containing Sesshin's eyes.

•

The city was tense, many armed warriors thronging the streets, the red banners of the Kakizuki flying from gates and roofs. As he passed through the southern gate, where beggars and other vagrants sought shelter, he was recognised in the middle of the chaos by one of Lord Hosokawa's retainers, who was in charge of the guards.

The man greeted him warmly. 'Kiyoyori! You have come to defend the capital?'

'What is happening?' Kiyoyori shouted back.

The other fought his way through the crowd, grasped the horse's bridle and gestured to Kiyoyori to bend down. He whispered, 'The Emperor is finally dying, and the Miboshi are approaching from the east.'

'I would be more use at Matsutani, defending the high road,' he said, wondering if he should turn back. He felt every decision he made was the wrong one, as though whatever divine protection he had been under had been withdrawn.

'No, you are needed here. We fear an attack on the Crown Prince. How many men have you brought?'

'Barely fifty. You did not hear about the earthquake?'

'We felt it here, but it was not destructive. You had better report to Lord Hosokawa as soon as you can, and he will tell you what to do.'

Kiyoyori acquiesced and rode on.

There was no sign of Taro at his house below Rokujo and the place looked even more neglected than before. He unleashed his anxiety on the servants in a blast of rage that had them scurrying round, opening shutters, airing the bedding, sweeping floors and preparing food.

Hina was white with exhaustion. He himself bathed her face and feet and as soon as a room was ready made her lie down. Then he found paper and writing materials and sent Sadaike with a message to Ryusonji.

The man came back within the hour. The Prince Abbot would receive him even though it was getting late. Kiyoyori left at once, taking the ox carriage he reserved for travel within the capital, especially when he did not wish his face to be seen. The carriage was full of spiders and smelled of mould; the ox had not been in harness for months and had forgotten all its training. Other carriages packed the streets as the city's inhabitants prepared for flight. It took a long time to get to the temple and when he arrived it was already twilight. The sky was clear and stars were appearing.

The carriage was not allowed beyond the first gate. Kiyoyori descended and was led across the gravel and through the temple buildings to the same reception room he had been in last time. The Prince Abbot sat on the same purple and white silk cushions. At his side knelt a young man whose head was not shaved and whose hair was tied up like a warrior's. He raised his head when Kiyoyori came in, and Kiyoyori recognised Shikanoko.

His instinctive response was relief that the boy was alive but this was quickly replaced by rage. Shika did not look like a prisoner or a hostage. He must have allied himself with the Prince Abbot. How deeply Kiyoyori regretted sparing his life. But he could not waste time dwelling on that now. He knelt, waited for permission to speak and then said, striving for politeness, 'My lord Abbot, I heard that your monk Gessho was successful in tracking down the fugitives you sought. I see you have Shikanoko at your side, apparently in your service. So why has my son not been restored?'

The Prince Abbot answered him coldly. 'There are still outstanding matters that need to be settled between us. Where is the woman, the sorceress? And where is your allegiance now? Whose side will you take?'

For a moment he could not speak. *He thinks she is alive!* Then he said, letting his anger show, 'Who can I side with but my family, the Kakizuki? It is less than noble of you to expect me to betray my allegiance for my son's life.'

'You dare lecture me on nobility?' the Prince Abbot's voice took on a note of fury. He half-rose as if he would step towards Kiyoyori, even strike him, but then he gained control and sat again. He tapped a scroll that lay on its own cushion at his side. 'Do you know what this is? It is the Book of the Future. In it are inscribed the names of all the Emperors to come, down through the ages. I am not acting idly or through the desire for personal gain. I am following the will of Heaven. Prince Momozono's name is not in it. But his younger brother's is.'

'Show me,' Kiyoyori demanded.

'Only my eyes can read it,' the Prince Abbot replied.

*How very convenient!* Kiyoyori was assessing rapidly the attempted distraction, the apparent loss of control. He said boldly, 'Show my son to me, your Holiness. Just let me see his face.'

'Agree not to oppose me, to stay out of the coming confrontation, and you may see him.'

There was a note of uncertainty in his voice. Kiyoyori realised the Prince Abbot did not have Tsumaru. Had Taro been successful? He glanced at Shikanoko and saw that the young man was regarding him with pity. A jolt of fear struck him in the belly.

'Why do you waste my time?' the Prince Abbot said angrily. 'I regret even agreeing to see you. Go. We have nothing more to discuss, now or ever again. The next time I see your face your head will be on a stake, along with all my enemies.'

Kiyoyori left, half-expecting to be detained before he reached the gates and even more disturbed than he had been when he arrived. As he crossed the last courtyard, he heard the sounds of a lute and a voice singing:

*The dragon child, he flew too high*
*He was still so young, he tried his best.*
*But his wings failed and he fell to earth.*
*He fell to earth.*
*Now he dwells beneath the lake at Ryusonji.*

The plaintive tune sent a shiver down his spine.

He returned home, left the carriage and rode on horseback to his kinsman Hosokawa no Masafusa's palace. Armed men gathered in the courtyard, swords at their hips, quivers filled with arrows on their backs, bows in their hands. Night had fallen.

Masafusa greeted him tensely. 'You are here, Kiyoyori? I was afraid you would have been already defeated by the Miboshi. Is anyone defending your estates?'

'I left most of my men there, about a hundred. The place was badly damaged in the earthquake. We had several dead and lost many horses. I had no idea the situation had become so desperate so quickly. Why was I not told?'

'We didn't realise the extent of the Prince Abbot's intrigues or the Miboshi's war preparations. While the Emperor lived, there was no cause for alarm. He had always designated Prince Momozono as his heir. But now he is dying – indeed, come close let me whisper: it is rumoured he already passed away some days ago, but the Prince Abbot will not allow it to be revealed until the Crown Prince and his son, Yoshimori, are dead, and he can immediately place his favourite on the Lotus Throne.'

'Surely even he will not dare to harm his Imperial Highness?'

'Make no mistake, he will dare. He will accuse the Prince of rebellion and attack his palace – it could be at any time, maybe even tonight. The Miboshi are approaching from the east, ready to take the capital and defend the claim of the new Emperor.'

'Where is our lord and what are his commands?' Kiyoyori said.

'He believes we should flee. The years of power and excess it seems have sapped his fighting spirit. Our men have little taste for war. Maybe our time has come to yield to the Miboshi.'

'Not while I live!' Kiyoyori replied. He was glad the time for fighting had come. Nothing else would assuage his unease.

'I knew I could count on you. Lord Keita wants to take his grandson with him. That way he will protect the rightful Emperor even if Prince Momozono should not survive. Go to the Prince's palace, defend it as long as you can, but most importantly rescue the boy and bring him to Rakuhara, where our lord will take refuge.'

Rakuhara was a large Kakizuki estate to the west of the capital near the port of Akashi.

'Go at once,' Masafusa said.

Kiyoyori bowed his head. 'I will see you in Rakuhara.'

He reflected grimly as he hastened back through the dark street on how children were used as pawns in men's struggles for power. His son, Tsumaru, the Emperor's grandson, Yoshimori, were to be abducted, hidden, murdered, not for any crime of theirs unless it was from a former life, but because of who their fathers were.

The lute player's song came into his head. Why had he heard it at that moment and what message did it have for him? But in his heart he knew its meaning was that Tsumaru was already dead.

•

Hina had fallen asleep almost immediately after her father left and had slept deeply for a while, but the sound of men and horses awakened her. She was afraid her father was going somewhere and leaving her behind, and she ran out onto the verandah, but he had already gone.

It was a still spring night. The scent of blossom floated over the neglected garden and now and then a fish splashed in the pond.

Something moved in the shadows. She thought it might be a fox and pressed closer to the verandah's pillar. The figure approached, walking on two legs. She was about to scream when she saw it was Shikanoko.

He put his finger to his lips and beckoned to her to come closer, then put his hand on her shoulder and took her to the end of the garden. Azalea bushes had grown wild and she could see their blossoms faintly. She was happy to see Shika. She had missed him since he and Sesshin had been driven away.

'Hina,' he whispered, 'where is your father?'

'He has gone out. I don't know where.'

'He came to Ryusonji,' Shika said. 'I saw him there. But hasn't he returned?'

'I was asleep,' she replied. 'He must have come back and left again, for I thought I heard him depart with men and horses.'

'I wanted to speak to him, to try and explain things to him – but now it is too late.' Shika was silent for a few moments. 'Well, I suppose I must tell you, though it is a hard thing for a child to hear.'

'Is it about Tsumaru? Is he dead?' She was shivering. Shika put his arm around her.

'How did you know?'

'I dream about him and he is always a spirit in my dreams.'

Shika sighed and said, 'You must tell your father how it happened. Tsumaru disappeared from Ryusonji, the first night I was there. The Prince Abbot was distraught. He had grown very fond of him, and he had promised your father no harm would come to him. He performed a spirit-return ritual and learned that someone in your father's service had tried to snatch him away. While keeping him silent he had suffocated him by mistake. We found his body in the lake.'

Hina was crying silently. Shika said, 'He is with the dragon child now.'

'Father told me who it was,' Hina wept. 'He was going to rescue Tsumaru, and he killed him. It was Iida no Taro.'

'I will remember that name,' Shika said.

She leaned against him. 'I missed you. And the horses. How is Risu?'

'She is improving in temper. She is in love with Nyorin. I think she will have a foal next year.'

'I wish I could see it. I wish I could live with you and Risu and Nyorin and their foal. Why don't we get married when I am old enough?'

'Your father will want you to marry a great lord, someone of your high station.'

'I would rather marry you.'

There came a distant sound of shouting, the whine of humming arrows, the clash of steel, then screams of horses and men.

'What's happening?' Hina's fingers ground into Shika's arm.

'It has started,' he replied. 'I must go back to Ryusonji.'

'Shikanoko, are you on our side or someone else's?'

'I am on no one's side. Only my own.'

'So you are a sorcerer like everyone says?'

'I was made one against my will, and now it is my fate, it seems.'

'You sound so sad about it.'

'I wanted to talk to your father. I am sad that it is too late. If you see him tell him I am sorry . . .'

'Sorry for what?'

'I don't know, sorry he spared my life that day.'

'I'm not sorry! I'm glad. I thought he would kill you like all the others. I prayed and prayed that your life would be spared. And I was so happy when you took Risu as well as Nyorin. I was afraid you were going to abandon her. I liked you as soon as I saw you, but I really liked you after that.'

'Hina!' he exclaimed. 'What a gentle child you are!' Then he drew her closer and looked at her face intently.

'What is it?' she whispered.

'I want to remember how you look. We may never meet again.'

Neither of them spoke for a moment. Then Hina said, 'I have Master Sesshin's eyes. Shall I give them to you?'

'Why did you take them from the gate?'

'There was an earthquake,' she said in exasperation. 'Didn't you know? The house was destroyed and the stables. Lots of horses were killed and some people too. And my stepmother ran away.'

She was crying again.

'He intended his eyes to remain at Matsutani,' Shika said. 'But now you must keep them with you. Wash them with your tears and they will watch over you.' He held her for a moment, then released her, leaped over the wall in one bound and was gone.

Hina returned to the house. The clamour from the streets had awakened the maids. They clustered round her in fear. She sat on the verandah with the box containing the eyes and the Kudzu Vine Treasure Store waiting for her father. From time to time she allowed tears to fall in order to moisten the eyes, but she could not tell if they were watching over her or what protection they could give her.

# 15

# AKI

Aki woke from a vivid dream – she was standing by a stream, she saw splashes of blood on the rocks, then a young stag leaped towards her. She opened her eyes. Lamps burned feebly in each corner of the room but outside it was dark and still. No birds sang yet, not even the cocks were crowing.

Her father was kneeling beside her, wearing a hunting robe, beneath which she glimpsed green-laced armour. His long sword was at his hip. Her mother stood behind him, holding his quiver of arrows.

'They are coming to arrest the Prince,' her father said quietly.

Aki's heart was racing. She breathed slowly and deliberately in the way he had taught her, her gaze fixed on his. She wanted to relate the dream to him and hear his opinion of it, what it meant, whether it was auspicious, but there was no time now.

'He will not be captured,' her father went on. 'He will not let them execute him in secret so they can put their puppet on the Lotus Throne. We have sent for help. Kiyoyori is coming. We will defend ourselves for as long as possible. You must take his Highness and escape.'

He turned and took the quiver from his wife and fastened it to his back. 'Wake him up quickly and dress him in some old clothes.'

Aki's mother said, 'Better they should both cross the River of Death here with us. How will a girl survive on her own? Where will she go?'

'We must give Yoshimori a chance,' her father replied.

'I'll take him. I'll look after him. I promise.' She was on her feet now. 'What shall I wear? Do you have something old for me?'

Her mother brought a pile of maid's clothes. 'Even these are too fine,' she grumbled. 'Look at her, nothing can hide her appearance. There are bad men out there. What will they do to her?'

'This is why I have taught her to defend herself,' her father said. 'Take your knife, Aki, and promise you will stay away from men – you know what I am talking about. There are dangers women face that men do not. Kill anyone who tries to get intimate with you or who tries to hurt the Prince.'

'I promise,' she said.

'I will cut her hair,' her mother said and called for a maid to bring scissors. Aki's hair reached almost to the ground. Her mother held each strand close to her head and snipped through it, allowing them to fall around her until she seemed to be standing in a pool of black. Neither of them spoke or wept.

When it was done and Aki had finished dressing, her mother brought Yoshimori and changed his embroidered sleeping robe for one of rough hemp, tied with a rope cord. His eyes were heavy with sleep and he yawned deeply but he did not cry out or protest.

Aki's head felt light and cold. She wrapped a cowl round it, as though she were a town girl going early to market or visiting a shrine.

She had never met or talked to a town girl in her life; it seemed an exotic thing to pretend to be.

'Where shall I go?'

'Follow the north road around the lake and head for the temple, Rinrakuji. You remember we have often been there together. The monks will hide the young Prince there and you can be what you were dedicated to be, a shrine maiden in the service of Kannon. Stay with him until he is safe. You must take your catalpa bow, we have wrapped it with Genzo, the imperial lute – we cannot let that be destroyed.'

Her mother handed the bundle to her. She took it with reverent hands, and felt the lute vibrate through the carrying cloth. It gave a single soft, grief-filled twang, and the bow responded.

'Go now, my daughter,' her father said. 'The Prince Abbot's men will be here at any moment. We will hold them off at the main gate. You must slip through the moon gate at the rear and follow the river. There will be many people fleeing the city. Mingle with them.'

He knelt before the boy. 'Yoshimori, you must not be called Prince or Lord for a while. No one must know who you are. Do not speak to anyone. Obey Aki in everything. She is your older sister now. Do you understand?'

'What about Kai?' Yoshi said. 'I'm not going anywhere without Kai.'

'It is hard enough with one child, let alone two,' her father murmured.

'If Kai stays she will die,' her mother said, just loud enough for Yoshimori to hear her.

'I'll scream,' he said. 'If Kai doesn't come I'll scream and scream. And I won't go anywhere.'

'Wake her up,' Aki said. 'I can take them both. Kai will make things easier.'

Tears sprang from her father's eyes. Her mother was weeping silently as she thrust two pairs of clogs into Aki's hands. Aki bowed to the ground before her parents. She did not speak but in her heart she was crying, *Father, Mother, when will I see you again?*

Noise was erupting like a rainstorm: first the spattering drops, a single cry, the urgent thud of feet hurrying along a corridor, then the heavier fall, women wailing, the tread of men running, shouts, in the distance the shrill neighing of horses. Aki lifted Yoshimori in her arms and settled him on her hip. He was a slight child and she was strong, unlike most palace women who never lifted anything heavier than a writing brush or a hair comb; even so she did not know how far she would be able to carry him.

Kai appeared at her side, pale and silent. She was holding Aki's ritual box.

'Your mother told me to bring this,' she said.

'I can't carry it too!' Aki exclaimed, near tears for the first time.

'I'll look after it,' Kai said. She touched Yoshimori on the ankle and smiled up at him.

Lights flickered, throwing strange shadows on the brocade and bamboo blinds that covered the entrances to the rooms. Aki pushed the closest blind aside and stepped out onto the wide verandah. She set Yoshimori down on the edge and put on her clogs, fitting the other pair to his feet. Taking him by the hand she pulled him upright.

'Now you must walk beside me.'

For a moment she thought she would have to show him how, but, though he had been carried almost everywhere throughout his short life, his muscles were not yet useless and he was still young enough to want to walk, even to run, like any normal child. Kai followed barefoot. They went swiftly across the darkness of the Eastern Courtyard but as they passed the New Shining Hall a sudden light flared, revealing the face of Yoshimori's mother, known as Lady Shinmei'in.

Aki pulled the cowl lower over her face and tried to hide the boy in the skirt of her robe. For a moment she thought they would pass by unrecognised but the Princess leaned towards them.

'What are you doing with his Highness? Where are you taking him?'

'I must not be called that,' the boy said.

'Lady, I am his nurse's daughter. My father, Hidetake, told me to escape with your son, into hiding.'

'Why? What is happening?'

'The Prince Abbot has sent men to arrest your husband. The Prince intends to resist.'

Lady Shinmei'in's eyes were huge, her face as pale as snow. 'Then I must be at his side and share his pillow in death as in life. Our son must die with us. Come, your Highness. We will change these base garments and prepare your illustrious body for the next world.' She held out her arms, slender and white against the black hair that fell like silk around her. 'No one can escape his fate.'

The boy hardly knew his mother. He had been brought up by Aki's parents. He shrank closer to Aki's side and gripped Kai's hand.

What was she to do? Should she obey her father and defy the Princess? Or should she recognise the mother's right to decide the fate of her child, relinquish him and return to die alongside her own parents? What was there to fear in death? It lay all around, separated from life by only the thinnest of membranes. A moment's exhilarating pain and then you passed through to the other world, leaving behind honour and courage as your memorial, facing judgement and then rebirth.

In the dim light the mother's pale hands beckoned like a ghost's towards the grave. The child said, 'If I am to reign I cannot die now.'

Until they are seven, children belong to the gods and speak only truth. Aki knew she was hearing a divine message. Without saying anything she seized Yoshimori's hand. For a moment he resisted in surprise but then he surrendered to her grip and the three of them were running towards the moon gate and the river.

There were many people trying to escape, for the attackers, the Prince Abbot's men, were setting the palace buildings on fire, one after another. The wind that sprang up just before dawn was driving the flames westward towards the city. Already the Hall of Light From the East was alight, and next to it the Hall of New Learning stood gutted, its rafters black against the red inferno. Priceless treasures, irreplaceable scrolls were being consumed and reduced to ashes. She felt the lute in her hand vibrate again and moan softly.

Yoshimori was quivering too, tremors running from his hand to hers. She bent and whispered, 'Be brave. Remember your own words. Your destiny is to live.'

He made no reply but his grip tightened and as they hurried through the gate, rather than she being the guide, he was leading her.

Kai stopped for a moment and made a sign to Aki.

From behind Aki heard a great shout, as if one of the gods had appeared and was announcing his presence.

'I am Kiyoyori of the Kakizuki, lord of Matsutani and Kuromori.'

The girls looked at each other with wide startled eyes and then hurried Yoshi on towards the river.

# 16

# KIYOYORI

Kiyoyori had ridden straight from Hosokawa's residence to the Crown Prince's palace. It was not far away, on the east side of the Greater Palace compound where the Emperor lived (and presumably now lay dead). As he and his small band of men forced their way through the streets he thought of Hina left alone, wondered if he would ever see her again, if anyone would stay and look after her or if they would all run away, wondered what had happened to his steward, Iida no Taro, and then saw the man himself, standing on the corner of an alley.

Taro's face changed at the sight of Kiyoyori. It was as if he had been waiting for him. For a moment hope shot through him. *He brings good news. Tsumaru is alive, hidden somewhere in safety.* But then Taro made a helpless gesture and Kiyoyori understood.

*I must talk to him. I must find out what happened.* He was prepared to face death but he could not bear the thought of not knowing the manner in which his son had passed over before him.

There was no time. The horses swept past. Kiyoyori turned in the saddle briefly, and saw Taro begin to run after him, weaving through the crowd. His horse shied, and he looked ahead again.

It was around the end of the hour of the Ox, still a while before dawn. The gates of the palace were barred with armed men on both sides. He could see at a glance they were too few. He stationed his men on the outside facing the street, and then convinced the guards he was who he claimed to be and that they should summon someone to speak to him. A nobleman came out, leading his horse, and the guards closed the gate behind him.

Kiyoyori knew him slightly – Lord Hidetake.

'Kiyoyori,' Hidetake said in relief. 'You have arrived just in time. We received word an hour ago an attack is imminent. The Prince is putting on his armour now.'

'I would stay and fight alongside you,' Kiyoyori said, leaning down from his horse. 'But Lord Keita has ordered me to rescue his grandson and escort him to Rakuhara.'

'So, Keita is fleeing,' Hidetake said. 'He will not come to our aid?'

'At least we can save Yoshimori if we act quickly. Where is he?'

'I have already sent him away. My daughter is taking him to Rinrakuji.'

'I must go after them,' Kiyoyori said, but at that moment the sound of horses coming up the street made them both turn. Men carried torches that showed their weapons and their helmets. They stopped just beyond arrow's reach and their leader announced, 'I am Yoshibara no Chikataka of the Miboshi. I have been sent by Lord Aritomo and his Holiness the Prince Abbot of Ryusonji to arrest Prince Momozono for inciting rebellion against the Emperor.'

Kiyoyori rode towards them, announcing his name in a voice louder than thunder.

'We serve his Imperial Highness and we will never surrender him to you.'

'You should have stayed in Kuromori, Kiyoyori. The Shimaura barrier has fallen and fifty thousand Miboshi are advancing on the capital.'

'Then we will die here and you with us,' Kiyoyori replied, grim elation welling up in him, sharpening his vision and strengthening his arm.

The gates behind him opened and the Crown Prince himself rode out, at the head of a hundred men. As they swept past Kiyoyori, Hidetake leaped up onto his horse, took up his bow and set an arrow to it. The horsemen all had bows ready and a hail of arrows sped towards the Miboshi, making them fall back momentarily. Kiyoyori thought the Prince had the numbers and the will to prevail, but hundreds more men had been waiting out of sight in the alleys. Now, with white banners gleaming in the light of torches, they rushed into the broad avenue, letting fly a barrage of arrows. Prince Momozono was hit in the throat. Kiyoyori galloped towards him, but his own horse screamed and staggered, its chest pierced. He jumped from it as it fell.

A circle had formed around the wounded Prince as his men strove to defend him, fighting hand to hand with swords, pikes and daggers. One by one they dropped, their life blood mingling with that of their Prince. Kiyoyori saw there was no hope; they were completely overwhelmed by the mass of the Miboshi. His own men formed a larger semicircle, their backs to the gate. Kiyoyori remembered his orders to rescue the child, now almost certainly the Emperor. He did not want to be thought to be fleeing, but he had to save Yoshimori. Shouting to his men to fall back behind him and protect the entrance he ran inside the gate, closing it himself. His last sight of the battle was Sadaike, blood streaming from a head wound, gesturing to show he understood.

The palace was already on fire – attackers must have broken through the other gates, unless there were traitors inside the Prince's household – and women ran shrieking from the flames. Kiyoyori ran too, hoping to catch up with Hidetake's daughter before she left the compound. He was brought to a halt by the sight of Lord Keita's daughter, Lady Shinmei'in, the child's mother, standing outlined against the blackened pillars and rafters of what had once been a great hall.

'Lady,' he called, 'where is your son? I am sent to find him and you. Your father commanded me to come. I am Kakizuki.'

She held a dagger in her hand. Her eyes gazed on him without seeing him.

'My son, I come to join you,' she said, so softly he could hardly hear her against the roar of the flames and the crash of falling beams.

She slashed her throat with the blade. Blood flew, covering him. She stood for a long moment, her eyes huge, her hands fluttering. Then she crumpled before him.

Miboshi men burst into the courtyard. Kiyoyori turned to face them, his long sword in his hand. He had no fear, just a resolve to take as many as possible into death with him and on to Hell afterwards. The sight of him, covered in blood, surrounded by flames, made them pause for a moment, and in that sliver of time a man appeared at his side like a shadow. Taro.

'What are you doing here?' he shouted.

'I have to tell you about Tsumaru!'

'What is there to tell? That he is dead and you killed him?'

'The dragon child took him. It's true he died, in the lake, but he lives on in the dragon child.'

A Miboshi warrior ran screaming towards them. Kiyoyori felled him with one sweep of his sword.

'It was my fault,' Taro cried over the clamour. 'I am going to die with you and when we face the Judge of Hell I will take your place.'

'If we don't both die here I will pursue you and kill you,' Kiyoyori yelled, ducking to avoid a sword thrust, then parrying the returning stroke, disarming the blade's owner and skewering him. He wrenched at his sword to release it and slipped in the pool of blood. Taro stepped in front of him to protect him while he recovered his footing.

'I could not be a warrior in life,' he said, bending over Kiyoyori. 'Maybe I will be one in death.'

# 17

## AKI

Aki's father had trained her in the arts of war. She had practised for many hours on the polished floors of the halls of Rinrakuji, she had ridden horses and shot arrows at their country estate, Nishimi, on the shores of Lake Kasumi but she had never been out in the city on her own or mingled with common people. She did not know how to beg, or steal or barter for food. Yoshimori had hardly ever walked on his own two feet in the palace, let alone outside in the dark over a rutted road filled with people, oxen, carts, horses, all flooding towards the northern gates of the city, and the river.

The temple, Rinrakuji, where her father had told her to seek refuge was on the eastern side of the lake, a long way to the north. As her father had said she had been there many times before but she had only rarely gone there by road, more often by boat from Nishimi. It took a couple of hours across the lake, no more, but now she had to make her way from the south, either by road or over water from Kasumiguchi, where the two roads from the north converged at the barrier.

Cocks were crowing and in the east the sky was turning pale. Behind them the city burned like another fiery dawn in the south. Yoshimori's eyes were wide with shock and disgust at the smell, the rude jostling, the unpleasant closeness of so many bodies, but he did not cry out or complain, just clutched Kai's hand as if he would never let it go. Kai said nothing, her small face set in an expression of determination. Aki's mother had tied a scarf around her head, but it could not completely hide the long hair. She was limping a little.

Aki caught snatches of information: the barrier towns to the east had fallen, the Miboshi were pouring into the city from the south, the Kakizuki were fleeing . . .

Many in the crowd wavered, some deciding to follow the Kakizuki and taking the road to the west, some pressing on to Kasumiguchi. Aki reasoned the town would be in enough confusion to allow them to slip through the barrier. Maybe they could take a boat there; if not they would follow the road along the east side of the lake.

The boy was getting tired. He leaned against her, his feet dragged. The lute was heavy; she changed arms and felt its muted response to the movement. As the light grew she could see the river on their right. Horses and men towed boats upstream; none were returning to Miyako. Some of them carried produce, lumber, casks of rice wine and vinegar, barrels of grain. One boat was laden with musicians and young women dressed in robes of scarlet silk, holding parasols decorated with moons. The musicians played, lute, flute, harp and drum, and the women sang, their voices ringing out in the cool dawn air.

Kai was staring at them. 'What beautiful ladies,' she said.

Yoshi waved to them. 'I wish we could ride in the boat with them!'

His refined speech caught the attention of a man walking beside them. 'Beautiful ladies!' he scoffed. 'You're a bit young for a ride with them! But you're a handsome boy – get on that boat and someone will ride you. And those pretty girls too.'

He thrust his pockmarked face towards them, leering. Aki's hand was on her dagger as she pulled Yoshi away.

'You must not speak,' she whispered. 'Didn't my father make that clear?'

A few paces later they came upon a dead body. A man lay on his back, grinning vacantly at the sky, blood congealing round the wound in his throat where flies crawled. Who could he have been? Aki wondered. Victim of a robbery, perhaps, or the thief himself, dealt a rough justice. Or maybe just some unfortunate who had offended the wrong person. She wished she had not just mentioned her father, for now she could not stop thinking about him, and her mother, and them both dead.

Yoshi went white, swayed on his feet and vomited a rush of yellow liquid. Aki knelt beside him, wiped his face and mouth. He was crying silently. Kai was also in tears.

The same pockmarked man came close, saying, 'Here, I'll carry the little lord for a while,' but Aki saw something lascivious in his face and drew out the dagger, backing away, her arm round Yoshi.

'Oh, an armed girl, a young warrior!' The man's leer embraced her too. 'Never been opened by a man, I'll wager. I'll take you first and then the boy, and sell the little girl.'

They were at the water's edge. She could back away no further. A horse came between them and the man, its handler shouting at them to get out of the way before the two ropes fastened to the bow and the stern threw them into the water beneath the boat's hull.

A woman's voice called to her from the deck. 'Give us the children, little sister, and then jump yourself.' Aki just had time to realise it was another pleasure boat, filled with musicians, when many hands reached out and seemed to pluck Yoshi, and then Kai, from her. She tucked the dagger in her belt, a woman took her hand and she leaped onto the boat, clutching the bundle with the other, terrified the lute would fall into the water. It moaned with its almost human voice.

On the shore the man made a vulgar gesture towards her and yelled something she did not understand.

'Don't worry about him,' the woman said, the same voice that had told her to jump. 'Stay with us and you will come to no harm.'

They had placed Yoshi on a bench covered with scarlet cloth and cushions embroidered with dragons and flowers. Kai stood beside him, still holding on to him, still clutching the ritual box. A young woman was bathing Yoshi's face and hands and another pressed a cup of lukewarm broth into Aki's hands.

'I did not even bring water with me,' she said, horrified by her own helplessness. She had no idea how the world worked or who these people were. They had rescued her from one danger but were they not simply another? How was she going to keep Yoshi safe? They were almost certainly alone in the world now, her parents dead, Yoshi's too. Her eyes grew hot as she drank the broth, but she struggled not to let the tears fall.

'Where are you going, little sister?'

'I don't know exactly. Our parents are dead and we are fleeing from the fighting. Maybe we will go to Rinrakuji, maybe as far as Kitakami.' Aki remembered the name of the port on the Northern Sea, even though she had never been there. 'Where is this boat going?'

'To the fifteenth-day market at the Rainbow Bridge. We are entertainers. They call me Fuji.'

She said it as though Aki should know her name, but it meant nothing to her nor had she ever heard of the market or the bridge. They sounded otherworldy and she wondered if she had been rescued by spirit beings or if she and the children had in fact fallen under the boat and drowned, and were now on one of the streams of the River of Death.

*Father, Mother, I will be with you soon!*

There were several canopies on the boat covering soft-matted platforms, which could be made private behind bamboo blinds. Fuji led Aki onto one of these and the other women lifted Yoshi and laid him down beside her. His eyes closed but he still gripped Kai's hand. She climbed awkwardly up next to him, putting the box close to his head. Fuji lowered the blind on the eastern side against the sun's rays. The shadows fell, striped and dappled, across their faces. Fuji leaned towards Aki and unwound the cowl that covered her head.

'What happened to your hair?' she exclaimed.

'My mother cut it.'

'Did she intend you to be a nun? Is that why you are going to Rinrakuji?'

Aki nodded. 'I am dedicated to the shrine of Kannon there.'

'That explains the box.' Fuji made a gesture towards it. 'I thought it must be a ritual box.'

'It's mine, Kai was just carrying it for me.'

'How old are you?' Fuji said.

'Sixteen.'

'And your brother?'

'He turned six this year.'

Fuji narrowed her eyes. 'From a different womb?'

'Yes, but the same father.' Ten years was a long gap between siblings, two mothers was more plausible. So, had her mother died? Or been put aside for a younger woman? Suddenly there was a host of stories she might tell but she had to remember what she said and to whom. And then her sister came into her mind, the child born the same day as Yoshi, who had died at birth, leaving her mother with milk for an infant Prince.

'What about the little girl?' Fuji said. 'Surely they are not twins?'

'No, the child of another woman. My stepmother took pity on her and raised her with her son.'

'Come here, little one.' Fuji reached out to Kai and tried to pull her towards her, but Yoshi tightened his grip.

Kai shook her head. 'If I let go he'll scream. I always stay with him like this until he falls asleep.'

Fuji stood and went closer. Kai shrank back as the woman took the scarf from her head. 'What beautiful hair,' she murmured, and then swept it back, revealing Kai's half-formed ears.

'Ah!' she cried in surprise. 'That's too bad.'

Kai stared back at her with her usual steady expression.

'What are we going to do with you?' Fuji said.

She sat down next to Aki, ran her hand over Aki's cropped head and said nothing more for a few moments. Aki thought she looked disappointed. Fuji drew the dagger from Aki's belt and laid it down on the mat beside them, staring at it. Then she said, 'What do you carry in the cloth? Is it an instrument?'

'Yes, a lute. And my catalpa bow.'

'I can understand the bow, for it is part of your vocation, but the lute? It must be precious to you. You must play for us later.'

'I am not at all skilled,' she admitted.

'That's a pity, if it is true, for we need a lute player. Our last one was seduced away by a rich widow who fell in love with him and offered him a life of ease in Akashi.'

She had been removing Aki's clothing while she spoke, until the girl sat in her underclothes, shivering a little.

Fuji studied her appraisingly. 'It is a shame about your hair,' she murmured. 'You are well formed, even though your face lacks true beauty. Why don't you stay with us while it grows back, and then you can become one of us?'

'What would I have to do, apart from the music?' Aki said.

'We entertain men, soothe away their troubles, bring a smile to their faces, sing to them as their nurses or their mothers once did.'

'I am already dedicated to the shrine,' Aki said. 'I must go to Rinrakuji. I should not *entertain men*.'

'Nothing crude would be expected of you,' Fuji said with a smile. 'Your purity would not be compromised. Men come to us not in power but in supplication. They do not command, they entreat. Sex has a power of its own, which I know how to wield. This boat is my realm, my sisters and brothers are my subjects. Men visit us as ambassadors from a foreign country bringing tribute, seeking favours. But purity also has power. Your presence will strengthen us and bring us blessings. I already feel I love you like my own daughter. In return we will protect you and your little brother, and the other girl. Say you will at least come with us as far as Aomizu. It is only a day's walk to Rinrakuji from there. You can try life as a shrine maiden and if you don't like it you can come back to us.'

'Thank you,' Aki said, though she did not think there was any going back from the life that had been ordained for her. Fuji dressed her again with tender fingers like a mother's.

Aki lay down next to Yoshi and stroked his head. He was asleep now and stirred only very slightly at her touch. Kai had fallen asleep next to him. She listened to the noises of the boat, the musicians practising, a woman singing. Then suddenly dream images began to form, the Princess, her father's face; they dissolved and she was asleep.

When she awoke the boat had come to a halt. Fuji was brushing her hair with her gentle fingers. Yoshi still slept beside her.

'Little sister, we need to get ready for our guests.'

Aki looked around. She had no idea where she was, but the narrow river had widened into a vast lake, its surface as smooth and dark as steel. The boat, transformed with glowing red lanterns, was moored against a wooden pier that stretched out into the water. It was twilight and a thin grey mist rose from the lake, blurring the reflection of the lights and making the boat look as if it were suspended in the air. The musicians were warming up and the notes echoed in a random pattern that sounded enchanted.

'You will play with them?' Fuji said. It was only partly a question.

'Really, I have no skill,' Aki said. She had thought the older woman kind before in the way she expected women to be, in the way, all her life, servants and waiting women had been to her, but now she felt Fuji's strength and her dominance. No wonder she was the empress of her realm. Aki's flight had been driven by a mixture of excitement and desperation. Exhaustion had felled her. These emotions had given way to fear. She had entrusted Yoshi, Kai and herself to these people – and what else could she have done? – but the enormity of what her father had asked of her began to sink in. The Emperor of the Eight Islands slept beside her. The sacred lute of the Lotus Throne lay on her other side. How was she going to keep them hidden, when the lute would reveal itself by its gold and pearl inlay, its rosewood frame?

Yet she could not refuse to unwrap it, when Fuji told her to. Aki stared at the shabby old instrument, not recognising it. It had changed its appearance completely. What could have happened? Did her father pick up the wrong instrument in the dark and confusion? Had someone stolen Genzo while she slept and replaced it with this ordinary, plain lute? Was the imperial treasure, preserved through the ages, lost through her fault, while in her hands? Then Yoshi would never be Emperor and she had failed when she had hardly even begun.

She took it up with shaking hands, aware that Fuji was watching her intently. She knew how to hold the instrument, how to move her fingers over the strings, but she had no gift for music and, as a child and young girl, had always preferred her father's teaching and pursuits to her mother's. Now she began to pick out the notes to a children's song her mother used to sing, using her nail as she had no plectrum.

She made a face; even she could tell the lute was out of tune.

Yoshi awoke, rubbing his eyes. He began to sing in his high childish voice. After a few lines Kai sat up and joined in.

Aki felt Genzo come alive. She felt its surprise, as though no one had actually played it for hundreds of years, and then its joy and delight as it found its tune and the notes began to pour from it.

'Astonishing,' Fuji exclaimed. 'Really, the three of you are quite enchanting.'

Quickly they were dressed in red and white robes and placed among the musicians in the prow.

'Do you know this song?' the players asked, singing a few lines or picking out the notes, and Aki shook her head, only to feel Genzo vibrate beneath her fingers. There was no tune the lute did not know. So she played all night, watching the men – the guests, the ambassadors – come to visit the women and retire behind the bamboo blinds, to be entertained by them.

The moon rose and set, and it was almost dawn when the last guest departed. Gifts had been delivered in tribute: lengths of cloth, casks of rice, embroidery, sweet bean paste, fans, ceramic dishes. An early meal was prepared and then the women lay down and slept while the mooring ropes were cast off and the sail raised. A single helmsman steered the boat along the coast towards the Rainbow Bridge.

Aki rewrapped Genzo in the carrying cloth, and placed it next to Yoshi and Kai, bowing her head and thanking it. Before she slept she lifted a corner of the cloth to check it and saw the gleam of gold and pearl.

•

At one time, the island, Majima, had been part of the mainland, home to a lakeside village, but in the past fifty or so years the weather had changed, with long heavy rains in summer and huge snowfalls in winter, so the water level in the lake had risen and several villages had been submerged. Now Majima was a three-cornered island, its rocky western point thrusting out into the lake, a pine-shaded beach on its eastern side. On its highest spot stood a shrine to Inari, the fox god, from which a row of vermilion gates led down to the curved wooden bridge, the Rainbow Bridge, that joined the island to the mainland.

Fuji told Aki that the local lord dreamed he should have a market at the end of the rainbow and the next day he saw one fall on Majima, so he had the bridge built.

'Why didn't he have the market on this side and save himself the trouble?' Aki said.

'Men love to build bridges,' Fuji replied. 'They love to join things together. The bridge is beautiful and sacred and, you know, markets are best held on islands, or river banks, places that are thresholds, removed from the everyday world. For there is a sort of magic going on at markets. Goods are bartered, one thing transformed into another. Craftsmen create something from nothing. Men trade the work of their hands and muscles. Everyone is equal, there are no masters and servants, no lords and retainers.'

Kai was listening intently. Yoshi shrank close to Aki and pulled her head down so he could whisper in her ear.

Fuji seemed to divine what he was saying. 'You are afraid of pollution? What a little prince you are! Some would think your little friend a source of pollution with her shell ears. Where were you brought up? In the Imperial Palace? Let me guess, your father was a nobleman who either stayed to face the Miboshi and died in the capital or fled west with Lord Keita.'

Aki did not know how to respond. Fuji pressed her. 'Am I right?'

'Not really,' Aki said, creating a story rapidly. 'My parents were employed in a nobleman's palace. My mother cleaned and my father was a painter.'

'A cleaner's daughter does not have such soft hands, a painter's son has sulphur and cinnabar under his nails!' Fuji laughed. 'Don't worry. I won't tell anyone where you come from.'

Aki felt the older woman believed she now knew a secret that gave her power over them and brought them under her control.

'We are considered a source of pollution, like many here at the market,' Fuji said. 'Wandering women who present puppet plays, men who build gardens and dig wells, changing the face of the earth, those who deal with death and decay, who bury corpses and demolish buildings, children who train animals and perform acrobatics. But don't you see, little lord, we, being their opposite, are closer to the divine and the sacred than is the everyday world where most people live. Your mother may have been a lady or a cleaner, but she still went to the threshold of death to bring you into the world, and the afterbirth that nourished you had to be buried, like everyone else's, in the gateway. You began life in blood and excrement and you will end it the same way. What you call pollution is not defilement; rather it is the essence of life, dangerous and dirty, maybe, but full of deep pleasure and power.'

Yoshi gazed at her, not comprehending but impressed by her serious intensity.

'One day you will understand,' Fuji said and stroked his cheek with her slender fingers.

The blinds were lowered, the silk cushions spread out and the women prepared to receive their guests. Aki again sat with the musicians with the disguised lute. She made Yoshi sit next to her, Kai on the other side, and he sang with them; she could tell he was becoming bored but she was afraid to let him out of her sight. When the musicians took a rest and Fuji was occupied behind the blinds, she let the children go to the side of the boat and they hung over the railing, gazing at everything going on around.

'Can we go ashore?' Yoshi said.

'I'd like to, but I don't know how to get there,' Aki replied.

The boat was moored along with several others between the two shores. The visitors arrived in little vessels, hardly bigger than tubs, or were carried on the shoulders of porters, clambering on board with their feet wet and the hems of their robes soaked, making jokes about it that Aki blushed at, though she only half-understood them.

They asked for girls by name; they knew them well. Their eyes were bright with anticipation and excitement. They aroused in Aki a curious mixture of interest and scorn.

'Look!' Yoshi said. 'Monkeys! Children with monkeys!'

A strange troupe was making its way along the island shore. Not all of them were children though they all wore children's clothes, in every shade of red, and all had the same wild, free look as though they were part child and part animal. They stopped opposite the boat and waved. Even the monkeys, tethered by long silken cords and braided collars, raised their little paws.

Yoshi waved back eagerly. One of the men started beating rhythmically on a small drum. A boy of about eight threw himself in the air, turning and tumbling. Two monkeys watched gravely and when he had finished imitated his routine in a bored, offhand way that the onlookers found most amusing. The boy became angry, the monkeys pretended to be scared and when he turned his back imitated his anger perfectly. The crowd roared with laughter.

A competition ensued, boy against monkeys, leaping ever higher, turning more and more somersaults. The monkeys won effortlessly.

The boy fell to the ground, discouraged and miserable. The monkeys looked anxious, conferred with each other, chattered pleadingly at the crowd as though seeking advice. They approached him silently and wrapped their arms round him. He leaped to his feet, grinning, while the monkeys clung round his neck and kissed his face.

'Oh!' Yoshi sighed. 'I wish I was him!'

The acrobats were followed by a travelling physician selling herbs, oils and potions with long, complicated anecdotes that made the crowd laugh, though Aki hardly understood a word, and then an old man made his way through the throng, stood on the shore and waved to the musicians.

They waved back excitedly and quickly arranged for one of the porters to carry him over to the boat. When he was on board one of them dried his feet reverently with a towel and the others gathered in a circle around him, bowing their heads as he spoke a blessing.

Aki had never seen anyone like him, nor did she recognise the prayer. It was the time of the midday meal and food was served, prepared by the market women, carried across to the boat in baskets: rice with eggs stirred through it, fresh fern heads and burdock root, grilled sweet fish from the lake lying on young oak leaves, sweet bean paste in many different flavours and forms.

The old man ate sparingly. At the end of the meal he took the last of the rice and formed it into balls with his fingers, spoke a blessing over them and handed them round. When Aki took one his gaze fell on her, and on Yoshi sitting on her lap.

'They are like the Lady and her Child,' he said. 'Call on the name of Secret One, and he will save you and take you into Paradise.'

The musicians all murmured a prayer.

Aki divided the rice ball with Yoshi and Kai and put a fragment in her mouth. She shivered as she swallowed it. All the tastes in the world seemed embodied in its sticky grains, blood and bone, bitterness, salt and sweetness.

•

Slowly the boat made its way along the eastern coast of the lake until they came to the small town of Aomizu. Kai became something of a favourite with the musicians. They gave her a drum – she was sensitive to vibration and rhythm and she played with a natural talent. She began spending more time with the musicians, leaving Yoshi bored and restless. When he tried to order her around, the musicians teased him, calling him princeling and little lord. Several times Aki thought he was on the point of telling them who he was and she became even more anxious to get him away. As she was getting ready to leave, one of the female drummers came to her and said, 'We will miss you and your lute – we've never heard anything like it, any of us – and we hope you will come back one day. But we have a favour to ask: leave the little girl here. If you are dedicated to the shrine and your brother is to become a monk, what will happen to her? Rinrakuji will not accept her since she is blemished, nor will Lady Fuji take her on. But we accept her, we already love her. She has a divine gift. Heaven must have sent her to us.'

'I would gladly,' Aki said. 'But my little brother is devoted to her. I don't think he'll leave without her.'

The girl smiled slightly. 'We will arrange something.'

The boat had docked, Aki had the lute in her hand and their clogs ready when Yoshi came up to her, looking distressed.

'They say Kai is too sick to travel with us,' he said.

Aki went immediately to where Kai was lying under the canopy in the stern of the boat, the ritual box next to her. She seemed to have been stricken by a sudden fever. Her eyes were dilated, her skin burning.

'It is just lake fever,' the musicians said. 'We'll look after her. She will be recovered in a day or two.'

'We can't go without her,' Yoshi said, his voice trembling.

'Do you remember my father saying you must obey me in everything?' Aki replied.

'Yes, but . . .'

'Obedience means not saying *but*,' she rebuked him. 'We must go now. The boat has to leave and we must get to Rinrakuji. Kai obviously can't come with us. You'll see her again, but now you have to be strong.'

He opened his mouth and she thought he was going to argue or scream, but then he bit his lip, knelt next to Kai and stroked her hair. When he stood and let Aki take her hand he was fighting back tears.

'I am glad she is staying,' Fuji said. 'It is a good thing for her, and it means you are more likely to come back to us.'

Aki thanked her and then asked, 'Who was the old man who shared food with us at Majima?' She had not been able to stop thinking about him.

'Everyone just calls him Father; he is a travelling priest of some sort. The musicians belong to the same faith. He usually waits for the boats at the markets. They look forward to his blessing. Maybe one day they will tell you the story of the Secret One. It is very strange and moving.'

Aki found she longed to hear it but now there was no time. The boat was preparing to move on. She stared briefly across the lake towards Nishimi, her childhood home, lost in the haze. Then she took Genzo in its carrying cloth and stepped from the side of the boat onto the wooden dock. She had her bow on her back, no longer feeling the need to hide it. Yoshi was passed across to her. Cries of farewell and thanks rang between boat and shore.

The ropes were cast off and the sail raised. Aki and Yoshi watched and waved for several moments, then turned away and began to follow the steep narrow road that climbed through the mountains to Rinrakuji.

# 18

# SHIKANOKO

Through the courtyards at Ryusonji echoed the voices of singers, accompanied by lute players and by the old blind man, who, it was said, had once been a sorcerer but had lost his powers along with his eyes. He must have had some natural talent, for he had learned the notes and words swiftly in the course of the winter.

They had new songs to sing, about the victory of the Miboshi and the flight of the Kakizuki, poignant, stirring tales of courage in battle and nobility in defeat, of the shocking but necessary death of Prince Momozono, who had dared to rebel against his dying father, and the virtues of his younger brother who was now the Emperor Daigen.

Shika imagined it brought the Prince Abbot great pleasure to hear daily the recounting of his triumph, by his former rival, now fallen into senility. He was uncle to the new Emperor, and the Kakizuki, his old enemies, were in exile. The wives and children they had left behind were slaughtered, their palaces were rebuilt and occupied by the victorious Miboshi, their presence was being erased from the capital as though they had not dominated its life, its customs, its arts and fashions for nearly fifty years.

Yet Shika knew the prelate was not as satisfied as he might have been. Two things irked him, two missing bodies. The heads of the defeated were displayed on bridges and along the river bank, but Kiyoyori's was not among them. The Prince Abbot's men had combed through the wreckage of the palace and the surrounding streets. The corpses of Momozono and his wife were identified in the piles of dead, along with those of their retinue, male and female, who had died in the fighting or the fire, but Kiyoyori's body had not been discovered nor had that of Yoshimori, only son of the former Crown Prince.

It was reported that Kiyoyori had been last seen in front of the New Shining Hall. An arrow had pierced him and an unknown man who had dashed in front of him. Both had fallen into the flames just before the roof collapsed. Kiyoyori could not have survived, eyewitnesses said, but because his body had not been found fanciful tales had begun to spread about him, the most popular being that the dragon child of Ryusonji had carried him away to join his son Tsumaru, who, it was rumoured, had been kidnapped by the Prince Abbot, had died in some mysterious way and was now a manifestation of that same dragon.

Shika knew from his own experience that men hate above all those they have wronged, and the Prince Abbot's hatred for Kiyoyori had grown even more bitter since the discovery of Tsumaru's body in the lake. He blamed the child's father for the bungled rescue attempt at the same time as he resented Kiyoyori's spirited refusal to be coerced. The suggestion that Ryusonji's own divine being might have aided him in some way was intolerable. The Prince Abbot attempted to suppress the rumours and the tales; his secret police cut out people's tongues for repeating them.

Shika had spent at least part of every day throughout the winter with the Prince Abbot. For many of those days he had been required to fast, be subjected to ordeals of icy water and deprived of sleep. Slowly under these stern disciplines the natural power of the mask had been controlled. He had been taught words of power, some from sutras, others known only to the Prince Abbot, Gessho, and a few older monks. With the aid of all these things the mask took him to places beyond the human world, where the spirit of the deer spoke to him and through him.

But every step forward demanded a price. Often he would emerge from a trance and see in the hollowed eyes and slackened faces around him vestiges of some ritual he had taken part in, without his knowledge and against his will. The mask had been made with both male and female elements; it harnessed the regenerative power of the forest, the sexual drive of the stag. All this interested the Prince Abbot deeply.

He was delighted with his progress. Shika became his new favourite, replacing the young monk Eisei, who had been so burned by the mask. Eisei recovered from his injuries, but would always be disfigured. He wore a black silk covering across his face, behind which his eyes burned with despair.

Shika went every day to sit with Sesshin. The old man did not seem to recognise him, but smiled at him gratefully and patted his hand. The Prince Abbot often questioned him about Sesshin, but even when Shika was in trances induced by strong potions, the power that Sesshin had transferred to him remained hidden. It would reveal itself, he thought, when it was ready and when he was.

The Prince Abbot also questioned him about Kiyoyori. 'That scoundrel has become more popular since he died than he ever was when he was alive,' he complained. 'What magic arts did he possess to vanish without a trace? Did the sorceress come for him? Could she have flown into the burning building and carried him away?'

Shika had learned that many of the Prince Abbot's questions did not require an immediate answer. He did not reply now but he was thinking about how Lady Tora had visited Shisoku's hut in some supernatural manner during the making of the mask.

The Prince Abbot was watching him intently. Shika looked away towards the garden. It was the beginning of the fourth month, a warm day with more than a little humidity in the air. Outside the sun shone glaringly on the wisteria and the azaleas, giving their flowers an intense hue.

The waters of the lake rippled suddenly, a sign that the dragon child was awake, was aware of everything.

Did it remain a child, he wondered, or was it growing to its full size secretly, and would one day emerge? When he looked back into the room his vision was distorted by circles of light and dark.

'And Yoshimori?' the Prince Abbot questioned. 'Was he spirited away too? Perhaps by Hidetake's daughter, the girl they call Akihime, the Autumn Princess. As long as he lives, the Kakizuki will have a cause to reunite and inspire them.'

He sat in thought for a long time while the room grew warmer. Sweat began to trickle from Shika's face and chest. He longed for the cool shade of the forest, the dawn mists of the mountain. He remembered the waterfall.

The Prince Abbot's voice startled him, bringing him back suddenly. 'Is that where you will find them? That place where your mind just wandered? Is that in the Darkwood? Have they fled there?'

Shika still had not learned to hide his thoughts from the Prince Abbot.

'I think I will send you after them,' the Prince Abbot said slowly. 'She will be heading for Rinrakuji, for she was to be a shrine maiden, but she must not get there. The werehawks will accompany you so I know where you are. Bring me Kiyoyori's head and the child's. You can do what you like with the girl, let her live or die. Ride fast. They have already been on the road for days. You must overtake them.'

'I cannot go without the mask,' Shika replied.

The Prince Abbot smiled. 'I would never separate you from your mask. But be aware, I have cast spells on it so I can be sure my little stag will return to me.'

•

Shika left the next morning, riding Nyorin, Risu following. He had intended to leave the mare, who was just beginning to show signs of her pregnancy, but at the last moment decided to take her, telling himself he did not trust anyone there to look after her, not daring to admit that he might never come back. At one moment he thought only of disappearing into the forest, the next the mask whispered to him, reminding him of all he had learned during the winter and all there was still to learn. He was tied in some way through it to the Prince Abbot, who had become his master, but he did not fully understand how or to what extent.

The Prince Abbot had instructed him to ride north and then cut across towards the western edge of the Darkwood. He could picture it all in his mind, as if on a map: the track that led south to Shimaura, the stream that flowed from the mountains, the bandits' hut where they stored weapons and loot they had taken from travellers, for it was on the boundary of Akuzenji's territory and he had ridden all over it a year and a half ago when he had spent the summer in the service of the King of the Mountain.

With only the horses and the two werehawks for company he had many hours to recall the past and reflect on what his life had become. He found himself dwelling, in particular, on the last time he saw Hina, waiting in the garden of the house below Rokujo for her father to return. There had been no specific reports about her but he imagined she had been found and killed along with all the other Kakizuki children. He grieved for her and then forced himself to remember the last time he had seen her father, the expression on Kiyoyori's face when the lord had seen Shika at the Prince Abbot's side.

*He considered I betrayed him; he regretted sparing my life.*

The werehawks fluttered and cried around his head. When they needed to rest they sat on the mare's back, preening themselves and croaking and grumbling to each other. Risu hated them and often bucked or swung her head round to bite in an attempt to dislodge them. They fluttered upwards squawking in surprise and outrage and then returned immediately to their roost.

Shika did not know how the Prince Abbot communicated with them but from the first day he set his mind to understand them. How was it done? Did he have to become like a bird himself or did he have to use some deeper knowledge? Did all Nature understand itself, the pine trees and the crows, the hawfinches and the berries, the fox, the rabbit, the hare? Was there some vast web of communication that joined everything? And if so why should men stand outside it? The stag mask must have given him access to something like that, the power of the forest Shisoku had called it. If he wore the mask, would he understand the werehawks?

At first he thought they disliked him. After all, they had attacked him at Kumayama – he still had the scar – and before that he had shot and killed one at Matsutani. But after a while he realised they were trying in some obscure birdlike fashion to ingratiate themselves with him, even to please him. One in particular, who had a gold feather in its left wing, often sat on his shoulder and made remarks in his ear. He called it Kon, and the other Zen, for its wicked eyes and arrogant manner reminded him of Akuzenji.

They showed him the route to follow, along the eastern edge of the lake, and every night one or other of them flew off to the south, to report back to the Prince Abbot. He resented the fact that they were spying on him, but he knew they were not to blame for it and he treated them well, scratching their heads, feeding them the grain he had been supplied with, listening to their strange talk, trying to decipher it. They seemed to know something about him as though they could smell within him the sweet fiery nugget that Sesshin had fed him, and wanted to partake of it.

He meditated on that power, determined to learn how to use it, following the rhythm of the horses' pace. He noticed with his conscious mind the lush spring landscape, the fresh green of the new leaves, the flooded rice fields that reflected the sky, aware of his own youth and energy, excited by all that lay before him, glad to be free of the stifling atmosphere of Ryusonji. Farmers worked in the fields, a few monks and merchants passed along the road, all making the most of the fine days before the onset of the plum rains. There were no signs of battle. The Miboshi had confined their advance to the capital and were consolidating their conquests in the east. He wondered what had happened at Matsutani, and his own estate of Kumayama. Whose hands were they in now? Presumably his uncle had been rewarded for handing him over, and had allied himself with the victors.

*One day I will get it back*, he vowed.

He followed the Prince Abbot's command and rode fast, sleeping for a few hours at night in the woods using Nyorin's saddle as a pillow. The werehawks led him away from the lakeside road, through rice fields, skirting the small town of Aomizu. He had never been here before but in the distance in the east the mountains rose, their highest peaks still snow-capped, and he knew somewhere to the south lay the course of a stream that would lead him to the pass through to the Darkwood.

One afternoon he came to the road between Aomizu and Rinrakuji. It was a little before sunset. He did not know if he should turn east or west, so he let the horses graze for a while in a small grove and waited for the werehawks to show him.

Kon had flown towards the west, and suddenly returned, landed on Shika's shoulder and said distinctly, 'Prince Yoshimori!' Zen gave a triumphant squawk, flew upwards from Risu's back and settled on an overhanging branch, peering expectantly.

Shika crept towards the edge of the road, bow in hand.

Two figures were hurrying along the road from the direction of Aomizu. One was definitely a child; the other turned and looked back and he realised it was a girl, and that there were two men following her, flitting in and out of sight like wolves pursuing deer, like the wolf that had driven him to Shisoku. There was no one else around. She was running desperately now, dragging the child by the hand, tripping and stumbling. They were closing in on her.

He heard one call, 'I'll take the girl; the boy is for you. Then we'll swap.'

She stopped and spun around to face them. She was carrying a bundle, but she thrust it into the child's hands, and pulled out a dagger. She had a small light bow on her back.

Shika thought he could gallop past, seize the child and escape. The girl was not important. Who the men were he had no idea; they wore no emblems, crests or armour. But he could see their faces, their undisguised lust and greed. The girl's courage, her defiant stance, spoke to him. At that moment he decided to save her life.

He took the arrows from the quiver on his back, drew the bow and shot rapidly twice. Both arrows found their mark, one in each naked throat. The look of astonishment, the useless clutching at the shaft, the weakening of muscles and sinews, the loss of blood, all took place in a few brief moments. Both men fell dead.

The girl turned and looked at him, her face white. She did not threaten him with the knife. It was clear she knew she had no defence against his arrows, but she drew the boy closer, the blade at his throat.

Shika saw she was planning to kill Yoshimori and then herself. Her desperation and her resolve touched him even more deeply.

'Don't be afraid of me,' he called. 'I will help you.'

And he felt Sesshin's power come to life within him, and he knew he was going to defy the Prince Abbot.

# 19

# HINA

Yukikuni no Takaakira was riding through the capital looking for somewhere to live. Lord of the Snow Country, he was close to Lord Aritomo, advisor, confidant, and as much of a friend as anyone could be to that taciturn and suspicious man, who had been deeply scarred by the loss of his family and his years of exile. The Minatogura lord's temper was unpredictable, his nature unforgiving, his favour, once forfeited, lost forever. He never forgot an insult or an offence, never overlooked a mistake. Yet Takaakira respected him and even loved him, admiring his fortitude, his perseverance, and the unexpected high ideals that had led him to establish courts of law that demanded written records, title deeds to estates, signed testimonies to exploits in battle, and a system to hand out rewards fairly.

Takaakira saw, with sorrow, one beautiful house after another reduced to ashes, shrouds of smoke still hanging over them. Perhaps alone among the Miboshi, who now occupied the capital, he regretted the destruction of the Kakizuki. As a youth he had visited the city many times and had revelled in the richness of its art, poetry, music and dance. He admired with all his heart the flamboyant heroism of the Kakizuki warriors in the recent battle, who had sallied out to meet the Miboshi, one by one, as men used to, according to the old songs, calling out their names, demanding a worthy opponent. Under Aritomo's orders they had been brought down by a hail of arrows from an anonymous and united force. This new form of warfare had broken their spirit. They no longer understood how to fight. The men fled with Lord Keita, presumably to regroup at Rakuhara or some other stronghold in the west, abandoning their palaces and their residences, their exquisite gardens, now in the full flush of spring, and in most cases their wives and children.

Lord Aritomo, who understood the nature of both power and revenge, had ordered these to be put to death. Takaakira had admired his lord's ruthlessness while deeply regretting the extinguishing of young, innocent lives. And that, he reflected, was an essential part of his nature. He admired so easily – human qualities of courage or kindness, artistic talent, the beauty of nature, all the poignancy of existence expressed in poetry – and he felt loss so deeply, sometimes unbearably. He was riven by the sadness of things and these days, in the defeated city, had been more raw and unendurable than anything he had experienced in his life. He had never felt so agonisingly alive, never longed so much for the indifference and tranquillity of death.

The slaughter, now, was mostly over. Aritomo had moved into Lord Keita's palace, which had survived undamaged. Preparations were underway for the crowning of the new Emperor. Courts were being set up to share out the spoils of war. Miboshi elders were moving into official positions formerly occupied by their Kakizuki counterparts. Takaakira was one of these; his title now was Senior Counsellor of the Left, but before he could begin carrying out his duties he had to find a house.

On the edge of the city, below Rokujo, on the western side, he came upon a wall around a garden, neglected but, to his eye, not unpleasing. Wild flowers and long grass grew around the gate, which stood half-open, covered in morning glory vines. He dismounted and gave the reins of his horse to his companion, Gensaku, and walked quietly inside.

A long low building of excellent proportions stood on his left, looking out to the southwest. The garden was overgrown, the shrubs straggling, the pebbles and the pond choked with weeds. A cat had been sunning itself on a large flat rock near the house. At the sound of his footsteps it lifted its head, leaped from the rock and vanished under the verandah.

Apart from the cat, there did not seem to be a single living being. Dust lay, mostly undisturbed, on the verandah. He noticed the cat's paw prints and, lit by the afternoon sun, a child's. He felt regret. He did not want to shed blood in the place he had already decided he was going to take for his own. He considered calling Gensaku, and waiting outside until the deed was done, but something prevented him. He stepped inside.

He could not see anyone, all the shutters were closed and the interior dark, but he thought he could hear the child's light tread as it flitted from room to room. The pursuit excited him; it was like a childhood game. Finally he could see its eyes, shining in the half-light like a cat's. He had cornered it. He grabbed it. It made no resistance; in fact it seemed to be clutching something so its hands were not free. It did not cry out or struggle as he carried it out onto the verandah. He must call Gensaku and have him take it away and put it to death.

On the verandah the sunlight fell on a girl's face. She looked at him with a grave, resigned expression but she did not speak. When had she last eaten, he wondered. She was holding a box in both hands and under her arm a folded text. He prised open her hands and took the box, but when he went to open it she said sternly, 'No!'

He put the box down and took the text from her. It seemed to be a treatise on herbs and medicine, esoteric perhaps. His interest was piqued. He had read all the works of the yin-yang masters and had dabbled a little in secret arts.

'Why do you have this?' he asked.

She sighed in a way so knowing and so mature he was surprised and touched. *She knows she will die. Yet she cannot be more than ten years old. How can one so young be so adult and so aware?*

At that moment he seemed to be shown all the years of her life as they might have been: growing up, learning to read and write, becoming a woman, marrying. Was all that going to be extinguished in a moment on his orders? And then he saw the alternative: he would save her. It was so simple it almost made him gasp, simple and perfect. She would be Murasaki to his Genji. He had always dreamed of having a child he would bring up, like a daughter, to become a wife, a companion who shared his interests, who would be his equal in intellect and learning, who would love him. He imagined the clothes he would dress her in, the books he would give her, games of incense matching and poetry that he would teach her.

'What is your name? Don't be afraid of me. I'm not going to hurt you. I'll never let anyone hurt you, I promise.'

She continued to regard him unwaveringly, then the ghost of a smile flickered over her lips.

Takaakira thought, *She trusts me*, and a feeling of joy came over him.

'Tell me your name,' he urged.

'I don't have a grown-up name,' she said. 'Everyone's always called me Hina.'

'That's charming. And your father's name?'

'I don't remember.'

It would be easy enough to find out. But on second thoughts it might be better not to know. If she was from some high-ranking or important Kakizuki family it would mean a far more serious act of disobedience on his part. He guessed her family were provincial warriors who kept a residence in the capital but who lived on their country estate. The house was pleasant but not grand, on the west side and too far from the Imperial Palace to be fashionable – and luckily for him hidden from prying eyes.

'Stay here,' he told Hina and went to the gate to give instructions to Gensaku, to find serving women and cleaners, to put one of his men in charge of running the household and to buy food and wine. Then he added casually, 'There was a girl hiding in the house. Her father died fighting for us and she fled here. I will look after her for the time being until we can find her family. But there's no need to spread this widely.'

Gensaku bowed his head and designated one of his soldiers to inspect the house and find out what was needed.

Takaakira returned to the verandah. Hina had placed the box on the floor and was kneeling before it, her lips moving in prayer as if she were thanking it. A slight chill came over him; there was something uncanny about her as if she were a fox wife or had fallen from the stars. Yet this only made her more appealing to him.

When he approached her she sat back on her heels and smiled at him. It was a little hesitant but nonetheless it was a true smile.

'Father promised to teach me to read,' she said. 'But he has not returned.'

'I don't think he ever will,' Takaakira said quietly, grieving for a man he had not known, an enemy.

The smile faded and her eyes shone with tears.

'I will teach you,' he said, and while he waited for the house to be made ready he began to show her the characters, tracing them with his finger in the dust on the floor.

# 20

# TAMA

In Minatogura, Lady Tama waited anxiously for news. Life in the convent was tranquil but she was bored and restless. She worried about the children, she longed for Matsutani, homesick for its fields and streams and the mountains that encircled it. She wondered if the damage from the earthquake had been repaired, if the lake had been refilled, who was overseeing the preparation of the rice fields and the raising of seedlings, the airing of clothes, the spring-cleaning. She was certain that only she would do it properly.

She had seen the Miboshi army depart, thousands of them, some by road, some by boat, and, though no one had told her directly, she assumed Masachika had gone with them. If Matsutani and Kuromori fell he would be there to declare them his, by right of conquest, and probably by right of law as well. She had found out his claim had not yet been heard. The tribunal, made up of old men who had retired from the battlefield, was still working through cases, trying to clear the backlog before the victories of the new campaign brought a fresh flood of demands for legal recognition.

'We heard last night that Lord Aritomo has taken possession of the capital,' the Abbess told her one morning. 'It seems the Kakizuki incited the Crown Prince to rebel against his father; he was killed in the fighting and many Kakizuki too. The rest fled. The Emperor has passed away and his second son will succeed to the throne. We will observe a period of mourning and pray for the spirits of the departed.'

She spoke calmly but Tama could sense her distress.

'If only men truly followed the way of the Enlightened One,' she went on, half to herself. 'If they shunned ambition and the lust for power, refused to take life and were content with what they had, they would not unleash waves of suffering on the world.'

Tama bowed her head to show agreement but could not help asking, 'Is there any word of our thief?'

'It was he who brought me this news.'

'So where is he now? Why did you not tell me at once?' She could not hide her impatience.

'Your time here has not altered your determination to claim your estate?'

'I am more determined than ever but I am afraid it is all too late. I must speak with Hisoku.'

'Stay here with us,' the Abbess pleaded. 'Abandon your claim and find peace.'

'If Hisoku has returned without the deeds, I will have to. But if I have documentary evidence I intend to present it to the court.'

The Abbess sighed. 'Go to the pavilion. I will send him to you.'

•

Hisoku bowed to the ground before Tama and then they sat knee to knee on the small verandah. The cherry blossoms had all fallen and the tree's green leaves gave a dappled shade. Her heart was beating a little faster from his presence and she suspected his might be too. She had no intention of becoming intimate with him – she would not risk her reputation, but the knowledge that he was attracted to her was reassuring. It meant he would do anything for her.

From the breast of his robe he drew out a small package and placed it on the ground between them.

'You found them without any difficulty?'

'Lady,' he said, 'I don't know how much you have heard . . .'

'Tell me everything.'

'When I came to your estate at Matsutani, Lord Kiyoyori and his daughter had already left for the capital.'

'Kiyoyori left? I thought he would stay and fight for the estates. I imagined, if Matsutani were taken, he would retreat to Kuromori, which could be defended indefinitely.'

'That is what his men have done, apparently. Matsutani had been damaged by the earthquake and the garrison left there had no hope of taking on the Miboshi. They fled and are holed up in Kuromori.'

'Waiting for Kiyoyori to appear, I suppose. Where is he?'

'It is assumed he died with Prince Momozono, but it is not confirmed.'

She felt unexpected grief well up within her. Ah, she would never see him again, her husband of seven years, the father of her son!

'And the children?'

Hisoku had been speaking in a dry unemotional tone but now his voice faltered. 'All Kakizuki children in the capital were sought out and killed. Again there is no confirmation, there were so many and they were so young. Most of the corpses were burned without being identified.'

The bright day went dark and she could see nothing.

'Lady Tama? Are you going to faint? Let me call someone.'

'No,' she said. 'Finish your account.'

'All I have just told you, I heard by report. I have not been as far as the capital myself. I wanted to hurry back with your documents. Matsutani was deserted. The guards fled long before the Miboshi arrived.'

'Was it the damage from the earthquake? I did not think it was so bad – surely it can all be repaired?'

'It was not the earthquake,' Hisoku said. 'Rebuilding had already begun. Sawn planks were stacked up in piles, cut to the right lengths and ready to put up. But there were no workmen, no guards, no servants. I saw some farmers working in the rice fields, so I went to question them. They told me the residence had fallen under the influence of evil spirits; one of them who fancied himself an expert on these matters explained that Master Sesshin must have put them in place to protect Matsutani, but since his departure they had felt abandoned and neglected and had turned spiteful. It seems two men, a guard and a carpenter, had heard their names called in Lord Kiyoyori's voice and had run into the building only to be crushed beneath falling beams, dislodged with great force from the roof. Witnesses said they heard laughter and one even claimed to have seen the spirits crouched in the rafters. After that no one dared go in the building. The shrine priest came and conducted a divination from which he concluded the spirits were beyond his capacity to deal with and should be left alone until Sesshin or some other master could exorcise them.'

'I accused him of being a sorcerer,' Tama said, 'but I had not realised he was so powerful.'

'The priest told me you had his eyes put out and sent him away into the Darkwood.' His voice expressed no emotion that she could discern. She did not want to dwell on memories of that terrible day. What did it all matter now? Her son was dead, her home cursed.

'You should have killed me as you were ordered to when you came before,' she cried, and tears began to fill her eyes. 'Kill me now and put an end to my suffering.' She could no longer hold in her feelings and for many minutes she wept bitterly.

Finally Hisoku spoke with some hesitation. 'As I said, Lady Tama, I found the documents.'

'You went into the house? You weren't afraid?'

'A little afraid, yes, but very respectful. I spent several days talking with the spirits. I brought them placatory offerings, spring flowers, rice wine and so on. I know a little about these things – my father was a gardener at the Great Shrine in Miyako and often had to soothe spirits that were displaced or offended by garden works.'

'You really do have many talents,' Tama said.

'In my line of work, when I have so many enemies, I don't need hostile spirits as well. I try to keep them on my side. Eventually I told the spirits I had to collect something from inside the house and they let me in. The documents were where you told me, in the cavity in the well in the kitchen.'

She did not look at the package. 'It is all my fault,' she said. 'I have destroyed the place I love. If I had not treated Master Sesshin so cruelly, if I had not turned him away, he would still be protecting my house. I did not know he had been doing it for so many years. I thought it was thanks to Heaven's blessing, Kiyoyori's ability, my own efforts. But, in truth, it was not Sesshin I was punishing. It was my husband. He started it all by bringing another woman into my house. Jealousy of her, and fear for my son when he was snatched away, made me act so cruelly and unwisely.'

'You must have loved your son very much.'

'I did not know how much.'

'And his father too?'

'That is no concern of yours.' In fact Tama was amazed at how strong and painful her grief was for Kiyoyori.

'From all accounts,' Hisoku said, 'he was a better man than his brother. Well, you yourself admitted as much to me when you said Lord Kiyoyori would have come to kill you himself, rather than send an assassin like me.'

'Where is his brother, Masachika, now?' Tama said slowly. She was going to have to fight Masachika in the courts for Matsutani. But she found within her a determination to do it. She would rebuild and restore her home and make it the safe and beautiful place it had been when Kiyoyori, Hina and Tsumaru were alive.

'He accompanied the Miboshi forces into the capital,' Hisoku replied. 'I heard he fought with distinction at Shimaura and the Sagi River. Now he is assisting Lord Aritomo with the reassignment of official positions. He has been made a captain of the guard of the right.'

'One brother's fortune rises while the other's falls,' Tama said. 'Their father wanted to have one son on each side, so, no matter who prevailed, Kuromori would stay in their family and their line would survive. He was farsighted, I suppose. But he never took into account that Matsutani was mine and still is. I will make one final effort to claim it and if the judgement goes against me I will become a nun and pray that the departed will forgive me.'

Hisoku was staring at her with open admiration. 'I will help you in any way I can.'

# 21

# MASACHIKA

Masachika himself watched the Prince Abbot's men go through the ruins of Momozono's palace. He wanted to be sure Kiyoyori was dead and he wanted to give his remains a proper burial to pacify his spirit and put an end to the conflict and rivalry their father's decision had caused between them. People were already talking about the return of the murdered Crown Prince as a vengeful ghost and priests gathered every day at the site of his death in elaborate attempts to placate him. Their chants and the smoke of incense were the background accompaniment to Masachika's restless searching and waiting.

If anyone were to return as a vengeful ghost, he thought, surely it would be Kiyoyori. Even though no trace of his corpse was discovered, he concluded he must be dead – it was what he wanted to believe – and ordered the priests to add Kiyoyori's name to their prayers. No one told him the rumours that Kiyoyori had been rescued somehow; they did not want their tongues torn out.

Masachika went to the old house below Rokujo, but found the doors guarded and was told it had been taken over by Yukikuni no Takaakira. There was no arguing with that. Takaakira was too close to Lord Aritomo, and Masachika had no intention of making an enemy of him. He had never cared for the house anyway. It was where their mother had died and held only sorrowful memories for him. Tsumaru was already dead, he learned, and Hina must have also perished. He had never seen his brother's son, and had last set eyes on Hina when she was an infant. Naturally, he felt some twinges of grief for them, and for the brother he had known before the rift. Memories of their shared boyhood rose fresh in his mind: their horses, their hawks, their first bows and swords. They had been close friends then; he had admired Kiyoyori deeply, and sought his approval in everything, until he had grown old enough to realise his unenviable position as a younger son. Then he had begun to resent the brother who, by accident of birth, had everything while Masachika had nothing. His marriage, his wife's brother's unexpected death, had seemed to redress fortune's balance in his favour until his father's brutal decision had taken away his wife and his estate, and bestowed them on Kiyoyori.

He had gone to Minatogura burning with resentment and rage, but he had mastered his feelings and served his new family, the Yamada, and his new lords, the Miboshi, diligently. He had seen how he must make himself useful to those around him to survive, and he had become adept at willingly performing tasks no one else wanted to do.

He had obeyed his father, as sons were supposed to, and now he intended to enjoy the fruits of his obedience. He was even grateful now to his father who had ensured his position on the winning side. Matsutani and Kuromori were now his, with or without the tribunal's ruling. He was the only surviving heir.

Yet he did not feel secure. He began to fear that the estates might be bestowed on someone else, that Lord Aritomo might forget him or overlook him, that his Kakizuki blood might count against him. When it was reported that the last of Kiyoyori's men were holding out in Kuromori he requested permission to lead an attack on them before the rains set in.

He was given a hundred warriors, who had been waiting restlessly in the city for their next chance for a battle, a skirmish or a siege – anything was better than hunting down women and children. They were eager for a chance to prove themselves again. Most had no land and were hungry for recognition and rewards. Masachika, and his second in command, Yasuie, could both read and write and, even before they left Miyako, were beset with requests to record the men's names, their war history, the battles they had fought in, the wounds they had received.

It amused Masachika and he found it a useful means to learn each individual history and form judgements on this loosely associated troop of men who were only in the vaguest terms under his command. Some were braggarts, some brave (and of course it was possible to be both), some pragmatic and calculating. They were content to follow him for the time being, if only because he had some legitimacy: he was taking back what was his and he knew the country and the terrain, but each man would be fighting for his own glory and gain.

On the second evening they arrived at the barrier at Shimaura. It was still decorated with the heads of Kiyoyori's men who had died defending it in vain. Masachika, himself, had killed more than one of them. He had not thought about it in the heat of the battle, but now he felt uneasy. They had been his family's retainers. He had been taught by the older men, had grown up with the younger ones. Their sightless eye sockets (the eyes had already been pecked out by crows) seemed to reproach him. He would have liked to have the heads taken down and buried, yet he did not dare show weakness or any sympathy for the Kakizuki. Instead he addressed the dead boldly, by name, mocking them, making the living laugh heartily.

He slept badly that night, woke the others before daybreak, and rode with a sombre heart towards Matsutani.

The sun rose over the eastern mountains, dazzling their eyes. Ahead, slightly to the north, lay the Darkwood. On the flat land along the river the young rice plants glowed a brilliant green, swaying above their reflections in the flooded fields. Frogs croaked from the banks and butterflies flew up from the grass. The air was moist and heavy, the men sweated beneath their armour, the horses' coats turned dark.

In the early afternoon they approached Matsutani. Sensing they were near their destination the men began to break away to collect whatever food they could find: some eggs here, a bucket of millet there, fresh greens pulled from the earth. The farmers and their families did not protest or resist, but stared resentfully in Masachika's direction. He wondered if they recognised him. He wanted to say, 'I am your lord. Everything here is mine.'

Yasuie was eyeing him curiously. 'There's some strange history, isn't there, between you and your brother?'

'Nothing that need concern anyone, anymore, since my brother is dead.'

'Just seems a bit unusual that you ended up on opposite sides.'

Masachika urged his horse on, making no answer, but when he arrived at the west gate, alone, he called in a loud voice, 'I am Kuromori no Jiro no Masachika. I have come to reclaim my estate.'

Yasuie caught up with him. 'The men were told the house is occupied by evil spirits. That's why it is deserted. They were placed there as guardians by the old man, Sesshin.'

'Sesshin?' Masachika said in surprise. 'Well, no wonder they've gone bad.'

'They say it happened after the lady had his eyes put out.'

Masachika said, hiding a shudder, 'It is a feeble excuse for failing to carry out any repairs. I heard there was an earthquake, months ago. It's disgraceful that nothing has been done.' He dismounted and let the horse graze. He walked through the gate and spoke again in a loud voice. 'It is I, Masachika, lord of Kuromori and Matsutani.'

There was a long moment of silence, long enough for Masachika to observe the destruction and neglect of the once beautiful house and garden. The lake was a stretch of mud, the summer pavilion a pile of charred wood. Then a ripple of laughter came from inside the half-burned residence.

'Masachika, come here!'

'Kiyoyori?' he gasped. 'Brother?'

Yasuie spoke behind him. 'Don't go any closer. It is not your brother. It cannot be.'

'I'd know his voice anywhere,' Masachika said and stepped towards the verandah.

An iron pot hurtled towards him. He ducked his head to the side just in time. The pot struck him on the shoulder, knocking him to his knees.

A mocking voice, nothing like Kiyoyori's, came from the house, saying, 'Your brother's wife is the Matsutani lady, and your brother is the Kuromori lord. What are you, Masachika? Neither Kakizuki nor Miboshi, you are nothing!'

More shrieks of laughter followed, as the spirits hurled out kitchen utensils and household objects, a bamboo dipper, two small brooms, a lacquer tray and several quite valuable bowls, which smashed to pieces on the path.

'It must be some local urchins,' Masachika said furiously. 'I'll cut off their ears, I'll sell them to the silver mines.'

This threat only caused more hilarity among the spirits.

Masachika had retreated out of range back to the gate. Behind him he could hear that the men had regrouped. They were probably waiting, with callous curiosity, to see what he would do next. His authority was slipping away. He called out, 'Who will drive these brats from my house?'

No one moved or spoke.

'What? Are you all afraid?'

Yasuie said at his side, 'They are afraid of no one human. Beings from another world, that's another matter.'

A young man appeared in the gateway. He was of huge size, a head taller than Masachika, and carried a long spear heavier than most men could lift. He was Yasuie's younger brother, Yasunobu.

'I will get rid of them for you, Lord Masachika.'

'Brother, don't go in there,' Yasuie said. 'No one will despise you.'

'But I would despise myself,' the youth said, his voice light. 'Now I have offered, I must – or allow my name to be remembered as a coward's.'

Holding his spear out in front of him he ran to the verandah and leaped inside. There came two fierce shrieks followed by a howl of pain. Yasunobu came flying out from the house, pierced through the stomach by his own spear. He fell with such force he was nailed to the ground.

Yasuie and Masachika ran to him but there was nothing to be done. His life blood was pouring from him. As they tried to prise the spear from the ground a rain of small insects like bees fell around their heads, stinging them on their faces and hands, each sting an intense spark of pain. But Yasuie would not leave his brother, whose screams were subsiding into a ragged panting, and Masachika felt he could not retreat without him.

Finally, the spear came loose and, as Yasuie eased it out, Yasunobu's panting ceased. They lifted the body between them and carried it beyond the gate. Once they were outside the walls, the insects left them. Masachika could feel his face swelling, his eyes closing up.

He glanced up at the sun, its rays making his face ache even more. A few hours of daylight still remained. He must act to remove the humiliation the spirits had inflicted on him. He would go at once to Kuromori. The only hope of succeeding was in a surprise attack from behind, down the steep slope of the mountain at the rear of the fortress. The defenders would not be expecting that. He would go immediately before any reckless farmer thought to warn them.

Yasuie wept beside the corpse, tears oozing from eyes that had closed to slits.

'Stay and bury him,' Masachika said. 'The rest of you come with me. We will take Kuromori, and then we will return and deal with whatever evil it is that has possessed this place.'

There was a slight murmur from the men, not quite grumbling or dissent. Masachika said, 'If anyone prefers squatting here sucking eggs to battle, he can help Yasuie bury his brother. All names will be recorded, those who stay and those who come with me.'

All except Yasuie went with him. He led them up the valley along the stream that flowed from the Darkwood and had once filled the lake at Matsutani. As they left the estate, Masachika recalled the day he had married Tama, the thrill of having a young beautiful wife, the shock of her brother's death, how he had consoled her, rejoicing silently that Matsutani would now be his. And then the nightmare as the two old men, their fathers, put their monstrous plan into practice.

Kiyoyori, to his credit, had tried to persuade them to abandon it, had remonstrated with his father, persisting even in the face of the old man's terrifying rage. But if Kiyoyori had succeeded in making them change their minds, Masachika would still be Kakizuki, he would probably now be dead or in flight. He had been given a second chance. If he could take Kuromori, both estates would be his. The pain in his hands and face did not let him forget that Matsutani was haunted, but he did not dwell on it. He would find some sorcerer or other to get rid of the spirits and, in the meantime, no one else would be able to snatch his jewel from him.

He followed tracks he had often galloped along with his brother. How many hours of their lives had they spent exploring the forest and the mountain? Throughout their boyhood they had devised strategies to attack and defend the fortress that was their home, and had practised endlessly for their adult life as warriors, with their bows, swords and horses.

Now as he and his men rode further into the forest he ran through those strategies. They would ascend the mountain behind the fortress and drop down on it from above, as if from the heavens. But, to avoid lookouts and guards, they must leave the stream and strike out to the north, turning east once they were past Kuromori.

He was sure this made sense, yet his mind was clouding as though he had a fever, and he was having trouble seeing. The terrain was rough, scattered with boulders, and very steep. The horses quickened their pace into a clumsy canter, stumbling and plunging. When they reached the small plateau where they would turn east, they were breathing hard and sweating more than ever. A couple had grazed their knees and blood oozed through the hair.

Masachika did not allow any rest but led them on at a gallop. Between the trunks of the pine trees the last rays of the sun threw their speeding shadows before them. Then the red orb slipped behind the western mountains, turning the sky vermilion. The white moon in the east slowly became silver.

By the time they came to the top of the crag above the fortress, it was close to nightfall. Below them, smoke rose from fires and a few lamps gleamed. It was impossible to tell how many men held the fortress and too dark to see if the northern side was defended. But he would not wait till dawn; the chances of being discovered were too great. He had forbidden the men from speaking since the time they had left the plateau, but no one could keep a horse from neighing.

He allowed himself a moment to peer down on Kuromori, now at last within his grasp. Ignoring the pain and the fact he could hardly see, he made a sign the men should follow him, and led the way over the edge of the cliff.

There was a path of sorts, just as he remembered, made by foxes or deer. He and Kiyoyori had followed a stag down it, a lifetime ago. The horses crashed down, some squealing in fear while their riders whooped and shouted.

Masachika was in front but his sight was darkening, and then he realised he could not breathe. His throat was closing. He gasped and choked. *It is the bees*, he thought, *they have poisoned me.* His horse stumbled and he went over its head. He was aware of his face in the dirt, of his body struggling for breath, and then a hoof struck him on the back of his head and he lost consciousness.

# 22

# AKI

Aki tried not to look at the dead men and instead stared at the bowman and the two horses as they trotted towards her. She had to decide in seconds whether to cut Yoshi's throat and then her own or to trust the stranger when he said he would help her. Then she saw the werehawks and knew at once what they were and whom they served – the man her father had hated and feared above all others. One bird was already flying south to tell its master the fugitive Emperor was found. It was time to step into the River of Death.

But the birds distracted her, drawing her eyes towards them, making her hesitate. The other bird was now swooping after the first. It seemed faster and larger. She expected to see them both disappear in the direction of the capital but the second bird caught up with the other and attacked it, striking with its beak and attempting to grasp it with its talons. Both birds were shrieking and a flurry of black feathers fell, swirling, bloodstained, to the ground.

Then the horses, white stallion, brown mare, reached her, and the rider leaped down.

He took the knife from her, with a movement so swift and sure she had no defence against it, and whistled to the birds, as a hunter calls his falcons. One returned to his shoulder, the other fluttered to the ground a little way off. The man went to it and picked it up, carrying it back gently. Its eyes glazed and it went limp. He knelt, stroking its black feathers, his face intent.

The remaining werehawk had fluttered from his shoulder to the ground and now bowed its head to its dead fellow. Tears seemed to glisten in its eyes and it spoke in a broken voice that Aki did not understand. Then it hopped to where Yoshi was still hiding behind her, stood in front of him and bobbed its head three times.

'Kon killed Zen,' the man said. 'I did not expect that. He wanted to stop him returning to the capital.'

'They are werehawks,' Aki said. 'In the service of the Prince Abbot at Ryusonji. You understand their speech, they obey you – or one of them does – so you must serve the Prince Abbot too.'

'I did,' he said slowly. 'But Kon tells me this boy is the Emperor, and you are the Autumn Princess.'

She stared at him. He was tall and lean, with thick black hair tied up like a warrior's. He looked as though he had been sleeping in the woods, his face stubbled slightly, and dark, either from the sun or dirt. But his skin was smooth, his features pleasing, his leaf-shaped eyes deep black.

'I was known as the Autumn Princess,' she said. 'Akihime, people used to call me, in the capital.'

'And people call me Shikanoko or Shika. My name used to be Kazumaru, but I am no longer a child and I do not have an adult name.'

'Shikanoko? The deer's child? Why are you called that?'

She felt quite calm and unafraid now. She wanted him to keep talking to her. She liked the sound of his voice. She wanted to trust him. Then she remembered the dead men, the swift unhesitating killing, the werehawk.

Shikanoko said, 'I will tell you as we ride.' He knelt before Yoshi. 'I am going to lift your Majesty onto this mare, Risu. Akihime will ride behind you and hold you.'

Genzo sounded a warning, thrumming note.

'I must not be called Majesty,' the child said, 'only Yoshi. I must not tell anyone who I am.' He leaned against Aki, shrinking away from Shika. 'Does what you said mean my father and grandfather are dead?'

'They have gone to the next world and are awaiting their rebirth,' Aki told him. 'My father is there too, and my mother.'

'And my mother?'

'When we get to the temple we will pray for their spirits,' Aki said.

The child did not reply but tears began to trickle down his cheeks. He cried silently. The mare swung her head round and nuzzled him as if he were her foal.

'Kai,' he whimpered. 'I want Kai.'

Aki said to Shika, 'We were heading for Rinrakuji. My father told me we would find shelter there.'

'And then what? Sooner or later the Miboshi will attack that temple and the Emperor will be discovered.'

'Nevertheless, first we must go to Rinrakuji. I must obey my father.'

'Very well,' Shika said. 'I will take you there. But it's almost dark. Don't you want to rest a little, you and the child?'

'The moon is almost full and will be rising soon. Surely we can get to the temple before it sets?'

Shika did not say anything more, but lifted Yoshi onto the mare's back, made a rein from the lead rope and told Yoshi to hold on to it.

'You don't need to lift me,' Aki said. 'Make a stirrup with your hand and I can jump up.'

He did as she said. Risu had made no objection to the child but she swung her hindquarters away when Aki tried to mount. Aki slipped down into Shika's arms. For a moment she felt his body against hers, his hands holding her. Then he muttered an apology and stepped back, giving Risu a smack on her shoulder.

'Stand still!'

'I am not dressed for riding!' Aki hitched up her robe, baring her legs like a farm girl. 'I'll try again, I'll be ready for her this time.'

The mare's coat was smooth against her skin, her flesh warm. Aki put her arms round Yoshi and held the rope with one hand. Shika leaped onto the stallion's back and Kon flew up to his shoulder.

'What about those men?' Aki said as they rode off. 'Do we just leave them there?'

'Let them rot,' Shika replied, and then, 'Who were they? Did you know them?'

'One had been following us since we left Miyako. I thought we had shaken him off but as we left Aomizu I realised he had caught up with us.'

'That's a long way to keep following someone. Did he know who you were? Why was he so persistent?'

'I think something about us had roused his lust,' she said.

'What was he going to do to us?' Yoshi said.

'Don't worry about him. He is dead now and can no longer do anything, good or bad, to anyone.' Aki tried to speak reassuringly but thinking about what might have happened made her tremble. The days with the entertainers on the boat had awakened something in her. She remembered the suitors who had started hanging round the house in the city. Most girls her age would be married by now. She recoiled from the idea – she had made her vows of purity – yet she was drawn to it at the same time. Instead, neither a wife nor a shrine maiden, she was riding through the twilight, following a man on a white stallion who had just saved her life, the Emperor of the Eight Islands held tightly in her arms.

After a couple of miles they came to a crossroads. Rinrakuji lay some way to the east, while the track between Kitakami and Shimaura ran from north to south, following a small shallow stream, crossing and recrossing it as it wound between the mountains. The road was not much used. It was impassable in the rainy season, and people preferred to travel by boat over the lake. Now the crossroads was deserted. The mountains loomed to the east, their huge dark shapes outlined by the moonlight behind them. The wind had risen and was making the pine trees sigh and moan. The air was warm and humid and insects were calling.

The horses went forward nervously and just before the meeting of the four roads they baulked completely. Nothing would make them move on.

Kon flew in an upwards spiral above the crossroads and then came back to Shika's shoulder, chattering quietly but urgently.

'There is a spirit there,' Shika said. 'The horses will not go past it.'

'You are just making it up to persuade us to turn back.' Aki's earlier mistrust returned.

'Not back. We must go south a little way and then we will go into the Darkwood. I know a place where no one will find you.'

A voice came out of the dusk.

'Shikanoko! Is that you?'

Aki saw his face pale. 'Lord Kiyoyori?' he whispered.

'Yes, it is I.'

Aki could see nothing. Risu was trembling beneath her. Shika dismounted and gave the stallion's reins to her. 'I'm going to talk to him.'

'Who is it?'

'It is, or was, the Kuromori lord.'

# 23

## SHIKANOKO

Shika took the mask from the brocade bag and slipped it over his face. He stepped into the exact centre where the four roads met and found himself in a place between the worlds.

He had learned about such things from the Prince Abbot: crossroads, river banks, seashores, bridges, islands, were all points where the worlds came together and touched, where miracles took place, where saints and restless ghosts dwelled, where adepts might be shown their next lives, or Paradise, or the different levels of Hell.

The Book of the Future, in which, the Prince Abbot claimed, neither Yoshimori's name nor that of his father was written, had been disclosed centuries before to Prince Umayado in one such place, between the worlds.

He stood on the banks of the River of Death. He saw its black, still water, and heard the splash of the ferryman's oars. The moon cleared the last mountain peak and in its light he saw Kiyoyori. Pity and revulsion churned in his belly. The lord's skin was burned, his eyes sightless. As Shika went closer he saw that his chest did not move to draw in breath and there was no pulse of blood in his temple.

It was impossible that he was alive, yet he stood and spoke.

'Is that the young Prince with you, the true Emperor?'

'Yes, it is Yoshimori, and a girl called Akihime.'

The spirit reached out a charred hand, holding a blackened twisted sword. 'I will not let you take them back to Ryusonji.'

'I don't intend to. She wants to go to Rinrakuji. If that is no longer safe I will hide them in the Darkwood.'

'Then I must come with you, for am I not the Lord of the Darkwood, of Kuromori?'

'Can you leave this place?' Shika said, doubting it was possible.

'I am not sure. I have not been here long. I had crossed two of the three streams of the River of Death, and was prepared to meet the Lord of Hell, when I was told a man who wronged me had taken my token of death, given it to the ferryman and gone on in my place. You must have known about Iida no Taro, at whose hands my son died? It was he. One arrow took us both from this world at the same instant. His guilt and regret caused him to make this offer and the Lord of Hell accepted it. I was told my work on earth is not finished. While the usurpers are in power the realm cannot receive the blessings of Heaven. I have to return to the world to restore the Emperor.'

'How is it done?' Shika said.

'You must summon me back, Shikanoko. I resented you when I saw you in the service of the Prince Abbot, but now I understand that you were learning from him, you were stealing from him his knowledge and power, just as you stole Akuzenji's stallion, and the werehawk that has never belonged to anyone but the Prince Abbot but now does your bidding. Heaven uses us for its purposes. Bring me back so its intentions may be fulfilled. Or must I stay here forever, neither living nor dead, a ghost of the crossroads?'

Shikanoko did not answer. He recalled spells and words of power that the Prince Abbot used in rites of secrecy and magic, the spirit-return incense, the fire, the salt. He had nothing, except the mask and something he now became more acutely aware of: Sesshin's nugget. He could feel it glowing and expanding within him until the pain became so intense it took him beyond words, beyond even thought. He sensed the Prince Abbot's surprise and anger as this new power combined with all he had learned at Ryusonji and surpassed it. He saw Kiyoyori's spirit clinging to the burned husk, and then another's, a horse spirit poised at that moment to enter its mother's womb.

'I am ready,' Kiyoyori said, and Shikanoko commanded the two spirits to become one.

He felt a surge of power as they obeyed him. He saw Kiyoyori's spirit leave its ruined body and float above the ground. The body dissolved away into dust. The earth shook beneath them. Shika fell as if struck by lightning. Risu neighed wildly and Nyorin answered, their calls echoing back from the flanks of the mountains.

In the distance other horses neighed in response. The werehawk flew directly upwards, its ragged wings outlined against the moon.

Shika heard it calling desperately, 'Rinrakuji is in flames and the Miboshi are riding this way.'

Through the silence that enveloped him, numbing his senses, Shika heard the girl's voice, urging him to get up. It sounded a long way away. He stood, groggy and sick, as if he had been hit on the head, and felt for Nyorin.

'What happened?' she was saying. 'Are you hurt? Can you see?'

His hands found the stallion's shoulder and he leaned against him for a moment. Risu was circling anxiously, Aki trying to control her and hold Yoshi at the same time.

*What will your foal become, Risu?* He did not answer Aki, as he had no words for what had just taken place.

The moon was now fully overhead and something glittered in the dust. He stepped towards it and picked it up.

'What's that?' the girl said sharply.

'It's Lord Kiyoyori's sword.'

Blackened and twisted beyond recognition it was all that remained of the Kuromori lord.

He slipped it into his belt on his right side, took the mask from his face and said the prayers of thanks to it before placing it in the seven-layered bag. He went back to the horses and pulled himself up onto Nyorin's back.

No one knew they were on the road. Kon was still with him, flying down now to his shoulder and croaking in admiration. Whoever had taken Rinrakuji would probably go on to Aomizu. He had to take Aki and Yoshi deep into the forest.

He put the stallion into a canter. Turning his head he saw Aki and Risu were able to keep up. The girl was holding Yoshi tightly and the child was clutching whatever it was that was in the bundle. He was amazed at how well she rode.

The track towards the south ran straight for a while, the river alongside splashing swift and white under the moon. Now and then water birds flew up, startled at their approach, but they saw no one human. After some time, when the moon was starting its descent, they came to the place Shika was looking for. A small stream joined the river, through a deep valley from the east, which led to a pass through the mountains. It was the western extent of Akuzenji's realm and Shika had ridden through it once or twice with the bandits. The horses knew it too and crossed the stream eagerly as if they were going home.

Aki said, on the further bank, 'Yoshi keeps falling asleep. It's hard for me to hold him. Can we stop and rest?'

'There's a hut, it's not far. We'll let him sleep there.'

It was a place Akuzenji had taken over for his scouts, where they could watch for merchants and other travellers on the south road. It was built against the side of the hill, beside a large natural cave where several horses could be hidden out of sight. Shika halted the horses a short way from it and went forward on foot, Kon flying above him, sending an owl swooping away on silent wings.

*If owls roost there it must be deserted*, Shika reasoned, and indeed the hut was empty, full of dust and cobwebs. Fear of the King of the Mountain, even if he was dead, must have kept it undisturbed. He returned to the horses and led them to the cave. Water, dripping from the roof, had filled a small hollow in the soft limestone. The horses knew it even in the dark, and drank eagerly from it.

Shika lifted Yoshi down and, holding the drowsy boy against his shoulder, reached out his other hand to Aki. She took it and swung her leg over the horse's back to jump down.

He held her for a moment longer than he needed to, and felt again the spark of desire and longing that had been awakened when she had fallen against him earlier. Could she be the one who was meant for him, the one Lady Tora had told him he was to wed? She had been brought to him by Fate; she had been present when he had defied the power of the Prince Abbot and performed an unimaginable act of spirit magic. A sense of what he might be capable of had been welling up steadily within him.

It was still light enough, by the moon, to see a little. Kon flew up to the roof and sat on the ridge pole, a dark outline against the darker sky.

'Does the werehawk ever sleep?' Aki said, stepping away from him.

'They act like ordinary birds: they eat and sleep, and as you saw, they can die. Yet they are different. They are like humans in that they plot and scheme, seek favours and ally themselves with the powerful. Perhaps because they have language.'

'Which you can understand?'

'I can understand Kon. For some reason he has attached himself to me.'

'Why do you call him Kon?'

'He has one golden feather,' Shika explained.

'I think he has more than one,' Aki replied.

Shika glanced upwards but it was too dark to see. He stepped into the hut. There was no fire or light, but it did not seem worth the effort to make them. The night was warm and dawn was not far away. He remembered a pile of old coverings and, feeling his way to the corner of the room, found it, pulled out two of the cloths and put Yoshi down on the rest. The boy stretched and murmured something and then dropped into a deeper sleep. His grasp on the bundle loosened and it slipped to the floor, vibrating with a faint musical chord. Aki knelt to retrieve it.

'What is it that he carries so carefully?' Shika whispered.

'It is the lute, Genzo,' Aki replied. 'It is an imperial heirloom. It is magical. It can play by itself, if it wants to, and can change its appearance. Here, see how it looks, if it reveals itself to you.'

'It is too dark to see anything,' Shika replied but Aki had already removed the lute from the bundle.

The mother of pearl gleamed like moonlight. Aki touched the strings and the lute began to play quietly, an old song Shika recognised, a love song.

He knelt beside her. 'You can lie down and sleep too. I will wake you when it is daylight.'

She lay down and pulled the old quilt over her. 'It smells,' she said. 'I suppose it is full of fleas too.'

He heard the note of unease, almost of fear, in her voice. 'You mustn't be afraid of me,' he said.

'It's not that I'm afraid of you,' she replied, so softly he could hardly make out her words. 'Not in the ordinary way. Maybe I am afraid of myself, of my own feelings.'

She said nothing more and he thought she had fallen asleep. He stretched out, the bow and arrow behind his head, his sword beside his right hand. He let his limbs relax, though he did not intend to sleep.

After a little while Aki's voice surprised him. 'I am dedicated to be a shrine maiden. I promised my father that I would not let any man be intimate with me, that I would kill him. I still have my knife. I am just warning you.'

'Go to sleep,' he said, but he wished she had not brought the subject up. Now he was even more aware of the female body next to his. Memories of the day's events seemed to race through his muscles and his veins. First he had killed two men, dropping them like hares. Then Kon had attacked Zen and torn the other werehawk to pieces, and Shika had understood his speech and had wrested him from the Prince Abbot's control. He had walked between the worlds at the crossroads, had spoken to the spirit of the Kuromori lord and had summoned it from the entrance of Hell into the foal's developing body.

*Truly I am a sorcerer of power! What else am I capable of?*

Pride began to well up in him, sweet and seductive, telling him he deserved all things, that he was allowed all things, that he could take what he wanted, in this world and the next. This was the one meant for him, the one the sorceress had told him he would wed. She was here, alongside him. He had killed for her, he had rescued her.

The night was warm, filled with the sounds of spring, frogs

croaking from the stream, insects calling. The lute continued to play quietly, its plangent notes adding to his desire.

He turned restlessly and then sat up, deciding to meditate for a while to try and still his rebellious body. He fumbled in the dark for the seven-layered bag, took out the mask and slipped it over his face.

Immediately he felt himself transported from the hut, bounding on stag's hooves towards Ryusonji. He struggled to take control, reached inside himself for Sesshin's power. He stood on the verandah of the temple and saw the Prince Abbot, sitting in meditation by the open door.

The priest said without opening his eyes, 'So, my little stag has returned? Did you think you would escape me so easily?'

Shika tried to regain his will, to turn and run, but his limbs were frozen as if he were dreaming.

'Where is Prince Yoshimori? If you have found him why have you not brought me his head? What have you been doing and how did you evade me before, at the crossroads?'

The Prince Abbot opened his eyes and stood, and Shika felt the full force of his rage.

'I will punish you,' the priest said. 'You dare to try to oppose me? You have no idea how strong I am. Now go and do what you want with the Autumn Princess. I see your lust for her. Take her now, why wait for marriage? Then kill Yoshimori and bring me his head.'

The Prince Abbot raised his hand and spoke words Shika had never heard before. He found himself back in the hut. The power of the forest was all around him and the pure animal instinct of the stag swept over him. The girl turned in her sleep towards him. Her robe was open. Then she was in his arms and his mouth was on hers. She tried to push him away, he remembered briefly the knife, but then nothing would stop him, neither pity nor fear. He possessed her as the stag does the hind, with mindless domination. But even as he cried out at the moment of ecstasy, he realised what the Prince Abbot had done, and he had the first inkling of how complete his punishment would be.

He wrenched off the mask and threw it from him. She lay without moving or speaking. He wanted to hold her and caress her with tenderness but shame prevented him. He pulled his clothes around him and went to the door of the hut. Beyond him lay the Darkwood and all the sounds and shadows of the night-time forest. Far away wolves were howling. He recalled his earlier pride and exultation with despair and disgust. He went a little way down the side of the hut and leaned against the rough-sawn planks of the wall. He had no idea what to do now. He just knew he had failed.

From the hut he thought he heard sounds of weeping but the lute was still playing softly so he could not be sure. His own eyes grew hot, but he would not grant himself the relief of tears. He walked away into the darkness, stumbling over fallen branches, until he came up against the trunk of a huge cedar. He clasped it in his arms and leaned his forehead against it, then slid to its base, feeling the moss cool against his skin.

When he came to his senses it was dawn. He made himself get up and return to the hut. He was not sure what he would do: throw himself down before her, ask for forgiveness, seek her help. But she was not there. Had his actions forced her to run away, to abandon Yoshimori? He turned and called her name, 'Akihime! Akihime!'

Birds were singing and Kon answered them from the rooftop. Rain was falling softly, a drizzling mist that hid the mountains. He knew he had lost her, a loss that felt immeasurable as if it encompassed the whole world. Every tree dripped with moisture as though they wept with him. He had not rescued her. How arrogant to think that! She had been entrusted to him and he had broken that trust.

He called again, 'Akihime!'

The horses whinnied in response to his voice, and at the same moment he heard something stir in the hut. Was she there, had he somehow overlooked her? He went inside

The boy was awake, staring at him with puzzled eyes.

'Where is Aki . . . older sister?' he said.

'I don't know. She's gone. She ran away.'

Yoshi's gaze remained steady. 'Where to? Why did she leave me? What have you done to her?'

The mask lay on the floor, staring at him with its hollow eyes. Hardly knowing what he was doing, but seeking some relief from his remorse and regret, he picked it up and put it on. Immediately he felt the pull of the Prince Abbot's power, and knew what he must do. Perhaps it would assuage his immense pain. Yoshimori would never have become Emperor anyway. His family were all dead and those who would have fought for him scattered. Now Shikanoko had to put an end to his life and take his handsome head back to Ryusonji.

He picked up his sword and held his hand out to the boy.

Yoshimori shrank from the sight of the mask.

'Come, your Majesty must be brave,' Shika said.

'Shall I bring the lute?' Yoshi said.

'There is no need for it,' Shika replied and led him out of the hut.

The rain continued to fall softly, the birds were silent and there was no wind. The only sound was the rushing water and the pounding of Shika's heart. It was not the river bank at Miyako, where so many were taken to be executed, but the side of a mountain stream, which would serve equally well.

'Look away from me towards the mountains,' he commanded.

After one brief glance Yoshi obeyed him.

As Shika raised his sword, Yoshi said, 'The sun is rising.'

*How could he see it?* Clouds covered the sky, but the sun's rays must have penetrated them in some way, for the raindrops were reflecting the colours of the rainbow all around them. For a moment Shika was dazzled, seeing clearly the fragile beauty of the child before him. He hesitated, suddenly reluctant to do what he was supposed to do.

From the cave came the twang of a bow. Time stopped. The world held its breath, the sword outlined against the fractured light. Shika gripped it harder and inhaled deeply.

Kon swooped towards him, talons extended, beak slashing, and the horses burst from the cave, Risu leading, her teeth bared, her ears flat.

Shika dropped the sword, raising his arms to protect the mask. Kon seized it in his talons, tore it from his face and let it fall as Risu charged him, knocking him to the ground. He had seen her bad tempered before and she had bitten and kicked him many times, but he had never seen her so enraged she wanted to kill him. Nyorin was also lunging at him as he struggled to his feet, the stallion's lips drawn back from his huge white teeth, his eyes flashing as if in the midst of battle. Nyorin's head, solid bone, collided with Shika's and as he fell again the stallion whirled round, kicking him with both back legs.

Neither sorcery nor all his skill with weapons could help him. Risu seized his right arm in her teeth and snapped it. Nyorin kicked him again, then brought his forefeet down on him, striking him on neck and shoulder. The mask lay on the ground shattered in two. His vision went red with pain and then black.

When he regained consciousness the rain was falling more heavily. He crawled to the water and lay in it, feeling its icy coldness on every cut and bruise. One eye was closing and he could hardly see out of the other, yet he knew Yoshimori and the horses were gone. He could not raise his head to look upwards to see if Kon had too, but there was no sound from the werehawk. His arm throbbed unbearably and he could not move it, but the bone had not broken through the skin.

He began to tremble, not only from the cold water and the pain, but also from profound shock that the horses he had loved and trusted should turn on him. He could understand why Kon had attacked him as viciously as he had gone for Zen – the werehawk's instinct to protect the Emperor overrode any commands from either Shika or the Prince Abbot. But the horses? After many more minutes of confusion and pain the realisation came to him that it was Kiyoyori's spirit, within the unborn foal, that had driven Risu to turn on him, and Nyorin had followed.

*Even the animal world recognises that Yoshimori is Emperor, and fights for him*, he thought.

Eventually he managed to stand. He picked up the sword with his left hand and went to the hut. He could hardly bear to enter it – it seemed to reverberate still with his uncontrolled lust and he heard again his own cries with revulsion.

He gathered up the bow and the quiver of arrows, and the twisted metal that had been Kiyoyori's sword. The lute had gone – of course it would have gone with Yoshi: not only animals but also objects recognised him.

Outside he picked up the pieces of the broken mask and put them in the seven-layered brocade bag. He would go into the Darkwood. It would either kill him or heal him. If it healed him he would see the Prince Abbot destroyed and Yoshimori on the Lotus Throne.

*Part Two*

# AUTUMN PRINCESS, DRAGON CHILD

# I

# SHIKANOKO

Shikanoko, unable to sleep, racked by pain and fever, walked day and night through the Darkwood. His flesh alternately froze and burned; it did not seem to belong to him. He floated outside his body, watching it sweat and shiver, wondering why it still clung to life. Often he hallucinated. The dead seemed to walk alongside him, haranguing and accusing him. Once he heard the horses' shrill neighing, and did not know whether to run towards them or hide from them. His weapons, and the bag holding the broken mask and Kiyoyori's sword, grew heavier. One day he simply let his own sword and the bow and quiver fall to the ground. He could not imagine ever using them again. The following day he was tortured by the smell of death. *I am rotting away*, he thought. *It is all over.* He leaned against the smooth trunk of a young beech tree, and then half fell, half slid down it until he was sitting in the dried leaves at its foot. The forest, in high summer, reverberated around him with bird calls and insect cries. Once he had loved that sound, had known every bird. Now it was an unpleasant clamour that made his head ache.

He had buried his head in his arms but now a sudden strange sound, a kind of rough bark, made him look up. A crafted animal, a sort of wolf, stood before him. He saw the flash of its lapis blue eyes, and the dull gleam of its cinnabar lips. The clarity of the hallucination and his fever filled him with despair.

Then the false wolf spoke in a thick, halting voice. 'Welcome home,' it said, and Shika knew where he was and where the stench of rot and decay came from. It was over a year since he had ridden away with Akuzenji, the King of the Mountain, but now he had come back, to the mountain sorcerer, Shisoku.

It watched him struggle to his feet and then turned and padded stiffly away. He followed it, across the stream, past the carvings, the drying skins, the piles of bones, the live and dead animals, to the hut beneath the paulownia tree.

It stopped in front of the door. 'Master!' it called. The vowels in its speech were clear but it had trouble with the consonants: *Ma-er!*

Shisoku came out of the hut, shading his eyes with one hand.

'Shikanoko? Why have you come back? What have you done?'

Shika dropped the bag as Shisoku approached him. It lay on the ground like a dead bird, the hilt of the sword protruding from it.

'What is this? Whose sword was this? Nothing should be put in the same bag as the mask! Where is the mask?'

'It is broken,' Shika heard himself say.

'Aaargh!' Shisoku screamed like the mother of a dead child. 'It cannot be broken. No human power can hurt it. How did it happen?'

He drew the two pieces out and wept over them.

Shika tried to explain. 'It was the horses, they attacked me, not their fault, my fault.'

Shisoku's face was distorted by rage and grief. Without saying another word he rushed back into the hut. Shika sank to the ground.

His teeth clashed against each other as the fever sent violent shudders through him.

'Are you sick?' the false wolf said. 'Master, he's sick.'

'Let him die,' Shisoku called from inside. 'He destroyed my gift, my creation. All the power of the forest could have been his, and he threw it away.'

The false wolf called again. 'Master, help him!' and it began to lick Shika's face with a tongue that felt human.

The sorcerer appeared again. 'How extraordinary,' Shika heard him say. 'The creature feels sorry for him. Maybe I should too. Yes, I suppose I must.' He knelt next to Shika and felt his forehead, then, none too gently, examined the broken arm.

While Shika wept tears of pain, Shisoku disappeared and, after what seemed like an eternity, was again kneeling beside him, making him drink some potion. It dulled his senses enough for Shisoku to be able to align the ends of the broken bone.

He longed for sleep, for oblivion, but every time he closed his eyes he believed he was dead and in Hell, burning in fire, pierced by swords, knives, arrows and thorns, tormented by visions of demons and unquenchable thirst. He saw, over and over again, the horses' huge teeth as they tore into him, and his body arched and twisted as he felt again the hammer-like blows of their hooves.

Liquid poured from his body, both sweat and tears, the waters of remorse.

At one stage he dreamed Lady Tora came to him. 'Are you alive or dead?' he tried to ask her, but she laid her cool fingers against his burning lips and silenced not only speech, but thought too.

Then finally he slept, maybe for days. All that time the false wolf did not leave his side.

When he woke, he was inside the hut; he heard Shisoku say, 'It has become attached to him. It's the first time something like that has happened. I did not expect it. Even I have never inspired affection in my creations.'

'You are a greater sorcerer than you think,' a woman replied. Shika turned his head slightly and saw it was indeed Lady Tora. She went on. 'Perhaps it is because you bestowed the power of speech on it. How did you achieve that?'

Shisoku laughed. 'I gave it the tongue I cut from a human head, and I built speaking cords from gossamer and sinews.'

'And the head? Whose was that?'

'There have been plenty of dead between Miyako and Minatogura in the last year. This was a Kakizuki warrior who fled into the forest and died of his wounds. I came upon him while he was still fresh enough to use. That's his skull on the wall.'

Shika could see the new white skull grinning vacantly. Next to him the false wolf whined.

'Shikanoko is awake,' Lady Tora said.

They both looked in his direction. Their shapes were outlined against the flames of the fire and the candles round the altar. He saw the huge swell of Tora's belly and remembered what she had told him, that she would give Kiyoyori more sons. Whosever child it was, it was very close to birth.

'Shisoku was extremely angry with you,' Lady Tora said, 'but he has forgiven you, now.'

'I have?' the hermit queried.

'Either you have or you soon will. But Shikanoko should tell us what happened. See if you can get up,' she said to him.

He struggled to his feet and, leaning on each of them, went outside. They led him to the paulownia tree and, sitting between them in its shade, he related everything, from the blinding of Sesshin, their flight into the Darkwood, their capture by his uncle Sademasa, who handed them over to the monk Gessho, the knowledge Sesshin had passed over to him, the winter spent at Ryusonji with the Prince Abbot.

'There was an uprising,' he said. 'Well, it was started by the Prince Abbot who dispatched his men to arrest the Crown Prince, but, afterwards, it was said that Momozono rebelled against his father. He died but his son escaped. I was sent to find him and bring his head back to the capital. I caught up with him, and Akihime, the Autumn Princess, on the way to Rinrakuji.'

'Ah,' Lady Tora said. 'Now I begin to understand.'

'I killed two men who were about to violate her and the young Emperor, for he truly is the Emperor, you know. Everything recognises him. I had two werehawks with me and they knew him at once. I called them Kon and Zen. Zen tried to fly back to Ryusonji and Kon killed him. We rode on towards Rinrakuji, but we were stopped at a crossroads by a spirit. It was Lord Kiyoyori.'

'So he is dead?' Tora said, in a small voice.

'I called him back,' Shika said, remembering the immense power that he had drawn on, a power that had led him into pride and arrogance and betrayed him. 'His spirit entered the unborn foal within the body of my mare, Risu.'

'He drove the horses to attack you?' Lady Tora said.

'Yes, and that is how the mask was broken.'

He fell silent, and then said, 'The sword is Kiyoyori's. It is beyond repair too.'

'Nothing is beyond repair for Shisoku,' Tora said. 'Even if the results are sometimes unexpected, like this false wolf that has attached itself to you.'

*It must recognise my falseness*, Shikanoko thought. *We are two of a kind.* But his confession was not finished yet.

'We went to Akuzenji's old hut. I was planning to bring them here to hide them.'

'The last place you would expect to find the Emperor of the Eight Islands,' Shisoku muttered.

Shika went on steadily, 'But being in the hut, alone with the Autumn Princess, who I thought was the one meant for me, I put on the mask and found myself under the Prince Abbot's sway. I blame only myself. I thought I was all powerful . . .'

'Aha!' Shisoku said, 'He could teach you many things but he could not teach you brokenness.'

Shika wished he would stop interrupting. Every time he had to start again it was harder.

'The Prince Abbot told me to do what I liked with her. I did. But she was to become a shrine maiden. She fled during the night. In the morning he told me to kill Yoshimori, and I was on the point of doing it, when the werehawk and the horses attacked me. When I came to, I was alone and the mask was broken.'

'The gods must have been enraged against you both,' Tora said.

After a few moments Shika said, 'The werehawk, Kon, was turning gold. I remember seeing the light on its plumage.'

'It must be transforming into a houou,' Shisoku said. 'It is the sacred bird that appears in the land when the ruler is just and blessed by Heaven.'

'That must be Yoshimori. I have to find him and restore him to the throne.'

'These are concerns of warriors and noblemen,' Shisoku said. 'Leave them to it and become a mountain sorcerer like me.'

'I was a warrior first, long before I became a sorcerer,' Shika replied. 'Restore the mask for me, and the sword, and, when they are ready, I will begin my search for Yoshimori.'

'Nothing will change until your power matches the Prince Abbot's,' Lady Tora said. 'You are going to have to confront him and overcome him physically and spiritually. At the moment you can do neither. You have no men, no followers, not even a horse. In your first challenge to him, you failed. He forced you to make a terrible mistake, from which you may never recover. The horses and the werehawk, which should have been your allies, turned against you. You have a lot to undo and even more to learn.'

'How long will it take you to repair the mask and the sword?' Shika asked Shisoku.

'When you are ready they will be ready,' the old man replied grudgingly.

'Will it be days or weeks?'

'More likely years,' said the sorcerer.

'I can't wait that long,' Shika cried, his impatience signalling he was recovering.

Lady Tora said, 'There will be plenty to occupy you. As well as all you have to learn, you have to bring up my sons.'

'That will teach you something,' Shisoku murmured.

•

'The children cannot come into the world here,' Lady Tora said, 'in the midst of Shisoku's wayward magic, all these bones, skins and transmogrification.'

'Certainly not,' Shisoku agreed. 'Childbirth, especially involving one of the Old People, is completely disruptive and would unleash all kinds of uncontrollable forces, though possibly I could use some of those to repair the mask, so don't go too far away.'

'Shikanoko must help me build a dwelling,' she said.

*The Old People* . . . where had he heard that before? Then Sesshin's words crystallised in his mind. Just after he had transferred the nugget of power into Shika's mouth he had said, *From five fathers five children will be born. Find them and destroy them. They will be demons. She is one of the Old People.*

The words haunted him as, under her instructions, he built a small hut on the north side of the clearing, facing south. He cut the wood, from sweet-smelling maples and strong holm oaks, with Shisoku's sharp-edged axe and saw. They forged the nails together, blowing the fire into white heat with bellows made from deer skin.

Shika had never built anything before, and like most of Shisoku's endeavours, the results were not quite what was expected, but he liked the process of hewing the wood and shaping it into a human dwelling. It was like making bows and arrows, a kind of magic in itself, turning what the forest gave into something that had not existed before. When it was finished, and thatched with susuki reeds, it looked very pleasing.

Shisoku treated the tools as if they were children or servants. He never took them down from their place on the wall without asking their permission or put them back without thanking them. Shika saw how everything in his world was connected, how he knew intimately all the unseen strands and interstices, and how his power came from that knowledge, his ability to unravel and reconnect.

At the time when the silkworms began to spin their cocoons, Lady Tora also began to spin. Shika did not see where the threads came from, perhaps the gossamer that the morning mist turned into bright jewels, mixed with the soft underbelly fur of wolf and fox, or from the long tendrils of wisteria and briony, seeds of milkweed and dandelion, delicate and powerful strands of root and sinew of bark, everything pliable and tensile that could be turned into yarn.

From this she wove five cocoons, soft on the inside and hard on the outside, and hung them from the rafters of the hut. One morning, it was clear that each held some kind of egg.

Shika did not witness their birth nor did he hear any of the cries of pain that usually accompany childbirth. Lady Tora seemed exhausted. She did not want him near her, but lay all day without moving. From the door of the hut he could smell a distinctive odour of blood and egg yolk. At dusk, she asked Shika to bring water and rags and wait outside while she washed herself.

Afterwards, she gave him the bowl, saying, 'Give this to Shisoku. It is full of power.'

Her voice was faint, her face pale, and she seemed to have been drained of something essential. Over the next few days, while the creatures in the cocoons grew, she faded.

'My work on earth is achieved,' she told Shika when he tried to urge her to eat.

'Does she mean to die?' he asked the sorcerer.

Shisoku pursed his lips and then said reluctantly, 'It is the way of the Old People.'

'Who are the Old People?'

'Sometimes they are called the Spider Tribe. They are the ones who were here before.'

'Before when?' Shika said.

'Before people like you came from Silla, with your swords and your horses, your Princes and your Emperors.'

'I have never heard of them!' A suspicion came to him. 'Are you one of them?'

'My grandmother was. She died when my father was born, from a cocoon like this. His father raised him in the forest, as we will have to raise these children. They will not be like ordinary children.'

'Will they be demons?' Shika asked with a sort of dread.

Shisoku smiled. 'Not demons, just different.'

Shika had to ask. 'And me? Am I one?'

'Because you came here at the right time? Because you were able to become the deer's child? I wondered sometimes, and so did Tora. But we did not know of you, and there are so few left we know every one. Maybe there is some blood mixed in you. Maybe you were just lucky.'

'Or unlucky,' Shika said quietly.

'That too,' Shisoku agreed. 'Did you ever cross paths with a tengu?'

Shikanoko was silent for a moment.

'Did you?'

'When I was a child, I vaguely remember something, but perhaps it was a dream. Why?'

'When you first came I thought I discerned some tengu influence in your life.'

'In my dream, if that's what it was, my father played a game of Go with a tengu. He lost the game, his life, and Ameyumi, his bow. He left me hidden in the grass but the tengu flew overhead and they saw me. I remember their beaks and their wings.'

'Well, that's interesting,' the sorcerer said. 'That could explain a lot.'

•

A few days later Lady Tora called them into the hut. The creatures had grown into human-looking infants, now too big for the cocoons, which were beginning to tear as the children struggled and pushed with their hands and feet.

'Shouldn't we help them get out?' Shika said.

'No, they must do it alone, so we know who is the first and strongest.'

It seemed as though two would emerge at once, and even before the final rip of the silky fabric, they appeared to be racing against each other. They grew under Shika's eyes and by the time the first child stood before them he was the size of a two year old, wobbling on uncertain legs like the young animals of the forest.

'You shall be called Kiku,' Lady Tora said. 'It means Listen. You will hear everything. Because you were the first to emerge you will be the strongest and the cleverest.'

Almost immediately the second child was on his feet, looking around with inquisitive unafraid eyes.

'Your name is Mu,' his mother said. 'Both Nothingness and Warrior. You will exist between the two. No one will see you. It is your fate always to strive to be first, but you will never overtake Kiku.'

There was something enchanting about them. They were appealing, like fawns or baby monkeys.

'Come,' Shika said, and took a boy in each arm. Mu's pressure on his broken arm only caused the slightest ache. It was almost completely healed.

The third child crawled from the cocoon and Lady Tora gave him the name Kuro, Darkness, and told him he would walk alone.

'He will be like me,' Shisoku said, as he held him on his knee.

There was a short lull as the two remaining children struggled, with more difficulty, to emerge. The others watched, with no apparent emotion beyond curiosity. Shika felt the warmth of their bodies as they rested with complete trust against him. They were beautiful beings, with thick black hair and slender limbs. He thought of the five fathers whose seed had combined to make them: Akuzenji, Kiyoyori, Sesshin, Shisoku and himself. It was quite impossible for him to consider killing them.

One of the remaining two came free and crawled out, limp and exhausted. 'Your name is Ima – Now,' Lady Tora said. 'You will be a servant to your brothers, you will never know envy or disappointment.' She embraced him for a moment before giving him to Shisoku.

'And it is your fate to be last,' she said to the final child. He was noticeably smaller than the others and did not stand and walk immediately, but crawled on all fours, like a blind puppy. 'Your name will be Ku. You will love all animals and they will love and trust you. You will follow your brothers like a dog.'

•

As Tora grew weaker, she said she craved nature, the warm air on her skin, the dappled shade, the murmur of the stream and the sounds of birds and insects, the night sky and the stars. Delivering the children had made her gentle, as though her hardness and fire had all drained away into them.

At her request, Shisoku took a clear amber jewel from the altar and placed it on her chest. Shika carried her outside, where she lay for several days, neither eating nor drinking, but seemingly at peace. The children played around her, growing visibly every day.

'How did you escape from Matsutani?' Shika asked, one morning. 'We all thought you died in the fire.'

'I will burn,' she replied, 'but then was not the right time. I real-ised what Kiyoyori's wife might do; I would have done the same, or worse. I left then, but a part of myself – we call it the second self – remained behind long enough to fool anyone watching and make them believe I was still inside. I came to Shisoku, my mission complete. I had the gift of five men within me: the sorcerer, the bandit, the sage, the warrior and the youth who is or will be all these things – as will be my sons, my little tribe. I did not know that you would return but, now you have, I see I can entrust them to you.'

'Which one is mine?' Shika asked. They both turned their eyes to them.

'They are all mingled, so they are all yours. They're beautiful, don't you think? I am glad I chose handsome men like you and Kiyoyori.'

Shika saw how her face and voice changed as she spoke his name.

'What will happen to the lord's spirit?' he said.

'I don't know. When is it time for the foal to be born? Unless you can find your horses again, we will never know.' After a moment she said, 'I really loved Kiyoyori – in the way you people love each other, and we, not so much. I had never felt that before. I should be able to pass away without regret, as easily as the leaf falls from the tree in autumn, but the idea of never seeing him again, in whatever form, fills me with sorrow. I cling to life for his sake. This is what love does to you, Shikanoko. See how the false wolf grows more real every day, because it has become attached to you. It shivers at your approach and wags its tail at the sound of your voice. It has made you its master, it lives for your affection. But, as your saints teach and we have always known, attachment enslaves you. Only those free from it see the world as it really is and have power over themselves and all things.'

'I will never have that,' he said in a low voice. 'I cannot forget Akihime. I am tormented by love for her and terrible remorse that I betrayed her. I feel I must leave this place and search for her and Yoshimori. I have vowed to restore him to the Lotus Throne. How can I do that if I have to care for five children?'

Tora had closed her eyes and turned her face to the sun. She spoke so quietly he had to bend closer to hear her.

'Be patient. Teach the children how to be human, so they can pass in the world. Look after them well. When they are grown, they will help you in your quest.'

He thought her breathing stopped then, but he could not be sure. He felt heat glow from her and saw the rays of the sun had hit the jewel on her chest and had ignited her robe. The children stopped their play, and stood round, staring with their expressionless eyes. The flames grew quickly and in a moment had engulfed her, as though she were no more than dried grass. Nothing remained of her, no skull or bones, just the ash that Shisoku gathered up and placed in a carved box in front of the altar. The boys did not seem to miss her or to grieve and even Shika, who had grieved so much, did not know how to teach them.

•

Shisoku took the blood and other fluids from childbirth and spread them over the two broken halves of the mask. He bound the pieces together with what was left of the strands of the cocoons. They covered the face like a spider's web, silver and grey against the lacquer. He said many spells to protect it anew and placed it on the altar. When Shika knelt before it he thought he could hear tiny sounds as the edges knitted together, as had the bones in his arm.

Next Shisoku turned his attention to the ruined sword. Despite the heat he built up the fire, until the embers glowed white. He sent the boys, who were now the size of five year olds, out into the forest to the warm, sandy spots where snakes shed their skins. They found several dry papery patterned skins, and Kuro, who already showed an affinity with all poisonous creatures, brought back a live adder. Shisoku showed him how to hold its head and milk its venom. The skins were added to the fire, and the venom to the molten steel.

Shisoku killed the adder and skinned it carefully, putting the skin aside to bind the hilt, after the scorched mother of pearl had been removed. The steel was hammered and folded over and again, cooled in the clear mountain water, reheated, cooled again. Mu in particular was fascinated by the process and followed every step closely.

The essence of the snake was absorbed into the blade and Shisoku named it Jato, the snake sword. He would not let Shika touch it, but placed it outside in the cleft of two rocks. He tied a white straw rope around the rocks.

'The elements must temper it,' he said. 'And we must let it choose whether or not to come to your hand.'

None of the boys spoke much though they understood everything that was said to them. They were thin, with slender limbs, and were always hungry, eating voraciously to fuel their rapid growth. Their favourite food was meat and Shika went hunting, every day, to bring back rabbits and squirrels, sometimes wild boar, though he never killed deer. The skins were cleaned and dried to make winter clothes, but in the heat of late summer the boys went naked. They fought all the time, testing each other's strength and agility and endurance of pain, but at night they slept in a tumbled heap, like puppies.

One evening Shika saw Kiku seem to divide into two people, spontaneously, as though he had no idea what he was doing. He realised it was the second self that Lady Tora had told him about. Almost at the same time Mu vanished from his sight, and reappeared a few moments later on the other side of the stream. These abilities were innate; he could teach them nothing about them, nor could Shisoku. Instead both shared their own particular skills with them.

Shika fashioned poles and instructed them in the basic moves of sword fighting. He made small bows and showed them how to shape arrows. They trapped birds and collected the feathers for the fletches, and learned how to string and draw a bow.

Shisoku demonstrated how to forge sharp knives and other weapons, and he taught them all the poisons that could be found in the forest, as well as the snakes, aconite and briony, the kernels of certain nuts, toadstools and other fungi.

Ku, as his mother had predicted, loved the animals, the fake ones as much as the real, but Kiku and Kuro were indifferent to them, though they teased the false ones mercilessly, tripping up the water carriers, jumping out at the guard dogs. The real animals snapped at them, but the false ones never did. They had been created without aggression. But, one day, Kiku came bleeding from a wound on the cheek.

'Your wolf bit me.' It was the longest sentence Shika had ever heard from him.

He cleaned the bite, saying, 'That will teach you to leave him alone.' He realised he had spoken of the wolf as *him*, as though it were truly alive. Tora had said it was love that made the wolf become more real, but *he* had also become aggressive in a way the other false animals were not. Now he was truly alive the wolf seemed to need a name and Shika decided to call him Gen, which might mean either reality or illusion.

Shisoku had still not given permission for Shika to touch the sword, Jato, when, in the eighth month, a typhoon swept up from the southwest. The wind tore trees up by the roots and threw them down. Rain fell from the sky like a river. The stream roared through the night and raged across the clearing. Many of the false animals were swept away, their empty skins caught on tree branches, their skulls washed up on the bank miles away.

At the height of the storm, Shisoku said, 'Jato is outside.'

Shika went out. The wind seized him and shook him. A false dog flew past his head and crashed into a tree. He could see the rock where Jato lay but it was already almost submerged. He thought he saw the sword gleam beneath the rushing water and struggled towards it, fighting the wind, but the current dragged it loose. It disappeared with a flash of steel, a water snake in the flood.

When the wind and the rain abated, and the stream returned to its normal size, Shika and the boys searched the valley, but the sword had vanished.

'It must be buried in mud and silt,' he said to Shisoku after another day of fruitless searching.

'When it wants to be found it will be,' Shisoku replied.

It made Shika sad and angry. He had called Kiyoyori's spirit back from the gates of Hell, he had rescued the ruined sword. Now, both had vanished into the Darkwood, as if they had not thought him worthy of them.

At the end of the ninth month, Shisoku pronounced the mask healed. Though it was not perfect as it had been and one antler remained broken, it had different powers, attained through suffering and loss. Shika put it away in the seven-layered brocade bag, reluctant to face the Prince Abbot as he knew one day he must, and, in the calm autumn days, began to work at the fire, helped by Shisoku and Mu. They forged a new sword, and called it Jinan, Second Son, and a helmet mounted with iron antlers, one broken in the same way as the mask's, and armour, bound with leather lacing, dyed with madder and indigo. It seemed there was nothing Shisoku did not have stored away somewhere, and what was not stored he could find in the forest.

'Are you planning to go to war with someone?' he asked Shika when the armour was finished.

'With my uncle first. The boys cannot just grow up in the forest. They need a home, they need learning, far more than I can teach them. I am going to take back Kumayama. After that who knows? Maybe Kuromori and Matsutani. Maybe I will be like Akuzenji, become a bandit and control trade as King of the Mountain. Then I will be able to provide for the boys.'

'They are not ordinary boys,' Shisoku said dubiously. 'You are not going to be able to turn them into warriors.'

'Maybe not. I will turn them into something very useful to myself, though,' said Shikanoko. 'I suppose I'll need a bow, too,'

'I will make you one,' the sorcerer promised. 'Do you remember what Ameyumi looked like?'

'Only that it was enormous and no one could draw it but my father.'

But it seemed Shikanoko remembered more than he thought, or Shisoku somehow drew the knowledge from hidden memories. When the bow was finished, it felt the way his father's bow had, in his hand. They named it Kodama: Echo

'Will Ameyumi ever be found?' he wondered aloud.

'It will, but not by you,' replied the mountain sorcerer.

# 2

## MASACHIKA

Masachika opened his eyes on the familiar setting of his boyhood home – opened, he thought, was not quite the correct word, as he could barely see through the swelling. His skin burned and itched and beneath the inflammation he ached from head to foot. His tongue was swollen and his lips cracked.

He realised where he was from the outline of the mountains beyond the one open shutter – the rest were closed and barred on the inside. It was raining steadily but even the dull light of a wet day and overcast sky was too bright, sending a piercing pain deep into the back of his skull. He closed his eyes and tried to ask for water.

'He is awake,' a woman's voice said. He thought he knew it from his childhood. 'Go and tell Hironaga.'

Hironaga, he knew, was this woman's husband. Had they not been as close to him as foster parents? Was he a boy again, had he fallen from his horse? He could remember nothing.

'What happened?' he muttered. He did not really care about the answer. He was sure he was dying. A pitiful rage flickered within him; it was too soon, he did not want to leave yet, if only he could stay. But living entailed so much pain. Maybe it was better to slip away into the numbness of death.

The woman held a cup to his lips and he gulped down the lukewarm slightly salty liquid. It only partly quenched his thirst. His gullet burned and smarted.

He heard footsteps and a man knelt at his side.

'Lord Masachika? Can you hear me?'

The woman had taken away the cup and was bathing his face. The cloth felt cool and soothing. He nodded and felt it slide against his skin. Then it too was removed. He could see a little better. Hironaga, a man in his fifties, with greying hair and a weathered face, was bending over him.

'We found you after the attack. We were searching the hillside for spent arrows and uninjured horses. Luckily, it was I who came across you and I recognised you. You have been unconscious for a long time. My wife has been caring for you – you know she always loved you like her own son.'

'The attack?' He half-recalled the desperate plunge down the hillside.

'We knew it was coming. Young Chikamaru, Kongyo's son, came from Matsutani to warn us. The Miboshi horsemen plunged straight into a trap. None of them survived. If you had not fallen from your horse halfway down, you would have been killed too. We could see very little in the dark and we would never have known who you were.'

He remembered that he was Miboshi now. Didn't Hironaga know that? He frowned, confused, and pain shot around his eyeballs.

While his eyes were shut he thought he sensed someone else approaching. Again he knew the voice.

'Lord Masachika,' it said.

He peered through his swollen eyelids.

'It is I, Kongyo. Do you remember me?'

He nodded. 'You were my brother's friend.'

'I became his senior retainer, and will be yours too, I hope. We all know how your father commanded you to go to the Miboshi. You cannot be blamed for obeying him. But something prevented you from attacking your family home. If your brother, Kiyoyori, and his only son are indeed dead, then you are the last of the Kuromori lords. Your father made a difficult decision to preserve his family line. Who are we to put an end to it? Heaven spared you. We could not go against its judgement.'

'I feel more like Heaven punished me,' Masachika said and groaned.

'Heaven gives punishment with one hand and mercy with the other,' Hironaga said.

Masachika remembered how the older man had always been inclined to make these sanctimonious pronouncements. At that moment he realised two things. One was that despite the pain he would rather be alive than dead, the other that he was going to be given another chance. He closed his eyes again and began to prepare himself to take full advantage of it.

•

They were a tiny fortress, not quite under siege, but anticipating another attack any day. The men, almost forty in number, were bored and tense, and always hungry. They waited for news, of a Kakizuki counterattack or confirmation of Lord Kiyoyori's death, but none came. The bodies of the dead Miboshi had been burned, their swords, bows and arrows added to the armoury. No one came to avenge them or to punish the Kuromori group.

It rained frequently. The summer days were lush and humid. Farmers paraded outside with food: eggs, summer greens and other vegetables, and every day a handful of men climbed the hill behind the fortress to hunt rabbits and deer.

The farmers reported that the spirits were still in residence at Matsutani and no one dared go inside the garden walls. Weeds were growing rampant in the rains and the house was disappearing beneath them.

Masachika had many long hours in which to reflect on what the future held for him. As the swelling in his face slowly went down his memory came back, but the bee stings left after-effects, fierce headaches and night fevers. He dreaded confronting the spirits again, yet he became obsessed with ousting them. The idea of Matsutani rotting away, after all the sacrifices that had been made, gnawed at him constantly. He could not help thinking of Tama. He was sorry now he had hired the assassin. It had been an impulsive act and he regretted it. He didn't even know if the man had been successful; he had not had time to find out before he left with the Miboshi army. But to be on the safe side he offered prayers for her soul in the makeshift shrine that had been erected inside the fortress.

Hironaga and Kongyo, with their simple concepts of lineage and loyalty, seemed to assume he had returned not only to Kuromori but also to the Kakizuki. Of course he had not; he had a better idea of how things were in the capital. He knew who the real victors were. He was not going to join the losers' side at this stage of the war. But it was not hard to pretend his new retainers were right, nor to agree with them that what they most needed was information, and that he was perfectly placed to get it for them.

He made a convincing show of gratitude to Hironaga, respect for Kongyo, affection for his old foster mother, joy at being back in his childhood home. Just as he had in Minatogura he endeared himself to most of the men, already predisposed to accept him as their departed lord's brother, by undertaking any task alongside them, willingly and competently, by remembering their names, their characteristics and their exploits.

'Could you get to Lord Keita, who, it seems, has retreated with the Kakizuki forces to Rakuhara?' Kongyo asked him one morning. It promised to be the first clear day for several weeks. The plum rains were drawing to an end.

'I can certainly return to the capital. I served the Miboshi well during the years I lived with them. I believe they trust me. I could assess the situation there, and report to Lord Keita, get a message back to you or return myself.'

'Ask him if we should remain here or fight our way through and join him,' Hironaga said.

One of the men who was listening spoke up. 'Lord Masachika was with the Miboshi for eight years and was part of the force that attacked us. Forgive me, but someone has to say it. Can we really trust him?'

'Tsunesada,' Masachika replied, 'a man cannot forget his first loyalties. I longed to return to my true family, especially since my revered brother appears to have passed on to the next world. I was born Kakizuki and Heaven has decreed I should become Kakizuki again.'

'Even though the Miboshi rule the capital and the Kakizuki are in exile?' Tsunesada persisted.

'That makes my choice all the more honourable,' Masachika said smoothly.

Tsunesada pointed at the stack of reports that Masachika had written and that had been retrieved from the saddlebags of his fallen horse. They had sat for weeks on the floor of the room in which the men were now gathered as no one could decipher them. 'What do all these mean?'

'They are records of the warriors. The men dictated them to me because I can read and write.'

'Not much use now they are all dead!' Tsunesada scoffed.

'The records give them immortality. Their names live on. If I take them with me, they will be sent to Minatogura and their families may be able to claim compensation.'

Hironaga was frowning. 'Do the Miboshi do the same in everything?'

'Keep records? They do. It is Lord Aritomo's method to know everything, remember everything, control everything. Memory cannot be trusted. Five men will remember the same event in five different ways, but written accounts become legal records. Aritomo loves legality.'

The men shuffled uneasily.

'If I present them in the capital I can make myself seem more credible,' Masachika said, 'but burn them if you like.'

Tsunesada looked at Kongyo. The older man said, 'I suppose Masachika is right. He had better take them with him.'

A few days later, supplied with a new horse and his own sword, Masachika slipped away from Kuromori before dawn and rode towards Shimaura. But he did not follow the western coast road towards the capital. Instead he turned east towards Minatogura. He had been thinking about this plan for weeks and had decided he must confirm his legal claim on Matsutani. Only then would he return to Miyako.

•

Compared to the half-destroyed capital, Minatogura looked peaceful and prosperous, hardly touched by war. Its ships sailed to and from the port, laden with goods that its wealthy merchants bought and sold with even more vigour than usual. The news of the Miboshi victory and the Kakizuki defeat had given the city an atmosphere of triumph. In offices and courts, scribes and lawyers recorded these victories, and the exploits of individual warriors, and calculated the rewards in land that would be granted, and from whom, among the defeated, such lands would be taken.

Masachika went to his adoptive family's house, riding through the familiar streets, past the port and up the slope to the north. It was very hot, the sun was blinding in a brilliant sky, yet shivers ran through him and his head ached. He was aware that, unless the onset of war had delayed it, his claim would have been decided. He told himself there was nothing to be nervous about – the estate could only be granted to him; there were no other heirs; he had served the Miboshi faithfully – yet his anxiety persisted. What if he had been ruled dead, or worse, a traitor? Only legal confirmation that Matsutani was his would bring him reassurance and tranquillity.

His adoptive father, Yamada Keisaku, came hurrying out to the gate as Masachika dismounted and handed the horse's reins to a groom.

'You are home, and safe! We heard rumours that you had been killed in an attack on Kuromori. Heaven be praised! My wife has prayed for you day and night, and our daughter – how she has wept, believing you dead and our family bereaved.'

Masachika brushed aside his effusive welcome. Keisaku was a pious and jovial man who wanted everyone around him to be happy, but Masachika had never had much respect for him, despising his excessive religious faith and what he considered shallowness.

Inside the house he caught a glimpse of his betrothed, her plump pretty face flushed with excitement and joy, her eyes all the more sparkling for her tears. He pretended not to see her.

'Is there any news from the tribunal?' he asked immediately.

'About your claim?' Keisaku replied. 'We want you to know you will always be our son. We have a country estate, more remote and not as wealthy as Matsutani, of course, but which will always be yours. You will never be landless.'

'What are you talking about?' Masachika demanded.

Keisaku was rubbing his hands together nervously. 'I am grieved to be the one to reveal such disappointing news. Despite my deep affection for you I am the one who must inflict a grave wound. Accept it as Heaven's will for your life. No doubt good will come of it in the end.'

'Are you trying to tell me my claim has failed?' Masachika said, incredulous.

'Your former wife, Lady Tama, produced documents that stated clearly the land was left by her father to her and whomever was her husband – Matsutani, that is. No ruling was made on Kuromori, which I suppose would still be yours.'

Masachika stared at his adoptive father, speechless. So, Hisoku had failed. Tama was not only alive but had dared to approach the tribunal in her own right. He was outraged and furious, but at the same time he couldn't help admiring her audacity, and he felt the stirrings of old longing.

Oblivious to his future son-in-law's inner turmoil, Keisaku said, 'Lady Tama has a powerful ally in the Abbess at Muenji . . . however, the reasons are not important; the court found in her favour.'

'But she is a woman!' Masachika could think of nothing else to say.

'As the only surviving child of her father, and the widow of the Kuromori lord, she was considered to hold the greater right,' Keisaku said. 'As the father of an only daughter, I have some sympathy with this judgement.'

'Surely I have a chance to appeal? I would have been here pleading my own case if I had not been fighting for the Miboshi, and nearly dying, I might add!'

'I cannot answer you on that subject. You could try speaking to someone of higher rank. Yukikuni no Takaakira, for example; he is here in Minatogura for a few days. Our meagre estate borders his, so I have some channels through which to approach him.'

'Takaakira? He has taken over Kiyoyori's old house in Miyako.'

'That is good,' Keisaku attempted a smile. 'He will consider himself beholden to you.'

'Do you think so? If a man wrongs you once, he will find it easier the next time. I can't expect much help from him.'

'My dear son, you must not be so cynical. I will do my best with him. Meanwhile, let us put our trust in the Enlightened One and bear whatever Heaven sends us.'

Masachika could not hide his irritation, thinking, *What Heaven sends is one thing but to bear the platitudes of the old is quite another.*

•

He tried to see Tama but when he went to Muenji he was refused admittance. He was told the lady was practising a religious retreat.

'For how long?' he demanded.

'It is hard to say.'

'Will she see me if I come back in a few days?'

'It is hard to say.'

That was the only answer he received.

His adoptive father began to make delicate attempts to contact Yukikuni no Takaakira while Masachika waited impatiently, avoiding his betrothed and her mother, and putting off any discussion of marriage. Tama had suddenly become desirable to him once more. He recalled the early days of their marriage, her ardour and eagerness, his terrible pain when she had been taken from him. He convinced himself that she was still his wife. Had she not made it clear she wanted him back last time they met? This time he would not refuse her.

Even the nagging memory of the spirits did not discourage him. He would face them again with Tama, whom they had called the Matsutani lady, by his side. Together they would find a way to placate or remove them.

Four days later he was told a messenger was at the door. He rushed out and immediately recognised Hisoku, the rogue he had hired.

'Lady Tama wishes to see you before she leaves,' Hisoku said.

'Where is she going?' Masachika could not hide his surprise.

Hisoku met his gaze insolently. 'We are leaving tomorrow for Matsutani.'

'We?' The word shocked him. He could not bring himself to believe all its implications.

'Lady Tama has graciously taken me into her service.'

'She will soon find out how incompetent you are,' Masachika said with scorn.

Hisoku did not reply but Masachika saw a muscle twitch in his cheek. It did not worry him that he had made an enemy. He despised the man and had already decided he would kill him at the first opportunity.

However, he had to follow him to the temple, where they were taken to the garden pavilion. Even here in the shade by the lake, where water trickled from the spring, it was unbearably hot. Cicadas droned deafeningly from the woods.

Masachika went forward, leaving Hisoku waiting on the step. He studied his former wife with respect. She seemed both unaffected by the heat and possessed of a new calm authority.

'Your religious retreat has been beneficial,' he observed.

She did not respond to his trace of sarcasm, simply indicating he might sit next to her.

'You desired to see me?' she said.

'Tama,' he began.

'Lady Tama,' Hisoku corrected him.

'Can we speak in private?' Masachika tried to mask his impatience.

'How can I be sure you will not make another attempt on my life?' Tama replied.

'That was a mistake, I apologise ...' His excuses trailed away under her level gaze. 'Forgive me,' he said simply.

Without turning her head, she said, 'You may wait a little further away, Hisoku.'

The man moved a few paces to the edge of the lake, but did not take his eyes off them.

'What do you want, Masachika?' Tama said.

'I want us to live together as husband and wife.'

She continued to look at him without speaking and a slight smile began to curve her lips.

'You will agree?' he said eagerly. 'I may come with you to Matsutani?'

Now her eyes were alight with emotion. He leaned forward to take her in his arms, but in one swift movement she was on her feet.

'It is too late.'

Then she was gone, hurrying down the path by the side of the lake.

'What?' he shouted after her. 'You won't even listen to me?'

'I think Lady Tama has made her feelings clear,' Hisoku said, giving Masachika a triumphant, sneering look before he followed her.

•

Two days later, still burning with regret and rage, Masachika found himself in the presence of Yukikuni no Takaakira. He did not want to be there, he would have preferred to leave meeting Takaakira until he returned to Miyako, but his father-in-law had gone to great efforts to obtain the audience, eager for Masachika to seek support for his appeal. However, Takaakira was not inclined to help him or even to listen to him. He cut short Masachika's explanation saying, 'That has no interest for me. What does interest me is Kuromori.'

'My lord?'

'You left with a hundred men. All of them, save Yasuie, appear to be dead. The fortress is still in the hands of your late brother's retainers, yet you have not only survived but were permitted to leave. What deal did you strike with them and whose side are you on now?'

His voice was deliberately insulting. Masachika knew Takaakira could be both charming and generous to those he respected, and it wounded him to realise he was not one of them. He began to defend himself.

'I am, and for years have been, Miboshi. Does your lordship not recall how well I acquitted myself at Shimaura and the Sagi River?' It did not seem to be the time for false modesty. 'I deeply regret the failure at Kuromori, but I was attacked by evil spirits and rendered unconscious before the actual battle.'

The mention of the spirits, he could see, aroused Takaakira's interest, and he found himself relating the strange occurrences at Matsutani, Yasunobu's death and the crippling bee stings. Takaakira heard him out and then said, 'That is one of the most fanciful explanations for a defeat I have ever had to listen to. So, you did not agree to spy for the Kakizuki, and to try to get to Keita in Rakuhara?'

Again Masachika felt the flick of contempt. He hid his anger and affected a penitent air. 'I can hide nothing from such a great and wise lord. I did agree, but only so I could escape, and return to Lord Aritomo's service. I have even brought with me the records of the warriors who died. The men at Kuromori trust me and regard me as Kiyoyori's heir. Surely that can be turned to our advantage?'

'Kuromori will have to be dealt with eventually,' Takaakira said. 'In the meantime I have a task for you. I do want you to go to Rakuhara. Everyone suspects you of spying for the Kakizuki, so you will return to them, but you will be spying for us. Now you have lost your inheritance it will be a consolation for you.'

When Masachika did not answer, Takaakira went on, 'I am doing this for Keisaku's sake, since we are neighbours. I know you do not lack courage, Masachika. I have seen you in battle. But you have a self-serving nature that makes you untrustworthy. This is your chance to redeem yourself. If you refuse, Lord Aritomo will require you to take your own life in compensation for your failure, and to wipe out the suspicions that are growing around you.'

'I will do whatever you and Lord Aritomo command,' Masachika said, prostrating himself. But beneath his feigned humility his mind was searching desperately for some new strategy that might improve his position.

'Good. You will leave tomorrow. That will be all.' Takaakira gave a brief nod and turned away but Masachika did not want the interview to end on such unequal terms, nor did he like the idea of his life and future held in the other man's hands.

'May I ask one question?' he said, as he sat up.

The lord gave his permission with another slight nod.

He was playing for time, not even sure what question he was going to ask, when an image of the house in the capital came into his mind and he made one of his intuitive stabs in the dark.

'I believe your lordship has taken over Kiyoyori's old house in the capital.' He felt Takaakira's flash of surprise and anger and knew he had hit on something. 'Don't misunderstand me; it is an honour for our family. But was his daughter there? Did she survive?'

'I did not know whose the house was, or even that Kiyoyori had a daughter. The place was empty,' Takaakira replied. 'That's all I can tell you.'

But something in his face told Masachika that the noble lord of the Snow Country was lying.

# 3

# AKI

When Shikanoko left, Aki lay rigid with shock, tears pooling in her eyes and spilling over her cheeks. She could never become a shrine maiden now, never undo what they had done. She was filled with regret and fear – surely the gods would punish them? After a while she picked up the catalpa bow and went to the stream to wash herself, her blood disappearing into the cold water. She was shivering, not only from the chill but also from emotions she did not recognise. She blamed herself as much as him. The world was colourless, leached of enchantment and mystery. Yet there had been both earlier, something had taken place, some spell had been cast over them, girl and boy, that neither had been able to resist.

*I could have fought him off,* she thought, as the water flowed over her, *I could have killed him. Why didn't I?* And she answered herself, *Because I wanted to touch his skin, place my mouth on his, be held by him and hold him, and I have done so ever since I saw him, when those men lay dead, killed by his arrows. But I did not know it would be like that, so brutal, so painful. And now I have done*

*exactly what my father told me not to do. It can never be undone.*
*I am another person now.*

Like a wild animal, she longed to flee into the forest. Then she thought of killing herself, but she had left her knife in the hut; and, she could not leave Yoshi. While he lived she must live too.

It began to rain. Not wanting to return to the hut, yet needing to think clearly, she stood up, pulled her robe round her, and walked to the cave, where the horses were tied up on long lines.

Nyorin was standing, and whinnied softly at her approach. Risu was lying down, and did not want to get up. They must have been restless during the night, for they had stepped over the loose ropes several times and had entangled themselves. She untied them and pulled the ropes free. Then she lay down next to the mare, within the cradle of her legs, and rested her head on her belly. She imagined she could hear the foal's heartbeat. Could the spirit of Lord Kiyoyori really have taken possession of it? She remembered him from the few times she had seen him, his courageous bearing, his imposing looks. How pitiful his fate had been. Tears formed in her eyes. She could hear the soft dripping from the rocks and trees around the cave, a gentle, soothing sound. Nyorin stamped. Risu whickered.

Her mind began to drift. Suddenly she was dreaming of monkeys. She awoke to hear someone calling her name.

'Akihime!'

Nyorin neighed loudly and Risu began to struggle to her feet.

He called again. 'Akihime!'

She did not want to go out to him. How could she meet his gaze? She shrank back for a moment, listening to the dawn's birdsong, the constant dripping of the rain, the babble of the stream. Yet she wanted to see him; almost against her will, her feet led her outside, the bow gripped in her hand.

She saw the masked figure come from the hut with Yoshimori. It looked like a being from a dream or from the distant magical past. The antlers gave it height and authority, and it moved in a way that was neither human nor animal but that exuded force and power.

Hardly believing her eyes, she saw the kneeling boy, the drawn sword, as if they were part of the dream. For a few moments she stood without moving, the horses, as motionless, beside her, their ears pricked forwards, their eyes startled. Then she raised the catalpa bow and twanged it, she heard the scream of the werehawk and, as if it released them, the horses bolted from the cave, Risu in the lead.

Aki ran after them, and watched as they attacked Shikanoko.

She thought they had killed him. Sobbing with grief and shock and fury, she ran to Yoshi and held him close against her. Kon fluttered round her head saying something she did not understand. Yoshi clung to her, trembling. He muttered something.

Aki bent down. 'What?'

'I was brave, wasn't I?'

'You were very brave,' she said.

'Was Shikanoko going to cut my head off?'

'Yes!' she screamed, then tried, for the boy's sake, to control herself.

'Why? I thought he was going to protect us.'

'I thought so too. But he is in the service of a very powerful man, who wants to kill you. Shikanoko has to obey him.'

'I liked him,' Yoshi said, sadness in his eyes.

'Like, *like*? What does that mean?' Aki replied. It was far too tame a word. 'Luckily, some other force is looking after you. Heaven itself is protecting you. But we must get away from this place.'

'And leave him here?'

Shikanoko's eyelids fluttered briefly, he cried out in pain, but did not wake. Yoshi looked down on him. 'Shouldn't we take care of him?'

'He was going to kill you,' Aki said. 'He will try again.'

'We should love our enemies,' Yoshi said stubbornly.

'Where did you get that idea from?' Aki was wondering if she should finish Shikanoko off, before he regained consciousness.

'I heard the old man on the boat tell the musicians. I liked it.'

'I remember him,' Aki said. It seemed like something from a different world.

'I don't want anyone else to die.' Yoshi was close to tears.

'Come,' she said gently. 'We are going to get away before he wakes; we will leave him to Heaven to deal with. Fetch Genzo and my knife while I get the horses ready.'

He nodded, gave one more worried look at Shikanoko, and went to the hut, the werehawk fluttering after him. It had more gold feathers than ever, Aki noticed. They gleamed through the misty rain.

The horses, calm now, lowered their heads to their unconscious master and drew in his smell. Then they followed her docilely to the cave and stood, while she fumbled with the saddle and bridles. When Yoshi returned, she put the knife in her belt and tied the lute on her back. Was that the faintest echo of the love song?

'Traitor,' she said to it silently. 'I should burn you!'

She lifted Yoshi onto Risu's back.

'You don't have to hold the reins. I'll knot them on her neck and lead you.'

'I can ride,' he said. 'Anyway, Risu won't let anything bad happen to me.'

Aki was surprised he knew the mare's name. 'What's the stallion called?'

'Nyorin. It means silver. And the werehawk's name is Kon – gold. That's funny, isn't it? Silver and gold.'

'Do you listen to everything, and remember it?' she asked.

He nodded. 'I understand it, mostly, though sometimes not till later, after I've thought about it for a while.'

*He will be a fine Emperor*, Aki said to herself. *And he will have seen life in a way no other Emperor has.*

'Where are we going now?' Yoshi said, as she scrambled up onto Nyorin's back. The stallion was much taller than the mare, but he waited patiently, and let her settle in the saddle and take up the reins, before he moved off.

'I'm not sure.' Aki was trying to form a plan. They had the horses, the werehawk – if it too did not betray them and fly back to Ryusonji – and the untrustworthy lute. She had her knife and the catalpa bow and she knew a little about the herbs and seeds of the forest. But they could not hide out there forever, not in winter, though that was still half a year away. She decided to ride north, keeping away from the roads, to Rinrakuji, as her father had told her to. Maybe someone who could help them had survived there. If not, she would go on to Kitakami and from there down the western side of the lake to Nishimi.

'I will show you where I lived when I was a little girl,' she told Yoshi. Nishimi was closer to where the Kakizuki were in exile. There she would find the men and the arms Yoshi was going to need.

She explained this out loud, as though she expected the werehawk and the horses to understand it, and let Nyorin have his head. He immediately set out up the valley to the east. She thought they should be heading north, but the valley grew narrower and the forest thicker; east was the only direction possible unless they turned back. But the fear of finding Shikanoko dead made that impossible.

After a couple of hours it stopped raining. The sun had climbed high in the sky and now its rays pierced the clouds. It became very hot, the earth steaming around them. The horses stopped in a grassy clearing, where the mountain stream had formed pools filled with bulrushes and lotus stems. They drank deeply and then began to tear at the long grass.

'It looks like we're taking a rest,' Aki said. She slid down from Nyorin's back, flinching at the pain, noticing she had left smears of blood on his silver coat, and helped Yoshi dismount. A dove was calling from the forest and she could hear the pretty whistle of something she thought might be a grosbeak, though she knew it only from poetry.

Yoshi said, 'Older sister, what are we going to eat?'

'Good question,' Aki said. 'We could always eat grass like Risu and Nyorin.'

Yoshi pulled up a few blades, crammed them in his mouth, chewed bravely for a few moments, then spat them out.

'No? I'll have to see what else I can find. You rest here, under that tree. Keep an eye on the horses. Don't let them stray out of sight. And look after Genzo.'

She waded into one of the pools and pulled up the rushes, throwing them to the bank behind her. The mud was cool and soothing to her feet. Little fishes darted away through the tawny water but she had nothing to catch them with. Further up the stream, she saw a flash of gold and Kon flew up with a loud squawk, a small sweetfish in his talons.

'Take it to Yoshi,' she called but Kon was already flying back to the tree. He returned and took another fish from the water. Aki felt her stomach ache at the thought of food. How long was it since they had eaten? She could not remember.

She cut the succulent roots from the rushes and chewed on one. The grosbeak sang again and this time she saw it, grey and black, flying to a rock in the stream. A wagtail answered, and then above the birdsong came music. Genzo was playing, the same love song from the previous night, awakening the longing and the fear she had been trying to forget.

'I will smash that lute,' she cried, 'heirloom or not!'

She ran back to the tree where Yoshi sat cross-legged. Kon was tearing pieces off the fish and feeding him like a baby bird. The lute's decoration sparkled in the sun as the music poured from it.

And around them in a half-circle, just like in her dream, sat ten or more grey-furred, rosy-faced, green-eyed monkeys.

Aki stood still. She had never been so close to wild monkeys and she was uncertain how they would behave. She did not want to be attacked by them nor did she want to scare them away. Was it the lute that enchanted them, or Yoshi? Did they recognise him in some way as the divine Emperor? Of course, she reasoned to herself, they should, all creatures should, since the true Emperor was the link between Heaven and Earth. It was his prayers and rituals that kept both in balance and harmony, affecting the wellbeing of monkeys as much as men.

A usurper on the throne would cause disasters and catastrophes, earthquakes, plagues, fires and floods. Maybe these were already occurring in the capital. She had no way of knowing. The forest was so peaceful, the birds singing, the grass lush and bright with wild flowers.

Yoshi saw her and called out, 'Look, older sister! Monkeys!'

She remembered he had called that out once before, at the island market at Majima, by the Rainbow Bridge, when he had seen the boy he had so much admired and his monkey friends. And she had dreamed of monkeys. Was it a sign that fate had brought them together for some purpose?

In the middle of the semicircle a large female sat nursing a baby. Something about her suggested authority and Aki approached her with deference. Genzo stopped playing and the monkeys all turned their heads and chattered softly. Aki fell to her knees as she would to a court lady, or the Crown Princess herself, held out the catalpa bow and laid it down, and bowed to the ground. The monkey matriarch put out a hand and gently scratched the girl's head, put her fingers to her nose and sniffed them, then shuffled a little closer, shifting the baby to the other nipple and began to run her fingers through Aki's cropped hair, searching for fleas, grooming her.

Aki submitted without moving, and felt some deep wordless connection with the old monkey, acceptance, the assurance of protection and support. Tears formed in her eyes suddenly. Somehow under the gentle fingers she went from a kneeling position to lying down. She could hear the horses tearing at the grass. Through the foliage the sun cast leafy patterns on her closed eyelids. The monkeys chattered to each other. Yoshi laughed. Kon called in response, almost tunefully.

The day passed and at dusk they followed the monkeys to a place where hot water bubbled up into rock-edged pools. Here the monkeys lived. Yoshi wanted nothing more than to stay with them, and Aki could not refuse him.

# 4

# TAKAAKIRA

Takaakira had kept the girl hidden in her old home in the capital for several months. When he returned from Minatogura, he had made more searching enquiries and found the house had indeed been the residence of Kiyoyori's family, as he had learned from Masachika. The girl must be Kiyoyori's daughter.

The realisation made him both angry and surprised at himself. He prided himself on knowing all the secrets of the city; how could he not have seen what was in front of his eyes? Kiyoyori might have been only a provincial warrior, but his unwavering support of the Crown Prince, his noble death, the mysterious death of his son and the legends that were growing up around them, ensured his name was still very much alive. The Prince Abbot, who had grown even more powerful now he was uncle to the Emperor, hated Kiyoyori, even more in death than in life.

Takaakira had told Masachika that the house was empty but when he recalled the other man's expression it made him uneasy. He did not want to give Masachika any influence over him. He was the girl's uncle, after all. What was to prevent him turning up at his former home and discovering her? Would he recognise her? Did she resemble her father? Why had he suddenly asked about the house? Had something made him suspect that Kiyoyori's daughter had survived? The risk of being betrayed by Masachika, or anyone else, began to disturb him. He must either hide her somewhere else or kill her himself. If she were discovered, she would be tortured and put to death and he – he could not imagine what punishment Lord Aritomo would devise for him.

He knew he could never bring himself to end her life. Every day she delighted him more with her intelligence and wit, and her beauty, on the cusp of womanhood. He loved her like a daughter, but he dreamed of holding her in his arms as his wife. She seemed to adore him; she sought to please him, she learned rapidly. When he was away, the servants told him, she spent her time studying, fretting for his return. By the end of summer she was reading fluently. He brought scrolls for her from his own library in Minatogura, works of literature and history, essays and poems. She grasped the essentials of poetry swiftly and began writing poems every day for him.

He educated her taste in clothes, colours and materials. He taught her to discern incense and perfume, he played music and demonstrated dance steps, found women to instruct her and moved them into his household.

She was a consolation to him during a difficult time. The city was hit by a series of disasters. A fire broke out in the sixth month and destroyed most of the newly completed buildings. An epidemic of sickness raged for weeks, leaving thousands dead. Smoke from funeral pyres darkened the skies and many of those who survived succumbed to starvation as the rains came for three weeks and then dried up. Rice crops failed, beans withered on the stem, fruit did not ripen. The new Emperor offered prayers for rain and as if in mockery Heaven sent a ferocious typhoon that swept across the country, flooding rivers and washing away bridges. Water ran waist deep through the streets of the capital, gravid with the bodies of the drowned.

People began to say openly that Heaven was outraged, that they were being punished for the crimes of their rulers. These mutterings eventually reached the ears of Lord Aritomo, he who prided himself on his fair government and his justice, who had sought to remedy the excesses of the Kakizuki and had expected Heaven to smile on him.

After the water receded a little, and the mud and debris had been cleared from the streets, Takaakira was ordered to go to the Prince Abbot at Ryusonji to find out what had gone wrong.

Trees had fallen in the garden of the temple and stone lanterns lay smashed. The lake was muddy, brimming over, logs, branches and leaves swirling in a whirlpool around its centre. It was still raining and the sound of water was everywhere, not the usual pleasant trickling, but thunderous and threatening.

He was shown into the reception hall by a young monk with a badly scarred face. Takaakira was surprised someone so damaged served the Prince Abbot. He wondered if that, in itself, might be an insult to the gods. One could never be too careful.

A mournful singing echoed in the courtyard; he looked towards the sound and saw an old blind man, with a lute, sitting cross-legged on the verandah. The words of the song were inaudible in the rain. Something felt wrong to him. The back of his neck prickled. He had come to Ryusonji hoping to discover the cause of all their problems. Now he began to suspect that Ryusonji itself was the cause.

It was the first time he had met the Prince Abbot face to face, though he had seen him at a distance at the ceremonies to give thanks for the Miboshi victory and install the new Emperor. Then and now, the priest had an impressive authority. If he was disturbed by recent events he gave no sign of it. He seemed completely in control of himself and of all he commanded, seen and unseen.

Yet water dripped through the roof, puddling on the wooden floors, staining the matting, punctuating their tense exchange.

The young monk with the scarred face knelt on one side of the Prince Abbot. On the other was an older man, strong and serious-looking, who was making notes of their conversation with a small badger hair brush. After formalities had been traded, Takaakira sat in silence for a few moments, wondering how best to broach his concerns, which he realised were more complicated than he had at first thought. The Prince Abbot had been responsible for the success of the Miboshi, the death of the Crown Prince and the accession of the Emperor. It went without saying that Lord Aritomo needed his support in the spiritual realm, as the priest needed his in the physical. Despite the Prince Abbot's calm air, Takaakira sensed an imbalance here in the heart of the realm. He thought, *A man is at his most dangerous when he senses his powers begin to slip from him.*

Finally the Prince Abbot spoke. 'The former Prince's son, Yoshimori, escaped from the palace with his nurse's daughter.'

'He is still alive?' Takaakira felt the shock of this revelation deep in his gut.

'He was a few months ago. In the fourth month the man I sent caught up with them. But he has not returned with the child's head as he was ordered to.'

'Do you know where Yoshimori is now?'

'Presumably somewhere in the Darkwood, if he has survived.'

'You should have informed us earlier,' Takaakira said sternly. 'Lord Aritomo would raze the Darkwood if it meant he would find Yoshimori there. What sort of man did you send? A monk? A warrior?'

'A young acolyte of mine. It's possible I made a mistake . . . I cannot reveal too much to you as these are esoteric matters. I can tell you that he is known as Shikanoko. He is the nephew of Kumayama no Jiro no Sademasa. He has an affinity with the forest, which is why I believe he will be found in the Darkwood.'

Sademasa, who had been a vassal of Kiyoyori's, had sworn allegiance to the Miboshi during their advance on the capital. Takaakira stored that information away without comment, and said, 'I am an initiate. You may speak of these things to me.'

The Prince Abbot gave him a quick sharp glance, as though seeing him with new eyes and needing to reassess his opinion.

'Very well. I believed Shikanoko was destined by Heaven to be a powerful sage, for fate led him not only to me but to two or three other people of great ability and deep knowledge of the other worlds: a mountain sorcerer, a woman of whom I know very little, and the old man you might have seen on your way in.'

'The lute player?' Takaakira said, in surprise.

'Yes, once my equal in all spiritual matters. He had been living in Kiyoyori's household for years, unknown to anyone until I discovered him. I sent Gessho to bring him to me.' He indicated the older monk who stopped writing for a moment and bowed his head in response.

'Gessho found him with Shikanoko. In fact they had fallen into the hands of Sademasa, which would be neither here nor there but for the fact that Sademasa subsequently decided to abandon the Kakizuki and ally himself with the Miboshi. He is still waiting for his reward from me.'

'When the old man arrived here,' Gessho said, 'he was as he is now, practically senile.'

'Was he always blind?' Takaakira asked.

'Kiyoyori's wife put out his eyes,' Gessho said. 'I saw them fixed to the gate at Matsutani.'

'Did they still see?' Takaakira tried to keep his voice emotionless, but in fact the cruelty, and the casual way Gessho spoke of it, shocked him.

'Yes, they saw everything,' Gessho said quietly. 'We said prayers over them and I hope we placated them. But Matsutani was badly damaged by the earthquake. Who knows if the eyes are still there?'

'Well, Sesshin and his eyes are not my main concern at the moment,' the Prince Abbot said. 'Shikanoko is, and, even more, Yoshimori. If he falls into the hands of the Kakizuki he will become an inspiration to them, a rallying point.'

*He is the true Emperor,* Takaakira realised. *No wonder the realm is so afflicted by disaster and suffering.* And then he thought with dread, *What have we done?*

There was no turning back now. He put the fear from him and said, 'It is a most unfortunate state of affairs. I hesitate to report it to Lord Aritomo, yet he must be told. But I need some strategy to soften the blow. Do you have any suggestions?'

'Let me send someone into the Darkwood. Gessho tracked Shikanoko once; he can do it again.'

'I will go gladly,' Gessho exclaimed, his voice sounding suddenly loud, for they had all been almost whispering.

'My lord Abbot!' The young monk with the scarred face spoke for the first time. 'Send me with Gessho. I have my disfigurement and weeks of pain for which to claim payment.'

'I am to blame for that.' The priest took him by the hand and drew him close. 'Leave your revenge to me and be assured Shikanoko will pay ten-fold.'

Takaakira sat in thought for a few moments. To launch a major manhunt for the fugitives would signal clearly that Yoshimori was

alive, and rekindle all the Kakizuki hopes. It might be better to
follow the Prince Abbot's advice, at least in the first instance.

'Do nothing until I have spoken to his lordship,' he said, and
abruptly took his leave.

As he passed through the courtyard he heard the blind man's
voice again. This time he could make out the words.

*The dragon child, he flew too high,*
*He was still so young, he tried his best*
*But his wings failed and he fell to earth . . .*

Takaakira decided the old man needed to be questioned a little
more forcefully.

•

'Yoshimori escaped?' Lord Aritomo had been glancing impatiently
around the room in the former Kakizuki palace, but now he turned
his fierce gaze on Takaakira. 'Who rescued him? I'll burn them alive!'

'The girl they call the Autumn Princess, apparently,' Takaakira
replied.

'Ah, Hidetake's daughter. Only child, sixteen years old. Her
mother was Yoshimori's nurse.'

Takaakira was not surprised his lord knew this. He had a
phenomenal memory for details of lineage and relationships, the
complex interlocking of noble families. 'And a young man called
Shikanoko was involved, an acolyte of the Prince Abbot's, also the
nephew of the Kumayama lord.'

'Sademasa? He's an ally of ours now. Shikanoko is a strange
name. Why would he be called that?'

'I can't tell you,' Takaakira replied. 'All I know is, he is on his
way to becoming a sorcerer.'

'Is it his sorcery at work? Does that explain all these disasters,
I wonder?' Aritomo mused to himself, looking away from Takaakira

to the garden. Another typhoon was imminent, the sky almost as dark as night, a warm wind moaning over the curved roof and sighing in the eaves. Loose shutters were banging and a dog was howling. 'Surely the typhoon season should be over?'

Aritomo was of small, slight stature. Had Takaakira been standing he would have towered over him but he would rather face ten men at once, as he had at Shimaura, than bring bad news like this to his lord. Aritomo had already mentioned fire, which was an ominous sign. He liked to watch people burn. His punishments were as severe as his pride in his justice.

'Have we offended Heaven?' he dared to suggest, but Aritomo cut him off.

'We are carrying out the will of Heaven!' he shouted. He did not often raise his voice but when he did it was terrifying. 'If Heaven is displeased it is because we did not exterminate the whole nest of vipers but let the young escape! So, where is this snakeling?'

'His Eminence, the Prince Abbot, is of the opinion Shikanoko fled into the Darkwood and took Yoshimori with him.'

'I will cut it down and burn him out!'

Takaakira had said the same thing to the Prince Abbot but the truth was this was beyond even Aritomo's great power. The Darkwood stretched as far as the wild northern coast, over the spine of the country with its huge snow-covered mountains. He did not think it wise to mention this but instead said tentatively, 'There is a monk who wants to pursue them . . .'

'A monk? What good is a monk? Better to send a hundred warriors.'

'This monk is a warrior, and he can be sent without drawing attention to Yoshimori's existence.'

Aritomo clicked his teeth and shifted his jaw from side to side, a habit of his when he was thinking. 'Who thinks they can survive the winter with a seven-year-old boy in the Darkwood? Hidetake had an estate on Lake Kasumi; Nishimi it is called. It is quite remote, but easily reached from the west, from Rakuhara. If I were trying to get the young Emperor – not that he is the Emperor, let that be understood – to his Kakizuki supporters I would try to take him there, to my father's old home.'

'That is a brilliant deduction, lord,' Takaakira said.

'I am trying to think like a girl,' Aritomo replied. 'It is not hard. Where else would she go? I suppose she would try Rinrakuji . . . yes . . . her father would have told her to go there, but, finding it burning, she would turn towards the west.' He gave a slight, tight-lipped smile. 'I always try to see through the other person's eyes. Once you understand your enemy, you have defeated him. The Prince Abbot is a powerful force. I do not wish to offend him but nor do I wish to fight his battles for him. Let his monk go after the sorcerer. You may go to Nishimi. Take a few men, not too many. We don't want to frighten our princess away. I guarantee she will turn up there before winter, with her young charge.'

'You are sending me away from the capital?' Takaakira tried to sound reluctant, tried to hide the fact his mind was racing with plans for Hina.

'Your work here is mostly completed, isn't it?' Aritomo said. 'This mission, anyway, is far more important.'

'I will leave as soon as the storm is over,' Takaakira said.

He touched his head to the ground and began to shuffle out backwards. As the door slid open behind him, Aritomo said, 'By the way, the fellow you recruited as a spy, Kiyoyori's brother.'

'Masachika,' Takaakira said unnecessarily.

'Make sure he is not changing sides again. Is he doing anything useful? If not, you can get rid of him. No one's going to miss him.'

*Maybe I should*, Takaakira thought. *If he brings nothing useful back from Rakuhara, I will.*

The wind had risen to a shriek and the rain grew heavier as he went home. The ox baulked and the wheels of the carriage stuck in the mud. He got out and walked to the house, arriving soaked. Rain poured from the eaves. Behind its curtain, Hina waited on the verandah.

'I was worried about you,' she cried artlessly.

'Yes, another typhoon is coming. I got back just in time. We will be shut indoors for a few days. After that we are going away.'

He led her inside, as the servants ran to close the shutters and light lamps. He changed into dry clothes, noting with faint distaste how the room already smelled of mildew.

Hina knelt on the floor to pour wine for him. He thought she looked more mature, her face rounder, her figure slightly more curved. He longed for her to be old enough. Impatience coursed through him, made worse by the incessant wind.

'Come and sit by me. I have a headache.'

She moved closer. 'I will stroke it away,' she said.

He lay with his head on her lap while her small fingers ran over his temples and scalp. After a few moments she began to sing softly.

*The dragon child, he flew too high,*
*He was still so young*

'Where did you hear that song?' he asked, his eyes closed.

'I don't know. I like it, it's sad.'

'I heard an old blind man sing it today. Sesshin.' Did her fingers alter their gentle rhythm? 'Did you know him?'

He had never spoken to her about her life before and she did not talk about it, either to him or, as far as he knew, to anyone else. They both acted as though she had fallen from the moon and had no past and no earthly ties.

'I don't remember,' she said, dreamily.

Did she really not remember? Had shock and grief wiped out her former life? Or was she dissembling, in which case she was even cleverer than he thought?

Neither of them spoke for a few moments. Then Hina said, 'Where are we going?'

'To a place on the lake, quite far away.' *I must start making plans*, he thought. *How will I transport her there? I can hardly take her openly.*

He remembered Lord Aritomo's face when he talked of burning and tried not to think of the risks he was taking.

•

By the time the storm was over, Takaakira had decided Hina should travel in a palanquin, with Bara, the woman who looked after her. Bara was not the sort of person whom Takaakira would usually have employed, but most of the servants in the capital, men and women, had fled with their Kakizuki masters, and many of the rest had died in the fighting, the fires or in the famine during the summer. There was an annoying dearth of working people, maids, cooks, gardeners and grooms. Hina seemed to like Bara, and when he bothered to notice her, which was not often, he thought she was intelligent and kind.

There were two rather elderly, elegant women who instructed Hina in various arts and skills, but he did not want his travelling group to be too large, so he made arrangements for them to follow by boat across the lake from Kasumiguchi, when the weather allowed.

The palanquin waited at the stone step; the horses stood ready at the gate. It was daybreak and, throughout the city, roosters were crowing and birds singing in the gardens. After the storm, the air was fresh, almost chill, with the first hint of winter. Bara was on the verandah, but there was no sign of Hina.

'Where is the young lady?'

'She ran back to fetch something. She did not want to tell me what it was,' Bara replied. 'She gave me this.' She showed Takaakira the Kudzu Vine Treasure Store.

He nodded. 'I suppose she would not go without that. I will go and find her.'

As he went inside he saw Hina walking towards him. She was wearing travelling clothes and holding the same box that had been in her hands when he had first discovered her, in the deserted house. He had not seen it since then and had put it out of his mind. Now he realised she had kept it hidden from him for months. He thought he knew everything about her, controlled every aspect of her life, but here was something secret.

'You don't have to bring that with you. Leave it here. It will be quite safe. Most of the servants are staying in the house.'

She clutched the box more tightly and said, 'I have to bring it.'

'Show me what is inside,' he said, anxious to get away. 'I will decide.'

She said as she had before, 'No.'

'I am like a father to you and, one day, I will be your husband. I expect you to obey me. Let me see what is in the box, what is so important to you.'

She sighed in the same adult way as when he first met her and his heart twisted with love for her. He wanted to say it did not matter, she could take whatever she liked, but now he had insisted he could not back down.

She opened the box. The eyes lay there perfectly preserved, the dark iris, the black pupils, the whites glistening, viscous. They gazed at him unblinking, as if they saw everything he was and would ever be, and suddenly he could only see that too. He saw his outward appearance, his own body beneath the green hunting robe, his long limbs, his angular features, his dark hair and eyes. He struggled to find his own vision again, to see Hina, the room, anything.

The eyes peered deeper into mind, memory and soul. He saw the men he had tortured and killed, the intrigues and betrayals that had brought him to Lord Aritomo's side, the women abandoned, his wife in far off Yukikuni, the Snow Country.

'Close the lid,' he whispered to Hina.

Of course he should take the box at once to Ryusonji, to the Prince Abbot. For the eyes must be Sesshin's, plucked out at Matsutani, and now able to work some powerful magic. But then he would have to explain how he had come by them, and Hina would be discovered. His only desire, at that moment, was to get her away from the city where she would be safe.

'Don't ever show them to anyone,' he said, and hurried her into the palanquin.

# 5

# SHIKANOKO

The monk, Gessho, left the capital around the same time, early in the tenth month. He travelled alone, apart from a werehawk the Prince Abbot had entrusted to him. He did not need anyone else; he had complete confidence in his physical and spiritual powers and he had a certain contempt for Shikanoko, despising his animal affiliation, knowing he had never been through the extreme discipline of body and mind through which older monks, like himself, became initiates.

The lord, Aritomo's favourite, who visited the Prince Abbot, had claimed to be an initiate. Gessho had been laughing inwardly, so much that he had made a rare mistake in his writing. Now the memory made him smile again. Noblemen and warriors dabbled in the mysteries but the distractions of their lives, in particular their attachment to their women and children, prevented them from achieving true knowledge. No human ties held him down, and he knew his master, whom he admired more than anyone in the world, was the same. The Prince Abbot might seem to have great affection for his acolytes and his monks, but he would sacrifice them without hesitation in his pursuit of authority and knowledge.

His orders were clear. All three fugitives were to be killed. Yoshimori's head was to be brought back to the capital. The other two, the Deer's Child and the Autumn Princess, could be left to rot in the forest. *Let the animals he loves so much feed on him,* he thought.

He did not think it would be hard to track them down. He was armed, with sword, knife, bow and arrows. He had been provided with a fine horse – he was equally at ease on horseback or in prayer; in fact, riding put him in a state, both relaxed and alert, which he found to be quite meditative. He knew the Darkwood well, having lived in it for over ten years as a mountain hermit. The last the Prince Abbot had known of Shikanoko had been on the road to Rinrakuji, when one of the werehawks had apparently died, spending its last heartbeat to reach its master's mind and say farewell, and then outside a mountain hut, where he had seen the stag manifestation.

Gessho thought he could place the hut, recalling Akuzenji who had ruled the mountain in the days when he had lived there. He decided to go towards Rinrakuji, taking the coast road to Shimaura and then turning north. However, his road took him directly past Matsutani and on the spur of the moment he decided to call in there. Shikanoko had lived there for several months, the estate had been a Kakizuki stronghold under Kiyoyori, there were probably servants left who would be loyal to their fallen lord and sympathetic to his lost cause. There was a slight chance those he pursued might have taken refuge there.

He arrived at the residence just before dusk. He had heard it had been badly damaged by an earthquake at the beginning of the year. There were signs of new stonework round the lake, and repairs had started on the gate where he had seen Sesshin's eyes, but the eyes were no longer there, the house still stood half-burned, the former stables a pile of charred wood, while unused lumber lay on the ground, half-buried by rank autumn grass.

He thought the house was deserted, but he could sense the spiritual realm in a way others could not and slowly became convinced that there was *something* inhabiting the house. He wondered if it had been possessed by supernatural beings. He did not want to risk an encounter with them that would delay his mission, and had decided to ride on, a little disappointed as he had hoped to find shelter for the night, when he saw a man approaching, carrying a flask of wine, sprigs of bush clover and a pot filled with honeycomb.

He greeted the monk, making an awkward bow and saying, 'Welcome! I saw you coming and wanted to prevent you entering. The house has been taken over by spirits. They allow me to go in with gifts for them but anyone else is attacked. They are quite malicious, there have been several deaths.'

Gessho frowned. 'What sort of spirits are they?'

'From what I've been told I believe they are guardians, put in place by Master Sesshin when he lived here. Since his unfortunate downfall, they have become spiteful. Only he can control them, I fear, but will he ever return?'

'I am Gessho from Ryusonji,' the monk said. 'Sesshin is there now. He has become a lute player. My master with great kindness took him in and had him taught music. But even if he were here he would be no use. His powers are gone.'

'Lady Tama is growing desperate,' the man said, with unpleasant familiarity. 'The estate was granted to her, it has been her home all her life, but she cannot repair the house or live in it. Yet if she abandons it, she has nowhere else to go and no other choice but to become a nun.'

*Which no doubt would not suit you,* Gessho thought.

'I am just a retainer,' the other hastened to say, as though reading his mind. 'Hisoku is my name. I am completely at your service and would appreciate your favour.' He paused and then said, 'Well, I must make these offerings before the spirits grow impatient. But come with me afterwards to the house where we are staying. We would be very grateful for any advice a wise monk like yourself could give us. You must stop for the night before you ride on. Where are you going? Few people ride towards the Darkwood these days.'

'I will tell you later.' Gessho watched Hisoku approach the verandah of the ruined house. He had to step carefully between an array of household objects, brooms, cushions, pots, ladles, scoops, which had all obviously been flung out of the house. They had been crafted with care, they were once precious and useful, but for weeks they had lain neglected under sun and wind and now had something forlorn, almost repulsive about them. Gessho felt a shiver of disgust touch his spine. All that mess should be cleared away for a start, though he himself was reluctant to touch anything.

Hisoku went cautiously forward, stepped onto the verandah and placed his gifts just inside the open door. He struck a bronze bowl, which rang out in a clear, piercing note, and bowed deeply.

Gessho heard indistinct voices, making another shiver pass through his spine. His horse put its ears back and tried to spin away. While he was controlling it, Hisoku came back looking anxious.

'They asked who you were and, when I told them, they said you should go back to Ryusonji, at once.'

'I will deal with them,' Gessho said. 'In the morning, I will get rid of them.'

A shadow passed over their heads and the werehawk settled on one of the gateposts. It gave a shriek, and from the house came an answering yell. A small writing desk and an inkstone were hurled out, landing with a crash in the garden.

'Oh, don't make them angry,' Hisoku cried. 'It will only make things worse.'

'You have spoiled them and indulged them,' Gessho said, making little effort to hide his contempt. 'Spirits have to be treated with a firm hand and shown who is master.'

'At least they let me go into the house from time to time, and so far have not killed me. Many others have died.'

Gessho thought the situation was intolerable, and he told Lady Tama so, after she and Haru, in whose house they were staying, had served dinner. The food was surprisingly good, river fish with grilled yams, quail's eggs and bean curd.

'Your estate is obviously rich – you cannot let these errant spirits destroy it.'

'You must have been sent by Heaven,' she replied. 'Surely a monk of your learning and holiness can exorcise them. I am afraid it is my fault for treating Master Sesshin so badly, but I am filled with remorse now and ready to make whatever amends I can.'

'I will do my best to remove them, but I cannot stay long. I have my own mission.'

He asked if they had seen or heard of Shikanoko in the past few months.

'Who is that?' Hisoku replied.

'He was the Prince Abbot's acolyte,' Gessho explained briefly, 'but he did not return from a journey he was sent on in the fourth month. We fear he died and his Holiness wishes to retrieve his body, due to his great affection for him.'

'I have not seen him,' Tama said. 'Poor young man, I treated him badly too.'

Gessho wondered how genuine her remorse was. He discerned her character to be deep and possibly duplicitous.

'I will now spend some time in meditation,' he announced. 'I will speak to the spirits tomorrow, before I leave.'

•

He took fresh flowers and rice gruel from the morning meal. As he approached the house, he heard the spirits talking to each other.

'Oh, here he comes, the fine monk from the capital.'

'He thinks he will make us do what he wants.'

'We don't do what anyone wants, do we?'

'We only do what *we* want.'

Gessho laid the offerings down on the verandah, and knelt in silence, his eyes closed, summoning up all his spiritual strength, calling on the name of the Enlightened One.

'Oh, he's a mighty monk!'

'He is mighty! Are you frightened?'

'No, I'm not frightened yet. Are you?'

'Not yet. But I might be soon.'

They both began to cackle with laughter.

'I command you to leave this place,' Gessho said in a booming voice.

'Haha, he's wonderful, isn't he?'

'He's so wonderful, I think we should leave.'

'But we're not going to.'

'We should do something for him, though.'

'We could tell him what happens to him when he goes into the Darkwood.'

'What, that he loses his head? No, that's too sad. Tell him something nice. Tell him about the eyes.'

'Oh, yes, the eyes are nice. Gessho!'

'I am listening,' the monk replied.

'We can only leave if our master's eyes are replaced. Then we will go back to the gateposts where he first established us. There, that's fair, isn't it?'

'I don't really want to go back. I like it here.'

'I like it here too. It's much better than the gateposts. But don't worry, the eyes are lost. No one's ever going to find them. We can stay here forever.'

'They are not lost,' the second spirit said sulkily. 'Kiyoyori's daughter took them.'

'She's dead, isn't she? Kiyoyori's daughter, isn't she dead?'

'Maybe she is and maybe she isn't.'

There was the sound of a smack and a yell of pain.

Gessho said, 'So, if your master's eyes are found, you will leave the house and return to the gateposts?'

'Yes, we will have to.'

'But if you go into the Darkwood, you will not live to see it.' They both shrieked with laughter again.

Gessho next tried flattery, thanking them for their warning and praising them for their insight, but though that seemed to please them in so far as they did not throw anything at his head, he could not persuade them to move.

He returned to Haru's house, eager to ride on into the Darkwood. The spirits' warnings had not dissuaded him but rather the opposite. If he risked losing his head it could only mean someone of great skill and power was waiting for him. He relished the idea of the encounter.

'What happened to the daughter?' he asked Haru, finding her alone in the kitchen.

'Lady Hina?' Haru said. 'We believe she is dead. My lady has been grieving for her as well as her son, and her husband. You will have noticed how low her spirits are.'

'Could Hina have perhaps survived?'

'How would we ever know unless she found her way back here?'

'It will be more difficult to remove the spirits than I thought. The house will have to be abandoned. I suppose Shikanoko might be able to control them.'

'But you believe Shikanoko to be dead, don't you?'

Her eyes were fixed on his face and he regretted saying so much.

'The Prince Abbot must be a warm-hearted man to send a great monk like you in search of a pile of bones!' she said.

Gessho made no direct response but remarked after a few moments, seemingly idly, 'There are no men around apart from Hisoku. Where are they all? Where is your husband?'

'Most died at Shimaura. Their heads were displayed there all summer. The rest perished in the capital alongside Lord Kiyoyori.'

'Your husband among them?'

She nodded her head, looking away, like a woman not comfortable with lying, then busied herself with preparing food for him to take on the journey.

Gessho watched her all the time and made her eat one of the rice balls before tucking the rest away in his pouch. As he rode away he glanced back over his shoulder and saw her talking to a boy aged about ten, her son presumably. All morning, as he followed the stream towards the northeast, he was aware the boy was following him. He wondered if it was just some childish game – he remembered doing the same thing as a boy – or if Haru had sent him with some other purpose in mind. He did not trust her nor did he believe her husband was dead.

The path forked and Gessho went a little way up the left-hand branch and guided the horse into the bushes. The boy appeared and took the right-hand branch without hesitation. Gessho waited a short while and then dismounted, tied the horse to a tree and, silent and unseen, followed the boy.

The path looked tangled and overgrown but he could see that brushwood had been cut and dragged over it. Beneath the branches were signs it was well trodden. He did not want to go too far from his horse but just as he was about to turn back the undergrowth cleared and he found himself on top of a steep crag. Below was a small wooden fortress. On its roof flew the red banners of the Kakizuki and the three black cedars of Kuromori.

There was no sign of the boy. Either he had moved faster than Gessho thought or there was some secret path he had taken, maybe a tunnel he had slipped through, to get to the fortress.

Smoke rose from cooking fires and men's voices carried across the ravine. The morning sun glinted on spearheads. It outraged him to see this Kakizuki stronghold in what should have been Miboshi-held land, as far as Minatogura. So, the last of Kiyoyori's men were holding out here, that lying woman's husband, no doubt, among them.

He slipped back into the undergrowth and for a few moments considered what he might do next. He wondered what message the boy had taken to his father and if it had any bearing on him. He did not think the men would leave the safety of their stronghold to pursue a solitary monk. All the same, their defiance would have to be dealt with. The next estate to the east was Kumayama, where he had caught up with Shikanoko before. He decided he would make his way there in a few days, if he had not had any success in his early search. He would replenish his food supplies, and suggest to Sademasa, the uncle who had switched sides, that it would be in his interests to deal with the men at Kuromori.

He returned swiftly to where he had left the horse and continued up the left-hand path, riding for the rest of the day. At nightfall he dismounted, let the horse drink from the stream and graze, while he slept for a few hours, drifting in and out of dreams in which he was a boy again. He saw his mother's form in the distance and ran to catch up with her, but fell down through the earth, waking with a start. He rose shortly after midnight, as had been his custom for years, washed his face in the cold stream water, and sat in meditation, listening to the sounds of the night-time forest. Once a wolf howled far in the distance, and he heard the feathery sigh of an owl's wings as it returned to roost. He saw it blink its yellow eyes at the horse, which stood dozing, one hind leg locked in, beneath the owl's tree. The werehawk slept, perched on the horse's back. Overhead, the stars shone in a clear sky across which, from time to time, drifted swathes of haze. While it was still dark, the first birds began to pipe up, pigeons, doves, robins, and as day broke, thrushes. It was not the exuberant chorus of spring, but autumn's more melancholy song, breeding and nesting over, winter's cold ahead.

He recognised the track he had followed in his earlier pursuit of Shikanoko, but in his meditation he had become aware of a strange presence, some dark magic at work, so instead of turning southwards to Kumayama he decided to follow it, towards the north at first, and then, when the mountains rose as an impassable barrier, to the east. The horse grew more nervous, laid its ears flat against its head, and shied frequently, once at the skeleton of a stag lying at the foot of a huge cliff. Gessho stopped and dismounted to see if its antlers remained, for they had many uses in medicine and ritual, but the skull and the antlers were gone. However, the shoulder blades remained and he took them with him. After that he noticed more piles of bones, stripped of all flesh, mostly bleached white but some green with age. The horse trembled and jigged past them. The werehawk flew down and inspected them, its golden eyes glinting. They seemed to be mostly animal, but two or three were human, though no trace of clothing, armour or weapons could be seen. Foxes and crows might have picked their bones but a person, or people, must have pilfered everything else, unless it was the tengu who were said to dwell in the Darkwood.

On the fourth day the smell began, at first a faint whiff that from time to time hit his nostrils, then, as he felt he was growing closer to the source of the magic, an odour so strong it blotted out everything else. Gessho urged the horse forward and it obeyed reluctantly; they were both alert to every sound.

Gessho heard the wolves before he saw them, a snarling rush, a pad of feet. The werehawk screamed. The horse spun and bucked in terror, then reared upright, so high Gessho thought it was going to fall backwards. He leaped from its back, drawing his sword in the same moment. The horse lashed out with its rear legs and hit one of the wolves in the flank, hurling it a few paces away, where it lay whimpering. Gessho thrust his sword into the chest of the second as it came at him, teeth bared. The horse galloped off, crashing through the undergrowth. The third wolf backed off, snarling, then turned and ran away in the opposite direction.

Gessho pulled the bow from his back and set an arrow to it. The forest grew so thickly it was hard to shoot properly. The first arrow hit the trunk of a tree, the second skimmed over the wolf's back, making it somersault but it found its feet rapidly, and ran on. Gessho ran after it, branches lashing and clawing at him. The first wolf recovered from the horse's kick and pursued him, limping but swift, made fiercer by pain.

The smell grew fouler, making him double up and gag. He crossed a stream, jumping from stone to stone. The wolf caught up with him on the farther bank. It tried to attack him but its injuries hampered it, making it easy enough to dispatch with his knife. He drove it deep into the animal's throat and let the body fall into the stream.

He stood on the bank, trying to catch his breath, wondering if he was dreaming, for, though he had travelled all over the Eight Islands and had taken part in countless extreme secret rituals, he had never in his life seen anything like the scene before him.

Rocks like animals turned to stone; carved statues with lacquered skulls; animals that had once lived and were preserved, still lifelike; creatures that had never been conceived within a mother or borne by her, but that had a sort of life and that moved and walked and watched his approach with their blue gem eyes; birds that flapped the carefully woven and glued feathers of their wings and turned their empty skulls towards him.

He transferred the knife to his left hand and drew his sword with his right, raising it threateningly if any animal came too close. They made his skin crawl in disgust. He realised the pollution and profanity he was exposing himself to and feared he would never be clean again. Even when he had lived in the Darkwood himself, he had never imagined such a place might exist within it. *The whole thing must be cleared*, he thought. *We will scour it from end to end and rid it of this vile old magic.*

Muttering incantations, the hidden names of the Enlightened One, the secret words known only to initiates, he went forward into the clearing, towards a hut with walls of animal skins and a roof of bones. There was no way of approaching silently. The horde of animals and birds was already uttering cries and howls of alarm, which rang through the clearing and echoed back from the surrounding mountains. Gessho, characteristically, turned this to his advantage, shouting at the top of his voice, 'I am Gessho of Ryusonji. By the authority of the Prince Abbot, I command whoever is the source and cause of this abhorrence to reveal himself.'

He saw a movement on the slope behind the hut. Someone was hastening down, taking great leaps over logs and boulders. Gessho sheathed his sword and quickly put an arrow to his bow, muttering a binding spell to it. Even as he loosed it he felt an opposing magic and knew it would go wide.

He took another and shot swiftly. A crow-like bird with an eagle's head dived onto the arrow in mid-flight, grasped it in its beak and flew away with it. The werehawk pursued it, shrieking in rage.

Gessho flung the bow down and drew his sword again. He sensed someone behind him and turned, slashing wildly, but there was no one there, or no one visible, for he was sure he caught a shadow of movement.

Then the throb of magic in the air grew stronger, making him spin back. Someone – it had to be the sorcerer – was standing at the edge of the clearing, a few hundred paces away.

Gessho called, 'I command you, in the name of the Emperor, and his uncle, the Prince Abbot of Ryusonji, to submit to me and surrender any fugitives you are hiding.'

'There are no fugitives here,' the man replied. 'Only those who belong to the forest. You are the stranger, the intruder. Or maybe you are the fugitive, escaping from an unjust, cruel master. In which case, lay down your weapons and be welcome.'

'There is worse perversion here than I have ever seen in my life,' Gessho shouted in response.

'Then you do not know your master's heart,' the sorcerer called back, in a voice of extraordinary clarity.

Enraged, the monk rushed forward, sword raised. In his path the air seemed to shimmer and suddenly a young boy stood before him, a handsome lad with a calm face and an ethereal smile. Gessho halted, his reason telling him it must be an imp of some sort, or an illusion created by the sorcerer, his mind wondering if it could be Yoshimori himself, his heart pierced suddenly by the innocent beauty before him.

In wonder, he leaned forward to look at him and the boy smiled more widely, opening his mouth, showing small white teeth. From behind those teeth came a stream of tiny darts, spat into Gessho's eyes.

He knew at once that they were poisoned, for they burned agonisingly, like a bee's sting. As he gritted his teeth against the pain, he felt an invisible being leap onto his back and slip something round his neck, a leather strap that he struggled in vain to break. He arched his back and flexed his huge shoulders, and felt the leather give slightly. He thrust his fingers under it and wrenched it away. As he flung it down, the creature holding it came shimmering into view. It was another boy, the same age as the first and strikingly similar, although his features were distorted by an animal-like snarl.

Shadows blurred Gessho's vision, but his enormous strength was not yet exhausted and he still held his sword. It was protected by powerful prayers and would not be subject to the sorcerer's magic. He struck out at the second boy, only to see him leap into the air, like a monkey, out of his range. Then he realised imps surrounded him on all sides. They were tormenting him like a swarm of hornets, disappearing and reappearing, darting in to stab his legs, or flying past him leaving wounds in his neck and face.

He was bleeding from a dozen cuts but was still far from giving up, when he heard hoof beats and splashing and, turning, saw his horse cross the stream with Shikanoko on its back. The boys fell back, giving him a moment's respite.

'Shikanoko,' Gessho called. 'The Prince Abbot commands you to return to Ryusonji. Where is Yoshimori?'

'So, this is your horse, Gessho,' Shikanoko replied, leaping to the ground. 'But why have you come on this doomed journey? Now I'll have to kill you.'

'Come back with me and you won't have to kill me,' Gessho said boldly.

Shika replied, 'I would tell you to inform your master that I will return to Ryusonji for one purpose only, which will be to destroy him, but you will not see him again until he meets you in Hell.'

Gessho called to the werehawk, circling overhead. 'Fly, fly to Ryusonji. Tell my lord what became of me, and where.'

Shikanoko snapped his fingers and the bird flew to his shoulder.

Gessho knew then that all was lost and his life was over. He heard the voices of the spirits in Matsutani.

*We could tell him what happens to him when he goes into the Darkwood.*

*What, that he loses his head? No, that's too sad.*

And it was too sad, that he should be undone by sorcery and magic, he who had never yet lost an argument or a fight. His eyes filled with water, tears mingling with his blood. He remembered his dream of his mother.

'Stand back,' Shikanoko said to the boys. 'We will fight with swords, now.'

'Where is Yoshimori?' Gessho demanded, as they began to circle each other.

Shikanoko did not answer.

'Do you have him here? Tell me!'

The animals had fallen silent. Out of the corner of his eye Gessho saw the sorcerer approaching, his straggling hair, his gleaming eyes. He sensed his aura of magical power. He could fight a swordsman, he could strive against a magician, but he could not do both at the same time, and he feared the magic more than the sword. The animals, false and real, turned their heads towards their master, waiting for his command. It would only take one word from them and they would attack him. The idea of his death being delivered by their fake mouths, their wooden teeth, their metal claws, filled him with revulsion and desolation.

Shikanoko was becoming impatient, making ever fiercer thrusts and slashes, which Gessho parried, able with his greater strength to drive the younger man back. With each circle he moved closer to the watching sorcerer. When he judged the distance was right he leaped backwards, as though avoiding Shikanoko's sword and, turning in mid-air, his knife in his left hand, stabbed the sorcerer in the throat as he landed.

For a moment he regretted not taking the old man hostage and forcing Shikanoko to submit, but he did not think he and his troop of imps would be swayed by any human compassion. Gessho pulled out the knife, marvelling that the sorcerer's blood spurted red and warm like any other man's, and then turned to face Shikanoko.

•

A howl of fear and horror came from the animals, as their master and maker crumpled to the ground. Shikanoko, too, cried out in fury.

'The fight was between us! Well, now you will pay!'

His sword, Jinan, descended, slashing Gessho from shoulder to waist. Its returning stroke whipped through his neck, severing his head. The eyes stared for one final moment, blinked one last time. The body swayed and crashed like a felled cedar.

Shika stepped between the body and the head, ignoring the flowing blood, and knelt beside Shisoku, gripping his hands.

'You made me what I am,' he said, tears falling down his face. 'You brought me back from the edge of death and despair.'

The old man was beyond answering, he would never move or speak again, would no more create his strange creatures nor practise his powerful haphazard magic. The five boys gathered round.

Kiku said, 'He asks you not to waste that fine skull.'

'And to take care of the animals,' Mu added.

Then they all wept bitterly for their teacher, one of their five fathers, who, without knowing, taught them human grief.

They gathered wood and made a pyre, watching as the old sorcerer's corpse was reduced to ash. The animals howled mournfully and even the insects gave out strange sad susurrations, all the melancholy sounds of autumn distilled like one of Shisoku's potions.

Shisoku burned like grass, but when they rolled Gessho's body onto the pyre it smoked and sizzled like a roasting boar, the smell mingling with the fragrant cedar branches. Shika was going to burn the head too, but Kiku took it from him and buried it beneath a wooden marker.

The boys caught the werehawk in a net and killed it. Kuro removed the beak, skin, feathers and claws, and after boiling the bones carefully so all the flesh came loose, buried the remains deep so the animals would not dig them up. The boys ate many birds but some instinct told them this half-magic bird was poisonous. Kuro put the rest out to dry, adding them to the bones on the roof, covering them with the same net to keep the real birds away.

Shika was both sad and relieved the werehawk was dead. It could have been a useful spy, but on the other hand it might have switched allegiance at any moment and flown back to the Prince Abbot. He already knew that the birds were capricious and untrustworthy. He had the scars on his face to prove it. He mourned the death of Shisoku for many weeks, wishing he could have saved him, regretting that it was because of him that Gessho had found his way to the sorcerer's hut. The monk's appearance brought back memories of Ryusonji, of the Prince Abbot and his secret rituals. They made his skin crawl; he wondered if he would ever be free. At night he took out the mended mask, purified it with prayers and incense, and finally dared wear it again. Deep in the forest the stags bellowed and from their calls he learned the movements of the autumn dance and its knowledge of resignation and death.

•

The boys grew and learned with supernatural ability. Kiku knew how to embalm and lacquer and could combine secret elements to make spirit-returning incense. Mu could forge steel and mend broken tools. Kuro was familiar with all the poisons of the forest, the plants, and the five deadly creatures, which he kept live, and tried to recreate when they died. Ima was good at tanning skins, and also knew all the forest plants and insects, though he was more interested in their healing properties and in the many remedies Shisoku had recorded in his own idiosyncratic code. He and Ku mostly looked after the animals, fed them and patched them up. Morning and evening, all the boys repeated Shisoku's prayers and chants that protected the forest.

They played on the horse, a mature and good-natured creature that put up with them vaulting on its back and making it gallop round the clearing and jump over rocks and statues. They named it Kuri, for its coat was the same glossy shade as the chestnuts they collected in the forest.

Kiku, being the eldest, was usually the leader in all their activities and games but he had a cruel streak that made the younger boys wary of him. Mu had a better sense of humour – Kiku never laughed from amusement or pure joy but only in mockery – and was kinder to the two youngest. There was a rivalry between the two older boys that led them to test each other and fight constantly. Shika had to forbid them to use actual weapons; instead their tools of combat were the strange talents they had been born with, the second self and invisibility, and these they practised endlessly. They were like fox or wolf cubs, perfecting, through play, all the skills they needed for adult life. They seemed to age a year every month, and not a day passed that Shika did not recall Sesshin's words, *They will be demons.* Sometimes he reflected he should have killed them the moment they were born, but now it was impossible. They had become precious to him. Their strange skills intrigued and delighted him. He loved them as much as any man loves his sons, and he trained them as warriors' sons, for all the time he was planning strategies to take Kumayama.

About a month after the deaths of the sorcerer and the monk, when winter was setting in and the clouds filling up with snow, Shika was skinning a hare by the fire, watched hungrily by Gen, who had become enough of a wolf to eat real meat. He had just slit open the carcase and was scooping out the entrails when Kiku, also waiting by him, quivering like a dog at the smell of blood and raw flesh, said, 'Someone is coming.'

Shika could hear nothing besides the crackling of the fire and the panting of the animals, but he trusted Kiku's hearing which grew more acute every day.

He skewered the hare and set it over the coals to roast. 'Someone human? One or several?'

'One man on a horse.'

Shika wiped the blood from his hands and stood. 'Go to your positions,' he said quietly. They had prepared for unwanted visitors. 'Don't move unless I give you a signal.'

Kuro held Kuri's muzzle to stop the horse neighing. Ima and Ku summoned the pack of dogs and wolves and hid with them behind the hut. Kiku and Mu picked up the bows Shika had made for them and took up position, on either side of the ford across the stream, concealed behind rocks.

Shika waited in front of the hut, sword in hand.

A man rode across the stream on a dull-coated black horse, so thin Shika was surprised it could still move. Its hip bones stuck out, its back was swayed, its eyes sunken. He felt a pang of pity, for he recognised it as one of the famous Kuromori blacks, brother to Kiyoyori's own stallion. With that clue he identified the rider: Kiyoyori's retainer, Kongyo, husband to Haru, the children's nurse.

Kongyo looked as half-starved as the horse. He slipped from its back and walked forward warily, his hand on his sword. His eyes glanced quickly round the clearing, taking in the skulls, the bone thatch, the clumps of feathers, the drying skins. He seemed to master a quiver of disgust, and some other emotion when he smelled the roasting hare. The horse lowered its head and began to tear at the dying winter grass. Its belly gave a hollow rumble.

The two men stared at each other. Shika wondered if Kongyo knew him. It was over a year since they had both served Lord Kiyoyori at Matsutani. Kongyo had been sent to Miyako before Lady Tama had put out Sesshin's eyes and turned him and Shika out into the Darkwood, but in the previous weeks they had seen each other daily. Then, Kongyo had been the Kuromori lord's senior retainer and Shikanoko the dispossessed son of a dead warrior, tainted by his association with the bandit chief, Akuzenji. Now they stood on a more equal footing, determined by the fact that Kongyo was starving and Shika had food.

'Do you still call yourself Shikanoko?' Kongyo said finally.

Shika nodded briefly.

'I am Kuromori no Kongyo . . .'

'I know who you are,' Shika interrupted. 'How did you find your way here?'

'My son told me the monk Gessho had come back to find you. I sent him to follow Gessho; he marked the trail. He saw Gessho die and he recognised you. You may remember him: he is the same age as Lady Hina and often played with her and her brother. We call him Chika.'

'I remember him,' Shika said, wondering how none of the boys had noticed him. They must have been too involved in the fight with Gessho, and then distracted by the death of Shisoku. And hadn't Chika prided himself on being able to flit around Matsutani unseen?

'He said you overcame Gessho partly by magic,' Kongyo said, seeming to choose his words carefully as if anxious not to offend Shika. 'That you employed spirits in the shape of children who could appear and disappear.'

'Perhaps his shock at witnessing the death made him see delusions,' Shika replied.

'But you have children here? We hoped one of them might be Yoshimori. Why else would the Prince Abbot send Gessho after you?' Kongyo's eyes were shining with a kind of mad hope. 'If Yoshimori is alive, my lord did not die in vain.'

Shika hesitated for a moment, but then decided he had nothing to fear from this starving man, who had been Kiyoyori's most loyal warrior. 'Yoshimori is alive, but he is not here,' he said. 'I was with him, but I was injured, we were separated, and then, as your son saw, some other children came into my care and I could not leave them to go and look for him. Now it is nearly winter and soon it will snow. What can I do before spring?' He made a sign and one by one the boys appeared and gathered around them. Kongyo looked at them, taken aback by their appearance.

'They look as well suited to the forest as wolf cubs,' he said finally. 'But will a child of imperial blood, who has been raised in a palace, survive a winter in the Darkwood?'

'He is not alone,' Shika replied, thinking with sorrow of Akihime, and the horses. 'I can't explain everything to you now, but I believe he will be safe, until the time comes when he can be rescued and restored to the throne.'

'We all pray that Heaven will decree it,' Kongyo said solemnly. 'But I have something else to tell you that I hope will encourage you to act. The night my son returned and told me he had seen you kill Gessho, I had a dream about you. I saw you as tall as a giant. Your head rested on the mountains of the north and your feet on the southern islands. I woke convinced Heaven has a plan for you. Why else should you have escaped death so many times? You were believed to have died when you fell off the mountain. Akuzenji could have killed you but he did not. My lord, Kiyoyori, spared you alone among the bandits. Your uncle captured you but handed you over to Gessho. The Prince Abbot did not put you to death but took you as his disciple. You escaped from his service, and now I find you here, alive, in this place of death.'

'Maybe I have been lucky,' Shika said. 'You know a great deal about me.'

'After the dream I pieced together all I had heard about you. And my wife told me she thought, along with everything else, that you had a kind heart, for you looked after Sesshin with tenderness after he was blinded. But it is not your luck, nor your kindness, important as they are, that will defeat the Prince Abbot. It is what you have learned from him, from Master Sesshin and from the sorcerer who made these strange creatures.'

'You are very flattering,' Shika said, 'but what exactly are you proposing?'

'We are confined to the fortress at Kuromori. We are starving – you can probably see that. We are not besieged as such. There is a secret passage through which individuals can slip in and out, but the roads all around are guarded and we believe Aritomo is planning another attack on the fortress. Masachika, Kiyoyori's brother, tried once before, but my son brought us a warning.'

'He seems a useful lad.'

'He is fearless and quite clever,' Kongyo said with pride. 'All Masachika's men were wiped out, but Masachika was spared. He agreed to switch sides, so we let him go – well, he is Kiyoyori's heir and Kakizuki by birth. None of us wanted his blood on our hands. We believe he went to the Kakizuki in Rakuhara, to tell them of our plight, but we have heard nothing since then. But we feel Aritomo will launch an attack on Rakuhara in the spring. If you have taken your estate of Kumayama by then, you can relieve us at Kuromori and together we can surprise the Miboshi from the rear.'

'And how will I take Kumayama with no men?'

'If Sademasa is dead his men will accept you for your father's sake. Matsutani is unoccupied, as it has been taken over by guardian spirits, but you will be able to deal with them. You will force a wedge between Miyako and Minatogura and cut off their supply lines.'

'You have great confidence in me! How am I going to kill Sademasa?'

'With your imps and their magic, of course!' Kongyo gave him a sly glance. 'Do you think that hare is cooked by now? You can think it over while we eat.'

# 6

# AKI

Akihime worried about her monthly bleeding, how she would manage in the forest, what she would tell Yoshi, if she should stay away from him – surely Emperors had nothing to do with such polluting matter as menstrual blood – but the bleeding never came. She watched the monkeys mating, giving birth, nursing their young ones, the babies playing with the long pink nipples, and her own breasts ached and swelled. The old matriarch treated her like one of her many daughters, groomed her hair, which was growing out matted and wild, and gave her the pick of the seeds and fruits they collected, as summer warmed the forest.

When it rained, the monkeys sat in the hot spring and, one damp day, Aki took off her clothes and joined them. She could see that she had lost weight, her limbs no longer pleasingly plump as they had been in the palace. Her collarbones protruded, but her stomach was very slightly rounded.

Yoshi had abandoned his clothes – once the rains began they were always wet – and he was turning as brown as a beech nut all over. His arms and legs were covered in cuts, scratches and old scars.

He never spoke of Kai – Aki wondered if he had forgotten her. He had joined the pack of young males and climbed and played with them all day long, coming to understand their chattering and facial gestures, sleeping in a heap with them at night. When they fled the palace Akihime had expected him not to be able to walk, but now he ran everywhere.

She tried to speak to him as much as possible, concerned he would forget human language. She sang to him and told him stories. The lute came alive under her fingers, enchanting the monkeys. He told her the names he had given to them. He called the matriarch Ame, and the strongest male Hai, his two special friends Shiro and Kemuri.

He rode the horses and persuaded Shiro and Kemuri to join him on their backs. To Aki's surprise, both horses put up with it. Yoshi never used saddle or bridle; he seemed to have developed a way of communicating with the horses as easily as with the monkeys and both of them, even bad-tempered Risu, did whatever he asked them, in a spirit of play.

The rains ended and the great heat of summer began. One day, the monkeys seemed unusually agitated. They gathered in groups, clutching each other, sniffing the air, peering towards the northwest and chattering anxiously. Now and then, one of the young males, Shiro or Kemuri, bounded outwards, calling threateningly, though Aki could not see or hear anything strange.

'What's wrong with them?' she asked Yoshi, who was sniffing the air too.

'Someone is coming, someone they are afraid of.'

Aki heard a pitiful crying, the noise the monkeys made when one of them died. It sent the group around her into even greater distress. A young female, in particular, began screaming in response. The distant crying became louder.

'It is one of them,' Yoshi said. 'One who was lost, a long time ago. I think he is tied up. He cannot come closer. He is calling for help.'

'Don't go,' Aki said. 'It might be a trap.'

'But he needs help.'

'Someone might be using him as a decoy,' she warned.

'What is a decoy?' Yoshi said, puzzled, but Aki did not have time to answer, for the whole monkey group, led by Ame and Hai, began to leap through the trees towards the sound. Kon hovered overhead, and Risu and Nyorin followed, with Aki walking between them. At first, the monkeys seemed cautious and furtive. They were drawn to the crying as if they could not help themselves, yet they were afraid. They wanted to keep silent, but the closer they came the more their fear made them chatter and squeal. The monkey who was tied up cried even more loudly but now with a heartbreaking note of hope.

As they came to the edge of the clearing, Aki could see him clearly, a half-grown male, with a green collar round his neck, tethered to a post driven into the ground. The elders, Ame and Hai, made warning noises. Hai ran the length of the troop, cuffing the young males into submission, but Shiro and Kemuri dashed forward with Yoshi on their heels. Aki cried out to him, as he and the two monkeys ran into a net and were immediately trapped in its invisible, unbreakable mesh. The monkeys squealed in the same note as the captured one. Yoshi was shouting in rage.

The watching monkeys howled in horror, jumping in the air, thumping the ground with their fists. Aki was about to run forward, but Ame held out a hand to restrain her, tapping her own belly and then patting Aki's. Her bright knowing eyes held Aki's for a moment. When the girl looked away she saw that three men had come into the clearing. They wore strange red clothes, and, even though two were fully grown, something about them, their hair maybe, was childlike.

Aki recognised the third. It was the boy who had performed with the monkeys at Majima.

He went to the tied-up monkey and gave him some food as a reward, which the monkey crammed into his mouth, chortling gently as though pleased with himself. His previous distress had completely disappeared. When his owner untied him he jumped straightaway onto the boy's shoulder and began grooming his hair.

The other two men went to the net, shouting in surprise. 'A good catch! Two young males and a boy!'

Again she wanted to run forward – but she was naked, and unarmed. She had left her knife and bow, along with Genzo, in the cave. The men carried knives and sticks. She remembered the men on the road to Rinrakuji. Shikanoko had appeared from nowhere and killed them, but if he had not, they would have raped her, and probably murdered or enslaved her. She was afraid these men would do the same. Then Yoshi would be lost completely. No one would know who he was and he would soon forget.

And she was stunned by something else: the realisation that she was carrying a child.

She looked at the horses, who stood watching, ears pricked forwards.

*I will follow Risu*, she thought. *Kiyoyori's spirit will tell me what to do.*

Risu did not move, nor did Nyorin. Yoshi did not look towards them, he did not utter another word, even when his captors questioned him. They were too amazed at their catch to notice anything else in the trees on the edge of the clearing.

'He must have been brought up by monkeys,' the boy marvelled. 'Maybe he never learned to speak.'

Aki remembered him at the market on the shore. He had seemed bold, kind to his monkey partners, and not slow to laugh at himself.

Perhaps Yoshi would be safer away from her. He could disappear among the people of the river bank. The Prince Abbot would never look for him there. He would be searching for a young noblewoman with a boy, and, of course, he or his monks would quickly recognise her. But none of them would have seen Yoshi since his first haircut ceremony at eighteen months of age. He would be indistinguishable from all the other orphans and urchins struggling to survive. She would always know where to find him, with the monkey boy.

But watching him and his two friends being bound with ropes and led away made her heart break. Risu bent her neck and nuzzled Aki's shoulder. She took that to mean that Kiyoyori's spirit approved of her decision. She leaned against the mare's flanks.

'Hurry up and be born,' she whispered. 'I need you. You and my child will grow up as brothers.'

From far above she heard a low fluting call and, looking up, she saw Kon, half gold, half black against the deep blue summer sky. The werehawk fluttered its wings as though to say farewell, and flew off after the Emperor and his monkeys.

•

The lute lost its gold embossing and its mother-of-pearl inlay and went into a sulk. It refused to release its tunes, no matter how many times Aki took it out, polished it, cajoled it, even prayed to it. She wanted to be able to play it on her journey to give her a plausible reason for being on the road.

She knew she had to leave the Darkwood. She did not think she would survive a winter there, even with the hot springs, not with a baby, which she had calculated would be born in the first month. She did not want to give birth in the forest, alone. She needed other women around her to help her bring the child into the world. The only place she could think of to go was her old country home at

Nishimi. Even though it was years since she had been there surely the women, who had known her as a child, would look after her.

She began to make preparations, took the saddle and bridles from where she had stowed them in the cave and wiped the mildew from them, washed her clothes in the spring, and tried to comb out her hair. It had grown enough to tie in bunches, like a country girl's. She bound the ends with strands of the tough reeds that grew in the shade around the pools.

The day she planned to leave, the monkeys' behaviour puzzled her. They did not go out into the forest as they usually did from dawn, but stayed close to the caves, chattering nervously. The horses, too, seemed restless, their coats dark with sweat.

By midday the air had turned metallic and the sky had darkened. The tops of the trees began to lash against each other, as a hot wind drove through them. Then rain fell, the drops sizzling as they hit the rocks and the ground. The surface of the pools churned. Soon the rain was so heavy it seemed to rise from the earth as much as it fell from the sky.

The whole world was made of water. Every tiny channel filled and overflowed. The wind howled more fiercely, driving the rain horizontally. There was a crack like thunder and the ground shook as a huge cedar was torn up by its roots and thrown down.

The monkeys huddled together, surrounding Aki and Ame, whimpering at every loud noise. Risu laid her ears back and stamped nervously. Nyorin stood motionless, gazing out at the curtains of rain.

When the typhoon had passed, they ventured outside. The earth steamed and a carpet of leaves and branches covered the ground. The monkeys investigated the fallen tree warily, finding grubs and insects in its roots. The storm had delivered a feast as well as destruction.

Everything was washed clean and the air was sweet-smelling. One by one, the forest birds began to sing.

The young monkeys went out exploring, though they were still subdued and nervous after the capture of Shiro and Kemuri. Aki led the horses to find new grass. She could hear the monkeys chattering ahead of her and could follow the trail of twigs and seed casings they let fall from the trees. The horses grazed on the long lush grass. Aki was hungry too. She sucked on roots of grass and chewed unripe beech mast, but these made her stomach ache even more.

They were following some sort of path, made by foxes or deer, that led towards a stream. There were tracks in the mud, paw prints and hooves. The monkeys' chattering grew louder and then she heard a cry of pain. Risu neighed in reply and rushed forward, barging past Aki, almost knocking her down.

On the far bank stood a young stag, its new antlers shining and hard. She held up the bow and twanged it. The stag raised its head and sniffed the air, then turned and bounded away. She realised she was trembling with fear. For a moment she had thought the stag would transform into Shikanoko. Had it been just an animal or was it a sign, a symbol perhaps of the child they had made together? She was suddenly certain it was. *I am carrying his son*, she thought with a mixture of sorrow and joy. And then she remembered her dream, the night she had fled the palace. She had seen the same stag in her dream.

The rocks at the stream's edge were covered in debris from the storm, washed down by the torrent of water, left there when the stream subsided. The monkeys had been sifting through it. Now there was red blood on the rocks and one of the monkeys was sucking its paw and crying. The others were jumping round something that gleamed on the rocks and making warning noises as if they had surprised a snake.

Risu gave a long groaning whinny and for the first time Aki saw her belly ripple as the unborn foal kicked and struggled within her. She went to the mare and tried to soothe her. The monkeys scattered at her approach and ran back to the treetops. Behind her, she could hear their noise as they made their way home.

Before her on the rock lay a sword, without a scabbard. Its hilt was wrapped in snakeskin, she could see it through the mud. Its blade had a few drops of blood on it. The monkey must have picked it up and it had cut him. She looked around uneasily. Where could it have come from? Had some warrior dropped it? Was he hiding somewhere or lying dead in the stream? She wanted to run like the monkeys and leave it where it lay, but Risu would not move.

Aki bent down warily. Risu gave her an encouraging nudge and she picked up the sword by its hilt. It alarmed her but at the same time it comforted her. It cleaved to her hand as if it belonged to her. It was a long time since she had held a sword. It reminded her of her father and the training he had given her secretly, at Rinrakuji, so no one would know the girl they called the Autumn Princess could fight with a sword, like a man.

Now Aki held the sword, Risu was happy to follow her, walking so close she almost stepped on her.

*It must be Lord Kiyoyori's sword*, Aki thought. *His spirit recognises it. As soon as the mare saw it the foal quickened.* She was shivering despite the warmth of the sun. The sword had been recast and repaired, but by whom? Why had the stag been at the stream? Was Shikanoko nearby? Was he alive or dead? Was it longing or fear that made her tremble?

She walked swiftly back to the cave, on the way stopping at the bamboo grove and cutting a length of bamboo to act as a scabbard. She washed the sword clean of mud and blood and slipped it into the scabbard, attaching it with a cord she wove from kudzu vine and strips of bark.

The old matriarch, Ame, watched her carefully, but kept her distance, as did all the monkeys. The sword frightened them. Aki tore her under-robe into wide strips and wound one of them round her head, covering her face except for her eyes. With the others she bound her legs so the saddle would not chafe them. Then she strapped the lute to Risu's back, saddled Nyorin and using a tree stump climbed up onto him.

She bowed her head to Ame and said aloud, 'Thank you for everything.'

The old monkey sat impassively, her child at her breast, as Aki rode away from the Darkwood, back to the world of swords and horses and men.

# 7

# YOSHI

Yoshi was told to walk, his hands tied in front of him, the rope held by the oldest man, who carried one of the monkeys, Shiro, wrapped up like a bundle, on his shoulder. The other man held Kemuri, while the boy followed with the decoy, holding the cord attached to its collar in his left hand. The monkey gambolled happily, turning somersaults, jumping on to the boy's shoulder, then down to the ground again, chattering all the time.

Shiro and Kemuri screeched in rage and fear and tried to bite and scratch, but the men did not grow angry with them, just laughed in amusement, preventing the monkeys from hurting them, or themselves, with practised gentleness.

The boy made monkey noises, the kind of sounds an older male might make to young ones, slightly threatening but mostly reassuring. Yoshi began to trust him.

They followed the same path to the edge of the forest that Yoshi had taken with Aki and the horses, and came to the old hut and the place at the stream's edge where he thought Shikanoko was going to cut off his head. He couldn't help shivering. There was no sign of

Shikanoko. Maybe he was still alive. Or maybe the horses had killed him, after all, and wolves had carried away his bones. He wasn't sure if that made him sad or not. Shikanoko had saved him and Akihime from the men, who he knew were going to do something bad to them, and Yoshi had liked him then, but Shikanoko had been prepared to kill him with the same sudden ruthlessness, and liking had turned to distrust. He knew his father was dead, which was why he was now Emperor, though he must never tell anyone, and his mother was dead too, and Akihime's father and mother, and probably everyone he had ever known, except Akihime and Kai. He felt sorry for them all; he wanted no one else to die, ever.

In the same cave from which Risu and Nyorin had come galloping, the monkey hunters had left a packhorse with two baskets, and another smaller basket, which contained fruit, loquats and apricots. The boy fetched water from the stream in a bamboo flask, put his hands together and said a prayer over it, and gave it to Yoshi so he could drink. Then he fed him fruit, cutting small slices with a sharp knife and putting them in his mouth. The other men did the same with Shiro and Kemuri, holding them on their laps.

The monkeys were not so distressed that they could not eat; indeed, the food calmed them and they allowed the men to put them on the horse, one in each basket. Yoshi was lifted onto the horse's back, where he sat between the baskets, gripping the mane with his tied hands.

It must have been quite dark inside the baskets, for Shiro and Kemuri went quiet, as if they had fallen asleep. The boy walked beside the packhorse, the tame monkey on his shoulder, and told Yoshi the names of everything they saw, rock, stream, tree, sky, speaking slowly and clearly as if he were teaching him. After a while Yoshi repeated a word, horse, and the boy shouted in delight.

'He can talk! He can talk!'

Yoshi continued to say the words after him, and there was something quite funny about learning to speak again, not in the polite, complicated language of the court, but in the direct slang of the riverbank people. He started laughing with every word, and the boy laughed too, and then the men joined in, feeding him words he suspected were rude, arse, cock, balls. Saying them made him feel like a different person, stronger and older.

'Sarumaru,' the boy said, pointing at his own nose. 'My name is Sarumaru.'

'Kinmaru,' the older man said, and the younger one, 'Monmaru.'

'Yoshi.' He could not point to himself as his hands were tied, but he bobbed his head up and down.

'We will call you Yoshimaru.' The boy laughed. 'We all have children's names. We don't cut our hair, we never grow up. We are children of the road.'

Yoshi liked the sound of that. He remembered seeing Sarumaru at Majima and wanting to be him. All the time he had been practising acrobatics in the forest with the wild monkeys and the two horses, he had been pretending he was that boy. Now he had met him, and was going to live with him. He was young enough to believe in the magic of his own thinking. It made him laugh again.

'Children of God,' Monmaru said and drew something quickly in the air with his index finger. The others murmured as if they were saying a prayer.

They travelled on through the day, resting in the shade for a while when it was hottest. Yoshi's hands were untied then and, afterwards, no one seemed to think they should be tied again. There were few people on the road, though they saw farmers in the distance working in the fields, bringing in beans and rice. Most of the paddies were already harvested, and crows gathered in them, picking up every last grain, every insect left exposed. Herons stalked on the banks, looking for frogs. Now and then Yoshi caught a glimpse of gold and black plumage and knew the werehawk was following him. He was not altogether happy about it. Kon was too closely connected with his former life and knew who he really was. Though most people would not understand the werehawk, maybe someone would, maybe the Prince Abbot who, Yoshi knew, was his most dangerous enemy.

In the afternoon they came to the crossroads where the ghost had not let Risu and Nyorin go any further, and Shikanoko had summoned it back from the shores of the River of Death and into the foal. He remembered the mask, how it had transformed Shikanoko into a supernatural being. He shivered again.

'Usually we would go from here to Rinrakuji,' Sarumaru said. 'The monks there always used to welcome us and watch our performance. Then they would give us food and shelter. They were good people and truly devout. But the temple was burned by the Miboshi in the early summer and has not been rebuilt.'

'And when it is rebuilt the Prince Abbot will install his monks there and bring it under the sway of Ryusonji,' Kinmaru said gloomily. 'The Prince Abbot does not approve of us or our monkey brothers.'

*It will never occur to him to look for me among them*, Yoshi thought.

That night they camped under the stars. Yoshi was used to this – he often slept in a tree with Shiro and Kemuri and he loved being outside at night, listening to the insects and the night birds, talking to the rabbit in the moon, and gazing at the vast sweep of stars, wondering why some shone more brightly than others, where they went in the day, what lay behind the dome of the sky.

Mon lit a fire of green wood and fragrant leaves to keep away mosquitoes. It was only partly effective, the insects whined around their heads, but none of the three tried to swat them. They either brushed them away or watched them as they pierced the skin to suck blood.

'So does the Secret One feed us,' Kinmaru said and again Mon drew the sign in the air.

'We have taken a vow not to kill,' Sarumaru whispered to Yoshi later. 'All beings desire to live, just as we do, and the Secret One has a plan for each life. Who are we to interfere? Our deaths, and everyone else's, are ordained by him and already written in his book. If we interfere with that we are destroying the harmony and beauty of his great design and letting evil into the world.

'Men fight and kill endlessly. When they are not engaged in battle great lords hunt for sport taking thousands of birds and animals, in a single day, decking themselves out in the plumage and fur of the slaughtered, fletching their shafts of death with feathers taken from the dead, so heron kills heron, pheasant, pheasant. Even monks and priests, who claim to follow the Enlightened One, kill for their esoteric rituals, using monkeys' skulls and wolves' hearts. But there is another kingdom, alongside this world in the midst of which we live, both within and without it, where there is no killing, no blood-soaked earth. By refusing to take life, we bring it into being.'

Yoshi listened, without saying anything, but in his heart he knew it was in this kingdom that he wanted to live.

'You understand everything, don't you?' Sarumaru said.

Shiro and Kemuri whimpered in their baskets. Sarumaru's monkey, whom he called Tomo, sat next to them, occasionally pushing a piece of fruit under the lid, chattering to them reassuringly. Yoshi wondered if they would ever trust Tomo, after he had deceived them so shamelessly. He had seen the monkeys in the forest outwit each other, either in play or to steal a piece of food, but he had not expected one of them to dissemble so successfully, at the command of a human.

He nodded in reply to Sarumaru's question and smiled tentatively at him.

'So, you haven't lived with the monkeys all your life? You were brought up among people. Where did you come from?'

'I don't remember,' Yoshi said.

'I was brought up in the village of Iida,' Sarumaru said. He didn't seem tired at all; he was prepared to chat all night. 'My family sold me to the acrobats when I was a child. I don't remember much about it. I had a lot of brothers, some older, some younger. Everyone blamed me for everything; they would take it in turns to give me a beating. I tried to run away, I remember that, but someone always came after me, my father or my older brothers, and then I would get two beatings, one on the spot and one when I got home. I still cried when I left. I didn't know any better. But Mon and Kin have always been kind to me, and now Tomo is my best friend. People laugh when we perform together; they love our act. And when I hear them clap, I'm saying to my brothers in my heart, "You couldn't do this in a thousand years!"'

'You must forgive them,' Kinmaru said.

'Mmm, I do forgive them, but I can't help feeling pleased all the same.'

'Stop chattering and let us get some sleep,' Monmaru said wearily.

Saru gave an exaggerated sigh and seemed to fall asleep, but a little later he said suddenly, 'My oldest brother was very clever. He could use an abacus and even read and write a little. He went to Miyako and worked in the house of a great lord. But I don't know what happened to him after that. One day I'll go and find him and I'll say, "Look, older brother, Taro, look what I can do. You never imagined that back in Iida, did you?"'

'Go to sleep!' the two older men said simultaneously, and then both laughed.

'Come here, Tomo,' Saru said, and, clasping the uncomplaining monkey in his arms, he settled down. With his other arm he pulled Yoshi close to him. He did not say any more, awake, but Yoshi heard him call out in his dreams.

Two days later they came to Aomizu, where Aki and Yoshi had said goodbye to Kai and the women of the boats, at the end of the third month. He had thought about Kai every day since then and wondered if he would meet her again now, hoping he would, hoping she would not give him away, but he couldn't see any of the beautifully decorated boats or the musicians or the elegant lady who had talked to him so strangely about pollution.

They went to a house by the lakeside where the other monkeys of the troupe had been left, in a yard at the back. Some women lived there, perhaps they were the older men's wives, though Yoshi never really knew for sure, with three or four very young children. The house was noisy; the women shouted and sometimes burst into song, the babies cried, the toddlers were always falling over and sobbing, the monkeys screamed from their enclosure, especially when they saw the new arrivals.

Shiro and Kemuri were kept in a separate cage. They moped and fretted, and Yoshi spent a lot of time with them, comforting them and feeding them titbits. There always seemed to be plenty of these; the acrobats received many gifts for their performances, and the merchant guild, which oversaw the markets around the lake, provided the house and looked after the families.

Gifts were of food and rice wine, lengths of cloth, gold statues, lacquer bowls, and sometimes even copper coins, which no one was quite sure what to do with. They seemed magical and slightly dangerous in their power to transform goods and transfer ownership. They were usually buried in the yard, as a charm to keep the monkeys safe.

But despite the charms and the titbits, Yoshi worried about Shiro and Kemuri. 'They're so sad,' he said to Sarumaru. 'They want to go back to the forest. We should take them back.'

'It's good that they are sad,' Saru said. 'That way they'll come to depend on you and me and that makes them easier to train. They'll get over it, they'll forget their old life and this will be all they know.'

*Like me*, Yoshi thought. Already memories of his early childhood were fading. Perhaps he really had died on the river bank, and now he had been reborn into a new life. Nothing seemed real before the morning when Shikanoko had intended to kill him, the horses had saved his life and he had lived in the forest with Akihime and the monkeys.

The acrobats had travelled throughout the summer, attending the great festivals as well as the fifth-day markets, held on the fifth, fifteenth and twenty-fifth of each month. Now as the typhoon season began they stayed close to home, training the new monkeys and practising with the old.

Training was slow, but the men and Saru were patient. They were never cruel, though they would reprimand any misbehaviour with a sharp word or a tap on the culprit's paw, just as they did with the toddlers, who, Yoshi saw, were also being trained to learn the same tricks and be as attentive and obedient. Shiro and Kemuri were smarter than the children and learned more quickly. This seemed to please them, and they began to seek rewards and to treat the toddlers like younger, less intelligent monkeys, with a mixture of concern and scorn.

They still squealed with delight and ran to cling to Yoshi whenever they saw him, but they also came to love Sarumaru, as all the monkeys did. They competed for his attention and tried to please him, not only for the rewards but for his words of praise, the way he scratched their heads and let them climb all over him.

Saru developed an act where he would appear among the crowd, covered in monkeys, a walking fur creature with six faces. Children ran screaming, as if from an ogre, only to run back in delight as Saru peeled off the monkeys, one by one, and sent them somersaulting into the air.

The first typhoon of the year came roaring across the lake, dumping rivers of rain from its dark heavy clouds, turning day to night, flooding the roads around the lake and tearing roofs from the flimsy dwellings. When it was over everyone set to, cheerfully, to dry out clothes and bedding, repair houses, clean mud from walls and floors. Typhoons were a part of life, to be dealt with like everything else, with the mixture of good humour, patience and gratitude that was the acrobats' way.

At the end of the ninth month, when the storms had cleared and the fine weather of autumn had set in, they began to get ready to take to the road again. The monkeys were excited; the women seemed sad and relieved at the same time; the children cried because they wanted to go too. Saru told Yoshi they would take him, Shiro and Kemuri.

'We will go down to the Rainbow Bridge for the fifth-day market, then back here for the fifteenth. That way, if you don't like it, or the new monkeys get upset by the crowds, you can stay here with them until we come back for the winter.'

'I will like it,' Yoshi said, 'I know I will.'

'You have to be prepared for anything, think on your feet, turn a bad situation into something good. All eyes are on you: people waiting for you to make them laugh, many hoping you will fail so they can jeer at you. It takes a bit of getting used to. And sometimes the monkeys just don't want to perform. They are in a bad mood or they don't feel well, it's windy or the crowd are hostile. Then you have to make the best of that as well, not freeze up or show that you're flustered.'

'You make it sound hard, but it looks so easy,' Yoshi said.

'Wait till you see me in a real crowd,' Saru boasted.

Yoshi opened his mouth to say he already had, at Majima, but then he thought better of it. He did not want to say anything about his past. He just wanted to be the boy who had grown up with the monkeys.

That night the old man who had visited the women's boat, the day Akihime and he had left it, came to the house to share the evening meal. Yoshi pretended he hadn't seen him before but he remembered him well and all the things he had said. He kept his head lowered and stayed at the back of the circle. The old man prayed before the start of the meal, the others responding in low, reverent voices. Then he served food to each of them, as he had done before, as though he were one of the women, not an old priest who deserved respect. Yoshi felt the old man's keen eyes on him, but he did not speak to him until the end of the meal when he began to say the words of blessing for the departure.

Kinmaru, Monmaru and Saru, who were leaving the next day, shuffled forward and knelt before him. Saru reached out behind him and pulled Yoshi alongside them.

'He is coming with us,' he said. 'And he needs blessing more than anyone, for he is alone in the world, apart from us.'

Yoshi knelt, keeping his head down, and felt the old man's hands rest lightly on his hair.

'May the Secret One guide you always,' he said quietly. 'You have taken a different path from the one set out for you, but it will lead you back to the same place, in the end.'

*I hope not*, Yoshi thought. *I want to be a monkey boy like Saru. I don't want to be Emperor.*

# 8

# SHIKANOKO

'If you wait for winter to be over, months will be lost,' Kongyo said to Shikanoko. 'But act now and take Kumayama and it will be you the snows protect.'

He had made the same argument several times since he had arrived at the hut and found Shika and the boys there. 'You are not going to stay in the forest forever. You may as well leave now. Besides, we cannot survive another winter in Kuromori. We must either escape or take our own lives. You would have us fighting for you, seventy men.'

'Half-starved,' Shika said, with scorn.

'Desperate and capable of anything. Hungry not only for food but, even more, to avenge Lord Kiyoyori.' Kongyo clutched his belly. The hare meat had been too rich for him and had given him the gripes. He had had to dash off into the bushes several times and now his face was pale and, despite the chill of the winter afternoon, sweaty.

'You're in no condition to travel,' Shika said. 'Rest another day. Let your horse recover too. I will discuss your suggestion with the boys.'

He wondered what Kongyo made of them. The older man had seen them all now, though he could not tell them apart. He had expressed surprise to Shika that they looked so ordinary. They had lost the striking beauty of their early months and now resembled the thin, half-grown boys found in any small village of the Eight Islands. It pleased Shika. He could see it made them less conspicuous. They had become unremarkable. They blended into the forest and he was sure they would blend into any surroundings in the same way.

'I think I will lie down,' Kongyo said, 'but not in that accursed hut.' Cold had driven him the previous night to sleep there among the skulls, masks and bones, the animal skins and the feather cloaks, but he complained of nightmares the next morning.

'The hut is not accursed,' Mu said. 'It is something you don't understand, but there is no need to fear it.'

The warrior looked astonished to be addressed in this familiar way.

'Nightmares are messages from the gods, like dreams, like the one you yourself said you had,' Mu said. 'You should be grateful for them. No harm will come to you, unless Shikanoko commands it. Go and lie down inside. It's too cold out here. Ku will keep you company and the dogs will keep you warm.'

Shika was surprised by Mu's words too. They were more than he had ever heard Mu say at one time and there was something strange about them. He realised Mu was copying Kongyo's intonation and vocabulary, as though he were absorbing them directly from the older man's brain. The boys were like the forest leeches, the tiny monsters that Shisoku, and now Kuro, tried in vain to replicate, that sucked blood and consumed earthworms whole.

Ku led Kongyo into the hut, followed by two real dogs and three fake ones. After a few moments the boy came out again and joined Kiku by the fire.

'He is lying down,' he said, 'but he needs to sleep to get better.'

Kiku was boiling something in an iron pot; it smelled of aniseed and rhubarb root.

He took the pot from the embers and poured the contents into a small cup. He handed it to Ku. 'Give him this. It will settle his stomach and send him to sleep.'

'You aren't planning to poison our guest, I hope,' Shika said.

'Of course not,' Kiku replied, adding, 'I will if you want me to.'

'Thank you,' Shika said. 'I'm pleased to see you all being so considerate.'

'If he is soundly asleep, you can discuss your plans freely with us,' Kiku replied. 'We are not being considerate, we are being practical.'

'We are learning a lot from him too,' Mu remarked. 'What did he mean when he said *avenge*?'

'It is when you want to harm or punish someone who has injured you. Payback. It is a sort of justice.'

Mu considered this reply for a few moments. Then he said, 'Who was Lord Kiyoyori?'

'He was a great warrior; they called him the Kuromori lord. Kuromori is the fortress where our guest, Kongyo, has been hiding out.' After a pause Shika said quietly, 'He was one of your fathers.'

'As well as Shisoku?' Kiku had been listening carefully to every word. The boys knew nothing of normal human relations, so they accepted this more or less unquestioningly.

'You had five fathers: Shisoku, Kiyoyori, a bandit chief, Akuzenji, a great sage and magician, Sesshin, and me.'

Kiku and Mu both laughed.

'You are very young to be our father,' Mu said. 'Aren't you?'

'You are our older brother,' Kiku added.

'I am old enough to make children,' Shika said. 'And, I suppose, the way you are growing, you soon will be too.'

The boys were silent while they thought about this. They were both smiling. Kiku gave Mu a shove; Mu punched him back.

*Something else I will have to teach them about,* Shika thought. *But who will they marry? Will they take human wives? And what will become of their children?*

'Do you want to avenge Lord Kiyoyori too?' Mu asked.

'I do, and I will. But first I need to kill my uncle,' Shika replied, and thought, *And then I have to destroy the Prince Abbot, and,* he hardly dared to put his longing into words, even silent ones, *find Akihime and marry her, and restore Yoshimori to the throne.* Kumayama was the first step towards all these goals.

'This is Kumayama, where my uncle lives now.' He picked up a charred stick and began to draw a rough map on one of the firestones. 'This is where I grew up.'

He was suddenly besieged by memories, the daily humiliations and cruelties, the helpless rages he had fallen into, when everything went red and he wanted only to lash out, to kill and destroy, the sense of outrage and injustice that the man who was supposed to care for him, who held his inheritance in trust, wanted him dead and was driving him either to suicide or to an act so uncontrolled it would justify his execution.

He was deeply grateful he had fallen over the cliff, grateful to the stag that had cushioned his fall and to the men who had spared his life and in their own strange way nurtured and educated him: Shisoku, Akuzenji, Kiyoyori, Sesshin. They had all been like fathers to him, so, in a sense, he was the boys' older brother.

He became aware they were watching him, the stick still in his hand, waiting for him to go on. He said, 'I was there briefly a year ago. I was a prisoner, so I could not see how my uncle had changed and fortified my old home since I had been away – it is nearly two years ago now.'

Kiku said, 'Explain *uncle*.'

'My father's brother. If Mu had a child, you would be the uncle.'

This made them laugh again. Kiku dug Mu in the ribs with his elbow. 'Who is your child's mother going to be? One of those bitches you sleep with? Your children will be puppies!'

Mu hit him and they tumbled over on top of Gen, waking him from sleep. He leaped to his feet, snarling and snapping. Shika silenced all three with a look, and went on. 'This is how it was when I lived there – we called it a castle but really it was just a fortified house, with a high wooden fence around it, a ditch in front of the fence, strong gates at front and rear, and a watchtower. Just inside the rear gate are cells with wooden bars, and between them and the house is an open space where horses are exercised, and where anyone who annoys my uncle is put to death.'

He moved on to the adjacent stone. 'The stable is also at the rear. It's an open shed with ropes for the horses to be tied to. Fodder and water buckets are stored here. The roofs are all thatch, reeds, not bones.'

'It looks interesting,' Mu said. 'It's so big!'

'Yet it is small compared to many other fortresses,' Shika said. 'Small but very important. Difficult to take, easy to defend.'

'I'd like to see it for myself,' Kiku said.

'I hope you will soon. Now leave me in peace for a while.'

Shika went to the hut, saw that Kongyo was deeply asleep, and took the shoulder blades of the stag from where they lay on the altar. He had found them among Gessho's possessions after the monk's death. He said a few words of prayer over them and placed them in the embers of the fire. Then he sat cross-legged, meditating, until the sun set. At nightfall he took the cooled blades from the ashes and studied the fine hair-like cracks that had appeared on them. He felt he heard their message in his own bones.

Kongyo did not wake, but that night his horse became colicky from the sudden large amounts of food it had eaten so hungrily, and, despite Shika's efforts to save it, it died in the early hours of the morning. As soon as Ima woke and saw it, he set about skinning it. The head and hooves were buried, like Gessho's skull, to rot away the flesh. The mane and tail were cut off and given to Ku, who washed them carefully and combed them out, so they regained in death the rippled silkiness they had lost in life. The dogs and wolves sat around, mouths dripping strings of saliva. When the belly was slit open Ima threw the still-steaming entrails to them and they snapped and fought over them.

Shika re-read the message in the shoulder blades.

'I am going to Kumayama,' he informed Kongyo. 'If you're well enough to ride, you can take my horse. Return to Kuromori and tell your men to expect me. I suppose I will be there in about ten days. If I'm not, you can assume either we are snowed in or I have failed. Your future will be in your own hands then.'

'You will not fail,' Kongyo said, his eyes gleaming. 'We have my dream to trust in.'

'You're taking us with you, aren't you?' Mu said.

'Are we going to kill the uncle?' Kiku asked.

'Do you want to?' said Shika.

Kiku looked around at the bone-thatched hut, the animals assembled from various parts of corpses, the carcase of the dead horse, and said, 'I don't mind.'

The middle boy, Kuro, emerged from the forest carrying a pole across his shoulders from which hung several small bamboo cages. He set them carefully on the ground and crouched down, his eyes fixed on his oldest brother.

'What have you got there?' Shika asked.

'A giant centipede, two golden orb spiders, a viper and a very angry sparrow bee,' Kuro replied.

Kongyo shuddered. 'I would rather face a hundred Miboshi warriors than any one of those – apart from the snake. Snakes are easy to kill, you just lop off their head.'

'This one is half-asleep,' Kuro interrupted him. 'It will not wake up properly till spring.'

Kongyo ignored him. 'But insects! You don't see them until it's too late. They lie in wait in dark corners and shadowy places, and they sting and bite without discrimination or mercy.'

'Are all warriors cowards when it comes to insects?' Kiku said. The question sounded innocent but Shika knew Kiku intended to insult Kongyo and unsettle him.

'It is not a question of cowardice,' Kongyo began.

Shika held up a hand to calm him. 'We will find out.' A plan was beginning to form in his mind. 'Kiku and Kuro will come with me. Mu, you will stay with Ima and Ku.'

'I'd rather go with you,' Mu pleaded.

Shika did not want the two older boys squabbling and competing, leading each other into danger. Kuro was the most solitary, usually, but he had more respect for Kiku than Mu did, and his poisonous insects could be useful. 'I'm trusting you to look after your brothers and the animals. You must be what Shisoku was, the guardian of this place, of the forest.'

This seemed to placate Mu a little and he was smiling as he went away from them and joined Ima, who was now slicing strips of flesh from the dead horse and threading them on sharpened sticks. Mu began to place these on forked poles above a bed of embers. Shika hoped the weather stayed fine. If the meat dried quickly, it would feed the boys for half the winter.

The sparrow bee had found it could not escape and was buzzing furiously against the narrow bamboo bars. Kongyo looked at it, fascinated and horrified.

'Lord Kiyoyori's brother, Masachika, was half-dead from what he said were bee stings when we found him after the attack. He told us they had stung him on the orders of the guardian spirits at Matsutani. I thought he was hallucinating but maybe they were giant bees like this one.'

'He would not be half-dead but all dead,' Kuro replied. 'But there are many kinds of bees, wasps and hornets, and many different levels of poisons.'

'Aren't you afraid they'll sting you? Then you'd be all dead!' Kongyo laughed, but no one else did.

'I let them sting me,' Kuro said. 'I am immune now.' He flashed a look at Kongyo from his expressionless eyes. Sometimes, Shika thought, the boys looked like insects themselves, and he recalled how they had been born from eggs in cocoons, like spiders.

•

Kongyo left at dawn the next day, and shortly afterwards Shika, Kiku and Kuro set out for Kumayama. Shika took his bow and Jinan, and the mask, in the seven-layered brocade bag, together with the shoulder blades of divination. The boys took knives, ropes, bows and venom-tipped arrows, and other poisons, carefully sealed with stoppers of beeswax in bamboo tubes, and the sparrow bee in its cage. It had gone silent and Shika thought it was dead but Kuro assured him it was sleeping; he had blown a drowse smoke over it and could waken it when it was needed. Gen, the fake wolf, came with them, inseparable as always from Shika.

They moved silently and swiftly through the winter forest. In low shady places the ground was white with frost. Most of the trees were leafless, only pines and cedars still deep green. Kuro said after a while, 'Will that man let our horse die of hunger, too?'

'It may happen, though I hope not,' Shika replied.

'If the horse was hungry, why didn't it run away and find food?'

'I expect it was tied up, somewhere inside the fortress. Horses suffer along with men in war. They are killed in battle, they starve in sieges.' Shika found himself thinking of Risu and Nyorin, and the foal. The time of its birth must be getting close. He wondered what would happen when it was born, if he would ever see it, ever know if Kiyoyori's spirit truly dwelt within it.

'And then they get eaten,' Kiku added.

Kuro said, 'Do men get eaten too?'

'Sometimes, I believe, starving, desperate people will eat the flesh of a dead human being, but generally not.'

'Why do horses submit to men? Why do they let themselves be tamed? I would never do that!' Kuro declared.

'I suppose it is in their nature,' Shika replied. 'Something in them longs to be mastered. When they submit, they feel safe. Most horses don't get to choose their owners. They are passed from hand to hand. If a new owner treats them properly, and feeds them, they obey and are content. There are many people like that in the world, you will find. They are happy to obey. But, like horses, while most will follow, a few others always want to be in front.'

'It is not *our* nature to follow,' Kiku said.

Shika laughed. 'I don't believe it is. Yet you and Mu are leaders over your brothers, and you all obey me, and must, until you are fully grown and understand how the world works.'

'Who do you follow?' Kuro asked.

'No one,' Shika said, after a pause. 'I am the horse that wants to go first.'

'What happens when several horses all want to be in front?'
Kiku said.

'They jostle and nip each other. Eventually they fight.'

'So, you are going to do a little jostling and nipping against your
uncle?' said Kiku. 'And then you will fight?'

'Exactly.'

•

On the evening of the fourth day they came to a place Shika
remembered, at the foot of a steep cliff. He found the stag's skeleton,
and marvelled that wolves had not scattered the bones. He helped
the boys build a rough shelter a short distance away, and shared
out the last of the food they had brought with them.

It was hardly enough to satisfy their hunger. Kuro set traps
for rabbits and then declared he was going to forage for nuts and
mushrooms. Shika told Kiku to keep watch, and went back to the
place where he had come tumbling down the cliff, expecting to
die. The stag had broken his fall, and in saving his life changed it
beyond imagination. Now he wanted to thank it, he needed to tell
the mountain, Kumayama, he was back, and he wanted to test the
power of the mask.

Kneeling beside the skeleton, he placed the mask over his face,
prepared to face the Prince Abbot, should he be taken into his
presence, and to remove the mask swiftly if he had to. It was over
a month since Gessho had died, and, even though the werehawk
messenger had been killed too, surely the priest would have divined
what had happened by now?

Shika breathed in and out slowly, bringing his thoughts under
control. Little by little, his mind quietened, and he felt his spiritual
power awaken. He was aware of everything around him. He could
feel the forest in its deep winter sleep, he knew its dreams. He spoke

to it and to the mountain, thanking them both for sustaining him, seeking their protection. Then he spoke to the stag. He saw it tread proudly through the forest, its antlers held erect, its nose twitching, its eyes bright. He heard its autumn cry of yearning and loneliness. He expressed his sorrow at its death, his gratitude for all it had done for him. He called it Father and told it his name, Shikanoko, the Deer's Child.

He felt no sign of the power of the Prince Abbot, nor was he taken into the realm of Ryusonji. The mask had been broken, he had been broken, but, in the mending, they had both become stronger.

He rose to his feet and began the movements of the deer dance. For a while he was transported by it. He thought he saw inside Kumayama, his uncle made cruel by his fear of attack from without and rebellion from within. He saw the fortress weighed down by hatred and repression; one push and it would fall. He saw the two great lords, the leaders of the Miboshi and the Kakizuki; he realised he could become greater than either of them. Kongyo's dream came into his mind as though he had dreamed it himself. He straddled the Eight Islands. He would put the rightful Emperor on the throne and rule through him.

But then his feet faltered. He did not know the rest of the movements, he had never learned all the steps. And now Shisoku was gone, there was no one to teach him. In that moment of doubt, he felt the pull of Ryusonji, as though the Prince Abbot had woken and turned his attention towards the east. He felt a surge of longing and regret. He saw all the wisdom and knowledge that dwelt at Ryusonji and longed to be part of it again. He missed the admiration and affection he had so often heard in the Prince Abbot's voice. He wanted to hear that voice again at the same time as he cringed from it.

He felt the bound beginning, as it had before, the stag's leap that would take him there in minutes. He would not go inside, he would just stand on the verandah . . .

He tore the mask from his face, his heart pounding.

That night he hardly dared sleep, lest he should meet his former master in his dreams. Instead his thoughts circled and returned over and again to all he needed to learn.

In the morning there were two rabbits in Kuro's traps. They skinned and cooked them, fed the entrails to Gen, ate one and took the other with them. The boys scaled the cliff easily, thanks to their skills in balance and leaping. They let down a rope for Shika to climb. Then the three followed the route along which he and his uncle had tracked the stag, two years before. He was in familiar territory now – he had roamed over this mountain as a boy, and, though there were no paths and it looked as if no one had been here in the past two years, they made swift progress. Did his uncle no longer hunt in this part of the mountain? Was he afraid he might meet Kazumaru's angry ghost?

The boys went ahead, for they could move more silently than Shika, and Kiku's sharp hearing would warn them of anyone in their path. They slept briefly for two nights, not making fires, sharing the rabbit, cracking and sucking the bones, then huddling together against the cold. Shika noticed that Gen's body, once as chill as the elements he was made of, now gave out a natural warmth.

Around midday on the third day Gen sniffed the air and said indistinctly, 'Dead people.'

At the same time Kiku appeared.

'There's a strange noise ahead,' he reported. 'Flapping and rustling.'

'Can you hear that noise, Gen?' Shika whispered.

The fake wolf turned his head and pricked the right ear, which had always worked better than the left.

'Birds,' he said.

As they cautiously approached the source of the noise, Shika saw Gen was right. A flock of crows swarmed over some thing, or things, mounted on poles. The birds did not caw, or even squabble. They simply pecked, relentlessly and silently, every now and then fluttering up into the air and then returning.

At the sight of Shika and the boys, they flew off into nearby trees, where they made the boughs hang down heavily, and watched with greedy, inquisitive eyes.

The things heaved and swayed, as if they still lived, but it was not life within them, but life feeding on them. Countless maggots teemed over them.

'That's a head,' Kuro said with interest. 'And those must have been internal organs. You can still see their shape and texture.'

'Not so unlike an animal's,' Kiku said, equally fascinated. 'There is the heart, liver, kidneys and look, even the private parts!'

They both laughed callously. 'Still with a mind of their own,' Kiku said. 'Even in death.'

One of the crows cawed, breaking the silence. Gen growled and snapped at it.

'Is this the sort of thing your uncle does?' Kuro asked.

'This looks like his work,' Shika replied.

'No wonder you hate him.'

Kiku said quietly, 'It takes many years to grow to a man, doesn't it? Many times longer than for us?'

Shika nodded. This man had been an adult. What remained of his hair suggested he might have been forty years old: forty years of human life, with all its complexities and intricacies, reduced to slabs of meat exposed in the forest, food for grubs and crows.

'Who was he? Did you know him?'

There was nothing to identify the dead man. Sademasa had many retainers and even more farmers, from whom he extracted tax in produce and labour. It could be any one of them, executed and dishonoured in death. How fragile were even the strongest of men.

'Can you find out?' Kiku persisted.

'How do you suggest I do that?' Shika said.

'You could use that mask, in the bag,' Kiku said.

'How do you know about that?'

'I saw you, the night before we climbed the cliff. And I've watched you before, at the hut. You put it on and go into some other place. Do it now.'

'Kiku's got a plan,' Kuro said, smiling in glee, seeming to read his brother's thoughts.

'We could tease your uncle a little,' Kiku said. 'Make it easier for you to kill him.'

With some reluctance, Shika took the mask from the brocade bag. The crows cawed wildly and flew up in one dark cloud. He prayed briefly, steeling his mind against his former master, and placed it against his face. He found himself on the bank of the River of Death, as when he had met Kiyoyori's spirit. He saw again the deep dark water and heard the splash of oars. Then he heard someone call out to him, in anguish and relief, using his childhood name.

'Kazumaru! Help me!'

'Who are you?'

'I am Naganori, your friend's father.'

Shika's throat closed up in horror and pity. His eyes were hot. He forced himself to speak. 'What happened to you? Where is Nagatomo? Is he dead too?'

'He was still alive when I died. Sademasa, your uncle, made him watch my agony and humiliation. My love and fear for my son has bound me to this place. I cannot cross the river until I know his fate, and until we are both avenged. My lord, Kazumaru, make your uncle pay. Make him suffer as so many have. People long for your return. Many of us regretted not helping you last year. We all knew who you were. Can you ever forgive us?'

'I will when my uncle is dead and I hold Kumayama,' Shika replied.

'Most of your house still consider themselves Kakizuki. They hate the Miboshi who are now our overlords. Some of us whispered about it, it was only talk, but we were betrayed. Sademasa has informants everywhere. My punishment was a warning to others.'

Shika had less time on this occasion before he felt the Prince Abbot's attention drawn to him. He saw his eyes turn and seek him out. Twice he had aroused the priest now. The Prince Abbot would not ignore such provocation. He would move against him, would send someone else after him. Not a lone monk, but armed warriors, maybe the whole Miboshi army.

'Farewell,' he said to Naganori. 'Today I will avenge you, Sademasa will die and your son will be saved. If I fail, you and I and Nagatomo will cross the river together.'

He took the mask from his face. The boys were watching him with more than usual respect, their black eyes wide and gleaming.

'How much did you see and hear?' he asked.

'We heard everything,' Kiku replied. 'We must go at once and save your friend's life.'

'That's a good thing, isn't it?' Kuro questioned.

'Of course it is!' Kiku gave him a cuff round the ear.

Kuro frowned. 'Sometimes I'm not sure when it's right to kill and when it's right to save a life.'

'Trust Shikanoko,' Kiku said. 'Just kill anyone he says.'

'Feel free to get rid of someone who's attacking me, even if I haven't specifically told you to!' Shika said, as they began to run.

'I just hope I don't get it wrong.' Kuro sounded unusually worried.

'It doesn't matter much,' Kiku assured him. 'Everyone dies in the end.'

•

The fortress stood on the slopes of Kumayama, overlooking a long finger-shaped valley, through which ran the Kumagawa. On either side of the river, on every inch of flat land and on terraces cut out of the hillside, rice was grown, but all the fields were bare now, covered in their winter blankets of mulch, dead leaves and manure, the higher ones white with frost.

Shika, Kiku and Kuro came down Kumayama at dawn and hid themselves in thick bushes, from which they studied the fortress for a long time, without speaking. In the year since Shika had last seen his childhood home, it had been even more heavily fortified, with a new palisade of sharpened logs around it and a higher watchtower on each corner. All cover had been cleared around the palisade and guards stood in the watchtowers and at the gates. All day, groups of men rode on horseback around the open area, and set up targets and practised archery.

Labourers were working on some huge earth-moving project, excavating tons of soil and moving it, bucketload by bucket-load, to the further edge of the clearing. Shika realised they were digging a moat and building ramparts for further defence. He wondered why it would be necessary, now the land from Miyako all the way to Minatogura was in the hands of the Miboshi. What was his uncle so afraid of? Was the control of the Miboshi not as secure as it appeared? Was Sademasa, like all turncoats, prey to guilt and suspicion? He had certainly made his fortress impregnable.

There were two strange machines on platforms on the ramparts and any rocks that were uncovered were lugged up to their base and added to the piles amassed there.

'Catapults!' Kuro said. The boys made small ones from strips of leather that they chewed for hours to render pliable.

'Could you get inside?' Shika whispered to Kiku.

'Kuro and I can get in at night,' Kiku replied. 'We can scale the fence at the corner, jump across to the roof and burrow through the thatch. No one will see us.'

'And then what?' Kuro said.

'Shika goes inside and meets his uncle. While they're talking we'll tease him and unsettle him. Then he gets killed.'

'That's more or less what I had in mind,' Shika said. 'A few details need working out. What about his men? I can't take them all on, single-handed.'

'We don't know about them,' Kiku said. 'They're your concern. You deal with them.'

'I will be disarmed as soon as I go in,' Shika said, thinking aloud. 'If I'm not killed immediately. You must take my sword, and get it to me somehow. I'll carry my bow and knife. They will think it strange if I arrive completely unarmed. And I must offer them something they want, so they keep me alive.'

They spent the short winter day watching and listening. Shika mapped the fortress as he remembered it and Kiku's sharp hearing enabled him to place its inhabitants within it. At the end of the day, Sademasa rode out to inspect the earthworks. They could all hear him clearly as he shouted at the foremen, complaining about the slow progress and the poor quality. His face lit up as he saw the piles of rocks and the catapults. He went to the nearest machine, dismounted and caressed its throwing arm, which was tied down, with a rock loaded in place. Then he peered down the valley, as if assessing how far the rock would be hurled.

Kiku and Kuro watched him with bright eyes. Shika's hand gripped his bow, but his uncle was beyond its reach and anyway wore a helmet and protective leather armour around chest and neck.

'We know him now,' Kiku said.

'You could offer him Gen,' Kuro suggested.

'Gen?' Shika said, surprised.

The fake wolf whimpered anxiously.

'He likes strange artefacts, man-made devices. Show him Gen and tell him you have the power to make things like this – artificial animals and men. He does not have enough warriors. He needs an army.'

Night fell swiftly. There was no moon and the sky was covered with low clouds that threatened snow. Shika made the boys embrace him before they left, and the feel of their thin, scarcely human bodies against his filled him with tenderness. He wondered if they felt the same, if they were like Gen and would grow more real through affection.

He could not see them once they had moved three feet away nor could he hear them. No sound came from the fortress, no clamour as intruders were discovered. The night remained peaceful, bitterly cold.

Shika barely slept. Gen crawled close to him but could not warm him. By daybreak he was so cold he could hardly walk. He forced himself to stand, to stretch, to run on the spot, in order to get the blood flowing into his extremities. He wondered where the boys were. He could see no sign of entry through the roof. He would have to trust that they were inside.

When he could move freely, he took up the bow and the brocade bag with the mask, slung the quiver with its twelve arrows on his back and, with Gen at his heels, walked swiftly down to the fortress.

Men were stamping their feet and rubbing their hands together at the gate. Just inside burned a fire in an iron brazier. For a moment

Shika thought how appealing the warmth was, and wanted nothing more than to sit by it for a while and thaw out. But he put aside this and all other distractions, hunger, fear, hope, revenge, and concentrated fully on what had to be done to bind the will of those surrounding him to his own.

He called at the gate, 'I am Kumayama no Kazumaru, known as Shikanoko, only son of Shigetomo. I have come to pay my respects to your lord, who is also my uncle, and offer him my service and a magic gift.'

One of the men moved towards the gate and peeked through it. A look of shock crossed his face and he stepped hurriedly back to confer with the others. They spoke quietly but Shika's hearing, though not as sharp as Kiku's, was keener than most humans' and he could hear them clearly.

'It's that wild boy who turned up last year, claiming to be Kazumaru.'

'Are you sure? He was taken away by the Prince Abbot's men to be put to death.'

'It's him.'

'Kazumaru? He died in the mountains two years ago.'

'But he was alive last year. Some people said they recognised him, Naganori for example.'

'Naganori! Look what happened to him!'

'What'll we do?'

Several men came to the gate to peer at him.

'Look at him,' said one. 'He's a vagabond, been living rough in the forest and wants to get out of the cold. Cut his throat and bury him without saying anything. Save us a mountain of trouble.'

'I'm not going to murder the old lord's son,' said the man who had first come to the gate.

His name suddenly came back to Shika and he called to him. 'Tsunemasa! Let me in and tell my uncle I am here.'

Tsunemasa approached the gate but the man who had wanted to cut Shika's throat pushed him back. 'What's the gift?' he said.

'I remember you, Nobuto,' Shika said quietly. 'I will not forget that you suggested murdering me.'

'You'll be praying for my swift knife later today,' Nobuto threatened. 'When our lord gets you in his hands, whether you are Kazumaru or some vagrant, you'll be begging me to kill you. Show me what the gift is.'

'Open the gate and I will,' Shika said.

'Who's with you?'

'No one. Just me and my gift.'

A man called from the watchtower. 'He has come alone.'

Nobuto drew back the huge bolts and the gate swung open.

Shika stepped inside and Gen followed him closely, his nose nudging the back of his legs.

'What is that?' Nobuto exclaimed.

Shika was so used to Gen by now he had forgotten how strange the fake wolf looked. Now he saw him afresh, the blue gem eyes, the human tongue, the wolf-skin coat through which the skeleton showed.

'This is my gift,' he said, feeling Gen quiver. 'It is an artificial wolf. I believe my uncle loves all strange devices. I can make these things for him, and more. I can make men.'

'I will take the creature to show him,' Nobuto said.

'By all means, but I must go with him. He is easily alarmed and quite fierce.'

'Wolves don't scare me, alive or not,' Nobuto said with a laugh.

'I do not want him destroyed, through stupidity or carelessness,' Shika said.

Gen snarled, showing his tongue and his artificial teeth. The thick wolf fur on his neck bristled. Nobuto stepped back as the creature lunged at him.

'Wait here,' he said. 'I will inform the lord.'

After Nobuto had left, Tsunemasa said, 'Come and sit by the fire, you look frozen.' Shika shook his head. He would accept nothing that was his uncle's; he would take it all when the usurper was dead.

He stood just inside the gate without moving. One by one people came out to take a look at him, men and women, warriors and maids, but he did not return their curious stares. With one part of his mind he was wondering where Kiku and Kuro were, but otherwise he was preparing himself for the coming confrontation.

Nobuto finally returned. 'My lord will see you and examine your gift. Give me your weapons.'

When Shika handed over the bow, the quiver and the knife, Nobuto looked at the bow carefully and then studied Shika with narrowed eyes. But all he said was, 'No sword?'

'A sword is little use in the forest,' Shika replied. 'I have not been fighting men for the past two years. But I have been hunting.'

'Hmm. What's this?' Nobuto had taken the seven-layered brocade bag that hung at Shika's waist and was opening it.

'It is a mask made from a deer's skull.'

'The one the monk was so thrilled to see? You should give this to the lord too.'

'No one can wear it but me. It destroys the face of anyone else who puts it on.'

Nobuto closed the bag without looking in it and handed it hurriedly back to Shika. He ran his hands over him to check for any other weapons, opened Shika's mouth and peered inside, pulled at his tangled hair. Shika submitted without emotion. He felt Nobuto's fear, the fear warriors had for anything they did not understand, especially the world of magic and sorcery. And he felt gratitude again that he had been taken out of their world and given the chance to know another, of great richness and strangeness, beyond human imagination. Fate dictated every man's path in life. His uncle's cruelty had been an instrument in his destiny.

*For that reason I will give him a swift death*, he resolved.

The crowd in the yard parted before him as he followed Nobuto into the fortress, Gen, panting slightly, at his side.

He remembered his old home well, despite the changes that had been made to it – the barred windows, the internal doors that had to be unbolted, at a password, and bolted again behind him. He glimpsed trap doors and sensed concealed rooms. He thought suddenly of his father, the tengu and the fateful game of Go. He heard the click and rattle of stones. And then a sharp recollection of his mother, whom he had not seen since he was a child, rose in his mind. Usually, he had only the haziest of memories – the feel of a robe, an outline against an open door – and he had never understood why she had left him, but he suddenly felt assured that she had never forgotten him and that she had been praying for him all this time. It was with a softened heart, then, that he faced his uncle.

Sademasa wore the same armour, leather laced with deep purple cords; his sword lay close to his hand. He sat on a raised platform, with no other concession to comfort or luxury than a thin straw mat. Fifteen retainers were in the reception room with him, five along each side wall, five at the back.

Shika knelt, lowering his head to the ground. Then, after an interval that was not quite respectful or long enough, he sat up and, without waiting to be addressed, said, 'I hope you are well, Uncle.'

Sademasa was frowning as he answered. 'My health is no concern of yours, whoever you are. I am surprised you have dared show your face here again. You must be eager to cross the River of Death. I will speed your journey. I can promise you, you will not leave alive this time, even if the Prince Abbot himself should come begging for you.'

'There is no need to be hasty,' Shika said. 'I can do you no injury, alone and unarmed as I am. Maybe I can be of service to you.'

Sademasa did not reply immediately but studied Shika's face intently.

'Stop pretending, Uncle. You must recognise me. You have looked long enough. You know it is I, Kazumaru.'

He heard the quick intake of breath from the men surrounding him.

'Kazumaru, alas, is dead,' Sademasa said without conviction. 'Show me the creature and explain how it works.'

Shika pulled the reluctant Gen around and placed him in front of him. Sademasa's eyes narrowed in disbelief.

'What half-aborted monstrosity is this?'

'It is a wolf, but man-made. I have many such creatures and can make many more.'

Sademasa said, without hesitation, 'Can you make men?'

'Men of a sort,' Shika said, lying, for even Shisoku had never attempted a man.

'How? Do you skin the dead, as a wolf was skinned for this, and stuff them with straw?'

'It is the same process.' Shika was thinking, *Where are the boys? How long can I keep up this strange conversation?*

'An army of half-men,' Sademasa said slowly. 'That would be something. Can they be taught to fight?'

'The wolf has grown more real,' Shika said. Gen snarled at Sademasa's intense stare and showed his teeth. 'You see, it snarls, it will bite, it feeds on meat.'

'Can it die? Would these men die?'

'They can only be destroyed by fire. Any other damage can be patched up. They are not truly alive, therefore they cannot die.'

'Well, I will have this one taken apart so I can see its workings.'

Gen gave a sharp howl, and Sademasa leaned forward. 'How interesting. It understands every word, doesn't it? I look forward to its dissection. Maybe it will tell me itself how it was made.' Sademasa smiled in satisfaction. 'Nobuto said you also have the magic mask, the one the monk would not let me see before.'

Shika bowed his head. *Kiku! Hurry up or Gen and I will both be dissected!*

'Show it to me,' Sademasa commanded.

Shika drew it carefully from the seven-layered bag and held it up with both hands, the face turned towards Sademasa. Stillness fell as, one by one, the men in the room became aware of its power. Even Sademasa was silenced. Eventually he said, 'Give it to me.'

'Uncle, it will burn anyone who tries to wear it, except me.'

Sademasa pursed his lips as he considered this.

'Fetch the traitor's son,' he ordered, and Nobuto and another retainer left the room. They returned, after a few moments, dragging between them a young man the same age as Shika. It was his childhood friend, Nagatomo.

He had been beaten so badly he could not stand. His arms were pinioned behind his back. Blood stained his face and hair. When the men released him he fell to the ground. Nobuto kicked him. He groaned but did not scream.

Shika's heart hardened immediately as horror, pity and rage filled it.

Sademasa said to Nobuto, 'Place the mask on his face and we will see if the vagabond is telling the truth.'

'It will burn him,' Shika warned again.

Nobuto smiled slightly, as if the prospect amused and pleased him. Sademasa leaned forward with cold curiosity.

Shika rose, intending to throw himself on his uncle and kill him with his bare hands, but two of Sademasa's warriors seized him and held him down.

One retainer held Nagatomo's face upwards and Nobuto pressed the mask against it. A scream of such pain erupted from the lips that even the most brutal retainers shuddered. Nagatomo writhed helplessly against the restraining grip. The smell of seared flesh filled the room.

Through the screams Shika heard something else, a voice that sounded like the dead Naganori.

'Sademasa,' it called, 'I am waiting for you!'

A ripple of shock ran through the room as the men registered the voice, but, before anyone could act, a high-pitched buzzing came from the roof. Shika looked up and saw a crack open in the ceiling and the sparrow bee burst through it.

Naganori's voice called again, 'Sademasa!'

Sademasa, distracted by the voice, did not notice the sparrow bee until too late. It flew straight to his face and stung him on the lips. He brushed it aside, and it immediately stung his hand. The men holding Shika let go and rushed forward.

The crack in the ceiling opened wider and through it dropped Shika's sword, Jinan. He was about to snatch the mask from Nagatomo's face, but instead he caught the sword by the hilt and raised it to strike Sademasa. But it was not needed. The venom had already done its work. His uncle was scrabbling at his throat with his hands, gasping for breath, his chest heaving against the tightly laced armour, his eyes bulging. He fell forward, his legs jerked and kicked, he lost control of bowel and bladder and the stench in the room grew worse.

The sparrow bee buzzed angrily as it swooped around, making the retainers shrink from it. One or two of them drew their swords, trying to hit it with the flat of the blade. But they only enraged it further. It had stung two more men, sending them to the same choking death as Sademasa, who now lay unmoving on the floor, before someone thought to unbar the door and the surviving men rushed out.

Shika stood with sword raised, but no one approached him. Then he went to Nagatomo, whose screams had subsided to moans. Shika removed the mask from his face and looked carefully at the damage. Through the scorched skin the eyes stared back at him, reduced by agony to something scarcely human. Yet, they saw Shika, and recognised him, and another light came into them.

Shika knelt beside him and gently untied his arms, rubbing the numb fingers as the blood rushed back. The eyes wept tears of pain.

'I am sorry,' Shika whispered. 'Forgive me. You will not die. We will save you.'

Kiku and Kuro dropped through the ceiling, restless with delight and triumph. They paid no attention to Nagatomo.

'That went all right, didn't it?' Kiku said. 'Did you like my voice? I told you we would tease him!'

'It was my sparrow bee that did it,' Kuro boasted. He inspected the corpses. 'I didn't know it was that poisonous! I hope they don't kill it. I want it back.'

'What happens next?' Kiku asked.

'Now this fortress is mine and everyone in it must obey me,' Shika said. 'I have to take control, but first I must help Nagatomo.'

'Oh,' Kiku said, looking at Nagatomo for the first time. 'Is he your friend? What a shame.'

'Do you have any salve or medicine for this burn?'

'I only brought poisons,' Kuro said. 'I thought we came to kill, not to heal.'

The fake wolf had wagged his tail at the sight of the boys and now he came closer to Nagatomo, who seemed mercifully to have lost consciousness, and sniffed at the ruined features, licking gently at the tears. Shika pushed him away, but Kiku said, 'Let him lick it. Dogs and wolves clean with their tongue. Maybe Gen will help soothe the pain.'

*I cannot delay any longer,* Shika thought. He ordered Gen to stay with Nagatomo and went to the door, signalling to the boys to follow.

'What can you hear, Kiku?'

'The men are in the inner yard. The one called Nobuto is trying to organise them to attack you. They sound reluctant.'

'Where's my bee?' Kuro demanded.

'It's buzzing. I can hear it, but I'm not sure where.'

'If they hurt it I'll kill them,' Kuro muttered.

The doors had all been left open as the men fled through them. Sword in hand, Shika strode through the passages and out into the courtyard.

The milling, arguing warriors fell silent. One or two set arrows to their bows and trained them on him.

He said, 'Kumayama no Jiro no Sademasa, brother of Shigetomo, uncle of Kazumaru, now known as Shikanoko, is dead. No man killed him. He was punished by Heaven for his faithlessness and cruelty. I have returned to take up my inheritance and challenge the tyrants in Miyako and Ryusonji. I will restore the rightful Emperor to the throne. Those of you who loved my father and who will serve me, kneel and swear allegiance. Anyone who wants to oppose me, can do it now, with the sword.'

One by one the men put their weapons away and fell to their knees. Only Nobuto remained standing. He looked around and saw he was alone.

'You cowards!' he screamed. 'You forget our lord so quickly? An impostor has scared you with his magic tricks and his accursed creatures. I will prove there is one man left in Kumayama.'

He rushed at Shika with drawn sword and gave such a slashing blow it would have cut Shika in half had he remained where he was. He leaped sideways, evading the blade, and immediately found himself parrying a frenzied attack. He had killed the two men on the road from a distance, with arrows, and Gessho had already been weakened by poison when he had fought him with the sword. Now he faced a grown man in the prime of life and full strength, a warrior far more experienced than he was, made fearless by desperation.

None of the watching men made any attempt to help him and he realised he was being put to the test before them. If he won this combat, as a warrior not as a sorcerer, they would follow him unquestioningly.

He had no time for any more thoughts. He was fighting for his life.

Time halted. Everything else faded away. The only things that existed in the world were his opponent and the swords. He was no longer Shikanoko or Kazumaru or anyone. He was a being of pure instinct and inexhaustible energy, with only one desire – to live. His will flowed through every stroke and every step, unbreakable and irresistible. His opponent was older and stronger, a better fighter in every way, a man who would not give up, even when blood streamed from ten or more cuts. When Nobuto's right arm was made useless by a slash to the wrist, he switched to the left.

Shika was also bleeding, and beginning to tire. He hated Nobuto for not surrendering, wondering how long he himself could continue.

Nobuto stumbled as something buzzed past his ear, distracting him.

Shika thought, *I must kill him before the bee does. He must die by my hand.*

With his last reserves of energy and strength he lunged forward, a clumsy brutal stroke that, for once, Nobuto did not foresee. In fact, he was moving towards the sword, and his own force thrust himself onto it, taking it deep into his throat and out through the back of his neck.

His eyes widened as blood gushed from his mouth. His legs gave way as the neck bones shattered. Hatred flashed briefly in his expression and then his soul fled his destroyed body.

The sparrow bee hurtled towards Shika, making him think he had won the fight only to die the same choking death as his uncle. He stood still, determined to show no fear. The sparrow bee buzzed briefly round his head and, when he did not move, swooped once more over the kneeling men and then flew beyond the palisade towards the forest.

•

After the bodies were burned and the ashes buried before the ground froze, Shika cleared the fortress of all traces of his uncle, adding his clothes and all his possessions to the fire. Once Nobuto was dead, the men were all ready to serve Shika, and within a few days he took half of them with him to Kuromori. They surprised the small besieging Miboshi force, killing all but a few who fled. After relieving Kongyo and his men, Shika would have advanced on Matsutani, but the first snowfall of the year made him retreat to Kumayama for the winter.

As Kongyo had advised him, the snow would protect him but, within the fortress, he had another problem, the women: Sademasa's wife, several concubines, and children. He did not know what to do with them.

'You should be ruthless,' advised Kiku, who seemed to have absorbed the essential elements of warrior culture after only a few weeks. 'They will only create more trouble for you later.'

'Your uncle would have killed you,' Kuro added.

'Yes!' Kiku exclaimed. 'And look what happened because he did not. That proves my argument.'

'They are my cousins,' Shika said. 'If I spare them and bring them up, they will be grateful and loyal.'

'I would hate any man who spared my life,' Kiku said.

'Me too,' Kuro agreed.

'But why? Wouldn't you be grateful?'

Kiku frowned. 'I would feel in his power, as if I owed him something. I couldn't bear it.'

'We could kill them,' Kuro offered. 'It would be good practice and I could try out some of the other insects.'

The fortress was freezing, despite braziers placed here and there, and the boys' words and their calm faces made Shika feel even colder. He forbade them curtly to do any such thing, yet over the winter, one by one, the children died. Two suffered vomiting and diarrhoea, one bled to death from mysterious puncture holes as if she had been attacked by leeches, one had convulsions, another croup. Of the women, two begged to be allowed to shave their heads and become nuns, one went mad after the death of her child and ran out into the forest. They found the body half-eaten by wolves in the spring. The others, including Sademasa's wife, took their own lives, like warrior women, a knife in the throat.

From this Shika learned that the boys did not obey what he said, but followed what they perceived were his secret desires, and were themselves unmoved by compassion or pity. He was torn between regret at the deaths and relief that the problem was solved, in a way that gave him a reputation for ruthlessness.

# 9

# HINA

Hina had been in Nishimi for four months. She was kept busy with the endless lessons that Takaakira had arranged for her: lute, poetry, classics, history, literature, genealogy. Mostly she enjoyed them, and she worked hard at her studies, practising music daily and writing poems in reply to the ones Takaakira sent her. He returned hers, with corrections and suggestions, which both annoyed and saddened her, but also made her determined to write just one that he could find no fault with.

He supervised her progress, coming to her rooms every afternoon to listen to her sing and play. He did not praise her often, with the result she remained unaware of her gifts and retained the unselfconsciousness of a child.

Her teachers were the two elegant women who had come from Miyako, across Lake Kasumi. The younger one, Sadako, provided instruction in poetry and music while Masako, older and stricter, was an expert in classics and history and had a passion for genealogy. Both women brought their own servants. Bara looked after Hina, and there were also cooks and maids, grooms and gardeners, and various warriors, Takaakira's retainers, who had appropriated the long low building to the left of the stables, as their quarters. They challenged each other to horse races and archery competitions, went hunting in the forest and along the lake shore, and kept themselves busy while waiting hopefully for orders to attack the Kakizuki forces, who had retreated to Rakuhara, several days' journey further west.

The house was built in the style of a country palace, both rustic and luxurious. Its rooms stood around three sides of a square whose fourth side was open to the lake to capture cool breezes off the water in summer. On the west a bamboo grove, with a garden in front of it, shaded the residence from the setting sun. A stream had been diverted from the lake to flow through the garden. Towards the north was a stretch of pasture where many horses were kept; the stables stood on its edge, facing south to keep the horses warm in winter.

The lake itself protected the house from the dangerous northeast, and a shrine stood on the shore where, Hina had learned, the Goddess of the Lake was worshipped and honoured with offerings of wine, fruit and rice.

Mostly the shore was sandy, but the house was built on an elevated piece of land, where cliffs rose above the lake and the water below was deep. Wooden steps led down over the boulders to a jetty, where fishing vessels were tied up and trading boats came whenever the weather permitted.

Lady Masako told Hina that the beautiful house had belonged to a nobleman, Hidetake, who was a close friend of the former Crown Prince, and held a high position in the court when it was under Kakizuki sway. His wife, Masako told her, had been wet nurse and foster mother to the Prince's son, Yoshimori, who was now, some still dared think, though not say openly anywhere east of Rakuhara, the true Emperor, if he was still alive.

Masako was careful to emphasise that this was an error, that the current Emperor, the nephew of the Prince Abbot, was legitimate and blessed by Heaven, but her devotion to the truth would not allow her to omit the other line altogether.

Even in Nishimi, far removed from the capital, they could not escape the disasters that had afflicted the country since the death of the Crown Prince and the defeat of the Kakizuki. The once prosperous estate, which had traded produce and goods from the west across the lake with the merchants of Miyako and Kitakami, which had cultivated wet and dry fields, rice, millet, beans and taro, had hundreds of mulberry, apricot and mandarin trees, raised silkworms and wove silk, had fallen into disrepair, hit by the natural disasters and the defection of most of its stewards and managers. Takaakira spent the first months he was there trying to organise replacements, save what he could of the harvest, and prepare the house for winter.

One day, in the eleventh month, a messenger came by horse from Miyako, wearing Lord Aritomo's crest on his surcoat.

'His lordship will be returning to the capital, no doubt,' Bara said as she combed Hina's hair in preparation for Takaakira's afternoon visit.

'Why? I thought we were staying here all winter,' Hina said.

'Lord Aritomo isn't going to keep his most important retainer buried in the country forever, is he? But he won't take you with him. You will stay here, where you are safe.'

'I wish I could go home, to my real home,' Hina said wistfully.

'Don't fret, my chick – I mean, Lady Hina – you are luckier than most.'

Bara often called her pet names and treated her like her younger sister, but not in the presence of the teachers or Takaakira.

When Takaakira came, he seemed preoccupied and reluctant to leave. Hina played for him, and sang an *imayo* that Sadako told her had been popular in the court a few years before. She read to him from a book of poems, but nothing penetrated his dark mood.

'Do you still have your Kudzu Vine Treasure Store?' he interrupted.

'Yes,' she said. 'I try to read a little every day. Shall I fetch it now?'

'No, I just wanted to know it was safe. And the box, do you still have that?'

'Yes,' she said.

He nodded, without saying anything. Then he remarked, 'It has been very cold today. It will be snowing in the mountains, and in my country, in the north. Bara must take great care of you, so you do not fall sick. No one must come in here, unless they have been purified, and prayed over.'

'I wish you did not have to go away,' Hina said.

'I wish it too, my dear child. I don't want to leave you. I will find out what Lord Aritomo wants and return as soon as I can. But I am afraid it may not be before spring.'

•

Hina missed him. The palace seemed empty without his presence and, though her lessons continued in the same manner, she was less inspired to study hard without his criticism and occasional admiration. Apart from music, which she truly loved – she would play the lute all day if she could – her attention wandered. She began to dwell on the past in a way she had not allowed herself until now. She recalled her life at Matsutani, the games with her little brother, Tsumaru, and Haru's children, Kaze and Chika. She missed the outdoor pastimes, the horses her father taught her to ride, the dogs that ran through the woods with them. She missed the Darkwood itself, its mysterious presence always around them. She began to sing the songs and ballads she had learned at Haru's knee, after her mother died, and often she included the lament for the dragon's child, who in her mind had become one with Tsumaru.

It made her sad, reminding her of the night in the capital when Shikanoko had told her how Tsumaru had died, when she had waited in vain for her father to come home. Grief and her childish love for Shika were inextricably entwined in her heart.

Many of the songs were sad, set in the season of autumn, which suited her melancholy mood. Sometimes she pretended she was the Autumn Princess, which was what she had learned everyone called Lord Hidetake's daughter. She liked the name, it sounded sorrowful and beautiful at the same time. She had suspected for months that that was why Takaakira had been sent here. It suited him as a place to hide her, but all the time he was listening to her music and poems, supervising her lessons and the restoration of the estate, he had expected the Autumn Princess to turn up here at her old home.

'He waited for her all autumn,' she said to herself. It suggested a poem and she let her mind play idly with the words, but really it would only work as a love poem, and she did not think Takaakira was waiting like a lover. Rather he and Lord Aritomo had set an ambush, a trap from which the Princess would not escape alive.

Where was she now? Had they decided she was dead and so there was no need to wait for her anymore? And Shikanoko, had he also departed for that other world, like her father and her brother, her mother, everyone she had ever loved? These thoughts saddened and subdued her. Her teachers and Bara noticed her changed mood and thought she was pining for Takaakira. They suggested more outdoor activities, when the days were fine.

It continued very cold, with overcast skies. The palace was constructed for the hot humid weather of summer and the airy rooms were freezing. Sadako and Masako both caught colds and kept to their own quarters for several days. Hina's fingers were too numb to hold a pen or a plectrum; like her toes, they were chilblained and itched and ached. She and Bara slept under piles of quilted clothes, snuggling together to keep warm.

One morning, there was a sudden change in the weather. The wind blew from the south and the sun appeared, low in the sky, but warm. Hina woke early, and Bara, who was usually restless all night from the cold, was still deeply asleep. Hina was seized by the desire to go outside.

The pasture had been white with frost every morning for weeks but this day it was bare and brown. The horses, with their shaggy winter coats, were grazing on the stalks of dried grass. Hina leaped down the cliff path – there was no one around to tell her to walk sedately. Some fishermen were already at the water's edge preparing boats and nets, taking advantage of the sudden warmth. She skirted them, not speaking to them. Further along the shore, beyond the cliffs, a flock of plovers rose into the air at her approach, uttering plaintive cries.

A horse whickered in the distance and she turned in the direction of the sound. It neighed more loudly, then began to trot towards her, slowly, clumsily because of its swollen belly. Behind it, cantering freely, was the silver white stallion.

'Risu!' Hina cried. 'Nyorin!'

The mare reached her, almost knocking her over in her eagerness to nuzzle her. Hina held her head, stroking the broad forehead, then put her other hand on the belly and felt the foal kick. She was filled with an emotion so intense it brought tears to her eyes. Nyorin lowered his head and breathed in her face. She stroked his soft pink nose.

'Where is Shikanoko?' she said aloud, and then called, 'Shikanoko!' Her voice sounded tiny, fainter than the plovers' cries.

The horses wore harness and on Risu's back was a bundle from which the neck of a lute emerged. Hina could not reach it to touch it.

It was like a dream, filled with strange images that must have some significance but that she could not interpret. All she could think was that Shikanoko had fallen and was lying injured somewhere nearby, in the rice fields or on the lake shore.

'Show me where he is,' she said to the mare, and took the reins in her hand. She would have liked to ride but she was afraid of hurting the unborn foal, and Nyorin was far too tall for her to mount without help.

Risu seemed to understand, for she began to walk purposefully along the shore towards the little shrine to the Lake Goddess. A vermilion bird-perch gate stood right in the water, and opposite it was a small hut. It was empty, only occupied at the seasonal festivals, and, though the farmers and fishermen left offerings at the outside altar, ringing the bell and making requests, no one ventured inside. The Lake Goddess was known to be unpredictable and capricious and no one wanted to risk inadvertently offending her.

Hina looked around. There was no one in earshot. The fishermen had launched their boats and were slowly rowing across the lake. She climbed the steps and listened at the door, then called quietly, 'Is anyone there? Shikanoko?'

She heard the smallest of creaks from the floor within, as if someone were tiptoeing over it. Then a woman's voice replied, 'Who are you? Why do you say that name?'

'Who are *you*?' Hina whispered. 'And why do you have his horses?'

'You know them? Tell me their names.'

'The mare is Risu and the stallion, Nyorin,' Hina said. 'Let me in, we cannot talk like this.'

'I will let you come in, as long as you are alone. But be warned, I have a sword.'

'I am alone,' Hina said, and pushed open the door.

It was still dim inside the shrine. The room smelled of mildew and dust, and a faint scent of lamp oil, like a memory of summer nights. A young woman stood before her, the sword in her hand, on her back a small ceremonial bow. Her matted hair was tied in a horse's tail, held back from her face by a head band. She wore leggings under a short jacket, the clothes filthy, hardly better than rags. Her face was dark from dirt and weather.

They stared at each other for a few moments, then Hina said, 'I am Kiyoyori's daughter. But can you be the Autumn Princess?'

'I used to be called Akihime.' She lowered the sword and said formally, 'Your father was a brave and loyal man. I am grateful for his sacrifice. He and my father died on the same day.'

Hina felt one sob rise in her chest but she fought it down. 'No one knew for certain. Did you see him die?'

Akihime looked at her with pity. 'No, but – well, I will tell you one day, but not now. Why are you here? How did you survive the massacre in the capital?'

'A warrior saved me. Yukikuni no Takaakira. He brought me here to hide me.'

'For what purpose?'

After a pause, Hina said, 'He wants to make me his wife. He is educating me to be a perfect woman, while the rest of the world forgets that Kiyoyori's daughter ever existed.'

'But you are still a child,' Akihime exclaimed.

'Not for much longer,' Hina said.

'Let's hope the Miboshi are overthrown before that time! I did not know that Takaakira would be here. I came because my family own this estate. I thought I could hide here.'

'He has been waiting for you,' Hina said. 'They expected you to come. You are not safe here.'

'I don't know where else to go,' Akihime said. 'I would have come before, or hidden somewhere else, but I had the horses. I could not abandon them. I've had to fight to hang onto them, so many people wanted to steal them from me. I have been travelling up and down the highways, but, even though I now look like this, people were beginning to talk about me. Men were seeking me out to challenge or capture me. My father taught me how to fight but I did not expect to be defending myself against thieves and rogues on the road. I can't fight, or travel, much longer.' She opened her jacket and showed Hina the swell of her belly.

Hina felt her eyes narrow and a wave of jealousy and anger flooded through her. Barely controlling her emotions, she said, 'Is that why you have Shikanoko's horses?'

'You are quick to guess! What a clever child you are. Yes, he is the father.' Akihime's expression turned sombre, but her voice suggested something else.

The last thing Hina wanted to be told was that she was a child. She lost all desire to help Akihime. She just wanted her to disappear, or be dead. But then she remembered that this young woman served the Emperor, for whom both their fathers had died. They were tied together by powerful bonds.

'Where is Shikanoko now?' she said.

'I don't know. The horses attacked him. He was unconscious when we left him.'

*I would never have left him!* 'Is he dead?'

'I don't know,' Aki said again.

'You said *we*? Were you with the child Emperor?'

Aki nodded.

'And where is he now?' Hina said, looking around, as if Aki might have hidden him somewhere within the shrine.

'I will tell you the whole story, I promise you, but not at this time. I must decide what to do next.'

'Takaakira is away,' Hina said. 'Some crisis arose that meant he had to go to the capital. I'm not sure when he will return. Most of the former servants ran away. I wonder if there are any left who would know you?'

'It is years since I have been here. I don't think they would recognise me.'

'The men are on the lookout for you. But they are expecting a young Princess, not ...'

'A vagrant with child.' Akihime smiled bitterly.

'Stay here if you are not afraid,' Hina said.

'I have been afraid for months, but here I ... I was going to say I wasn't afraid. I was dedicated to the Lake Goddess, who is a manifestation of the All Merciful Kannon, as a child. I used to hide here from my nurses and no one dared come to find me. I even ate the rice cakes and other offerings – the Goddess never punished me. But now she no longer protects me. I broke my vow of purity – I was supposed to be a shrine maiden at the Goddess's shrine at Rinrakuji. She is punishing me now.'

She looked so sad Hina was moved to pity. 'I'll look after you. I'll fetch some food and leave it here, and later I'll send Bara to bring you to the house.'

'And what will the men say when they see two strange horses, with saddle and bridles?'

'I'll take them to the stables now and say I found them. It's not the first time stray horses have turned up.' Hina could not help smiling. 'And Risu will have her foal safely here. Do you think I'll be able to keep it as mine?'

'No one is more worthy of it,' Aki said, smiling too.

'I saw the lute,' Hina said. 'Do you play?'

'I try but I cannot master it.'

'May I play it?'

'I will tell you a secret,' Aki said. 'It is Genzo, the Emperor's lute. Take great care of it and keep it hidden.'

Hina went outside cautiously. The horses waited close to the shrine. Hina stood on the steps to reach Risu's back, untied the bundle with the lute and tucked it under one arm. Then she took Risu's reins in one hand and Nyorin's in the other, and began to lead them towards the stables.

She had gone less than halfway when she saw Bara running across the pasture. The other horses tossed their heads and ran away from her, kicking out and bucking as if it were spring. Then they circled back to inspect the newcomers, sniffing the air and neighing loudly.

Bara cried out, 'Lady Hina, what are you doing?'

'Look what I found,' Hina shouted back. 'Stray horses!'

'Be careful, they may be dangerous.'

'No, they are gentle,' Hina said, but when Bara came closer and tried to take Risu's reins, the mare laid back her ears and showed her teeth.

'Behave!' Hina said and smacked her lightly.

'I don't like horses,' Bara confessed. 'They are so heavy and clumsy, they put their feet everywhere without looking, and they seem to be moody.'

'They don't like people who are afraid of them,' Hina said, remembering what her father had told her. 'It makes them nervous.'

'But what are you doing out so early?' Bara asked. 'I woke and you were not in the house. The lord will be so angry if he finds out. Anything might have happened to you.'

'I couldn't go back to sleep, and it felt suddenly warm. I just wanted to be outside on my own.' Hina felt some contrition at Bara's concern, but it also irritated her.

Bara looked at her. 'Well, it seems to have done you some good. Your eyes are bright and your cheeks rosy. But Lord Takaakira does not want you to look like a farm girl. He likes you languid and pale, like a lily.'

'I would rather be a rose, like you, Bara!'

Bara smiled. 'Next time, wake me up and I'll come with you. Here. Give me that bundle before you drop it.' She took it from under Hina's arm. 'What's in it? Is it a lute?'

'Yes, it was on the horse's back. I'll try it out later,' Hina said, and then, 'You would do anything for me, wouldn't you, Bara?'

'I would, my chick, as long as it does not get me into trouble with the lord.'

Hina smiled, but did not reply. They were now on the lower track that led to the stables and two men came running down to meet them, exclaiming in surprise at the sight of the horses. One was a groom Hina particularly liked, though she could not say why since she had hardly ever spoken to him. But he looked cheerful and open-hearted, and he treated the horses gently. Now she noticed for the first time that Bara liked him too, and perhaps he liked her back, for they exchanged a swift, almost secret smile and Bara's cheeks flushed, much more than Hina's.

He took Risu's reins from Hina and the other man took the stallion's. A boy ran from the stables and chased the herd of horses, which had been following them, back to the pasture. They cantered away, a wave of brown, black and grey. Nyorin pulled back as if he would gallop after them.

'Whoa!' the groom cried, and Hina said, 'Stay, Nyorin.'

'Where did these beauties come from?' the man holding Risu said.

'I found them in the pasture.'

'The mare is in foal,' the man observed. 'Getting close, by the look of her.'

'You must take care of them,' Hina said. 'They will be mine. What is your name?'

'Saburo, lady.' He bobbed his head to her. 'You called the stallion something?'

'Nyorin,' she said, adding quickly, 'it means silver, so I think it suits him.'

'And the mare?' Saburo said. 'Are you going to give her a name too?'

Hina pretended to think. 'How about Risu?'

'Very well, lady. I'll clean them up and feed them.'

'I will come and see them later,' Hina said as she patted the horses goodbye. They turned their heads to watch her go and whickered after her.

Bara made Hina sit on the verandah while she fetched water to wash her feet. It was as good a place to talk as any.

'Bara, dear,' she said quietly. 'There is someone hiding in the shrine.'

'So the horses did not turn up alone?'

'No, it is a young woman and she is going to have a baby. She has nowhere else to go.'

Bara continued washing Hina's feet with even more vigour, splashing water unnecessarily.

'Is it the person the lord has been waiting for?'

'How do you know that?'

'People talk about it. They wonder why Lord Aritomo allowed Takaakira to be absent from the capital for so long. There are a few left here who served Lord Hidetake and still consider themselves

Kakizuki. That groom, Saburo, for example.' Saying his name made Bara smile.

'And you, Bara?'

'I am from Akashi, the free city. I am neither Miboshi nor Kakizuki. But Lord Takaakira employs me and trusts me. I can do nothing against his wishes.'

'Well, it could hardly be her,' Hina said. 'She is not a Princess, she is a vagrant.'

She sat quite still while Bara dried her feet, afraid she had already betrayed Aki, wondering how she could warn her.

'If Lady Hina expressly commands me to do something, I cannot disobey her,' Bara said very quietly.

'What should I command you?' Hina said.

'The men will almost certainly search for the owner of the horses,' Bara said.

'I thought you could fetch her to the house after dark, but how can we stop them looking in the shrine and finding her?'

'Better to hide her in plain view. So that someone else finds her, who is not looking for her.'

'The fishermen,' Hina whispered. 'If they found her in the water they would think the Lake Goddess had delivered her to them.'

'A young pregnant woman who tried to drown herself, but was saved by the Goddess,' Bara said, thinking aloud.

'Let's take offerings to the shrine now, in thanks for the horses,' Hina said. 'We will tell her our plan.'

'I've just got your feet clean,' Bara complained.

'You can do them again afterwards. Go quickly, bring rice cakes and whatever else we have.'

While Bara hurried off to the kitchen, Hina turned her attention to the lute. She untied the bundle and took it out, surprised at how shabby and ordinary it looked. She plucked a string; it responded reluctantly. It needed tuning but beyond that she felt some deep-grained obstinacy that resisted her fingers and her will.

She was about to lay it down and put her sandals on again when she thought of something else. She decided to take the eyes to the shrine too, so they would protect Akihime. Carrying the lute, she went quickly to her room, where the box that held them was hidden beneath a silk cloth. She could hear her teachers coughing from their quarters. They still sounded very unwell; there would be no lessons today.

She took the box out and left the lute in its place, then raised the lid and prayed quickly, recalling how, when Takaakira had opened the box in the house in Miyako, she had seen him transfixed by the eyes, unable to move until she closed the lid. She had never dared ask him what had happened to him. When she opened the box it was to pray to Sesshin and to water the eyes with her tears. Once Sadako had come up behind her and looked over her shoulder, saying in her gentle voice, 'What have you . . . ?' which was as far as she got. She stood without moving, staring at the eyes, and then tears began to slide from her own eyes and trickle down her cheeks.

'Ah, what a wasted life,' she murmured. 'Yes, I see myself, shrivelled and old, with no man's love and no children.'

Hina had closed the box quickly and had been especially diligent and affectionate to Sadako for the next few days. Though she cried over the eyes to cleanse them and keep them moist, sometimes telling herself she was an orphan, alone in the world, hidden by a man who would one day force her to marry him, unlikely ever to see again the boy she truly loved, they did not really show her the devastating insights that others seemed to see.

In truth, when she kept her thoughts firmly in the present, neither grieving for the past nor fearing the future, she was not unhappy. Learning was a joy, her teachers were kind to her, Bara loved her.

She heard Bara call her name, and she closed the box and went back to the verandah. The sun was warming it now, and it felt pleasant to sit in the sunshine and let Bara rub her feet and then fasten her sandals.

Bara had placed a tray on the boards. It held two small rice cakes, a slightly shrivelled mandarin and a sprig of red-berried sacred bamboo. 'I did not dare make it too lavish,' she said. 'I didn't want to make anyone suspicious.

'You have your precious box, I see,' she remarked as she lifted the tray and stood up.

'I am going to lend it to the Lake Goddess,' Hina replied.

'What's inside, my chick?'

'Have you never looked in?' Hina returned, knowing Bara's inquisitive nature.

Bara went red. 'I did take a peek once, but all I saw was myself, all my regrets from the past, the stupid things I'd done, the way I treated my mother. It upset me, I'm telling you. I'd never look again.'

'They are a man's eyes. Perhaps he was a sorcerer, perhaps he was a saint. He was blinded, unjustly, by my stepmother. I am their guardian until I can return them to Matsutani.'

Hina was silent as they walked back to the shrine, wondering if that day would ever come.

The warmer weather had brought everyone outside. Retainers were exercising horses in the pasture. Fishermen were in their boats off shore, their wives and children were on the beach, their gossip and laughter loud in the clear air. The surface of the lake was as still and smooth as a mirror.

The presence of so many people made Hina very nervous. She was sure someone would find their behaviour unusual and would come to investigate. At the steps of the shrine she put the box down, so she could clap her hands to waken the Goddess and alert Akihime. Bara laid the offerings on the step and pulled at the bell rope. It clanged above Hina's head as she spoke softly to Aki in between her prayers.

*Goddess of the Lake, protect your child.* 'Lady, when there is no one around, come out and throw yourself in the water.' *She was dedicated to you as a child, act now to save her.* 'Let the fishermen find you.' *Hide her in your depths and let your waves bring her to shore.* 'My maid, Bara, will make sure you are looked after. I am leaving something here to protect you, but do not look at it.' *Goddess of the Lake, bless these eyes and enable them to see clearly.*

There was a large gap between the top step and the bottom of the door and Hina pushed the rice cakes and the mandarin through it. She heard the faintest whisper.

'Thank you. I will do as you say. I will leave my sword here, for the Goddess. Please look after it. I will keep my knife so I can kill myself if I am discovered.'

'That is not going to happen,' Hina said. She had complete confidence in the Goddess and in Sesshin's eyes.

# 10

# AKI

After Kiyoyori's daughter and the woman left, Aki ate the rice cakes, though they barely satisfied her. The baby was growing large and she was always hungry. She was also terribly thirsty. The mandarin was dry inside. She chewed each segment and sucked the peel but its bitterness made her mouth and tongue sore. Then the baby shifted position, stretching and kicking, making her need urgently to urinate. She squatted in a corner close to the door, hoping the Goddess would not be offended, praying no one would see the water drip through the floor. The stream seemed endless, its noise deafening.

She scattered the remains of the mandarin peel over it to mask the smell, took the sword and placed it behind the small altar at the back of the hut. Then she sat, leaning against the wall, gathering her strength and her courage for the next move. She could see the merit in Hina's plan, but she did not look forward to committing her life to the chill water of the lake and the mercy of fishermen.

She must have slept a little. She dreamed of Kai and Yoshi, the last time she had seen them, a few weeks ago. She had been riding along the lakeside road when she noticed the boats plying their way along the edge of Lake Kasumi, had followed them, and that night had watched the performers on the shore. Yoshi and the monkey boy whose name she did not know tumbled with a group of monkeys. The older men threw them through the air. And Kai sat on the side with the other musicians, and beat her drum. Aki was happy, for Yoshi looked content and healthy, and he and Kai had found each other again. They would look after each other. She crept away back to where she had left the horses, put her arms round Risu's neck and cried into her mane. She thought of going to join them, for hadn't Lady Fuji told her to come back if she didn't like life as a shrine maiden? But she was afraid of facing Fuji and the other women of the boats, and she did not want to be made to give up the horses. So she had ridden away, but in her dream she went down and called out to them. They both turned towards her and she saw their faces, and then she woke up. A strong wind was shaking the hut and it had grown much colder. She was shivering and her legs were cramping. She was about to stand up and move around when she heard men's voices. Her heart seemed to fill her throat and pound deafeningly in her ears.

*This is the end*, she thought, and felt the baby shudder inside her. 'I'm sorry, I'm sorry,' she whispered to it and grasped the knife.

Footsteps came closer, two or three men, on the steps.

'Could someone be hiding in the shrine?'

'It's possible, better check to make sure.'

'What's in that box?'

'Are those . . . eyes?'

Aki hardly dared breathe. For a few moments no sound came from outside. Then inexplicably she heard sobbing, accompanied by broken phrases filled with regret and grief.

'Those men I killed treacherously.'

'Those infants we slaughtered in Miyako!'

'I used to serve the Kakizuki. I betrayed them!'

'My favourite child – dead at six years old.'

'Those girls we raped, how they screamed.'

The wind howled more loudly and sleet pattered on the roof.

'Have we angered the Goddess?' she heard one man ask, and another replied, 'Let's get out of here.'

'Look at the lake!' cried the third. 'A blizzard is coming!'

Their feet pounded down the steps and then Aki could hear nothing but the wind. She waited for a while, trying to control her breath, then opened the door a tiny crack. The wind forced it open further and snow flurried in, melting on the floor. She caught some flakes on her hand and licked them. The lake and the shore had disappeared; everything was turning white.

On the steps lay Hina's box. She forgot she had been warned not to look in it and her gaze fell on the eyes.

All the sorrows and regrets of the past year rose within her. If only she had not yielded to Shikanoko. If only she had not hidden from him afterwards. She relived again the shock of seeing him broken on the ground. Why had she run away from him? She would never see him again and the baby would grow up fatherless. She had abandoned the Emperor, when she should be with him, protecting him with her life.

Her tears fell mingling with the snow. Her despair was complete. It was not to save her life that she ran into the lake. It was to drown herself.

# II

# MASACHIKA

Masachika knelt before Keita, the Kakizuki lord. It was months since he had arrived, on the orders of Takaakira, in Rakuhara, where the remains of the Kakizuki army had fled after the battles of Shimaura and Sagigawa, when they had lost Miyako. He had been welcomed as Kiyoyori's brother, and indeed heir, for he was now legally the Kuromori lord, though no one actually called him that. In his usual way he had made himself useful, offered to carry out tasks no one else wanted to do, listened sympathetically to the endless recountings of battles lost, and even wrote many of them down, recording all the blame-erasing excuses of betrayal and injustice with murmurs of outrage. No one suspected him of being a spy, and, in truth, he had done little spying worthy of the name, though he now had a very clear idea of the strength and state of mind of the Kakizuki leaders.

An unusually severe winter, with two months of gales and heavy snow, kept him, along with the rest of the Kakizuki, shivering in Rakuhara, where the cold winds penetrated every corner of the inadequate buildings, and snow drifted up to the eaves.

He had plenty of time to compare the two lords, Keita and Aritomo, and concluded on the whole he was lucky to have spent the winter in Rakuhara rather than Miyako. For, even in exile, Keita had not given up his love of luxury, his fondness for music, dancing and poetry. The roof might leak, the ill-fitting shutters rattle, the chinks in the wall let in icy blasts, but Keita still slept under silk, ate from celadon bowls, and was entertained by his many court ladies and concubines. Aritomo possessed the capital and occupied two-thirds of the Eight Islands, yet he chose to live frugally and despised ostentation. The craftsmen of Miyako were plunged into gloom and longed for the spendthrift Kakizuki to return so their businesses might prosper again. The craftsmen in the towns around Rakuhara rejoiced in the lively trade in ceramics, weaving, lacquer ware, paper and musical instruments.

Next to him, one of the elders, Yasutsugu, who had been a friend of his father's, said quietly, 'A spy has come from Nishimi. We think the Autumn Princess is there. Only she knows what became of Yoshimori. It has filled everyone with hope. They are bringing the man here now so we can all hear what he has to say.'

'What wonderful news,' Masachika murmured.

A young man, in the clothes of a groom, was escorted in and prostrated himself before the gathering. When he sat up, Masachika could see he had the honest open face that elicited trust, so useful for a spy. He told them a girl had been pulled from the lake by fishermen as the first snowstorm of the winter swept over Nishimi. She was pregnant and everyone assumed she was some vagrant who had tried to end her life. Her survival was considered something of a miracle and she was given shelter, though at first no one thought she would live. The icy water brought on a severe chill, followed by a fever, almost too fierce for her weakened frame to bear. But she survived and gave birth to a boy, who was thriving.

'How can the Autumn Princess be a mother, and abandoned?' Keita said doubtfully. 'What was she doing alone? Who is the father of the child?'

It was so far from any noble person's experience it seemed unthinkable.

'Is she an impostor, hoping to gain some advantage?' Yasutsugu said.

The groom answered, 'She herself has claimed nothing. She hardly speaks. I know this from Lady Hina, by way of my informant, Lady Hina's maid.'

'Who is she, this Lady Hina?' Lord Keita was frowning slightly.

'Some young girl whom Yukikuni no Takaakira brought to Nishimi and is keeping there, without Aritomo's knowledge. The maid, Bara, showed me a knife that the pregnant woman had on her, and I recognised it as belonging to Lord Hidetake, whom I served in Miyako and Nishimi. I realised the woman must be his daughter, and the maid confirmed it.'

'If she is truly the Autumn Princess we must bring her here and speak with her. But do we need to concern ourselves with Takaakira's plaything?'

Masachika tried to mask his intense interest. Hina had been the pet name for Kiyoyori's daughter. What if the child had been too young, too innocent to realise she should change it? He had thought Takaakira had been lying. Now he knew for certain he had been, and why.

'She is more than that,' the groom said. 'Inexplicable things have happened. The day Akihime was found, two strange horses turned up. They had harness that had once been of high quality. One, a mare, was pregnant, and gave birth to a foal the same day the child was born. The other is a stallion, fine-looking but strong-willed and stubborn. When they arrived Lady Hina gave them names, but they already answered to those names as if they had been called them before, for a long time, and I would swear they knew her. Horses cannot lie! Later, Bara told me the lady retrieved a magnificent sword that had been left in the shrine. She also took back to her room a box containing eyes.'

'Eyes?' Lord Keita repeated.

'Eyes that make you look into your heart and see everything you ever lost, all your failures and regrets, all your hidden secrets. Those eyes apparently kept Takaakira's warriors from searching the shrine, where the Princess was hiding. They would have found her if they had gone inside. And then the Lake Goddess sent a storm, at Lady Hina's request.'

Masachika knew it was his brother's daughter. Takaakira had told him she was dead so he could keep her for himself. His heart swelled with joy at this knowledge, which gave him power over the man who had humiliated him. Takaakira's contempt had stayed with him for months, fuelling the jealousy and resentment he held for Aritomo's favourite. And all the time Takaakira had been deceiving his lord. *This will bring him down. I'll make sure of it.* He had to go to Nishimi himself, at once.

'So,' the groom concluded, 'Lady Hina is much more than a young girl who has caught the eye of Takaakira. I believe she is a warrior's daughter but, even more than that, she is a sorceress in the making.'

Lord Keita looked troubled. 'We will consult the genealogies to find out who she is.'

Masachika cleared his throat and said, 'May I speak, lord?'

When permission was granted he went on. 'Kiyoyori's daughter was known within the family as Hina. Perhaps this is her.' He addressed the groom, 'I am his brother, her uncle. I thought my beloved niece was dead.' He allowed his voice to choke and raised his sleeve to his eye, as if to wipe away tears.

'I am happy to be the source of such good news,' the man exclaimed, and directed a cheerful smile at Masachika, which he immediately suspected was false. His fears that he might be unmasked, never far from the surface, now rose to disturb him. Did the man know something about him? What did the smile really mean?

'What is your name?' he said.

'Saburo, lord,' the man replied.

'You should return to Nishimi as soon as possible. What reason did you give for leaving?'

'My father's funeral.'

'Very sad. And how did you get through the barrier?'

'I came over the mountains. There are many secret paths.'

'You can show me,' Masachika said. 'We will return to Nishimi together and I will verify the truth of your report. If my lords agree,' he added hastily, looking round at the elders and Lord Keita.

'Should we not rather prepare to attack Nishimi and rescue both the girls, before they are discovered?' Yasutsugu suggested.

'Takaakira has many men there,' Saburo said. 'Such an attack would only reveal the importance of the girls and put their lives in danger. Better to try to spirit them away. I can bring them here.'

'If she truly is the Autumn Princess and if I recognise Hina as my niece, we will do that together,' Masachika said.

Saburo could not hide his reluctance. 'It is a hard journey over the mountains, and how will I explain who you are at Nishimi?'

'I have had worse journeys,' Masachika replied. 'I will dress as a groom, pass as a relative of yours, seeking work.'

'I mean no offence, lord, but you do not speak like any relative of mine.'

'You think I can't mimic you?' Masachika said in a familiar way, immediately regretting it, as the elders all stared at him in astonishment.

'You are a man of hidden talents,' Yasutsugu remarked.

'All in the service of Lord Keita and the Kakizuki,' Masachika said hastily.

'Do you swear it?'

'On my brother's soul,' he said and prostrated himself before them.

•

Clothes were brought for Masachika, and some food prepared for travelling. As soon as it was ready and he had changed, they set out.

Saburo looked him over critically, as they walked through the north gate of Rakuhara, past the guards, who wished Saburo a safe journey, and screwed up their faces at Masachika, not recognising him.

'Your hands give you away,' Saburo said. 'How long is it since they have held reins?'

'I have not ridden all winter,' Masachika replied. He thought he heard contempt in the groom's voice and decided he would kill him before they came to Nishimi. However, he knelt and rubbed his hands in the spring mud on the path. Small yellow flowers bloomed along its edge, attracting early bees. The sun was warm, but there was still a trace of winter in the air and snow lingered on the slopes of the mountains they had to cross. It was a little after noon. Night still fell early; they had less than half a day of walking ahead, unless Saburo intended to walk all night. Masachika tried to recall what phase the moon would be in. Surely it was coming up to full, so there would be plenty of light. If he'd known he was going to make this sudden trip, he would not have stayed up so late the night before, nor would he have drunk quite so much. His head ached already.

Saburo set a fast pace, even after the slope steepened and the climb began. The path gradually became more overgrown until it was scarcely more than a fox track and they often had to go on hands and knees to crawl through the undergrowth. After they passed a den, where they could hear newborn cubs mewing and could smell the rank fox odour, the path disappeared completely. Saburo seemed to be following some course he had marked on his descent, carefully placed stones, bent twigs, marks scratched on rocks. Masachika tried to pick them out and realised he could not. Without Saburo, he would be lost. Reluctantly, he decided to let him live until they arrived at Nishimi. He spent the rest of the day devising his punishment and death.

When it was too dark to walk further, Saburo stopped by a rocky outcrop. The ground next to it was flat, sandy rather than stony, and the rocks offered a little shelter.

'We will rest here until moonrise. Sleep if you can. I'll keep watch.'

Masachika sat down, trying to hide the fact that his limbs were trembling from the climb. He had no appetite but he forced himself to swallow the rice ball Saburo held out to him. It was flavoured with dried shrimp and salted plum and increased his intense thirst. Snow melt had gathered in small hollows in the rocks, and they drank from that, licking the last moisture with their tongues.

He did not want to sleep, too aware that while he needed Saburo to guide him, the groom did not need him. If the man suspected him, as he was sure he did, he could easily dispatch Masachika in the mountains and no one would ever know. Masachika was determined to live, for if he could deliver both the Autumn Princess and Kiyoyori's daughter to Miyako, he would win the most profound gratitude from Lord Aritomo, and avenge himself on Takaakira.

However, when he lay down exhaustion overtook him, and dreams began to appear behind his eyelids. He slept without meaning to. He heard familiar voices speaking to him: his father, Tama. He could not catch what they were saying but it seemed important. Then, suddenly, a dark brown foal stood before him. *It looks like Kiyoyori*, he thought in surprise. *How can a horse so resemble my brother?*

He woke, his heart pounding. He sat up swiftly and looked around. The moon had cleared the mountain peaks and lit up the rocks around him. He was alone.

He leaped to his feet, cursing aloud, but then he heard a rustle from the bushes and Saburo appeared.

'What's the matter?' said the groom. 'I just went for a piss. Did you think I'd abandoned you?' He was regarding Masachika with unpleasant shrewdness.

'You are a Kakizuki lord,' Saburo went on, 'brother to the great Kiyoyori. I have been entrusted with the task of getting you to Nishimi, and helping you rescue the Princess and your niece. I know nothing about you, except what the mountain forces you to reveal of yourself. But, already, you have shown you do not trust me. Only the untrustworthy find it impossible to trust others.'

Masachika did not reply. He relieved himself behind the rocks, then followed Saburo as they began to climb upwards, under the third-month moon.

# 12

# HINA

Throughout the long cold winter, Hina had worked at mastering the lute. She had never known an instrument like it. Many times she felt like consigning it to the fire. She would gladly watch it burn, for all the pain it had caused her. It went out of tune, its strings snapped for no reason or seemed to turn sticky under the plectrum so it slipped from her fingers. Even Sadako could not persuade it to play. Yet every now and then it relented and a burst of music would come from it, filled with such purity and yearning it brought tears to her eyes.

At those times she wanted to take it to Aki, but it seemed wiser not to spend too much time with her. The girl lived in the servants' quarters and Hina only saw her once or twice, when she pretended to be more of a child than she really was and went with Bara to the kitchen to be given precious treats, dried persimmons, pickled plums, red bean paste, which grew more scarce as winter dragged on.

When she recovered from her fever, Aki worked in the kitchen, after a fashion, for it was obvious she had neither training nor natural skill, but, as her time drew nearer, it was considered unsafe for her to be there, both for her sake and the household, for if childbirth were to take place suddenly in the kitchen the residence would become polluted. She was confined, with another woman who was expecting a child, to a small detached hut. It was dark and cold, and Hina, who saw it once, thought it a most inauspicious place to give birth.

Aki's labour was long and agonising and no one expected her to survive it. Risu went into labour on the same day. It was also long and difficult – the groom, Saburo, had to pull the foal from her body – but the mare recovered quickly from the delivery, with Saburo's help, and nursed her foal immediately.

Hina had not known it was possible to adore a horse so much. From the moment she set eyes on the foal, the morning after his birth, when he was already standing on wobbly legs beside Risu, she had been in love with him. She had to go and see him several times a day and she lay awake at night longing for morning so she could feast her eyes on him again. She made garlands of spring flowers and hung them round his neck, brushed his coat and polished his little hooves. His mother was brown and his father Nyorin almost white, but the foal's coat was as dark as coal, so she called him Tan.

'He will turn grey, or silver like his father, after his first year,' Saburo said. 'All greys are born brown or black. He is going to be a fine horse. And see how he loves you, Lady Hina.'

Whenever she went to the pasture the foal ran to greet her and followed her closely, breathing at her neck. Sometimes he fixed his huge dark eyes on her as though he would speak at any moment.

'What is it, my darling Tan?' she crooned to him, bringing her face close to his, and felt she was on the point of understanding him.

She loved the baby, who had been born on the same day, almost as much. Both had been difficult births for different reasons. The mare was so old, the girl so young. Aki was very ill after the delivery and could not feed him; the other woman luckily was able to nurse him along with her own baby girl. Aki whispered that his name was to be Takeyoshi, and for now they called him Takemaru: little bamboo shoot, little warrior, for *take* could mean both. He had a shock of black hair and a face that seemed old and wise. He was active and did not sleep much. His foster mother's young sister sometimes carried him around on her back, but mostly Bara looked after him. Often she walked with Hina to show the baby to the horses.

'This is your twin, Take,' Hina would say, taking the baby from Bara and showing him to the foal. 'He will be your horse, for you were born on the same day at the same hour.'

Yet, even as she spoke, she felt all the uncertainty of the future. They would not be able to conceal Aki and the baby forever. Snow still lay on the slopes and the nights were very cold, but one day the wind turned and blew from the east. Spring had come, and surely Takaakira would return soon.

The next day, Saburo was not at the stables. Bara told Hina his father had died and he had gone back to his village for the funeral. His absence added to Hina's unease. She realised she had come to depend on him and to trust him. Bara also was on edge and anxious.

The wind blew more and more strongly and spring came in a rush, leaves appearing on the trees, birds calling in the early morning. One day, Hina went with Bara and the baby to the pasture. She was carrying the lute, for she had dreamed in the night that she had offered it to the Lake Goddess and it had begun to play on its own. It had looked different in the dream, no longer shabby and battered but gleaming rosewood, inlaid with gold and mother of pearl. She could still hear its exquisite music in her head. She also brought Sesshin's book, the Kudzu Vine Treasure Store, intending to read a little in the quiet of the shrine, while Bara entertained the baby.

As usual Tan cantered up to her, nuzzling her and breathing in her breath, wrinkling his lips and snorting over Take, who laughed and wriggled with delight.

'Look,' Bara said, pointing out over the lake. 'A boat is coming!'

Hina's heart plunged to her belly. 'Is it Lord Takaakira?'

'It could be.'

They stared out over the water, dazzled by the sun, the wind bringing tears to their eyes. From the boat came strands of music and laughter, and a strange high sound, like an animal squealing.

'That doesn't sound like the lord,' Bara said, and they both gave a gasp of relief at the same time. Bara looked guilty as she smiled. 'It must be one of the market boats. They have been driven across the lake by the wind. I suppose they were trying to get to the Rainbow Bridge, and Majima.'

'What beautiful names,' Hina said. 'Where are they?'

'On the other side of the lake. They will be holding the twenty-fifth-day market there today. I think they might be performers, for those cries are monkeys.'

'Monkeys!' Hina exclaimed. 'Let's go down to the dock and see them. Little Take would like that, wouldn't you?'

The foal gave a strange sound, startling them. He was gazing intently towards the stables. His body trembled all over.

'Oh, it's Saburo,' Bara said. 'Did Tan recognise him?' She waved, holding the baby in one arm.

Saburo and another man were walking past the barracks, where the warriors were preparing for another day, getting out their bows to practise archery, repairing and polishing armour.

'Who's that with him?' Hina said.

'I don't know,' Bara said, sounding puzzled. 'Another groom, perhaps? I haven't seen him round here before.'

Hina was watching the way Saburo walked, nonchalant but wary, eyes flicking round as if searching. He saw Bara and made a slight gesture with his head. *What does it mean*, Hina wondered. She would never know. Suddenly Saburo was not walking anymore. The man alongside him grabbed him, twisted him into a strange position, one arm behind his back. The knife at his throat. Shouts of surprise. The men on their feet, swords drawn. Saburo on his knees. The sudden gush of blood. Bara's scream. The foal pushing her, pushing her towards the shore.

*Run, daughter. It is your uncle. He will hand you over to the Miboshi.*

'Akihime!' she cried. 'Bara, we must warn Akihime.' Then she stopped, terrified the murderer had heard her.

Bara stood whimpering in shock. Hina held the lute and the text in one hand and with the other seized the baby from her. She looked around, frantic. Where should she run to?

The boat had reached the shore. The easterly wind had dropped. She could hear laughter, the careless laughter of ordinary people. She thought of what she was leaving behind. Takaakira, her life of music and learning. The eyes? How could she leave the eyes? They were in her room. And the sword? Akihime's sword, which she had returned to the shrine as an offering to the Lake Goddess.

Bara was stumbling, like a sleepwalker, towards Saburo's fallen body. The other man, Hina's uncle, was gesticulating, explaining to the men who surrounded him. Hina heard their cries of amazement and triumph. Akihime was betrayed.

She felt the lute pull her. She ran to the dock, Take bumping and chuckling in one arm, the lute and the scroll in the other. The lute was changing before her eyes just like in her dream. It became beautiful, gleaming in the morning sun, and as she approached the boat it began to play, the glorious music echoing through the sudden calm.

Then with a rush the wind rose again.

'Ah, here comes the westerly!' called the helmsman. 'We will get to the market, after all!'

'Take me with you!' Hina cried, as the oarsmen turned the boat and the west wind filled the sail. The lute was almost deafening her. Behind her Tan was neighing.

Two boys, a few years younger than she was, stood on the deck, surrounded by monkeys.

'What are you doing with that lute?' one of them shouted to her, as the boat skimmed the side of the dock.

'Take it!' Hina put Take down for a moment and threw the lute to them and then the text. Then she picked Take up and holding him tightly in her arms jumped after them. But the boat had already veered around and the baby hampered her. She fell into the deep water next to the dock. She did not dare release her grip on Take. He struggled and screamed, choking on the icy water. The beautiful robes Takaakira had given her were now deadly, filling with water, as heavy as iron.

# 13

# MASACHIKA

The following day Masachika took Akihime to Miyako, crossing the lake by boat, using the same westerly wind. He did not go to Aomizu but directly to Kasumiguchi. He was troubled that Hina and the baby had disappeared, apparently drowned in the lake, though there was no trace of their bodies – it would have been tidier to scoop all three up in the one net – but he had the main catch secure in his hands. The weather was worsening and he did not want to get caught on the open lake in a storm.

He searched the house and the shrine before leaving and found enough evidence to prove that Takaakira had been keeping the young girl in the house for nearly a year. When he questioned the two women, who were teachers of some kind, they swore they had not known who their pupil was, but attested to her intelligence, gentle nature and talent for music and poetry, none of which interested Masachika in the slightest. But in her room he found the box and that interested him greatly.

He remembered what the groom had said, but could not resist the temptation to look inside. Immediately sadness swept over him. He felt anew the loss of Tama and Matsutani. He saw himself always, all his life, compared to Kiyoyori, and falling short. He saw his self-serving nature, his jealousy, his treachery. Bitter regrets assailed him for all that might have been. While his mind was so open and vulnerable, one of his flashes of insight came to him. The eyes were Sesshin's and would give him mastery over the spirits at Matsutani. He closed the box, and made sure it travelled with him.

He came upon the sword in the shrine. It had been placed behind the altar, and he marvelled that no one had stolen it, for he had never seen a finer blade. He felt an unusual reluctance to touch it, and when he lifted it it felt heavy and unwieldy, but after a few moments it settled into his hand and he was aware it had acquiesced in some way. It thrilled him, giving him hope that his life was about to turn around, that he would be well rewarded, that he would become a better man as a result. To his surprise, a prayer formed on his lips. He also found a ceremonial bow made of catalpa wood, but it made him feel uneasy and he decided to send it to Ryusonji. He was holding it in one hand and the sword in the other when he came out of the shrine. The horses were standing in front of it, as if they had been waiting for him. They stared at him fixedly, and a shaft of terror pierced him as he recognised the foal from his dream.

Masachika did not dare voice his fears. He gave orders that the horses should be brought to Miyako, resolving to present them to the Prince Abbot. If the foal were possessed, the Prince Abbot would recognise the spirit.

The maid, Bara, was hysterical at the loss of her lover, which Masachika realised Saburo must have been, and useless, so he took the younger of the teachers, Sadako, with them, to wait on Akihime, for even though she was a fugitive she was still a nobleman's daughter. Akihime refused to speak and did not respond to any of his questions regarding Yoshimori, or the child that she had recently given birth to, though when his patience gave out and he told her the boy had drowned, she wept silently.

•

Lord Aritomo inspected Aki as if she were a piece of art. Takaakira was in the room with them, but so far he had not spoken. Masachika glanced at him from time to time, trying to assess his reactions, but the lord of the Snow Country remained impassive.

The rain was teeming down. As Masachika had feared, the westerly had increased to a gale. Rivers were breaking their banks, destroying the spring plantings of rice and vegetables.

'You see,' Lord Aritomo said, 'I was right. She went to her childhood home. We only had to wait for her.' He smiled tight-lipped, then addressed Masachika.

'Well done. You will be rewarded.'

Masachika bowed. He had related how the groom, Saburo, had come to Rakuhara, but so far he made no mention of Hina or the baby, nor did he say anything about the eyes or disclose the sword.

'Why are her arms bruised?' Aritomo said.

'She was about to cut her throat. I had to prevent her. She struggled against me.'

Aritomo nodded.

'May I present the knife to you?' Masachika said.

Aritomo took it and inspected it carefully. 'It is very fine. In a way I am sorry it does not come fresh with the blood of a Princess, but, of course, she will be more use to us alive.'

He turned to Takaakira, showing him the knife. 'You would have had the honour of finding her, and earlier, if I had not summoned you back here to advise me on this upstart at Kumayama. What does he call himself?'

'Shikanoko,' Takaakira replied.

'Tell Masachika about him.'

'He is causing us some trouble by establishing a garrison between the capital and Minatogura. He attacked his family fortress at Kumayama and killed his uncle, who had become one of our vassals. Then he took over Kuromori at the beginning of the winter. Next will be Matsutani.'

'What possible claim can he have to Matsutani?' Masachika exclaimed.

'Right of conquest, it is called,' Aritomo said dryly. 'Don't be too concerned. He won't be there for long. We are going to use the Autumn Princess to draw him out. According to the Prince Abbot at Ryusonji he has strong feelings for her. Isn't that right, Princess?'

Akihime did not raise her head.

'He will try to rescue you, but he will die in the attempt,' Aritomo said pleasantly. 'But first you will tell us where Yoshimori, the false Emperor, is.'

'I don't know where he is,' Akihime replied. 'He was kidnapped from me. I have not seen him for months. But, as you well know, he is the true Emperor. Isn't Heaven itself telling you that? If he is restored to the throne, these disasters will end.'

The rain fell more heavily, as if the river itself had been drawn up from its bed and was emptying itself out, over the city.

'Neither Shikanoko nor anyone else will be moving if this continues,' Takaakira said. 'All the rivers between here and Minatogura are in flood and the country is devastated.'

'It is your evil doing that has caused it,' Aki said. 'You know how to bring back harmony between Heaven and Earth.'

'Silence!' Aritomo had gone pale and a muscle was twitching in his cheek. 'Takaakira,' he said in a tight voice. 'Send the Princess to Ryusonji. We will see what the Prince Abbot can find out from her. And have Masachika make a full report on the situation at Rakuhara.'

•

The guards escorted Akihime out of the room. Takaakira and Masachika bowed deeply to Lord Aritomo and left together. Masachika followed the other man to a small room overlooking the garden. He was slightly worried Takaakira would comment on the sword, but it was disguised in his old scabbard, and, in some way, he knew it was not going to draw attention to itself. The eyes were in their carved rosewood box, tucked inside the breast of his hunting robe. He wondered how much Takaakira knew about them.

A solid curtain of rain fell from the eaves and the once beautiful garden was sodden. Water lay on the paths in huge puddles and all the pools were overflowing.

Masachika reported all he had learned during his months with the Kakizuki army, weapons, numbers of men and horses, fighting spirit, and described the luxury Lord Keita lived in, and, finally, Keita's hopes of finding Yoshimori.

Takaakira listened without comment, saying at the end, 'Well, write it all down and bring the document to me at my house tomorrow. You can write, I suppose?'

Masachika noted the contemptuous tone and said blandly, 'Of course,' while thinking, *Don't be too quick to antagonise me, noble lord. You will be begging me, before too long. And don't forget that what you call your house is as much mine as yours.*

After Takaakira left, Masachika called for writing materials and something to eat and drink. All were supplied swiftly and politely. His status had risen, he concluded with considerable gratification. It took him some time to compose his report – his writing was adequate for recording the various exploits of warriors on the battlefield and he was familiar with that vocabulary, but, in striving to make his work both clear and elegant, he realised there were many words he was not sure of. He had to spell them out, rather than using their ideograms, and he feared it made the report look womanly, childish.

By the time he had finished, it was almost dark; the rain was heavier than ever. A servant came to remove the utensils, and he said he would spend the night where he was.

'Certainly, lord,' she said, prostrating herself. 'I will fetch some bedding.'

When she returned, she brought new robes. 'From Lord Aritomo,' she murmured.

Masachika settled down for the night, under the padded silk, feeling reasonably pleased with himself.

•

The next day he presented himself at the house that had been his father's, and then Kiyoyori's, and was now occupied by Takaakira. He wore the new clothes, a brocade hunting robe and embroidered trousers. Together with the eyes in their box and the sword at his side, they gave him confidence, but even more than these, it was the secret he held in his heart that would put him on an equal footing with Takaakira.

The lord of the Snow Country looked as if he had spent a sleepless night. Masachika wondered, as he had several times already, what the man's purpose was in keeping Kiyoyori's daughter alive, in defiance of Aritomo's orders. Perhaps he had fallen in love with her – some men did lust after young girls – but why take such a risk? There were plenty of maidens in the city. Why choose Kiyoyori's daughter?

*No doubt you are regretting your rashness now*, he thought, raising his eyes insolently to Takaakira's pale face and hollow eyes.

He had presented the report and it lay on the floor at Takaakira's side. They were alone in the room and the rain was so loud, there was little chance of being overheard. Nevertheless Takaakira gestured that Masachika should move closer and whispered, 'Did you find anyone else at Nishimi?'

Masachika pretended to look puzzled. 'Lord?'

'A young girl was living there, my ward.'

'Your ward?'

'Yes. She is called Hina.'

'My niece, Hina? My brother's daughter?'

Takaakira did not say anything but the expression on his face nearly compensated Masachika for all the petty humiliations he had endured. Nearly but not quite.

'She was believed to be dead,' he said. 'Can it be that she lives, after all? What joy!'

'What a scoundrel you are,' Takaakira said. 'How could you and Kiyoyori be brothers?'

'I'm surprised you are so free with your insults! I only have to mention my niece, and her lucky escape, to Aritomo and your life will be over.'

'My life is over, if she is dead,' Takaakira said, sombre.

Masachika stared at him. 'It's true, isn't it, that no man is without at least one weakness? A little girl has aroused your lust and you will throw everything away for that?'

'It's nothing like that. If I love her, it is as a daughter. She is a miracle, so intelligent, so gifted – but I will not discuss her with you.'

'Well, many men sleep with their daughters,' Masachika said crudely. 'You would not be the first.'

'Is she alive?'

'She ran away.'

'Where to? Did anyone see her go?'

'I'm afraid I only have conflicting reports. One person said Hina jumped aboard a boat with the baby.'

'What baby?'

'Akihime's son,' Masachika said.

'You did not mention that earlier in the report,' Takaakira said.

'I thought that information should rest between us for the time being. It may not matter, at all, for the other eyewitness said Hina fell into the lake with the baby in her arms. The water is very deep by the dock, and I believe they both drowned.'

Takaakira covered his eyes with one hand. When he could speak he said, 'I presume you searched the house and questioned the servants?'

'Of course,' Masachika replied.

'Did you find a box containing . . . something unusual? A small, beautifully carved box of rosewood?'

'No, lord,' Masachika said, feeling the box burn against his ribs.

'Then she must have taken it with her.' The idea seemed to console Takaakira somewhat. 'I cannot believe she is dead.'

'Shall I make a more detailed report for Lord Aritomo?' Masachika managed to convey sympathy and menace at the same time.

Takaakira gave him a long, unwavering look of pure contempt. 'I suppose we must come to some arrangement,' he said. 'If she is dead you can tell him what you choose. I will offer him my life in atonement. But if there is a chance she is alive, I must live and I must find her. What must I do to persuade you to keep this to yourself for now?'

'Are you suggesting I have a price?' Masachika said, pretending affront.

'We all have our price,' Takaakira replied bitterly. 'I just hope yours is not too high.'

•

After this, Masachika found it easy to obtain permission from Takaakira to do whatever he desired. He rationed his requests, not wanting to push the lord too far. At one time he thought he would demand Kiyoyori's old house for himself, but he decided against it. First he would secure Matsutani. Now he had Sesshin's eyes, he was sure he could pacify and control the rebellious spirits. He proposed he should be the one to find Shikanoko and tell him they held the Autumn Princess in Miyako.

Takaakira agreed to approach Lord Aritomo who gave his permission readily. It had been necessary to apply pressure to the Princess, enough to persuade her to talk but not so much as to kill her. Aritomo wanted her alive. She was watched day and night lest she try to take her own life, but despite the pain and the lack of sleep she revealed nothing other than that Yoshimori had been stolen away from her. She would not say where or how.

'If we bring them together,' Aritomo said, 'we will easily persuade the Princess to talk, and we will prevent any further Kakizuki uprisings.'

'Secure Matsutani, send a message from there and let me know Shikanoko's response immediately. Don't try to capture him or engage him in battle. The Prince Abbot wants him to be drawn into the capital so he can be taken alive.'

Once again Masachika found himself at the head of a band of men riding towards Matsutani. The Prince Abbot sent one of his monks with him, a young man with a fine muscular body and a face ruined as if by fire. His name was Eisei. He covered his features, what was left of them, with a black silk cloth, above which his lashless eyes darted, like a lizard's. Masachika learned his injuries had been caused in some way by Shikanoko. Eisei was an adept in esoteric practices, which would be useful, for everyone knew by now that Shikanoko was not only a warrior but also a sorcerer.

Their journey was delayed by downpours, flooded rivers, and a kind of sullen hostility among porters, innkeepers, ferrymen, in fact almost everyone they had to deal with. Horses went lame, provisions disappeared, mildew sprang out on everything, reins and tempers snapped. People grumbled openly that the Miboshi lords had offended the gods and they were being punished for it.

'You should cut out their tongues,' Eisei said to Masachika.

'Then I would make an entire population dumb,' he replied. He pretended to be unaffected by the unrest that seethed just below the surface of everyday life, but as usual he was calculating his best chances. The Miboshi were powerful and well armed, Aritomo single-minded and ruthless, blessed by the support of the Prince Abbot, but if Heaven had turned its face against him . . . Masachika was keeping all possible choices in the balance.

Once again, he passed through the barrier at Shimaura. The Kakizuki skulls had long been removed, but he thought of the living, at Kuromori, now immeasurably strengthened by Shikanoko. They would consider themselves betrayed by him, and were no doubt thirsting for revenge.

He learned here that Shikanoko was still at Kuromori, his forces growing in number daily as disaffected and dispossessed men found their way to him. The guards at the barrier were tense and resentful, tired of the constant rain, the flooding river, the gales that kept ships confined to port. They complained to Masachika that their supplies were dwindling, they were too few to fight off an attack and if they were overwhelmed the road would be cut between Miyako and Minatogura.

Masachika knew he had many failings. He was quite prepared to live with dishonour, rather than end his life prematurely, but he did not consider himself a coward. He was aware most of his small band of men mistrusted him; the disaster of the first raid, in which comrades and cousins had died, was still fresh in their memories, and everyone knew he had spent six months with the Kakizuki.

The capture of the Princess, and his rise in standing with Aritomo, counted in his favour, but there were still whispers. *Once a spy, always a spy. A man who turns once will turn twice.* He resolved he would ride to Matsutani openly, showing neither hesitation nor fear. He dismissed the guards' complaints, and scoffed at the rumours that Shikanoko had supernatural powers, employed invisible imps and artificial warriors that could not be killed, and talked to the dead.

Eisei took such rumours seriously, explaining to Masachika that that was why the Prince Abbot wanted him alive. 'He wants to understand the source of these skills so he can control them himself. Shikanoko has a mask, fashioned from a stag's skull; it gives him all the power of the forest, but only he can use it.' He touched the silk veil that covered his face. 'It burns anyone else.'

'Is that what happened to you?'

Eisei nodded. 'Before that, I was my lord's favourite. Now I am disfigured. I bring pollution into his presence. He looks on me with pity. He is good to me, and kind, but it is not pity I want from him, or from anyone. I used to be at his side during secret rituals of great power. He showed me wonders and took me to realms that are hidden from ordinary people. Now all that is barred to me. From time to time he graciously allows me into his presence but I don't like to accept too often. I am afraid I will infect him with my bad fortune. So I sweep the floors and tend the gardens. It is all I am good for.'

'You were lucky you did not lose your eyes,' Masachika said.

'If I were blind, I would not be aware of my disfigurement,' Eisei replied. 'I would not see pity and revulsion on the faces of others. I had lost all interest in life; indeed, I tried to hang myself.' He indicated marks at his throat, which Masachika had thought were scars from the same incident that burned his face. 'The branch I chose broke. It was not my time. My lord decided to find some purpose for my life and gave me this mission to accompany you.'

They rode in silence for a while. The rain had slackened to a drizzle; the mountains were swathed in mist. Biting insects buzzed around them, making the horses shake their heads and kick at their bellies.

'There are some guardian spirits at Matsutani,' Masachika said. 'Last time I was here they prevented me, or anyone else, from entering. I am hoping to be able to placate them this time.'

'Maybe I can be of help,' Eisei said. 'I know many spells and prayers of exorcism. Who placed them there?'

'An old man, Sesshin. I remember him from my childhood. He lived at Kuromori, for many years. We were not aware that he was a powerful sorcerer. After he left, no one knew the spirits were there and so they were neglected and have turned spiteful.'

'That can easily happen,' Eisei said. 'Guardian spirits can be quite petty and they take a lot of looking after. Sesshin . . . that must be the same old man who now plays the lute in the courtyards of Ryusonji. The monk, Gessho, captured him and brought him to my lord, along with Shikanoko. He had been blinded and apparently all his powers were gone. He turned out to be a fine musician, though. He and my lord had some past history between them – my lord had been looking for him for a long time. He was not pleased when Sesshin escaped him. He held his physical body but his sorcerer's spirit had fled with all its powers. And then Shikanoko slipped out of his control, and Gessho was sent after him again, but never returned. It is the first time anyone has challenged the Prince Abbot in this way. That is why Shikanoko must be destroyed.'

The rain began to fall more heavily. They spent a sleepless night in a group of hovels that hardly merited the title of village. There was little food other than a thin soup of mountain herbs. Masachika learned that Matsutani was still haunted and that Shikanoko was not there. Lady Tama lived nearby, alone, in theory, though Hisoku's name was mentioned once or twice in a way that made Masachika burn with anger. He had vowed to kill the man at the first opportunity and he hoped it would present itself soon.

The next morning they were met on the road by Hisoku himself, at the head of a band of ten or twelve men. They were all gaunt and ragged. Only two had horses, besides Hisoku, and their weapons were old-fashioned and inadequate. Moreover, they were not ready for battle. Masachika learned afterwards that most were Miboshi warriors, probably expecting him and his men to be reinforcements. Had the sun been shining he might have been inclined to negotiate and take the time to find this out, but the rain had put him in a vile temper and the sight of Hisoku enraged him further. He gave the order for an immediate attack.

The men on foot were cut down with swords; the horsemen tried to escape but fell in a hail of well-aimed arrows. Hisoku's devious skills were no use to him in an open fight. He was swiftly unhorsed and Masachika ordered his men to hang him from an oak tree on the edge of the forest.

'Make sure the branch does not break,' Eisei said.

The branch was secure. Hisoku cursed Masachika, then pleaded, to no avail. They left his body still kicking and struggling and rode on to Matsutani.

# 14

# TAMA

The long cold winter and the wet spring had given Lady Tama plenty of time to reflect on her situation, and she had realised her life was hopeless. As soon as the rain stopped, she decided, she would return to Muenji, shave her head and become a nun, and spend the rest of her life atoning for the sins she had committed and the hardness of her heart.

Matsutani had been granted to her in a tribunal of law, but she could not take possession of it because it was occupied by hostile spirits. She saw all too clearly the universal law of cause and effect. If she had not taken out Sesshin's eyes and driven him away, the spirits would have remained hidden, protecting the house and the estate as they had done for years without anyone knowing of their existence, save the man who had set them there, the very same Sesshin.

If even the powerful monk Gessho had not been able to control them, she did not think anyone could. Matsutani would have to be abandoned. Already the house was beginning to disintegrate. Most of her treasured possessions lay strewn around the garden, slowly rotting away and probably being possessed themselves by unwelcome elemental spirits. Holes had appeared in the roof, shutters hung lopsided and rattled in the wind, wild animals had made dens under the verandahs and birds nested in the eaves. A huge white owl had taken to roosting on the ridge of the roof. It hooted in an unpleasant way throughout the night.

Haru's house, where Tama now lived, was cramped and uncomfortable. Tama felt Haru despised her secretly, though the woman spoke to her respectfully and deferred to her. The abduction and death of Tsumaru lay between them; just as, while he lived, they had competed for his affection, so, now he was dead, each blamed the other and felt her grief was greater.

They did not speak of Hina. It was another of Tama's regrets, that she had not made more effort with the child, made pale and mute by grief, when Hina had become her stepdaughter. But she had had her own troubles, her brother's death, the loss of her first husband, the new marriage, the pregnancy. Somehow she had overlooked Hina and, when she had finally given her some attention, it was too late. Hina had withdrawn any affection forever.

Tama knew Haru's children disliked her, especially the older one, Chikamaru, whom everyone called Chika. He was an insolent and taciturn boy, who came and went without telling anyone what he was up to. She suspected he was going at night to Kuromori, where Shikanoko had been all winter, along with Chika's father, Kongyo, and the rest of Kiyoyori's men. He never told her what was happening there, but sometimes his eyes gleamed when he looked at her and his lips curved in a scornful smile.

And the final reason for giving up and returning to the temple was that she would be rid of Hisoku – she could see no other way to shed him, apart from having someone kill him, and among the few men at Matsutani the only one she could call on to carry out an assassination was Hisoku himself. He believed he was indispensable to her, that his adoration of her gave him some claim over her. He exaggerated his abilities and made much of the fact that he could approach the house with offerings, without having anything thrown at him.

'You don't see that you are their slave,' she said. 'You are not in any way their master.'

'Slowly does it,' Hisoku replied. 'I am working up to it, just as I am working up to you.'

He treated her with increasing familiarity and she knew he expected to be her husband soon. The thought made her skin crawl, yet again she could blame no one but herself. She had played on his devotion, using him to obtain the documents that proved Matsutani was hers, allowing him to accompany her, relying on him to take command of the Miboshi men who had fled after Shikanoko's attack on Kuromori, as if he were her husband and lord. It was only natural he would eventually demand payment. From Haru's remarks, she knew that everyone thought she and Hisoku were already man and wife, in all but name, and this filled her with revulsion, at the same time driving her towards him as if she were under a spell. Her sense of obligation, the lengthening days, the budding of spring, late and cold as it was, her own body with its frank needs and desires, all conspired to weaken her resolve.

In the fourth month, the rain lessened and late one afternoon Tama walked towards the west gate, trying to come to a decision. She resolved she would leave that week, walk to the coast and take a boat to Minatogura, as she had done a year ago. This time she would truly renounce all earthly desires and cut her hair. A weight lifted from her and she began to whisper her goodbyes to her childhood home, bidding farewell to the living and the dead.

Chika appeared beside her, seeming to materialise out of the drizzle. He was soaking, moisture beading his thick lashes and the smooth skin of his face.

'You startled me,' she said, trying to smile.

His stare was unresponsive and cold. 'Your man is dead.'

'What?'

'Hisoku is dead.'

She thought his eyes shone with secret glee. *Let me feel grief*, she prayed, *let me not feel relief.*

'They hanged him,' Chika went on.

'Who?' She looked round wildly.

'Some men from Miyako. They are coming here. One of them came before to attack Kuromori. He knew the mountain path because he grew up there. But the defenders were warned.' He glanced up at her, unable to keep pride and self-satisfaction from his voice. 'He was the only survivor. Can you guess who it is?'

'Masachika,' she said. He had been offended and humiliated by Hisoku and now he had taken revenge. To hang him was an outrage. Why could he not have simply taken off his head? She could feel tears threatening. So, she could experience grief – not only for Hisoku but for Masachika and herself, for the married couple they once were and the brief fierce happiness they had known in the house, once beautiful, now derelict and haunted.

Chika was watching her face. 'Is he friend or foe to you?'

'I don't know,' she replied.

She composed herself and went to the west gate to wait for Masachika. From the house behind her she could hear the spirits' voices. They sounded agitated.

'Matsutani Lady, who are you waiting for?'

'Where is Hisoku? We are hungry and thirsty.'

'Is it another great monk, like Gessho?'

'Gessho is dead. He lost his head!'

387

'Hisoku is dead too,' Tama said quietly.

'Oh yes! Oh yes! Born to be hanged!'

'It's the one that came before, that we sent the bees to sting.'

'Didn't the bees kill him?'

'We'll send more this time.'

'I beg of you, be still,' Tama said, 'until we know why he has come.'

'You should have been still, Matsutani Lady. You should have waited before you tore out our master's eyes.'

'Before you turned him out into the Darkwood.'

'I regret that with every fibre of my being,' Tama whispered.

'Too late, too late, too late!' they both jeered running the words together.

'*Toolatetoolatetoolate.*'

•

'I did not expect you,' she addressed Masachika when the men rode up and he dismounted. She recognised one of the riderless horses they led as Hisoku's and the sight of the horse alive, when its master was dead, pierced her unexpectedly. 'If anyone came, I thought it would be Shikanoko, who has been at Kuromori all winter.'

He bowed his head to her, and gave his horse's reins to the nearest man.

'Shikanoko is indeed the reason I am here.'

'Hisoku rode out thinking it was him, making an outflanking attack. You did not need to kill him. You were on the same side!'

'He and his men surprised us in an ambush,' Masachika said. 'They did not declare their names nor did they have any banners or crests. Anyway, they are all dead now.'

'*Toolatetoolatetoolate,*' sighed the spirits.

Masachika glanced towards the garden. 'So the house is still possessed?'

'Yes, and they will be more fractious now. Hisoku brought them offerings. He was the only person they allowed through the gate.'

'I have seen what they can do,' Masachika bent forward to whisper in her ear. 'But I believe I possess the key to controlling them.'

The horses were beginning to fidget impatiently. Masachika said, 'Let me organise food and shelter for my men. Then we will talk and I will show you what I have.'

Tama looked around for Chika but he was nowhere to be seen. He had vanished as silently as he had appeared earlier at her side.

The rain began to fall more heavily.

'Will it never clear up?' Masachika said.

'They say Heaven is outraged.'

'We all have to get over things. I suppose one day Heaven will too, and the sun will shine again.'

'Come to Haru's house,' Tama said. 'I am living there. But first, please bury the men with honour. We do not want any more offended spirits.'

There was no dry wood for fires; the ground was sodden and any graves dug immediately filled with water. Masachika's men carried the bodies up the mountain and threw them into one of the limestone caves, sealing the entrance with boulders. For weeks the northwest wind would bring the smell of death wafting down the valley.

Haru greeted Masachika coldly. 'On whose orders do you come this time? I hear you have been both Miboshi and Kakizuki.'

'I have been sent by Lord Aritomo,' he said. 'My mission is to speak with Shikanoko. I am sure you will be able to get in touch with Kuromori, through your son, like last time. Don't be alarmed. A year ago I would have slit his throat if I had been able to lay hands on him. But now he can be useful to me. Tomorrow he can take a message. I need to talk to Lady Tama in private. If I catch your brat eavesdropping I really will slit his throat. And that goes for you too,' he said, addressing the girl, who had been sitting silently by her mother. She stared back guilelessly as though she had no idea what he was talking about.

'I've learned women and girls are as dangerous as men when it comes to spying,' he said to Tama, when they were alone on the verandah of the attached room where she slept. 'More dangerous, as they are so often overlooked.'

'That's a mistake most men make,' Tama replied.

'Men make many mistakes.' Masachika gave a deep sigh. 'And many more are forced on them by circumstances.'

'Have you come to rake over the past, Masachika? That's a fire whose embers went cold long ago.'

But, even as she spoke, she knew her words were not wholly true.

'What I have to show you may cause you pain,' he said, taking a small carved box from inside his robe. 'This box contains the eyes of Sesshin. If we place them back on the gate, I believe the spirits will be placated.'

'Show me,' she said in a low voice.

He opened the lid. The eyes lay on their silk bed, still bright and glistening.

Tama began to weep silently.

'Let your tears wash them,' Masachika said, his own voice breaking.

'I have missed you every day since we were parted,' Tama cried, sobbing now. 'It was because I was taken from you that I became cold and cruel. I hardened my heart so I would not die of grief.'

'I feel the same. I have committed many sins, I have killed and betrayed. When the eyes see me, they show me everything I have ever done wrong and it all stems from the day when you were taken from me and given to Kiyoyori. My hurt was so great I wanted only to savage others. I felt that my own father and my brother betrayed me. I have trusted no one since then.'

'I am sorry, I am sorry,' Tama wept before the eyes' unblinking stare. 'Can I ever be forgiven?'

Masachika put his arms round her and drew her close to him. His tears fell on her hair. All the regrets of the past years rose before them, no longer suppressed, no longer hidden. 'I forgive you,' he said.

'Only you understand what was done to us.'

She felt the thrill of desire run through him at the same time as her own body leaped for him. The feel of his arms round her was so familiar, his smell, his skin, every muscle. She ached for him as she had when she was just a girl, newly married. He put his hands under her hair and lifted her face to his, covering it with kisses, finding her mouth. She loosened her sash and let her robe fall open, pressing herself against him as though she could absorb him through her skin.

She knew all his faults, as he knew hers, yet it seemed she had never stopped loving him.

'We are still husband and wife,' he whispered, as he loosened his own clothes.

'Nothing can change that,' she replied, as she did for him all that a wife does for a husband, and as they took and received bliss from each other she said silently to the spirits, 'You are wrong. I was wrong. It is not too late.'

The following morning, Tama sent for Chika, Haru's son.

'Lord Masachika has an errand for you. You are to go to Kuromori and tell Shikanoko to come here.'

Chika's eyes flickered at the word *Lord* and she felt he saw right through her. She did not care. Let the whole world know that Masachika was her husband again.

'*Tell* is not how you should address Shikanoko,' Chika replied. '*Ask* or *invite* or even *beg* might be more appropriate.'

'Tell him to present himself here,' Masachika commanded, 'if he wants to save the life of the Autumn Princess.'

'I believe he will be on his way, already,' Chika said. 'I will go and meet him and tell him you are expecting him.'

'Who is the Autumn Princess?' Tama asked after the boy had left.

'The daughter of the false Emperor Yoshimori's foster parents, and the only person, apart from Shikanoko, we think, who knows where he is. I will explain everything to you but first we must replace Sesshin's eyes.'

They took the box to the west gate and placed the eyes behind the carved frieze in the architrave. Both had dressed carefully, Tama in multi-layered robes in spring shades of pink, Masachika in a hunting robe that Haru had kept in a rue-strewn chest and that had been Kiyoyori's. He wore the sword he had found in the shrine at Nishimi. They wept again, knelt and asked for forgiveness for the mistakes and misdeeds of the past. For the first time in years they felt whole, each completing the other.

Tama had brought rice wine and spring flowers for the spirits, but these offerings did little to alleviate their distress.

'I don't want to go back to the gateposts, do you?'

'No, I don't. I like it in the house.'

Masachika said, 'Your master's eyes are restored. You are revered and honoured now. There is no reason for you to continue to be a nuisance.'

'Who is that speaking?'

'It is the husband of Matsutani Lady.'

'Matsutani Lord?'

'I suppose so.'

'Masachika?'

'Yes, Masachika.'

'So, the bees didn't kill him?'

'Obviously not.'

'Shall we try again?'

'You most certainly will not!' Masachika said. 'You will cease all your destructive acts. You will not throw anything or hurt anybody.' Masachika spoke with stern authority. 'You will dwell in the gateposts and watch over Matsutani as Master Sesshin commanded you.'

'Curses!'

'A thousand curses!'

'A hundred thousand curses!'

'No!' Masachika said. 'You are only allowed to pronounce words of protection and blessing.'

'Oh, all right,' they said grudgingly. 'Blessings, blessings, blessings. Are you satisfied now?'

'I will be when you are back in position,' said Masachika.

'It was fun while it lasted, wasn't it?'

'It was like Paradise. But all things pass.'

'Everything that has a beginning has an ending.'

'That is much better,' Masachika said. 'That is how guardian spirits should talk.'

There was a ripple of movement across the courtyard and the two gateposts seemed to glow with inner light.

'Back to work,' sighed the voice from the left one.

'I wanted the left. Why do I have to take the right?'

'What difference does it make?'

'If it makes no difference then swap over!'

'No!'

The bickering voices grew fainter and fainter until they could no longer be heard.

'They are funny,' Tama said, as Masachika opened the gate and they walked towards the house. 'I will miss them in a way.'

The years had fallen away. She felt like the young girl who had married him when she had been fifteen and he eighteen.

'Now at last we can make the house as beautiful as it used to be,' Tama said, stooping to gather up the various objects that lay scattered on the ground. 'Some of these things can be saved. Matsutani will be restored.'

When they stood on the verandah peering into the dark rooms, Masachika said, 'Kiyoyori's daughter was concealed at Nishimi.'

Tama stood frozen in surprise. All she could think of to say was, stupidly, 'Where is Nishimi?'

'It is on the western side of Lake Kasumi. It belonged to the father of the Autumn Princess, a nobleman, Hidetake. While I was with the Kakizuki at Rakuhara I learned she was in hiding there and I went to arrange her capture and transport to the capital. I was told Hina was there too. I did not see her myself. She ran away, and she is believed to have drowned in the lake.'

Tama said nothing for a while. She looked at the things she was holding and placed them on the floor, brushing the dirt from her hands. Then she said, 'Poor Hina. I was jealous of her, of Kiyoyori's love for her and for her dead mother. I tried to be a mother to her, but she was a cold little thing, always pushing me away, preferring Haru or her father. I was told she was dead, like my son. But how did she end up at that place?'

'You know Yukikuni no Takaakira? Aritomo's right-hand man?'

'I have heard of him.'

'He had taken Hina there. He must have found her in our family's house in the capital. For some reason he decided to spare her life.'

'Without Aritomo's knowledge?' She found it hard to believe. What could explain such a rash act? And then she remembered Hina's unnatural intelligence and, she had to admit, beauty. She felt the old jealousy stir and was both relieved and sad that its object was dead.

'Exactly,' he said. 'I could have guessed you would understand all the implications.'

'But how can you be sure it was her, if you did not see her?'

'From all the Kakizuki spy told me, it could only be her. And then I found the box with the eyes. Hina must have taken them with her when she left Matsutani. Afterwards Takaakira confirmed it – he even asked me directly about her.'

'I wondered why you had them,' Tama said.

'I also found this sword. Do you recognise it? Could it have been Kiyoyori's?'

He drew the sword from the scabbard and held it out to her.

'It may have been,' she said. 'There might be something familiar about it but, at the same time, I don't really recognise the hilt or the braiding. Could it have been recast after his death? It would have been burned with him.' She touched the hilt gently. 'You know, people say he is not really dead, but lives on in some form, and will return when the time is right.'

Masachika was silent.

'We must get to work at once,' Tama said, turning and stepping back into the garden. As they walked to the gate she asked, 'Masachika, are you with the Miboshi now or are your sympathies still with the Kakizuki?'

'The Kakizuki are doomed,' he replied. 'Only a fool would side with them. But I am first with Matsutani and its lady.'

Tama smiled. 'I suppose I have already abandoned the Kakizuki, since it is the Miboshi who endorsed my claim.'

'I am Aritomo's man now,' Masachika said. 'My main task here is to approach Shikanoko on his behalf.'

'Shikanoko is nothing,' Tama said. 'He was a wild boy whom the bandit Akuzenji found in the forest. Your brother spared his life because he considered him harmless.'

'He has Lord Aritomo and the whole of Miyako worried about him,' Masachika replied.

They passed through the gate and Tama bowed to the eyes and then to each gatepost, murmuring words of thanks.

On the other side the monk, Eisei, was waiting for them.

'I have come to help you deal with the spirits,' he announced.

'The matter is settled,' Masachika said. 'They are back where they belong.'

'But you wanted me to chant and pray.' Eisei's face could not be seen beneath the black cloth, but he sounded disappointed.

Behind them they heard whispering. Eisei turned back eagerly. The gateposts were quivering.

'Shikanoko!'

'Shikanoko is coming.'

'Who is Shikanoko?' Eisei asked.

'He's . . .' Masachika began, but Eisei silenced him with a gesture. 'I know who he is. But let's hear what they say.'

'Shikanoko is our master's heir.'

'Yes, our master gave his power to him.'

'What does that mean?' Eisei demanded.

'Find out for yourself.'

They all heard the sound of horses' hooves, and turned towards the east, Masachika drawing his sword.

Tama had described Shikanoko as a wild boy and at first she did not recognise the figure who dismounted from the leading horse. He had not only grown and filled out, he had gained an air of authority. Masachika's men were gathering around them, some with their swords drawn, others setting arrows to their bows.

Masachika said, 'Let no one attack. He is not to be harmed.'

Shikanoko's gaze swept over him and he gave a slightly mocking smile, but he did not speak to either of them or even acknowledge them. He walked past them to the gate and knelt before the eyes. A strange wolf-like creature followed at his heels until one of Shikanoko's companions dismounted and called the wolf to him. His face was horribly scarred as if by fire.

Tama was aware of the monk, Eisei, staring fixedly. Eisei took the silk covering he wore from his face and she saw that his scars were identical. Then both young men smiled, their ruined features assuming the same expression, their eyes full of emotion.

Shikanoko stood, his own eyes filled with tears. He brushed them away and said quietly, 'Hidarisama, Migisama, I am glad to see you obedient to your old master again.'

Tama knew he was addressing the guardian spirits, though they had given no sign of their presence, and he knew what to call them. Even Hisoku had not known that.

Shikanoko held up his right hand and said more loudly, 'Jato!' The sword Masachika was holding flew through the air between them and cleaved to Shikanoko's hand as though it recognised him. He said to Masachika, 'How did you come by this sword?'

Masachika shrugged and replied, 'It fell into my hands.'

Shikanoko considered this for a few moments and then said, 'It was your brother's sword, recast for me.'

'Kiyoyori's sword? How did you get it? Surely it was destroyed in the flames along with its owner?'

Shika laughed. 'Neither the sword nor its owner was completely destroyed.' He held it out and for a moment Tama feared he would cut Masachika down with it there and then. But he said, 'I don't think you came just to return Jato to me. You have a message for me?'

She truly admired Masachika at that moment for, showing no sign of fear, he announced loudly, 'I am Matsutani no Masachika, sent by Lord Aritomo, protector of the city of Miyako, to tell you he holds Hidetake's daughter, Akihime, the Autumn Princess. If you surrender and return to the lord you ran away from, the Prince Abbot at Ryusonji, her life will be spared. If you refuse, or if you make any attempt to rescue her, she will be put to death in the cruellest way that can be devised. Also, my lord commands me, if you have any knowledge of the whereabouts of the false Emperor, Yoshimori, you are to reveal it to me.'

Tama saw Shikanoko flinch slightly at Akihime's name but all he said was, 'I don't know where Yoshimori is, but wherever he is, he is the true Emperor. Nothing can change that, no matter whom you torture and kill. But you may take my sword in exchange for Kiyoyori's. Its name is Jinan, Second Son, like you, like your false Emperor. That is my only message.'

# 15

# TAKAAKIRA

While the rain poured down on the capital and while he waited for Masachika to return, Yukikuni no Takaakira reflected deeply on the grievous state of affairs, the imbalance in the realm, the obvious displeasure of Heaven. He tried to put aside his grief for Hina, and his anxieties about Masachika to do all he could, for Lord Aritomo's sake, to clarify the problem and put things right.

From time to time he regretted sparing Hina's life. He saw clearly all he had put at stake for her: his position at Aritomo's side, his domain of Yukikuni, his life. He should have had her killed the first time he set eyes on her, in this very house. But then he remembered the delight and joy she had given him, her intelligence, grace and beauty, and ached with love and grief. He dreamed that she was alive, and woke with hope, but then knew, if she did still live, he would sooner or later have to arrange her death, and wished for her sake that she had had the swift, gentle death of drowning.

Her presence was everywhere. She seemed to have just departed from each room he walked into. He heard her footsteps on the verandah, her voice in the garden. To escape her, wanting to see again the young woman, Akihime, who was defying both Lord Aritomo and the Prince Abbot, and remembering his intuition that there was some evil dwelling at the heart of Ryusonji, he decided to pay a visit to the temple.

His previous visit had been last summer, just after the first typhoon. Now the heavy rain had settled sullenly over the city. The lake was churned into foam and threatened to brim over its banks and join the river, which was rising every hour to meet it.

The Prince Abbot greeted him cordially, making no reference to the weather, as if by ignoring it he would deny its hostility. He inquired after Lord Aritomo's health and begged Takaakira to convey his messages of respect and devotion.

'We shall soon have reasons to celebrate,' he said. 'I am sure Shikanoko will attempt to rescue our prisoner. Once we have him under our power, we will soon discover Yoshimori's whereabouts. When they are all dead, harmony will be restored.'

*But he is the true Emperor*, Takaakira thought, as he had before, and immediately found himself trying to close his mind to the Prince Abbot's penetrating gaze.

'I would like to see the Princess,' he said.

The sight of her, lying in a small cage, her hands bound, shocked him. He did not understand how she could still be alive. In her twisted limbs and crushed body he saw Hina. This was what Hina would be subjected to if she ever fell into Aritomo's hands.

*Let her be dead*, he prayed. *Let her be drowned.*

'Was it necessary to be so cruel?' he said to the Prince Abbot, who was surveying Akihime with cold contempt.

'She knows where Yoshimori is and will not tell us. Her stubbornness must be punished, her will broken. And her suffering will reach Shikanoko and bring him to us.'

Takaakira gazed on her with pity, mixed with revulsion. There were many things he wanted to ask her, not about Yoshimori, but about her time at Nishimi. What had Hina been doing there? Did she still read the Kudzu Vine Treasure Store? How was she progressing with her music and her poetry? Did she talk about him? He wanted to know everything that had happened in the months he had been away. And where was the rosewood box with the old man's eyes? Suddenly he felt he was in danger of breaking down and weeping.

He tried to mask his weakness from the Prince Abbot. The thought of the old man reminded him that he had been going to question him more forcefully, before he had been sent to Nishimi. His excitement at having somewhere to hide Hina, and his absence from the city, had driven it out of his head.

'What happened to the blind lute player?' he said.

'He is still here,' the Prince Abbot replied. 'He still plays and sings but his mind is gone.'

'I would like to talk to him alone,' Takaakira said.

The Prince Abbot glanced at him sharply. 'What good can that do? You won't get any sense out of him.'

'I want to rule him out as a possible source of imbalance,' Takaakira replied. 'Perhaps proper restitution has never been made for the wrong that was done to him. We should look at everything.'

'You will find him in the cloister, I suppose. You may talk to him on your way out.'

There was a dismissive tone to his voice that irritated Takaakira. *This priest is full of arrogance and conceit*, he thought, and found himself wondering if the Minatogura lord might not be better off without him.

Sesshin was under the shelter of the cloisters, sitting cross-legged, his lute on his knees, his face turned upwards, his lips moving as if he were praying. The sight of his ancient, eyeless face made Takaakira shiver. This man's eyes knew his innermost secrets, all his mistakes and weaknesses, had made him weep. Did Sesshin know what his eyes saw, or were they forever separated?

He knelt beside him, speaking clearly in order not to startle him. 'Master Sesshin, it is Yukikuni no Takaakira.'

Sesshin made no response. Surely he was not deaf too? He spoke more loudly. 'Are you well? Is there anything you need?'

Sesshin said finally, 'It is gracious of such a mighty lord to concern himself with my wellbeing. I have no wants, no needs.'

He did not sound at all senile.

He then said, 'Are you well, Lord Takaakira?'

'Well enough.'

'And Lord Aritomo? Is he well?'

'I believe he is in good health,' Takaakira said.

'Tell him to make the most of it, for he will be very sick soon.'

'You could lose your tongue or be put to death,' Takaakira said warningly, but instead of being intimidated, Sesshin seemed to find this amusing and shook with silent laughter. He nodded his head for quite a while, making Takaakira feel perhaps his mind was wandering and he was wasting his time.

'Since you were so kind as to inquire after my health,' Sesshin said, 'I will give you some advice. The Prince Abbot has been very gracious to me lately, but for many years he has wanted to kill me. Do you know why? Because I was the only person ever likely to challenge him. We were equals once, can you believe that? And now he is bringing to Ryusonji the one person who can bring him down. Yes, he is about to fall. Sooner or later Aritomo will follow.'

'What are you saying?' Takaakira said. 'Is there going to be an attack on Ryusonji? Is it Shikanoko?'

Sesshin took up the lute and played a few plaintive notes. His face, which had been suddenly youthful and full of intelligence, now looked old and vacant again. He began to sing in a mumbling tone. Takaakira could not make out the words but he thought it was the song he had heard before, about the dragon child. He looked across the courtyard, through the heavy rain, to the lake.

Sesshin sang more clearly.

*He sleeps beneath the lake,*
*The dragon child,*
*But he will wake*
*And spread his wings again,*
*When the deer's child comes.*

'Is the deer's child coming?' Takaakira said urgently. 'Is it Shikanoko?'

A smile flitted across Sesshin's face.

Takaakira could see he would get no more sense out of him. He bade him farewell, stood, and began to walk towards the main gate. The courtyards were deserted and though he could hear chanting from within he did not see anyone. However, just when he had passed through the gate and was making his way to where his carriage was waiting, the ox up to its hocks in mud, he saw coming towards him the young monk with the scarred face who had gone with Masachika.

The monk recognised him. 'Lord Takaakira? I am Eisei. You came to visit our Abbot last year.'

'Yes, I remember you. You have been in Matsutani, haven't you? What news do you bring?'

'Lord Masachika is on his way to Lord Aritomo now.'

'Then I must hurry back there,' Takaakira said.

Eisei looked around. He seemed nervous, and he fixed his eyes on Takaakira as if he wanted to speak to him but did not dare.

Takaakira gestured to him to move under the shelter of the eaves of the wall. The rain dripped steadily around them. The ox lowed mournfully and shifted its legs. 'Where is Shikanoko now?' Takaakira said in a low voice.

'He is not far away. He came at once, as soon as he heard about the Princess.'

'Did he send any message?'

'He sent his sword,' Eisei said. 'It is a sort of message. Its name is Jinan.'

'Second Son?'

'Yes, like our current Emperor.'

*Masachika will not dare say that to our lord!* Takaakira thought.

'So, how many men came with him?' he asked.

'Just one. His friend, Nagatomo. So many rivers are in flood it wouldn't have been possible to move a whole army.'

'He has made himself vulnerable of his own free will?' Takaakira said in disbelief.

'He will give himself up if the Princess is released,' Eisei replied.

'Surely he will attempt to rescue her?'

'Lord,' the monk said. 'I must tell you. If you or my master have me put to death, so be it. Shikanoko has extraordinary power, far more than my master suspects. If he enters Ryusonji he will destroy it.'

It was just what Sesshin had said a few minutes earlier.

'But more importantly,' Eisei went on, 'Yoshimori is the true Emperor. Nothing can alter that.'

'How have you changed your thinking so much?' Takaakira demanded. 'You left a loyal servant to the Prince Abbot – now you will betray him?'

'It is not betraying someone to tell them they are wrong. Maybe it is the highest loyalty. Meeting Shikanoko again opened my eyes. I thought I hated him because my face was burned by his mask, but it wasn't he who deserved my hatred. He didn't force me to wear it. He warned against it, just as he tried to protect Nagatomo.' His face changed as he spoke. 'We have identical scars,' he said. 'We call ourselves the Burnt Twins.'

'Were you on your way to see the Prince Abbot now?' Takaakira said.

'Yes, I intend to tell him what I just told you.'

'Don't do that yet. You will be punished severely. I will talk to Lord Aritomo first. I will intercede with him on Shikanoko's behalf. Can you reach him, perhaps through your friend – Nagatomo?'

Eisei nodded.

'Then tell him to wait until he hears from me. I will come here tomorrow and meet you, at noon. I hope I may be able to save both him and the Princess.'

While listening to Eisei's words Takaakira had felt that his earlier misgivings had been confirmed and he had come to a decision. Ryusonji and the Prince Abbot were indeed at the heart of the country's suffering. It was his duty, and would be his greatest loyalty, to tell his lord. He got into the ox carriage and ordered the groom to go with all haste to the palace.

He met Masachika in the anteroom. It was filled with warriors, seeking to present petitions or awaiting orders. Masachika greeted Takaakira politely enough, spoke briefly of the difficulty of the journey, but there was no time to say more before they were summoned into the inner chamber.

Aritomo looked even more tense and suspicious than usual. A muscle twitched constantly beneath his left eye, betraying sleeplessness. His anger simmered beneath the surface, making both men nervous and deferential.

Masachika took his sword from his sash and held it out in both hands, bowing over it. 'Shikanoko surrendered his sword to me and I present it to you, lord.'

Aritomo looked slightly less grim as he took it and studied it carefully. 'It is very fine. I have never seen anything quite like it.'

'I believe it was forged in the mountains,' Masachika replied. 'Perhaps by tengu, perhaps by a sorcerer.'

*Are you not going to tell our lord its name?* Takaakira thought, but did not speak.

'So, you brought the upstart back with you?'

'He followed us. He is close to the capital now. He came alone save for one companion. I have his assurance he will give himself up if the Princess is released.'

'Well done, Masachika,' Aritomo said, his good humour apparently restored. 'I will give the sword to you as a sign of my gratitude.'

Masachika bowed to the ground. 'I must also tell Lord Aritomo that I am reconciled with my former wife, I have secured Matsutani, and dealt with the hostile spirits that had made it uninhabitable. The estate is firmly in Miboshi hands, and if you trust me I will regain Kuromori and Kumayama too.'

'Lord Aritomo,' Takaakira said. 'May I speak with you in private?'

Aritomo held up his hand. 'Shortly. You dealt with the spirits? How? I know you took one of the Prince Abbot's monks with you. Did he assist you?'

'I did it alone, lord. It was simply a question of replacing something that was lost.'

'How mysterious,' Aritomo said. His nostrils twitched, his jaw clicked from side to side. 'I am no adept. You will have to spell it out for me.'

'Kiyoyori's wife, Lady Tama, blinded an old man, Sesshin, a sage. After she turned him out, his eyes were placed over the west gate at Matsutani, where he had previously installed the guardian spirits. After the earthquake, the eyes disappeared and the spirits escaped. I was able to replace them and now the spirits are back where they belong.'

'All very satisfactory, no doubt, but how did you come to be in possession of the eyes?'

Takaakira could feel sweat gathering in his armpits yet he felt icy cold. His pulse was beating rapidly.

Masachika said slowly, 'Kiyoyori's daughter had taken them with her to Nishimi. I found them there.'

Aritomo's eyes bulged. He had been watching Masachika carefully, alert as always to any attempt at concealing the truth. Now he turned his stare on Takaakira.

A wave of heat rose from Takaakira's belly, staining his face red. He wanted to explain what Hina was like, why he had spared her, but, face to face with his lord, he knew there were no arguments and no excuses.

'You were concealing Kiyoyori's daughter, all this time?' Aritomo said in disbelief. 'Where is she now?'

'She tried to escape while I was securing the Autumn Princess,' Masachika said. 'It is believed she drowned. But she left behind the box containing Sesshin's eyes.'

Aritomo did not seem to be listening. His face was the colour of ash; his eyes filled with tears.

'I trusted you when I trusted no one else,' he whispered. 'We have been close friends for years, all our lives. Is it true that you have betrayed me?'

Takaakira could not answer. His own eyes grew hot. Finally he found his voice.

'It's true that I found Kiyoyori's daughter, let everyone believe she was dead, but spared her and took her to Nishimi. I disobeyed your orders. There was no betrayal. But neither is there any excuse and I am not asking you to overlook, or forgive. Allow me to take my own life; that is my only request. But first I must beg you to listen to me. You are making a terrible mistake . . .' *I am going to die,* he thought, *I can say anything.* But even on the threshold of death he feared Aritomo's anger.

'For the sake of our past friendship I will grant that request,' Aritomo said, his voice breaking. 'But do it now, at once, or I will burn you along with the Princess.'

'Now?' Takaakira said. 'Here?' Stray thoughts raced through his mind. *I did not suspect, when I dressed this morning, that I was putting on these clothes for the last time. Now they will be ruined by my blood. I must not hesitate or cringe. I must act bravely. I will never see the Snow Country again. Will I meet Hina on the far side of the River of Death? I can do nothing now for Shikanoko or the Princess.*

'You may use the knife belonging to the nobleman Hidetake,' Aritomo said with affection, as if he were bestowing a precious gift on his friend.

Takaakira took it, admiring its jewelled hilt, its perfect balance, its folded steel blade of exquisite sharpness. *I will hardly feel it*, he thought, as he unfastened his sash and opened his robes to expose his belly. He felt a rush of tenderness for his unblemished skin, his hard muscles. He felt sorry for his own body and the incurable wound he was about to inflict on it.

'Forgive me,' he murmured and with all his strength plunged the knife in, turned it and drew it sideways, feeling his own blood hot on his hands. At last he dared to say the words aloud, 'Yoshimori is the true Emperor!'

He did not seem to feel the cut, but then the agony began. His body, so strong and healthy, refused to die. Aritomo watched till the end.

The last sound Yukikuni no Takaakira heard, as his spirit finally broke free and began its journey across the Three Streamed River, was Aritomo sobbing.

# 16

# AKI

One morning Aki heard horses neighing and was convinced they were hers, the ones that had been Shikanoko's, her companions on the road. She could not recognise the girl she had been then, her courage and her freedom. She had been broken by pain, the pain of childbirth, the pain of torture, and by grief for the child she would never see again. But the horses restored a slight flicker of hope. She remembered the night at the crossroads, the ghost that had spoken from the shadows, Kiyoyori, the Kuromori lord. The foal had been born the same day as her son.

The room in which the cage was placed, part of the temple despite the use it was put to, held golden statues of the Enlightened One and wooden carvings of various saints, as well as the lords of Hell. It seemed especially evil to carry out such deeds of cruelty under their gaze. Aki stared back at the figures, wondering why they did not step down from their pedestals and come to her aid.

'Help me,' she whispered.

The next day she noticed that someone had placed a catalpa bow among the sacred objects at the statues' feet. She had mourned the loss of her bow, left behind at Nishimi; now as her vision sharpened she realised it was here. It had been miraculously transported to this place. She felt a wave of peace flow over her. It must mean that she had been forgiven. She thought of her ritual box, which she had been given at the same time as the bow, and which she had left with Kai. She comforted herself by picturing Kai and Yoshi as she had last seen them, their life together, the musicians and the acrobats performing around them. If she died now, no one would ever know where Yoshimori was, and she did not expect to live.

She was often feverish. Once she opened her eyes and thought she saw a warrior, one of Lord Aritomo's men, looking at her with pity. But what good was anyone's pity to her now?

For the rest of that day Aki's tormentors left her alone, while they turned their attention to another prisoner. From her wooden cage, in the depths of the temple, she could hear sounds that were too easy for her to turn into images. They awakened memory in her own limbs: the crushing rocks, the twisting ropes, the red-hot iron bars. She did not know who this poor victim was. He never cried out or spoke, though after the torturers had finished she could hear the faintest of groans and words of prayer.

She realised she no longer heard the lute music that had been such a comfort to her during her suffering, and she became convinced that the tortured prisoner was the lute player. She grieved for him and prayed for him.

That night she woke soaking, and realised she was bleeding. She did not know if it was her monthly bleeding or if the rocks of torture had injured her internally. Her whole body ached dully, the burns interrupting with fierce darting pains. She called for rags and water, but no one came.

She wept freely then, for her child. Bara had tried to tell her something, that Hina had fled with him, but then Masachika had informed her they had both drowned. And she wept for her own life, approaching its end, so brief, so filled with mistakes, grief and remorse.

A dim lamp burned in front of the statues, barely enough to light the room. For weeks no one had seen the moon. The sky was covered in dense low clouds and the nights were dark. Shadows flickered across the faces of the statues, giving them expressions of pity and horror.

'It is not pity I need but help,' Aki said aloud.

One of the shadows seemed to solidify and stepped towards her. Her heart fluttered, sending pain throbbing through her.

A boy stood at the bars of the cage, his eyes fixed on her.

She half-rose, forgetting the ties, wrenching her arms, increasing the pain so that she could not keep herself from crying out.

He made a sign to her to keep quiet, then moved silently round the cage and knelt so he could whisper to her.

'Are you the Princess?'

She nodded. His nose wrinkled, making her aware of how badly she must smell.

'I am bleeding,' she said. 'Can you get me some rags and water?'

'Don't worry about that now,' the boy replied. 'I have smelled far worse than you, believe me.'

Even her torturers had not spoken to her so bluntly. They had continued to address her in polite terms and call her Princess, even as they twisted her limbs and burned her flesh.

'Shikanoko sent me,' the boy went on.

Her heart thudded and for a few moments she could not speak. 'Where is he?'

'Not far away. I am to explore the temple and find the best way to rescue you.'

'It is impossible,' she said. 'Tell him not to attempt it. No one can attack Ryusonji. No one can defy the Prince Abbot.'

'You may be right. I had not realised how well protected this place was. It took me a long time to get in and that was only because whoever set up the protection had not allowed for people like me.'

'Who are you?' she said.

'My mother named me Kiku.' He moved around the cage checking the door and the fastenings, loosening the knots that bound her arms. Then he made a slight noise like a gecko and another boy, almost identical in size and looks, slithered out of the shadows.

'Shikanoko told us to bring medicine as well as poison,' Kiku explained, squatting down next to Aki. 'We didn't do that last time. What have you got, Kuro?'

'What does he need?' the other boy said, peering at Aki.

'*She*. It's a woman, it's the Princess.'

'Sorry, it's so dark. I didn't know women got tortured.'

'Something to dull pain, and stop bleeding,' Kiku said.

'Wound staunch, would that do?' said Kuro.

'Let's try it.'

Kuro passed a small flask to Kiku. He turned Aki's head gently and poured the flask's contents into her mouth. It was bitter and viscous.

'Are you poisoning me?' she said.

'We could if you want us to,' Kuro replied.

'Don't be an idiot,' Kiku said. 'Shikanoko wants her alive. That's what *rescue* means. You don't rescue a dead person.' Kiku addressed Aki. 'There's a lot about being human he doesn't understand. You have to explain everything to him.'

'I will be dead soon,' Aki said.

'So, we go back and tell Shikanoko not to bother?' Kuro said cheerfully.

'He mustn't risk his life for me,' Aki said. 'Tell him to find the Emperor. But before you go can you get that bow for me?'

Kiku went to the base of the statue and picked it up. 'Shisoku had some of these,' he said. 'Are they something magic?'

He thrust it through the bars of the cage. Aki felt its familiar shape, and some courage came from it to her. She twanged the string gently.

At that moment there came a sound from the adjoining room as if someone groaned in a nightmare.

'What's that?' Kiku whispered.

'It is the lute player, I think. An old man who sings ballads and war tales.'

'He is being tortured too?'

'What methods do they use?' Kuro asked. 'What causes the most pain?'

Kiku cuffed him. 'We'll find out later. Now we have to decide what to do next.'

The old man began to sing:
*The dragon child, he flew too high,*
*He was still so young, but now he's grown,*
*His wings are strong, his breath is fierce.*
*His breath is fierce.*
*He will rise from the lake at Ryusonji.*

They all listened without moving. Aki's heart was pierced by the poignancy of the human voice, frail and broken as it was, rising from the suffering and the darkness.

'Nice song,' Kiku said.

'I would like to see a dragon,' Kuro added.

Then Kiku cried, 'Someone is coming!' He grabbed the bow from her.

Torches lit the room, armed monks burst in, running to and fro, searching behind the statues and in every corner, uttering incantations and words of power.

'Who untied you, Princess?' one shouted at Aki.

She made no reply, watching in the torchlight as the boys flitted like bats, appearing and disappearing. Sometimes she could see three or four of them at once, sometimes none at all. The monks herded them, trying to corner them. She saw three trapped, but then one faded as one of the monks grabbed at him, and Kiku jumped upwards, seized a rafter and swung himself into the hole in the ceiling through which they must have first entered the room. He called back to his brother and Kuro leaped with astonishing agility to grab his outstretched hand.

Someone spoke a single word, someone standing in the doorway, a quiet powerful presence.

The Prince Abbot was asserting his authority over his spiritual realm and the intruders who had breached it. But it was too late. The boys had disappeared.

'They escaped, lord,' said one of the monks.

'I allowed them to. They will return with Shikanoko.'

'What creatures are they? Are they human?'

'Not really. I don't know exactly where they have sprung from, why they have appeared now, but they are at least part demon.'

'They could make copies of themselves and disappear into invisibility.'

'I have heard of such things,' the Prince Abbot said.

'What does it mean?'

'Nothing,' he snapped, but Aki thought she heard unease in his voice.

He moved towards her cage.

'She is bleeding,' he said. 'This place will not be purified until she is burned.'

# 17

# SHIKANOKO

Shikanoko, Nagatomo and the two boys had found rooms on the edge of the city, not far from Ryusonji. Shika traded the horses they had ridden so far and so fast for food and lodging. They were among hundreds of others who were escaping the flooded countryside to offer prayers and make petitions at the capital's many temples and shrines.

That night Eisei sent a message to say he would bring Takaakira to meet Shika the following day, and Kiku and Kuro went to explore Ryusonji. But the boys did not return until after daybreak, and Eisei did not come until late afternoon.

'I waited for Lord Takaakira for hours,' Eisei said to Shikanoko. 'And then I heard he was dead. Aritomo ordered him to take his own life. The Prince Abbot has had to perform a purification ceremony and the funeral will take place in a few days. Everyone, the whole city, is in shock. He was Aritomo's closest friend and very popular. No one understands the reasons, but it must be because he dared to speak up to Lord Aritomo on your behalf.' After a moment, he added, 'He was going to help you, I truly believe it. He wanted to spare the Princess and save your life. Yesterday he talked for a while with Sesshin and after that the Prince Abbot put Sesshin under torture too. I don't understand for what purpose. He is just an old man who is losing his mind.'

'I'm surprised he's been so lenient towards him till now,' Shika said. 'They are longstanding rivals.'

'But he is helpless now,' Eisei said. 'Is it because he gave all his power away to you?'

'How do you know that?' Shika asked.

'The spirits in the gateposts at Matsutani told us.'

'They talk a lot of nonsense,' Shika replied. 'And, regardless, I wonder if there is any power in the world that can help me now or save the Princess.'

'What will you do?' Nagatomo asked.

'Let me reflect for a while, and then I'll decide.'

It had taken Kiku and Kuro a long time to escape from Ryusonji. They had come back over-excited and unusually talkative. Now Kuro was occupied with his poisonous creatures, letting the centipede crawl over his hands and the snake through his hair. Kiku prowled restlessly round the room.

'Do you know, I think I miss Mu?' he said suddenly, coming to a halt in front of Shika.

'I do too,' Shika said. He had been worried about the other three boys all winter, had sent Chika to check on them once the snow melted, and had intended to bring them to Kumayama to be with him. But now he was glad they were still at Shisoku's place. They would be safer there, when he was dead.

'You must go back to the forest,' he told Kiku, 'whatever happens to me.'

'What is going to happen?' Kiku asked.

'I don't know yet. Leave me in peace for a while. I need to think.'

'Well, don't think for too long. He says he is going to burn her.'

'That can't take place till after Lord Takaakira's funeral,' Eisei said. 'So, we have a little time.'

'What else can you tell me about her?' Shika asked.

'She is very unwell,' Kiku said. 'I brought her bow. It was on the altar in the room she's imprisoned in.'

Shika held it, gazing on it in wonder. He knew it was a source of power to her. 'I wish I could take it back to her,' he said.

Kiku gave one of his rare smiles. 'Maybe we will.'

'There is a dragon in the lake,' Kuro said.

'Yes, Tsumaru's death awakened it,' Shika replied.

'Tsumaru?' Kiku questioned.

'He was Lord Kiyoyori's son. He was just a child when he died.'

'Lord Kiyoyori, our father?'

'Yes,' Shika said.

'So, he was our brother? We should avenge him.' Kiku gave a wide smile, as if both the idea and the word pleased him enormously. 'One more thing, speaking of fathers. Sesshin, the old man who plays the lute, he is also to be burned. We must save him too.'

•

Shika began to prepare himself, using the rituals he had learned from Shisoku and Sesshin. He brought out the mask and purified it with incense, and repeated the ritual for himself and his weapons. He fasted for the rest of the day, and at night sat awake on the small verandah, listening to the steady beat of the rain, calling on his masters and teachers, the living and the dead, Sesshin, Kiyoyori, Shisoku, Lady Tora, to come to his aid.

He heard Nagatomo and Eisei whisper together, quietly, intimately, and the boys have a brief muffled squabble over the snake. Then everyone fell asleep.

Gen lay with his head close to Shika's feet, neither waking nor sleeping, occasionally quivering. At dawn the fake wolf gave a sharp howl. Shika heard birds waken in the great trees that surrounded Ryusonji. Their song signified for him the power of the forest. Everything spoke to him, the birds' call, the wind, the rain, each tree that shook its branches and dripped moisture. Yet he felt all his own weakness, felt the old ache in his right arm, and then he heard the voice of the mountain sorcerer: *He could teach you many things but he could not teach you brokenness.* He had not understood what Shisoku had meant, but now he did. Both he and the mask had been broken. He reached out and felt for it with his fingers, tracing the tiny scars where it had knitted together, the broken antler. He placed it on his face and turned his attention towards the temple, let it slip under the great shutters, still closed, and through the courtyards and halls he knew so well. *I am coming. Are you there?*

With a jolt he came up against his former master's mind and will and saw for the first time their true immensity, dense and impenetrable, subtle and ever-changing. Nothing he had would prevail against the Prince Abbot, not the mask, not Jato, not the bow, Kodama, the dream echo of Ameyumi. He withdrew, shaken, aware of all he was facing: annihilation or enslavement, agony of body and soul.

He rose and took off the mask, staring out into the garden, longing to flee. Yet he could not. There was no other way but forward, even if it meant he would join Akihime in death. And he had to go in brokenness not in strength.

A rattle of stones distracted him. Nagatomo had found an abandoned Go board and was trying to show the boys how to play, with rain-washed pebbles they had filched from the garden. The sound recalled his father. He also had staked everything and lost. Now his son was doomed to follow him.

The three of them stared at him with expectant eyes.

'So, what's your plan?' Kiku said.

'I will go to Ryusonji now, alone, empty-handed,' Shika said. 'You must return to the hut in the Darkwood, as I said. Nagatomo, I release you from my service, if I can even call it that, it has been so short.'

'You are joking!' Nagatomo said in alarm.

'That's not a plan,' Kiku cried. 'Why don't you want us to help you? We got in before, we can do it again.'

'He will let you in but he will not let you out,' Shika replied.

'I refuse to be released,' Nagatomo said stubbornly. 'I'm coming with you.'

'I'm trusting you to take care of the boys, and Gen. See that all three get home safely.'

'I don't think Gen's going to leave you!' Nagatomo said, and the fake wolf shook its head and said 'Ne-er.'

'What about Jato, and your mask?' Kiku said. 'You're not leaving them?'

'I said, I must go with nothing, as if I am no one. If I die today, Nagatomo may have Jato, and my bow, Kodama, and you and Kuro must take the mask back to the hut and place it on the altar.'

'Can we use it?' Kuro said, frowning.

'Only if you want your face burned like Nagatomo and Eisei. Don't try it,' Shika warned. 'No one can wear it but me.'

'Then you should take it with you,' Kiku argued. 'And don't talk about dying!'

'You know what you said once,' Shika replied. 'Everyone dies in the end.'

'And the Princess's bow, which we went to so much trouble to bring back?' Kuro asked.

That made Shika hesitate, for the bow was not his to dispose of. 'I suppose you should take that to the forest too,' he said finally, 'if the Princess is also dead.'

He knelt before the sword and the mask, thanking them, relinquishing them. He washed his face and hands, untied his hair, combed and retied it, and brushed as much mud from his clothes as he could. Then he embraced the boys and Nagatomo, advised them to leave right away, and went out into the rain-soaked city. Gen padded at his heels, growling under his breath as if he were complaining, but Shika could not tell if it was about the wet, or his own actions.

The main gate at Ryusonji was surrounded by worshippers who had come to beg the Prince Abbot to stop the rain. They fell back at Shikanoko's approach, staring at him and Gen in alarm and surprise.

Eisei was just inside the gate as though he had been waiting for him, and he told the guards to let him in.

'You've come alone?' he whispered.

Shikanoko nodded.

'Where are Nagatomo and your boys?'

'I sent them home.'

Eisei's eyes widened. 'You're just going to give yourself up? I thought you would challenge him!'

'I'm giving myself up in exchange for the Princess's life,' Shika replied.

'They will never let either of you go until they find out where Yoshimori is, and will probably kill you then anyway.'

'Then we will die together,' Shika replied. 'Go and tell him I am here.'

He waited in the outer courtyard, Gen pressing against his legs.

On the southern side, there was a shrine to the horse god, where a pure white stallion was kept to be worshipped and honoured as a living god. A boy was futilely washing the horse's legs, but the rain splattered them again immediately. The horse stamped impatiently and swung its head round, taking deep breaths. Then it gave a loud whinny, both joyful and challenging.

'Nyorin,' Shika whispered, recognising his old stallion immediately. He wanted to touch him again before he died. He went to Nyorin and held out his hand, not sure how the horse would react to him. Nyorin lowered his head and allowed Shika to embrace him. Then he neighed again, more loudly still. An answering whinny came from the stables. Risu.

She was tied up just inside the entrance. The foal was loose, standing at her side. Risu whickered at him while the foal stared at him with bold, curious eyes.

'Lord Kiyoyori,' he said, seeing in amazement the embodiment of the spirit he had called back from the banks of the River of Death, all those months ago.

The foal gave a shrill whinny, and Risu nuzzled Shika, as though she had forgiven him.

'Thank you,' he whispered.

Eisei returned. 'Come with me,' he said. Risu whickered after them and the foal dashed from her side to follow them, and then back again, his hooves scattering gravel.

Chanting came from the main hall, the dragon sutra, its familiar words springing onto Shika's tongue. And then behind them he heard his old teacher's voice, singing plaintively.

*The dragon child, he flew too high*

The voice was silenced with a blow. Then came the Prince Abbot's voice, 'For the last time, you stubborn old fool, tell me how you gave your power to Shikanoko, or I will burn you alongside the Princess.'

Eisei said, 'They are in the interrogation room.'

As they approached the room, Shika heard Sesshin say, 'It is given. I cannot take it back. And you may burn me but you cannot destroy me.'

'What do you mean?' The Prince Abbot's voice was almost unrecognisable, husky with exhaustion. The interrogation must have been going on all night.

'I found it, my old friend. The secret we had both been looking for, all our lives. The elements that, combined together, cheat death.'

'You cannot die?' Disbelief was mixed with envy.

'I don't believe I can,' Sesshin said. 'Actually it's more of a burden than I thought it would be, but there is no unalloyed good in this world, just as there is no perfect evil. All is sun and shadow, darkness and light.'

'What is this magic?' the Prince Abbot said. 'Is it a potion? An incantation?'

'It was written down in one of my books, but they were all burned in Matsutani.'

'Do you not remember? Your memory was always faultless.'

'I am an old man. I remember very little.' Sesshin's voice lightened. 'Ah, here comes my boy,' he said with delight.

The Prince Abbot spun round to face the doorway as Eisei led Shika and Gen through it.

'Shikanoko,' he said, gazing at him. 'We have been waiting for you.'

Shika could not resist the look and felt his will begin to tremble and submit. Then Sesshin's words pierced his mind. *My boy*, he had said. It was the old blind man who was his true master. He felt the nugget of power begin to glow within him.

The Prince Abbot said to Shika, 'You have come to surrender yourself?'

'I am already a prisoner to your monk, Eisei,' Shika said.

'You will submit to me and refrain from challenging me?'

'Show me Akihime, promise to let her go, and I will do everything you ask of me,' Shika said.

'You are too late. You should have come earlier. The burning is already arranged. Lord Aritomo will attend it.'

'Then you can burn me with her.'

He heard a slight sound from the corner and turned towards it. He had not noticed her in the darkness, kneeling, hands tied behind her back, her head thrown back, her slender throat pale. She moved her head and looked at him. In her gaze he saw not trust, or forgiveness, but a steady acceptance of their destiny.

'I will, with pleasure,' the Prince Abbot said, the cruelty in his voice now undisguised. 'But first I will take from you what I want. Where is the mask?'

'I didn't bring it. In fact, I've sent it away.'

The Prince Abbot smiled slightly. 'It cannot be sent away. Remember I cast spells on it to make sure it would never escape me and nor will you.'

'Nevertheless, I came without it.'

The Prince Abbot was silent for a few moments, as if disconcerted. Then he said, 'What about those demon boys who were here last night? Have they accompanied you? Are they hiding somewhere?'

'They have been sent away too,' Shika replied steadily.

'I am sure they can be easily tracked down. Eisei reported to me what he learned at Matsutani. Sesshin gave his power away to you, though I still don't understand how. Is it through that power that you control the demons, or is it through the mask?'

'Neither,' Shika said. 'They are my sons. I brought them up.'

'Sons disobey their fathers all the time,' the Prince Abbot stated as from behind Shika heard his old teacher sigh and say, 'That soft heart is going to be your undoing, my boy, just as I said. I told you to kill the demons.'

'Bring Sesshin forward,' the Prince Abbot commanded. 'And the Princess. I want them to watch how I treat those who disobey me, who try to challenge me.'

Their hands were untied and they were dragged forward.

'I would have made you my follower,' the Prince Abbot said to Shikanoko, 'even my successor. Why did you run from me?'

Shika heard the sorrow in his voice. 'I will do whatever you command, give you whatever you want, if you will spare Akihime,' he said, falling to his knees.

The Prince Abbot made a beckoning gesture. 'Come here.'

Shika crawled towards him. The priest knelt, took Shika's head in his hands and raising it, placed his mouth over Shika's just as Sesshin had done before.

A gong sounded in the distance, and a cloud of perfume and incense enveloped him. For a moment he thought the whole magical process would happen in reverse. The snakes awakened in his veins, the catlike creature yowled in his brain, but they were fighting against being taken from him. Even if he consented to it they would not be released.

He tried to pull away but the Prince Abbot's grip was too strong. He could not breathe. He felt the teeth begin to bite into him. All the suppressed horror of the secret rituals of Ryusonji welled up.

He heard the Prince Abbot's thoughts as clearly as if he had spoken.

*And now I will send you down into Hell!*

Through the darkness that was rising around him came the sound of a bow twanging.

He knew at once what it was. Aki's catalpa bow, used to summon spirits. He had left it in his lodgings. How had it miraculously appeared here? In that moment the Prince Abbot released him, throwing him to the ground.

'You still resist me?' he said. 'You will not relinquish it to me?'

Sesshin said, as if from far away, 'I did give him my power, it's true, and in that very way that you divined when you tried to take it from him. But I haven't taught him how to pass it on, and won't for a long time, if ever.'

Shika tasted the blood in his mouth. For a moment he felt so sick and dizzy he wondered if he could stand. He felt Gen's tongue on his hands, licking, encouraging him.

The bow twanged again. Akihime called, 'Dragon child! Come to our aid!'

Shika turned to look at her and saw, not the tortured captive he had seen earlier, but a beautiful shrine maiden, powerful, pure, dangerous. A deep relief washed through him. His instincts had been right. Through his brokenness had been manifested her strength.

As he struggled to his feet the air parted and the mask emerged: the branching antlers, one broken, the lacquered surface, the reddened lips, the black-fringed eyeholes. It seemed more expressive than ever. It said to him, *You tried to leave me, but you cannot. Now I am here. Put me on.*

'Put it on,' Kiku said, becoming visible right in front of him, holding out the mask in both hands.

The boys had disobeyed him. Kuro had brought Aki's bow and Kiku the mask. The first act might save them but he feared the second would destroy him. 'I don't need it,' he said, stepping back but the mask leaped towards him and fastened itself over his features.

Kiku left a shadow of his second self as he slid away.

'Didn't I tell you it would return to me?' said the Prince Abbot and he spoke a word of power.

Without thinking, Shika countered it with one of his own. He felt something inside him purr with approval and tasted in his mouth a cleansing bitter-sweetness. But he knew he could not prevail against the Prince Abbot, here in Ryusonji, in the priest's centre of power.

Their eyes locked and the struggle began. Shika fought off a new terror as he penetrated deep into the priest's mind and soul. He saw the spiritual forces the Prince Abbot could call upon arrayed against him. He faltered, like a wary stag in the forest, catching the huntsman's scent, conscious of its broken antlers, seeing already the thicket that would entrap it.

Their minds circled each other, searching for weakness. Shika felt the older man's great strength and subtlety. Visions flashed before him, of endless pain and suffering. Demons rose from the underworld to taunt him. 'Soon you will be ours,' they jeered, revealing to him all the torments of Hell. Ancient sorcerers threatened him. 'You have dared to question one of us and rebel against him? Your soul is lost for all eternity,' and they showed him the barren, everlasting wastes that awaited him.

Gen, who was as close at his side in this realm as in any other, said, 'Something missing.'

Shika was holding on to the power of the forest, the world that existed before men were created and would endure long after they had disappeared, a world that re-formed and replenished itself endlessly. He called on the stag whose child he had become, on the greatest oak tree and the most delicate clover, the eagle and the hawfinch, the wolf and the weasel, the snake and the centipede. At Gen's words, for a moment, he saw that the Prince Abbot's guardians were counterfeit, a flashy show with no substance, less real than Shisoku's fake animals. Something was missing, something had forsaken the Prince Abbot, now when he most needed it.

The demons and the sorcerers rose in a huge cacophony, screaming at him. Maybe they were fake but he could not withstand them. Maybe something was missing, but the knowledge was no use to him. He felt the Prince Abbot's rage and, even more disabling, his pity and his regret, the affection of a father, the wise guidance of a teacher, the unmatchable power of the adept – all these were being withdrawn from Shika, the disobedient child, the rebellious disciple. He was on the point of calling out, *Forgive me! I surrender. I should never have tried to oppose you*, when again the gentle twang of a bow cut through the noise and the confusion.

Aki plucked the bowstring again and called, 'Dragon child! Representative of the gods in this place! Forgive me for offending you. Take my life as punishment, but come to our aid now!'

In the distance Shika could hear the foal's frantic neighing. *Tsumaru!* it seemed to cry. *Tsumaru!*

*Tsumaru, the dragon child.* In that moment he realised what was missing. The Prince Abbot no longer commanded the power of the dragon. Ryusonji itself had forsaken him.

The guardians surrounded him. 'Tsumaru is merely a dead child,' they wailed. 'There is no dragon.'

His spirit quailed, his body shuddered. *I am lost*, he thought, *I have failed.*

'Yes,' the priest jeered. 'In the end there is nothing. This is what awaits you – complete annihilation. You thought you would destroy me, but we will fall into the abyss together.'

'At least you will be destroyed,' Shika cried with his last shreds of defiance.

Then a lick of fire swept through the counterfeits, charring and shrivelling them like insects on a burning log. The ground shook. There was a roaring outside and thunder clapped directly overhead. Three lightning balls crashed through the walls and circled the room, crackling and flaring. They all converged at once on the figure of the Prince Abbot.

The fire consumed him instantly in a bright incandescent pillar. The dragon's roar filled the room, sending the monks fleeing in terror. The fire touched Shika's face, but the mask protected him. He fell to his knees, meaning to give thanks, but, at that moment, a rush of steam from the boiling lake, like a fine scalding mist, enveloped him, clouding his vision. He lifted his hands to his face but the mask seemed to have fused to his skin. He knew then that the forest had claimed him. It had given him power, and now he must pay for it. That would be the price of destroying the Prince Abbot.

A profound sadness swept over him, as though he already saw all he would lose. When his vision cleared, he looked around the hall. Flames were licking at the beams of the roof and smoke filled the air. Aki and Sesshin lay on the ground, their faces hidden. Eisei stood against the wall, his eyes reddened.

Sesshin raised his head and called, 'Shikanoko! You must kill the demons. I told you before.'

'What demons?' Shika said, confused, his ears ringing.

'The imps, the boys. Lady Tora's children.'

'They are your children too,' Shika replied. 'And mine and Lord Kiyoyori's.'

'Act quickly, my boy, or regret it for the rest of your life.'

Kuro had gone to Shika's side, as had Kiku. Now Kuro turned, the snake in his hand, and said, 'Why would Shikanoko kill us? He brought us up. He is our older brother.'

He threw the snake towards Sesshin. It spun through the air, hissing, writhing, its mouth agape, its fangs bared.

It fell short of the old man and seemed to disappear through a crack in the floorboards.

Shika went to Aki, who lay, trembling, still holding the catalpa bow, and tried to take her in his arms but she rebuffed him gently. Again sadness engulfed him. He had lain with her, he had longed for her, but he barely knew her.

'Shikanoko,' she whispered. 'I am sorry.'

'It is I who should apologise to you. Can you ever forgive me?'

'I do forgive you.' It seemed she wanted to say more but her strength was failing. The bow slipped from her grasp.

'Where is Yoshimori?' Shika said urgently. 'We will find him and everything will be right again.'

'Yes, you must find him. Promise me you will. But I cannot stay now, my life is forfeit.'

'No!' he cried, though he could see she was burning with fever. 'We can heal you. Sesshin! Kuro!'

No one answered him.

Aki's body shuddered and arched and she cried out. He looked down and saw that the snake had fastened itself to her ankle, its fangs sunk deep, the venom already coursing through her veins.

'Akihime!' he called, seeing her life flee from her before his eyes. He looked around. 'Sesshin, master, help her! Kuro, is there some antidote?'

'There is no antidote,' Sesshin said. 'I warned you.'

'You should have kept quiet, old man,' Kiku said. 'You upset Kuro. When he is upset he likes to hurt people. That's his nature, and mine too.'

Shika was barely able to speak. He could not look at either Kiku or Kuro. 'Go,' he whispered. 'Let me never set eyes on you again.'

'But you will see us again,' Kiku said. 'You know our lives are bound together. You know we carry out your secret desires.'

He hardly heard them, nor did he see them, as they faded into invisibility and passed unseen through the doorway. He continued to hold Aki close while his tears pooled behind the mask and spilled like a waterfall through the eyeholes.

'The Princess is dead,' Sesshin said.

'No,' he wept. 'No, she cannot be.'

'Lord,' Eisei said at his side. 'She is gone.'

Sesshin said, 'Be thankful for this moment for it is part of your journey. It shows you the true nature of existence. Everything suffers, everything will be lost.'

Shika said, 'Why should you be spared death, you who are old, blind and powerless? Why did you not die in her place?'

'It is not my fate. It is hers and yours. You have come into full possession of your powers. You overcame the Prince Abbot, with her help. The dragon child himself answered her call, then recognised you and helped you. I am proud of you, my boy.'

Shika would have killed him at that moment, except that the old man would not die.

Eisei touched his arm. 'We must go. The fire is taking hold.'

*Where shall I go?* he thought. *There is nothing left for me.*

Eisei lifted Aki. Her arm moved, making his heart leap with hope, but he saw clearly that life had fled from her.

'What about the old man?' Eisei said. 'Will he come with us?'

'No!' Shika said.

'I must stay here,' Sesshin said. 'My place is at Ryusonji now. I must turn my attention to the Book of the Future.'

The outer yard was flowing with water. Nagatomo was waiting with Shika's weapons, Jato and Kodama. Nyorin was stamping and fretting in the shrine. Shika could hear Risu squealing somewhere. The foal cantered up to him, its eyes huge and dark with meaning.

He took the sword and the bow from Nagatomo and said, 'Untie the white stallion and the brown mare.'

'But they belong to the horse god,' Eisei said.

'They were my horses before that. They will be mine again.'

He hoped the horses would attack and kill him, but Nyorin came with him docilely, and Risu followed, calling out to him in her old way.

They fastened Aki's body to the stallion's back. All three horses lowered their heads and moisture formed in their eyes as though they were weeping.

The water came up to their hocks as Shikanoko led them through the flooded city. The Deer's Child was returning to the Darkwood.

# AUTHOR'S NOTE

This book was partly inspired by the great medieval warrior tales of Japan: *The Tale of the Heike*, the *Taiheiki*, the tales of Hōgen and Heiji, *Jōkyūki*, and *The Tale of the Soga Brothers*. I have borrowed descriptions of weapons and clothes from these and am indebted to their English translators Royall Tyler, Helen Craig McCullough and Thomas J. Cogan.

I would like to thank in particular Randy Schadel, who read early versions of the novels and made many invaluable suggestions.